“Scorching, wrenching,

Shayla Black’s books are a

—Lora Leigh, #1 *New York Times* bestselling author

PRAISE FOR THE NOVELS OF SHAYLA BLACK

“If you like BDSM-themed ménage with strong, dominant males, you will enjoy this book.”

—*USA Today*

“A sizzling ménage.”

—*RT Book Reviews*

“Ms. Black is the master at writing a steamy, smokin’-hot, can-I-have-more-please sex scene.”

—*Fiction Vixen*

“The perfect combination of excitement, adventure, romance, and really hot sex . . . this book has it all!”

—*Smexy Books*

“Full of steam, erotic love, and nonstop, page-turning action.”

—*Night Owl Reviews*

“To die for. [A] fabulous read!”

—*Fresh Fiction*

“This one is a scorcher.”

—*The Romance Readers Connection*

“Wickedly seductive from start to finish.”

—Jaci Burton, *New York Times* bestselling author

“A wicked, sensual thrill from first page to last. I loved it!”

—Lora Leigh, #1 *New York Times* bestselling author

Titles by Shayla Black

The Wicked Lovers Novels

WICKED TIES

DECADENT

DELICIOUS

SURRENDER TO ME

BELONG TO ME

MINE TO HOLD

OURS TO LOVE

THEIRS TO CHERISH

HIS TO TAKE

Anthologies

FOUR PLAY
(with Maya Banks)

HOT IN HANDCUFFS
(with Sylvia Day and Shiloh Walker)

WICKED AND DANGEROUS
(with Rhyannon Byrd)

Specials

HER FANTASY MEN

WICKED ALL NIGHT

Titles by Shayla Black writing as Shelley Bradley

BOUND AND DETERMINED

STRIP SEARCH

His to Take

SHAYLA BLACK

BERKLEY BOOKS, NEW YORK

THE BERKLEY PUBLISHING GROUP
Published by the Penguin Group
Penguin Group (USA) LLC
375 Hudson Street, New York, New York 10014

USA • Canada • UK • Ireland • Australia • New Zealand • India • South Africa • China

penguin.com

A Penguin Random House Company

This book is an original publication of The Berkley Publishing Group.

Library of Congress Cataloging-in-Publication Data

Black, Shayla.
His to take / Shayla Black.—Berkley trade paperback edition.
p. cm.—(A wicked lovers novel; 9) ISBN 978-0-425-25125-6
1. Missing persons—Fiction. 2. Man-woman relationships—Fiction.
3. Sexual dominance and submission—Fiction. I. Title.
PS3602.L325245H57 2015
813'.6—dc23 2014038716

PUBLISHING HISTORY
Berkley trade paperback edition / March 2015

PRINTED IN THE UNITED STATES OF AMERICA

10 9 8 7 6 5 4 3 2 1

Acknowledgments

You've heard the saying that it takes a village. That's definitely been true for this book.

First, I have to thank all my awesome author friends of the sprint loop. (Clearly, we need a better name.) Lexi Blake, Jenna Jacob, Isabella LaPearl, Carrie Ann Ryan, Kennedy Layne, Carly Phillips, Stacey Kennedy, and Angel Payne—one of you was always there to write beside me, day in and day out, and share much-needed encouraging instant messages. I can't tell you how much I appreciate it. Without y'all, no clue how long it would have taken me to finish the book.

Thanks to my assistant, Rachel, for doing her best to keep me sane and for the words of encouragement as I wrote this story.

I'd be remiss if I didn't mention the lovely Liz Berry, whose invaluable insight has helped me see this book—and sometimes life—in a totally new way.

I must also thank the ever patient and kind Chloe Vale. She's been with me, picking out flaws in logic, continuity, and structure, for the last four books. I've come to rely on her grammar knowledge, Google ability, and, above all, patience. I appreciate you far more than I can express. You're awesome, which totally fits since we're birthday twins.

Last (but never least) I need to thank my incredible family for their support, patience, and understanding. I would never have been able to craft the emotional theme of this book without everything you've taught me through your unconditional love. Thanks especially to my husband, who believed in me enough to jump in with both feet and never look back.

Thanks, y'all!

Chapter One

NIGHT pressed in, along with the rage crushing his chest. As he crept through the unfamiliar house, it lay dark, silent. Every step through the shadowed family room cost him precious seconds during which more people could die.

If he didn't survive this endeavor, he damn well planned on taking a deserving bastard or two with him. No way were these assholes snuffing out anyone else.

He found the hall and crept down its length. As he peeked in each bedroom, he gripped a SIG SAUER in his gloved palm.

Finally, he found the master bedroom. He stepped in, then frowned. Too still. No snoring, no audible breathing. Dead silence.

Peering through the inky space, he found the bed rumpled but empty and bit back a curse. Where the hell—

The feel of something hard and cold pressing against the back of his skull had him grimacing and holding in a curse.

"You have five seconds to tell me who you are and why the fuck you broke into my house at three a.m. or I'll blow you away."

Despite the grim situation, amusement lifted a corner of his lips. "You could, Hunter, but I think your wife would remove your balls if you started offing her family."

"Joaquin?" the other man asked, but didn't ease up on the firearm aimed at his brain.

"Kata doesn't have any other brothers," he pointed out.

A muffled feminine squeal sounded from around the corner. The turn of a knob and the yank of a door later, bare feet scampered across a hardwood floor.

"Damn it, woman!" Hunter Edgington bit out at his wife.

In response, she flipped on a light and ran at him head-on. "It's fine, babe."

Joaquin Muñoz flinched against the bright beams stabbing his eyes. As he adjusted, he turned to face his sister. She barreled toward him in a pink, gauzy nightie that brushed the middle of her thighs and clearly demonstrated the fact that she wasn't wearing a bra.

Almost as bad, her very protective husband, Hunter, still pointed a gun in his face. No doubt the former Navy SEAL knew how to use it well.

With another feminine scream of delight, Kata reached him and launched herself into his arms. How long had it been since he'd seen her? Almost three years. A fucking lifetime ago, really.

Then Joaquin didn't think anything as he felt her hard belly against his own. "You're pregnant?"

Kata stepped back and rubbed a hand over her distended abdomen. "Yeah."

"Thirty-one weeks." Hunter lowered the gun, but the tone warned him not to upset Kata or there'd be hell to pay. "We're happy."

"We are," she assured with a smile. "I'm due May thirtieth. It's a boy. Please be happy for us."

Joaquin didn't get the whole pairing off and spitting out kids thing, but pregnancy agreed with Kata. Though she didn't wear a shred of makeup, she glowed. Glossy chocolate hair covered her shoulders. Her smile wasn't the only thing that revealed her apparently sublime joy.

If she was happy, he'd play happy for her. "Of course."

Kata relaxed, grabbing a nearby robe and belting it above her belly. "What brings you here?"

"Yeah. In the middle of the night without so much as ringing the doorbell?" Hunter's eyes looked chilly even when he was in a good mood. At the moment, they held the warmth of a glacier.

Kata elbowed her husband with an exasperated sigh. "Is everything all right? Do you need a bed? Can you stay this time?"

"Hold it right there, motherfucker!" Another Edgington blasted from the hallway, semiautomatic pointed in his face. Then he blinked. "Joaquin?"

"As you can see . . ."

"Logan, damn it!" Kata braced her hands on her hips. "Put the gun down. What are you doing here?"

"I was up helping Tara feed the twins when I looked out the window. Since that streetlight shines on your back fence, I could see someone sneak over. I found the French doors to the family room unlocked and I followed."

When Hunter whipped a censuring stare at Kata, she winced. "Sorry. I forgot to lock the door when I came back in after watering the plants."

"And you forgot to set the alarm," her husband added. "Again."

"Jesus, why didn't you just knock?" Logan sounded almost as annoyed as his brother.

"I didn't want to wake everyone in the house up."

"Everyone?" Hunter quipped. "There was no one else in the house with me except your sister. And the damn dog that's obviously sacked out. Freaking furball."

Joaquin rubbed at the back of his neck. He'd kind of figured that. He'd wanted help, not a family reunion. Right now, the family thing was just in his way, but he smiled at Kata. "I wasn't sure, and my time to be polite has run out."

"Danger?" Hunter asked sharply.

Despite his golden hair standing slightly on end, the scars on his shoulder where he'd been shot in virtually the same spot twice, and a pair of low-slung gray sweat pants, Joaquin didn't doubt that his brother-in-law could still kill a man with his bare hands. Exactly the sort of guy he needed now. Logan, also a former SEAL, was cut from the same cloth. He wore his dark hair a little long these days, and even though it curled up at the ends, Joaquin would never mistake Hunter's younger brother for a pussy. The pair of them had identical Navy SEAL tattoos on their biceps—an eagle with stars-and-stripes wings holding a trident—and piercing blue eyes.

"Yes," he answered his brother-in-law simply. "There have already been multiple murders, the last one less than twelve hours ago."

"Shit," Hunter muttered, then turned to Kata. "Put something on and go across the street with Logan."

"I'm not leaving my brother." She crossed her arms over her chest. "He just got here."

"That is a very direct order, Katalina." Hunter had become an immovable mountain.

Joaquin's sister looked agitated and defiant. Given the little collar she wore at her throat, he didn't think this was the simple request of a husband to his wife. It was the unequivocal command of a Dom to his sub. *Interesting . . .*

She drew in another angry breath, hesitated, then whirled on him. "If you leave again without saying good-bye, I'm going to kick your ass."

Joaquin smiled faintly. "As safety permits and Hunter allows, I will."

Was Kata keen to see him because she was on some family kick now that she was starting her own? He didn't get it. Blood aside, she'd gone her way. He'd gone his. He wished her all the best, but a picture-perfect, greeting card sort of brother he'd never be.

"You need more backup?" Logan asked. "Should I call someone to watch the girls?"

Hunter slanted a glance Joaquin's way, deferring to him. A little bit of a shock, but he supposed it was because he alone knew the situation.

"I think that's wise," Joaquin advised.

"On it." Logan pulled a phone from his belt and called someone named Tyler as Kata grabbed her slippers and her purse—sighing, banging, and slamming all the way. They disappeared out the door, and Hunter followed to the front window, watching them cross the street.

"When did you move into this place?" Joaquin asked his brother-in-law to pass the time until Logan returned. He didn't want to explain the hell going down more than once.

"Almost a year and a half ago." The man watched his wife like a sentry, not really breathing until Logan escorted her into the house and shut the door securely behind him. "I won't bother asking how you found me."

Yeah, he had ways. "And your brother lives across the street?"

Hunter nodded. "He and his wife, Tara, moved in about three months ago, just before their twins were born. We figured it would be good to have the kids close together."

More family closeness. Maybe Kata's desire for it had rubbed off on her husband. The concept of that much togetherness gave Joaquin hives. These days, he couldn't see past his anger. But he kept that fact to himself and shrugged. "Nice."

Within minutes, a big blond guy in a black truck pulled up and, piece in hand, knocked on Logan's door. The hulk entered. The other Edgington headed back toward Hunter's place. Now they could get down to business. That was a relief because he needed justice and . . . he really didn't know what to say to his youngest sister.

Logan let himself in and locked the door. Hunter secured the French doors and set the alarm. In the kitchen, he flipped on lights, started the coffeemaker, then looked at Joaquin expectantly. "Talk. Are you in danger?"

"No. But I need to figure out who might be this killer's next victim."

"Are you working a case?" Logan demanded.

He hesitated. "Not officially."

The brothers exchanged a look, like they had some sort of private speak that only they would ever understand. Finally, they broke contact, and Logan gave a little nod.

"Were you followed?" Hunter asked.

"No. I was careful. But if I don't move fast, we'll have more dead women on our hands."

Logan frowned. "Serial killer?"

"Not exactly, though the man wielding the implements has clearly had both training and practice. But if he were a simple serial killer, I would leave that to the police."

As the scent of coffee filled the air, Hunter opened a cabinet and withdrew mugs. "Cream? Sugar?"

Joaquin frowned. "Do I look like a pussy?"

"Hey!" Logan objected.

Hunter barked out a laugh. "Ms. Thang likes cream in his coffee."

"Fuck you both," he groused.

"No thanks." Against his will, the brothers amused Joaquin. He missed this banter and camaraderie. Nate had been a great friend, probably the closest thing he'd ever have to a brother. Joaquin still couldn't believe he was gone. The loss fueled him with fury all over again.

He shoved the blinding anger down and focused on the case. Nate had done the same until his dying breath.

"So what's going on?" Hunter asked, filling the mugs with hot brew and sliding them across the counter.

Letting out a breath, Joaquin settled onto a bar stool and leaned in, elbows surrounding his steaming cup.

"I have"—*shit*—"I had a friend. I worked with him before he left to become a P.I. He took this case . . . A young woman came in, saying she felt as if someone was following her. She never saw anyone, but 'knew' she was being watched. According to my pal, Nate, she wasn't involved with anyone and she couldn't think of any enemies. Even though he thought she was a bit paranoid, he took the case. It was a buck." Joaquin shrugged. "Then . . . about thirty-six hours later, he couldn't find her anywhere. No one had seen or heard a thing. She simply failed to report to work. So he called the cops. Her place had been turned upside down. Signs of struggle were everywhere, but no unidentified prints. No DNA. Nothing. The next day, she turned up dead. Tortured hideously before she died." He flashed them the crime scene photo on his phone.

Logan grimaced. "Then?"

"Nate was a good guy," Joaquin said, pocketing his mobile. "He thought he'd let this girl down. He was determined to figure out what he'd overlooked and solve her murder. He went through all her records. Financials looked good. Nothing wrong at work. Her phone records were pretty clean, just one number he looked into. But it turned out to be a burner phone, so IDing who it belonged to was as ineffectual as porn in a roomful of blind men."

Hunter snorted. "After that? 'Cause it doesn't sound like Nate is with you anymore."

"No." Joaquin clenched a fist and tried to breathe through the fresh grief. "He called the number. Got nothing. Didn't leave a message. He asked me to see what I could find out. I did and I got an earful."

"Earful?" Hunter prompted. "If you couldn't trace it—"

"NSA." He shrugged. Normally, Joaquin wouldn't tell anyone what he did or who he worked for, but if he wanted help, he was going to have to be uncomfortably forthcoming.

"That clears up the mystery," Hunter commented. "Kata has always wondered. Go on."

Joaquin spared them the boring history lesson about his previous few jobs. He'd worked for different fingers within Uncle Sam's tight grip. The NSA had simply been the latest.

"I tapped into the signal. And the conversation I heard between these two men shocked the fuck out of me. I tried to call Nate and tell him that he was onto something dangerous." He cleared his throat, wondering why it was clogged suddenly. Had to be his damn allergies. "He didn't answer, so I went to his house. He'd been shot execution style."

The scene had been branded in his memory. Nate's hands tied behind his back and his brains splattered all around him. Joaquin choked on a violent urge for vengeance. He'd repay these assholes, no matter what it took.

"Shit," Logan muttered.

"I must have interrupted whoever killed him. They'd started digging into his office, but hadn't touched the rest of the house yet. Given what I'd heard, his murder coinciding with this woman's wasn't random."

Logan cursed. "Did you find something yourself? Turn the evidence over?"

"I found a treasure trove of shit Nate had recently dug up. I swiped it from the crime scene and took it to my superiors at the NSA. I was told to stop using all the cool gadgets at work for my personal shit. Murder isn't their jurisdiction, so if what I found didn't involve eavesdropping on potential terrorists at home, I should drop it."

"But you didn't." Hunter didn't know him well, but the guy understood him enough not to phrase his reply as a question.

Joaquin scoffed. "No. A woman was mutilated so badly they had to use the serial numbers on her breast implants to identify her. My best"—*and only*—"friend is dead. From what I'd overheard, none of that was going to stop."

Hunter polished off his coffee, poured another, then looked at Joaquin and Logan. They both shoved their cups forward for refills. He tipped the pot. The dark liquid flowed. Joaquin had the feeling the elder Edgington was collecting his thoughts.

"Can you tell from the evidence who's responsible? Any theories?"

"No. I could use your help. Nate's dead client hadn't known who'd been after her. Nate himself hadn't figured it out, either. I overheard incriminating conversations conducted on that burner phone, but the two assholes never exchanged names. Nor did they state who or what they represented. One called the shots while the other did the dirty work. But to uncover their identities, I'd have to have approval to subpoena phone records, and with a disposable device, the odds of getting that information are long. I was hoping that if I figured out why someone killed them, that would lead me to who."

Logan nodded. "If you've got nothing else—"

"I don't."

"Then that's your best option. So no one you worked for gave a damn about these dead people and . . . ?"

"I've been suspended for a month. I'm pretty sure that when I go back I won't have a job, but I'm not giving up. I will figure this out. Which is where you guys come in."

"What do you need?" Hunter sipped at his brew again.

"Resources. Anything you can give me to help me find out who did this and why." Joaquin shrugged. "I figured you two would have ways."

Logan smiled smugly. Hunter's expression was almost a mirror.

So that was a yes.

Joaquin continued with his story. "The woman being followed was twenty-one, obviously of some sort of Anglo-European descent, probably Eastern bloc, but born in the U.S., and adopted in December 1998, somewhere around the age of five. When I found Nate's notes, he'd been working this furiously and found a string of mutilations over the last two weeks spread across the country. Four in total, but no one had connected the dots yet. All the women were the same age with the same ethnic background, adopted about the same time. The phone call I overheard between the two men indicated that they'd compiled a list of every female in the U.S. who met these criteria. They said they'd find Tatiana Aslanov if they had to kill a hundred women looking for her."

Hunter and Logan shared another quick stare, but neither said anything right away.

"What do you know about her?" Hunter asked.

"Nothing. All the usual searches turned up empty, as if she never existed."

"Some people would like to keep it that way," Logan asserted.

"You know about this girl?"

"We do," Hunter answered. "We'll get into it as soon as you finish your story."

Joaquin nodded, glad he'd followed his hunch to come here. "About fifteen hours ago, I overheard the two assholes talking about hunting the Aslanov girl. Then suddenly, they went silent, as if they knew someone listened in. Or maybe they just cycled out their phones. Whatever. But the conversation stopped abruptly. Another body fitting the description turned up in Atlanta this afternoon. Whoever's looking for this woman is looking hard."

"And obviously not finding who they're looking for," Hunter speculated. "If they were, they wouldn't kill their victim and move on to the next."

"Agreed." Joaquin nodded. "From what I gather, they want information. It makes sense that if a woman isn't who they're seeking, they dispose of her. After all, they can't let her blab."

"Exactly," Logan agreed.

"But why end her so brutally?" Hunter looked perplexed.

"My gut? Just because he can. This prick probably enjoys torture. I'll bet he gets hard hearing a woman plead for her life."

"Sick fuck." Logan's contempt couldn't have been more obvious.

"This creep started around D.C. and swept down the Eastern Seaboard, struck as far south as Miami, then headed back west. Every single one of these bodies is . . ." Joaquin shuddered as the crime scene photos flashed through his head, each more shocking than the last. The terrible deaths these women had endured made him flat fucking sick.

Logan slapped him on the back. "'Nough said on that. How can we help?"

"These killers are two steps ahead of me. I need help compiling a list of women who fit the profile so I can warn each before they become victims."

"We can help with that," Hunter promised.

"And that's everything I've got. Now tell me what you know about Tatiana Aslanov."

"Not much about her specifically, other than her name. I'm more familiar with her father's work." Logan cocked his head. "Do you know Callindra Howe?"

"The heiress who was missing for, like, a decade? I know of her."

"Yeah. I know her personally, so I know what she went through to escape the bastards pursuing her because of Viktor Aslanov's research. There's more to the story than they're saying on the news."

"You seriously know her?" Joaquin was about to call bullshit.

"Before he got married, he had the chance to know her up close and personal," Hunter added.

"And you passed that up?" Now Joaquin just wanted to call the younger Edgington an idiot.

"Hey!" Logan objected. "We were both in love with other people."

Was this guy for real? "So? That pic someone caught of her and her former 'boss' looking mighty cozy in Tahiti a few months back?" That had been one hell of a lip lock. "She looks insanely hot in a bikini. As long as her fiancé gets some, too, I kind of see why he just looks the other way."

The Edgington brothers exchanged another glance. Okay, they knew something else he didn't. He'd come back to it later. Right now, his goals were to avenge Nate and stop other women from dying, not worry about some pseudo-celebrity.

"So through Callindra Howe, you know something about the Aslanov case?"

Logan nodded. "Callie's fiancé, Sean, still consults with the FBI.

What we know is that the bureau is convinced that no scientist, especially one doing Aslanov's sort of groundbreaking genetic work, would intentionally hand over every scrap of his research to her father, knowing that he would only destroy it."

"What?" Joaquin hadn't had much time to devote to the news lately, and he was a little embarrassed to admit that he knew more about how Callindra Howe looked on a beach wearing next to nothing than about her case.

"Her father, Daniel Howe, hired Aslanov to find a DNA-based cure for cancer when Callie was a little girl," Hunter explained. "Howe threw millions at the Russian geneticist to try to save his wife from dying of ovarian cancer. When that didn't work, he pressed on, hoping no one else would have to suffer as he and his family had."

"Right." He remembered that part.

"Then when Howe figured out that Aslanov had stumbled across other genetic markers that had nothing to do with the grant he'd funded and the scientist had sold that information separately to make a buck, Callie's father demanded that Aslanov turn over his findings since it had been created on his dime. Aslanov supposedly gave Howe every bit of research he'd ever conducted with the funding. But the end of their business relationship was contentious, and the scientist had to know that the billionaire was going to turn his life's work into dust. Which is exactly what he did."

"But everyone thinks Aslanov left a copy somewhere else?"

"In his shoes, wouldn't you?" Logan challenged. "Would you endure years of advanced schooling, being ostracized in your own country for your controversial experiments, and work like a dog for a dozen years so that you could hand everything over and know it would all go up in smoke?"

His pride would never allow that. He didn't think most men's would, either. "No."

"So the FBI is speculating that another copy of this genetic-altering research is somewhere. What we know is that Aslanov sold his initial findings to some well-funded, fuck-all-crazy separatist group with delusions of a super army. They experimented with some U.S. soldiers they abducted in South America. When these loons came back to Aslanov for the rest of the research, the Russian told them he didn't have it anymore. They shot his family deader than dead—wife and two kids. They tortured him mercilessly for nearly two days before they killed him, too."

Joaquin absorbed all that and let it rattle around in his brain. "That's all terrible, but what does it have to do with my case?"

Logan clapped him on the back. "Well, the separatists never got their hands on all that research. Aslanov had *three* children, but authorities only recovered the bodies of two. This organization might seem insane, but they aren't stupid. I'd bet they found the obscure news story of a little girl covered in blood and walking a dirt road the same November day as the murders, less than a mile from the crime scene, then decided that she was Aslanov's missing daughter."

"So you're saying that's Tatiana Aslanov and she's still alive?" Joaquin's blood started to spark and race. Finally, after a frustrating few weeks, he might be onto something.

"Exactly. But you won't have an easy time tracking her down. According to Sean, the adoption records have been sealed tight. What we do know is the five-year-old girl wandering the side of the road was in shock and couldn't remember her name. The couple who found her took her to the local sheriff. She was adopted out shortly thereafter."

"She must be the one these people are after, just to learn what she knows about her father's research or where he might have hidden it." Joaquin blew out a breath. "I've got to find her."

"Before they do," Hunter added.

"Which means we don't have much time. Days at most. Probably more like hours."

Hunter plucked his cell phone out of the pocket of his sweat pants and made a call. Logan's materialized from his jeans. Within a few minutes, the place was crawling with people. First to show up was a big blond mountain of a man Hunter introduced as his brother-in-law, Deke.

The big guy shook Joaquin's hand. "I may have to leave suddenly. Kimber started having contractions this afternoon."

"My sister," Logan supplied to Joaquin, then frowned. "She's not due yet."

"We're only at week twenty-eight, so it's a concern. They'll stop her labor . . . if they can."

"No worries," Hunter assured him. "If you've got to go, just go."

"Jack's on his way. Morgan isn't due for months, so he shouldn't have any problems being here for the duration."

Joaquin frowned, staring at the men. What the fuck? A bunch of tough dudes all into their wives and kids. Were they trying to double the population of Lafayette, Louisiana, singled-handedly or go for some fucked-up record in that big Guinness book?

"Your wife is pregnant," he said to Hunter. "And so is yours," he addressed Deke. "This Jack guy's wife is expecting, and . . ." He turned to Logan. "Your wife just had twins."

"Yep." Logan flashed him a cheesy grin. "Don't forget my buddy, Xander. He and his brother are waiting for their wife to give birth, too. Six weeks to go."

"*Their* wife?"

Logan nodded, giving him a stare that dared him to say more.

Honestly, he didn't care much how these guys rolled, but . . . "What the fuck is in the water around here? If I get laid while I'm in town, remind me to tell her not to drink it."

Deke barked out a laugh. "It's not the water. We're all just horny."

Logan grimaced. "I don't want to hear that about my sister, dude. Eww! I need ear bleach."

"Get over yourself." Deke punched Logan in the shoulder. "My wife is hot."

Hunter rolled his eyes. "I'm ignoring your comments about my sister. Personally, I think everyone is trying to keep up with Tyler."

"This will be baby number three for them," Logan agreed with a nod.

"Delaney wants a girl this time."

Personally, Joaquin didn't give a shit, but just about the time he opened his mouth to remind them they had a case to work and that lives hung in the balance, Jack Cole showed up. He brought along a guy he introduced as Stone, who had a heavy brow line, a square face, and almost dead eyes.

Joaquin brought the newcomers up to speed. Within five minutes, they had multiple workstations up, humming on a super-secure Internet connection. Several of the guys were on the phone with their contacts as they quickly took Joaquin's list of all girls adopted in December 1998 at age five. Stone's fingers flew over his keyboard. He might look like a caveman, but the guy was definitely high-tech. In moments, he began whittling the list of names down to a handful that fit Tatiana Aslanov's profile.

Finally, as dawn crested over the Louisiana skyline, Logan made one last call, to a guy named Mitchell Thorpe. The name sounded familiar, but Joaquin couldn't place it.

"Callie with you?" Logan asked the man.

"Right beside me," said the voice on the speakerphone. "Aren't you, pet?"

A little feminine sigh, followed by a giggle. "Yes. Stop it!"

"Would you like to change your tone and rephrase that? It sounded a whole lot like a demand," said the man with the commanding voice.

"Sorry." She sounded almost contrite . . . but not quite.

"Because she's a little minx," said another man on the other end of the phone.

Joaquin frowned. The Callie on the line was Callindra Howe? Apparently. So Thorpe was with Callie and . . . who else? Her fiancé?

"Did you need to talk to her, Logan?" Thorpe asked.

"With your permission."

Permission? Did all these guys swing just left of normal? Whatever. If they could help him solve these murders and give him justice for Nate, nothing else mattered.

"Of course."

The speaker rumbled a bit, then a woman's voice took over. "Logan?"

"Hi, Callie. Sorry if we woke you."

"We're just being lazy. Sean's half-asleep, but you've got me. Tara good?"

"Absolutely. I called for your help."

"Anything. Name it."

"I might bring Kata's brother to Dallas to talk to you. How soon is the wedding?"

"Next Saturday."

"Can you squeeze a meeting in before then? I'm sure it's a crazy time, but it's about Aslanov. I don't think this shit is over. We're onto a new angle here."

"What do you mean?" The second male voice resounded over the phone again, sounding sharp.

"Half-asleep, Mackenzie?"

"Wide awake now," Sean grumbled. "Tell me what's going on."

"Time is of the essence, and I don't want to get into too much over the phone." Logan winced.

Joaquin nodded. *Never know who might be listening . . .*

"We'll make time for a meeting," Callie assured Logan.

"Thanks, hon. We'll be in touch when we're headed in that direction."

"Excellent," Thorpe assured him. "We'll be waiting."

Logan hung up and looked Joaquin's way. "They'll have information no one else will. You can interview them, see if anything helps your case along."

"Thanks, man."

Logan nodded. "No sweat. I hope we're able to stop anyone else from losing their life."

"I got it," Stone said into their discussion.

Since the guy barely talked, Joaquin had kind of forgotten he was there. Well, except for the constant tap, tap, tapping of his keyboard.

"You've got a list?" Jack asked, clarifying.

"Yeah." Stone nodded sharply. "I narrowed it down to women who fit the profile and are still alive. I went further and searched for women with blue eyes, since the only picture of Tatiana Aslanov I found shows she had them. She was only two at the time, but I'm rolling with it. That leaves us with four possibilities: Caitlyn Wells of Mobile, Alabama. Emily Boyle of Norman, Oklahoma. Bailey Benson of Houston, Texas. Alicia Allen of Casa Grande, Arizona. I pulled together brief bios of them all."

As Stone printed everything out and handed it to him, Joaquin stared in awe. "Where did you come from?"

The man never broke expression. "Prison. Jack just pays me to put my skills to good use now, instead of hacking into Uncle Sam's panties or department stores' customer payment records."

Joaquin didn't think Stone was kidding. On top of being good with a computer, between the ink covering his arms and the slabs of muscles lurking under his T-shirt, he just looked like a bad motherfucker. Nice to have the ex-con on his side.

"Thanks."

Stone inclined his head, his severely short hair like a dark paint over his scalp, matching his expressionless dark eyes. "By the way, Logan said you were wondering if you still had a job. You haven't been fired yet. I looked into it. There's a meeting on the subject this coming Tuesday."

Fabulous. "I appreciate it."

Jack slapped Stone on the back. "Good job."

Joaquin stared down at the list. The obvious would be to head to

Mobile first, but what if these violent bastards changed their M.O. or skipped around the country for some reason? "Any chance I can convince y'all to split up this list with me?"

"I'll hop on a plane to Mobile," Jack volunteered with a grin. "There's a place there I know with fabulous biscuits and gravy, so when I'm done, I know I'll have a great meal."

"I'll take Norman," Logan said. "I've been before and I know my way around. Shouldn't take me long."

"I used to live in Houston," Joaquin pointed out. "I'll be able to get in and out of there fast."

"I guess that leaves me with catching the next flight to Arizona," Hunter quipped. "Where is this place?"

"Halfway between Tucson and Phoenix. I passed through there once." Joaquin shrugged. "Look on the bright side. It's not a big town. It'll take longer to get there than to search it."

"Whoever finds her, I think we should take her somewhere with a lot of security, where we can watch her twenty-four seven. Like Dominion." Logan turned to Joaquin. "It's Thorpe's club in Dallas. Callie and Sean will be there, too. We can ask them questions at the same time."

"Club?"

"BDSM." Logan set his jaw. "You got something to say about that?"

Why would he? "Not a word."

"Excellent."

"I highly recommend you keep it that way." But clearly, Hunter wasn't suggesting.

Whatever. Impatience burned a hole in his gut. He just wanted to get this show on the road.

"Check in as soon as you've reached your target and either eliminated or identified her," Joaquin said.

"What do we do with the women we know aren't Tatiana? We

can't just leave them to this sadistic fucker and the prick giving the orders."

A heavy pall fell over the group. No one wanted to upend lives . . . but they all refused to leave another innocent woman to suffer so brutally at these killers' hands.

"We'll cross that bridge when we come to it," Logan suggested.

"All right." Joaquin didn't like it, but he agreed. "Now we need to get going. The more time we waste here, the more time someone else has to die."

Chapter Two

AFTER five hours of sleep and another four on the road, Joaquin drove through the historic Houston Heights neighborhood, cruising slowly past Bailey Benson's address. As sunset dipped closer, the golden glow backlit the cozy bungalow painted a pretty blue-gray with fresh white trim. Original stained glass graced a transom window over the front door. The little porch and dark wood front door gave the place charm.

It didn't look like a house where a murder could take place, but looks could be deceiving.

He didn't see a vehicle parked in the carport to the left of the house, but a bicycle was tethered to its back post. Vaguely, Joaquin wondered where this girl was now. He read the sketchy bio information Stone had given him again—more about dance than anything else. Nothing that told him precisely who she was.

As he scoped the house to find the best entrance to sneak in without being spotted, his phone buzzed. *Logan.*

"What did you find?" Joaquin didn't waste time with chitchat or preambles.

"I just got to Norman. Bad news. Emily Boyle was reported missing shortly after noon today."

His stomach balled and dropped. "Shit."

"I'm going to keep looking around, help if I can. But from what I can tell, she left her job as an assistant in a real estate office to grab some coffee this morning and didn't return. Of course, the police won't consider her an official missing person for another fifteen hours, but . . ."

"We know what happened, most likely." Joaquin sighed into the phone. "We're too late."

"As much as I hate saying it, the situation doesn't look good. But I'm not giving up yet. I'm trying to retrace Emily's steps and talk to anyone who saw her just before she disappeared."

"Thanks. Keep me posted."

He couldn't stand the thought that a young woman was probably, even now, being strapped down and scalpeled, punctured, then dismembered until she either admitted to being Tatiana Aslanov or she bled to death. Either way, she'd die eventually. If she wasn't the scientist's daughter, they'd snuff her out with no compunction. The best he could do was focus on Bailey Benson, hope she was the missing girl, and save her in case these brutal bastards came her way.

Then take them down for what they'd done to Nate and the other women.

Jack and Hunter had both climbed on planes to their respective destinations. Something between anticipation and dread bit into Joaquin's stomach. He hoped they'd have better news than Logan, but everything looked bleak.

As soon as the sun slid below the horizon, he drove a few streets over, slipped on a ball cap, and shrugged into a long raincoat. He climbed from the car and locked it, then strolled down the street, pretending to be a resident out for an evening stroll.

It didn't take him long to reach Bailey's little house. He ducked behind a row of hedges and crouched, following it to the side of the house, testing every door and window. He gave her credit for keeping the doors locked, but he found a loose knob on the door into the kitchen. A quick turn of the multi-tool he kept in his pocket, and he stripped away the hardware. From there, it wasn't hard to reach through and unlock the door. Predictably, no one had retrofitted the house with a security system.

Once inside, he reattached the doorknob and tightened it before making his way through the shadowed space, looking for a good hiding spot. He hoped like hell that she actually made it home, instead of disappearing like Emily Boyle. But since she wasn't due to work at the dive where she waitressed until Tuesday, he wasn't sure where else to find her but home.

Joaquin cased the place. Because the house was older, it didn't have a walk-in pantry or closet he could slip into. Nor did Bailey's place have a living room in the normal sense of the words. What it did have, however, was two walls of mirrors, gleaming hardwood floors, and a ballet barre.

The woman liked her dance. He'd never been to a ballet. Neither of his sisters had been into that sort of thing. His sister Mari had been a volleyball player. His mother had enrolled Kata for a time, but his younger sister had preferred to be one of the guys. Football, softball, soccer, even lacrosse . . . If Joaquin played a sport, Kata had joined in.

A jangling noise alerted Joaquin that someone had unlocked the front door. He dove into a floor-to-ceiling armoire Bailey had set up in one corner of the space and arranged himself around some ragged toe shoes, a few leotards, some tulle-like things, and a musty collection of old playbills from past ballets in a box.

Just as he settled with his knees somewhere near his throat, he heard a commotion at the front door. It opened, shut. Keys clattered onto a nearby surface.

"Blane, don't be that way," the voice said. "You know I love you."

Joaquin couldn't hear what the voice on the other end of the phone said, but Bailey laughed. "Of course no one is more wonderful than you. Didn't I follow you around like a puppy when we first met? I tell you all the time how incredible you are."

She paused, and Joaquin heard her footsteps drawing closer. The rustle of plastic told him that she had set a bag on the counter of the kitchen, which was open to her dance room. He leaned around in the cabinet until he caught a glimpse of her through the tiny sliver of space between the armoire doors.

Bingo!

Bailey Benson appeared, phone pressed to her ear, wearing a smile and a pair of killer dimples. She looked so fresh-faced, with rosy cheeks and her light brown hair in a loose bun. Wavy tendrils caressed her neck. He'd never seen a woman with such delicate shoulders and hands. Her fair skin would surely bruise easily. Even when she extracted apples from her grocery sack, the movements were graceful. He could look at a girl like her all day long.

Blood rushed to his cock like a flood, and he gritted his teeth. A man would have to be careful with a woman like that beneath him. He definitely liked sex physical and a little rough. Breaking her would be too easy.

He shoved the thought aside, reminding himself that he wasn't here to get Bailey into bed, but to save her. Because if this asshole Joaquin chased managed to abduct and torture her, he would be far more than a little rough.

A protective surge punched Joaquin in the gut.

"Aww, come on," she crooned into the phone, pursing a full pair of lips that he could imagine plump and rosy and wrapped around him as she sucked him deep. "It'll be great. You're gorgeous, Blane. We do hot and sweaty really well together. You know it."

Well, hell. She was talking to her boyfriend about sex. Joaquin didn't poach, and getting excited about some girl into another guy wasn't his speed. The fact that he currently spied on her through her armoire doors made him feel like a pervy letch. He shook his head.

She giggled. Her blue eyes sparkled. Fuck, she really was gorgeous. Then again, he shouldn't be surprised. She was young, blue-eyed, and nubile. And despite her conversation, she had a startling air of innocence.

"All right. I'll wait until tomorrow night. You're terrible to string a girl along and leave her panting, you know?"

The douche on the other end had turned down sex with her? Scratch that. That guy wasn't a douche, but a complete fidiot.

Bailey laughed, then hung up. She finished putting away her groceries, then stashed her purse on the kitchen counter and made her way to the open space of her dance studio. As she bent to retrieve a pair of toe shoes scattered on the floor, Joaquin got his first look at her form south of her shoulders.

Holy fuck, what a pretty thing. She wore some sort of gray spandex dance garment that covered her from shoulders to ankles yet revealed every dip and slight swell of her body. Along with the delicate shoulders, she had pert breasts that curved her leotard gracefully. Her narrow rib cage funneled down to an even smaller waist. The slight flare of her hips was just enough to be feminine. Firm thighs, muscled calves, and tiny feet that looked even smaller in those torture chamber shoes.

The woman weighed about a hundred pounds. She wasn't tall. God, had he ever even kissed a girl that fragile? No. But her lips looked like the least delicate part of her, pink and puffed. Soft. Sex ready.

Shit, the thought made him even harder.

As soon as Bailey finished lacing up her shoes, she ran back and grabbed her phone, then flipped through her playlists and chose a song. She set the phone down and struck a pose. Classical music filled the room, and she danced like a butterfly, flitting, floating. She looked so light. The woman came damn close to defying gravity. How could anyone stay in the air that long with her legs in the splits?

How could anyone turn on the tips of her toes seven or eight times like that without losing her balance, getting dizzy, or throwing up?

Through the thin, stretchy fabric, Joaquin witnessed every bunch of her thighs as she leapt, every ripple of her shoulders as she waved her arms in graceful expression. And her face . . . He had no doubt that she was never happier than when she was moving with the music to express the beauty of the dance and song together. Simply stunning.

He wasn't a dance sort of guy, but watching her made him fucking ache to touch her.

Time seemed without meaning, almost endless. When she pirouetted out of his vision, it frustrated him . . . but then she came back, and the sight of her was like something that soothed the savage beast inside him. The control she had over her body astounded him. Bailey lifted her leg, cradling her foot in her hand and hoisting it above her head, turning as she did, head flung back, eyes closed, as if in ecstasy.

Damn it, he was about to bust out his zipper.

One song bled into the next, then another. Even her graceful fingers turned him on, and he imagined his big dark hands all over her fair skin, enveloping her slight form as he drove into her sweet, tight cunt.

He drew in a deep breath. Mission objective: Save the girl from being horrifically murdered. He had no business thinking about sex with her. She had a boyfriend. He was a foot taller and outweighed her by at least a hundred pounds. The grooves on his face revealed the harsh danger in his life she would never understand. Bailey would probably take one look at him and scream.

As she raised her leg behind her, arched her back, and made some graceful sweep with her arms, the phone in his pocket buzzed. Thanking fuck that the music covered the sound, he pulled it from his pocket. Jack Cole. Caitlyn Wells's body had been discovered about four that afternoon. He'd thoughtfully included a picture. As he saw it, Joaquin hissed in a breath. She'd received the same treatment as the others—broken, sawed into pieces, mutilated almost beyond recognition. If Logan and Hunter's theory about who was behind all this was right, these separatists were working faster. Or maybe they were just losing patience. Either way, it wasn't good. They'd be done with the girl in Oklahoma soon. And they'd be heading down to Houston—if they weren't on their way already. Then they'd abduct Bailey and— Fuck no. He couldn't even think about that. It wouldn't happen on his watch.

He tapped out a quick curse to Jack and added that he'd call later.

About that time, Bailey turned off the music. Perspiration dripped down her neck, disappeared between her breasts. Patches of moisture discolored the back of her leotard. Her hairline was soaking wet. Joaquin found himself just as fascinated. Did she work that hard in bed with a lover, chasing pleasure with him to create an unforgettable experience?

She disappeared, and he saw the shoes fly across the room, back into the corner. The patter of footsteps over the hardwood floors grew quieter, fainter, until they disappeared. The creak of the old house's water pipes sounded in the walls next. Bailey had probably gone to shower.

Easing the armoire door open, he peeked out. All the lights were on and the coast was clear. Excellent.

First order of business: Secure the location.

Joaquin unfolded himself from the cramped space and backtracked to the front door. He wanted to throttle her when he found it unlocked. Was she insane? Even if she didn't know about the danger breathing down her neck, any run-of-the-mill rapist or killer looking for an easy thrill could just walk right in while she was in a tile box with her eyes closed and so damn vulnerable.

Shit. He'd never quite understood the urge to spank a woman, but he was starting to get a clue.

After locking them in tight once more, he swiped her phone and schlepped back to her bedroom. Sweat-damp clothes littered the floor. Running water pelted the walls and floor of the shower. She sang in a high, lilting soprano. He didn't recognize the song. Something about eternal love—vomit—but she could carry a tune. That shouldn't surprise him. She was both musical and talented.

Tucking himself behind a plush chair in a corner of the room, he prowled through her phone, just waiting for her to emerge from the bathroom. She didn't password protect the device, so he could see the name of her last caller. Blane looked young, fit, and boyishly handsome. They'd exchanged a series of texts with lots of flirting and hearts.

Somewhere in the back of his head, Joaquin wondered if her boyfriend would pose a problem by doing something inconvenient like dropping by unexpectedly tonight. Joaquin would almost wonder what she saw in a guy like Blane, except it was both obvious and irrelevant.

The phone in Joaquin's pocket buzzed again. He pulled it free to see a message from Hunter. The girl in Arizona was in Africa on a mission trip for the next six weeks. They exchanged a few texts, agreeing that she was safe for now and that if the case was still up in the air when Alicia Allen returned, they'd deal with her then. Hunter said he was catching a return flight home tonight. Giving him the thumbs-up, Joaquin had shoved his phone in his pocket again when he heard the bathroom door open.

Along with a cloud of perfumed steam, Bailey emerged. He caught a glimpse of her barely covered in a yellow towel, little water droplets raining down her pale skin as she scurried across the room.

She stopped right beside the bed, and a moment later the TV flipped on. She scanned a few channels, then paused.

"Welcome to Callindra Howe," said the male announcer with the buttery voice. "Thank you for being with us. Your story of survival and courage has inspired many in the face of adversity, and everyone is thrilled that your story has a happy ending."

"Thank you for having me here."

"In case you've been living under a rock . . ." The voice-over went into an explanation of Callie's history, surviving the murder of her entire family and repeated attempts on her own life. The backstory included a description of Aslanov and his research, along with a hint that this played a role in her tragic past. A little gasp escaped Bailey.

Joaquin inched his gaze above the back of the chair. She stood stock-still and staring. What had her so mesmerized? He cocked his head to see the TV. A picture of Viktor Aslanov appeared on the screen. He whipped his stare to Bailey again. She looked spooked and pale.

Suddenly, she made a frantic grab for the remote on the nightstand, stabbing her trembling thumb furiously against one of the buttons. Nothing happened on the first two tries.

"Damn it," she muttered, staring down at the device in her hand, her body taut.

"My story has a happy ending," Callie said on the screen. "But my mother's didn't. Every woman can live a longer, healthier life by having regular female exams. Pay attention to your body and report anything out of the ordinary to your doctor. If you can't afford a regular exam, please contact the Cecilia Howe Foundation. Besides cancer research, we're trying to help women with limited resources get the care they need."

"That's an admirable goal," the announcer said in praise. "Contact information is on the screen, folks. But let's talk about something very happy, Ms. Howe. You're marrying Agent Mackenzie soon. What can you tell us about the wedding?"

Bailey jabbed at the remote again, and the TV finally went dark. Into the shadowed room, she emptied her lungs. That action seemed to deflate her whole body. She clutched her towel to her breasts, shaking, looking like she'd seen a ghost.

Maybe she had.

Because she was Tatiana Aslanov?

Right now, that likelihood seemed pretty promising. With one possibility dead, one missing, and the other in Africa, Bailey Benson was his last hope for uncovering the truth and stopping these ruthless savages from killing again. Even if she wasn't the scientist's daughter, this sweet little ballerina wasn't equipped to deal with the danger about to knock on her door. Joaquin knew he had to be aggressive and act fast to keep her safe. Fuck the consequences.

* * *

RED splattered her once-pink shirt. She pressed her lips together to hold in a scream. If she couldn't stay quiet, something bad would happen.

Terror made her heart thump in her chest, drum in her head. As she looked around the ransacked house, splashes of red marked the walls in nearly every room. She was afraid to look closer. Time to get out. But as she ran down the hall, she slid in more of the red stuff, nearly losing her balance. It lapped at her toes, warm and sludgy. Some scent she didn't like tinged the air. Her stomach turned, but she kept running.

Finally, she made it to the door and reached for the knob. But her hands were covered in red. Horror assailed her.

The wind blew the back door open. With a silent screech, she darted outside. Cold. Snow had fallen recently. The ice bit into her feet, but she kept charging as fast as she could, until she couldn't breathe, until the tears turned icy on her face. Until she came to another road.

She walked what seemed like forever, past animal pens and pastures and dormant trees. Her feet had long ago gone numb. Quiet smothered her. The absence of noise—even the call of a bird—somehow scared her more.

Where was she going? Where could she hide? She didn't know. Would she walk forever and never see anyone again?

Then an old blue sedan pulled over. A woman with a kind face and brown hair opened the door and gave her a look that held both pity and horror.

"What's your name, little girl?"

She didn't know. She should, but all she knew now was that she felt cold and shivering and afraid.

The man dashed around the side of the car with a phone mashed against his ear. Concern creased his face as he held out a hand to her. She reached for him, praying he offered warmth and safety, but she caught sight of her hand again. The terrible red had seeped into her skin, dripped under her fingernails . . .

Bailey's eyes flew open and she gripped the sheet. That damn nightmare. Again. Even in her warm nightshirt, she shivered.

Panting in the silence, she looked around the room frantically. The dream still flashed vivid images in her head, as it always did. She'd been having these same visions almost nightly for as long as she could remember. Her parents had told her repeatedly it was just a dream, assured her that no part of it was real. Even the psychologist they'd insisted she see as a kid had explained that the subconscious can confront a person with their greatest fears and make the dream-state experience seem very real, yadda, yadda, yadda. But everything about the nightmares sure felt as if she'd been through that hell.

Squeezing her eyes shut, Bailey tried to compartmentalize the fear, remind herself that it wasn't genuine or rational. She lived alone in a little house close to downtown Houston, not in the middle of farmland somewhere snow fell thick and heavy. She'd never been covered in blood. For heaven's sake, she'd grown up in suburban Houston with every advantage a kid with two attentive parents could have. Mom had homeschooled her until ninth grade. Dad had worked for a small company that believed in family, so he'd been home for dinner every night. She had been to every dance class they could afford, then attended a high school for the performing arts. Everything had been picture-perfect in life—except their deaths in a car crash shortly after high school graduation and these damn dreams.

Why did the visions plague her almost every night when she closed her eyes?

Whatever. She refused to let the fear drive her from bed again. She'd danced hard today and she had another round of grueling rehearsals tomorrow. No way she'd get through it without sleep.

Roll over. Cuddle up to your pillow. Think of something happy.

Bailey sighed. That tactic hadn't worked before. It probably wouldn't work now.

Flinging her blanket aside, she opened her eyes, pondering what might be on TV. Maybe she'd just go into the kitchen and make some popcorn and watch a movie.

Suddenly, a shadow eclipsed her—one in the shape of a man. Before she could scream, his hand clamped over her mouth. She tried to scream around it, but the sound came out like a whimper. A thousand terrible possibilities pelted her brain at once. She remembered hearing on the news last week that there was a serial rapist in the area.

Oh, please God, no . . .

His other hand came closer. Would he rip her clothes? Defile her? Bailey tried to writhe and thrash. Escape—she had to. Somehow. She was an athlete. A fighter, damn it.

In the next instant, Bailey noticed something in his darkened hand. He brought it closer. Before she could fight or flee, she felt a prick in the side of her neck.

Shock jolted through her system. Then . . . nothing.

Chapter Three

BAILEY floated in and out, feeling hazy and in no hurry to wake up. Something nagged at her that she should. But rehearsal wasn't until later in the day, right?

Toasty warmth and a heavy head dragged her back under. She couldn't remember her bed ever being quite so comfortable. She still slept on her childhood mattress, which had always been too soft. But this felt firmer and a little bit perfect. She melted into it. Well, except her shoulders. Why were her hands above her head? It was making her nightshirt bunch around her hips. Something dug into her forearms. She never slept in this position. *Weird . . .*

She tugged to pull her arms down, but nothing. They were stuck. No, tethered. Restrained.

The realization jolted her eyes open, and she found herself staring at an unfamiliar room, unable to move. Her heart started thundering in her chest. She bit back a scream.

A black down comforter covered her. The walls were some shade of gray, as was the leather ottoman at the end of the bed. Everything else was a blend of woods. Floor-to-ceiling shutters in a cherry tone, a dresser in some rustic finish, the darker hardwood floors dominating the large space, even some of the art on the shelves. A nightstand with modern lines and a contemporary light fixture sat next to the bed. Nothing else. Not a personal picture or memento anywhere. Spartan. And totally alien.

Cold fear snaked through her system. The attacker in her house last night rushed through her memory, and the truth set in: She'd been taken.

Bailey couldn't hold her terror in anymore. She screamed.

The door flew open, and a man busted in, slamming it behind him, then rushed to her side. No hint of warmth softened his dark face or greenish eyes, though he appeared surprisingly concerned for a kidnapper. Looking more than a little rugged, the short, sharp cut of his black hair accentuated his severity. He stood tall, about six and a half feet. Muscles bulged everywhere under the tight black T-shirt seemingly painted over his chest. God, he was huge. Scary.

"Calm down, Bailey," he rumbled in a low voice that incited a shiver of fear.

Hell no! "How do you know my name? Who are you?"

"I'm not going to hurt you. I promise."

Said the spider to the fly . . . "Where am I? What do you want?"

"To save you."

From what? Was he planning to kill her in order to "save" her from the cruel world or whatever? Terror made her tremble again.

"I was doing fine on my own. Let me go. Please! I won't tell anyone about this."

Compassion tempered his face for a moment. "Even if you didn't, you'd be in far more danger. I know you're scared. I'm sorry I had to get this drastic, but there's a lot going on that you don't know."

"You have me mistaken for someone else."

"I don't. Just hear me out." The man's assurance rattled her even more. "We'll start at the top. According to your records, you were born Bailey Katherine Benson. You came into the world twenty-one years ago on December fourth in Houston. But I don't think that's true."

What? Obviously he was a few sandwiches shy of a picnic. "No, that's exactly who I am. If you're looking for someone else—"

"I'm pretty sure you're not, but let me finish telling you my theory."

"Let me the hell out of here!" she demanded, struggling against her restraints. But he didn't budge—and neither did they. "You have to let me go. People are going to miss me."

"Not the people you know as your parents. They're 'dead.'" He made air quotes.

"Yes, they are. Why are you doing this to me?"

"The identities of Jane and Bob Benson are dead, but I suspect the people behind them are very much alive. Didn't you ever think those names were a little too simple?"

"For what, good parents?"

They'd been supportive of her academically, except her weird love of science. Her mother had called that unladylike. Artistically, they'd been in favor of dance. They hadn't been the sort of parents to hug or tease her a lot, but at least one of them had dutifully attended every recital. Her dad had sometimes been preoccupied, wrapped up in his career, she supposed. Her mom had passed her time constantly gardening or sewing—neither of which had appealed to Bailey.

"I'll bet they were FBI agents with aliases whose mission it was to raise and protect you, but I'll check on that."

"No." The denial slipped out automatically.

Still, his words echoed in her head. She hadn't looked like either of her parents—not even a little. She hadn't shared any interests with them, either. As she'd gotten older, they had insisted she learn to defend herself, to fire a gun, to hunt and cook her own game, to box. She hadn't taken much of it seriously. Instead, she'd been hurt, assuming that her dad had wanted a son, and when he hadn't fathered one, he'd tried to morph her into one instead. But federal agents?

No, they'd been her *parents*. Maybe they hadn't been perfect, but they'd been hers. She wasn't going to let this psycho tell her otherwise.

"I'm not having this conversation with you."

He sat on the edge of the bed and leaned close, his face looming just above hers. "You are. You're cuffed, remember? I swear I won't hurt you, but you're not going anywhere until I let you. It's for your own good."

She bit her lip. He might have her in a bind—literally—but that didn't mean she had to share any part of herself with him. "Fuck off, creep."

He grabbed her chin in a firm but not painful grip. That surprised her. If he wanted to cause her pain, he could do it easily. She had no way to stop him, and he was certainly big enough. Then again, maybe he was toying with her or biding his time until he got whatever he wanted from her.

"Are you forgetting who has the upper hand?"

Like that was possible. "Why don't you tell me what you want so we can get this over with and I can go home?"

His big fingers left her face. He dragged them up her arms and curled a hot path around her manacled wrists, pinning her deeper into the mattress. A manly spice wafted from him. Cataloging it momentarily distracted Bailey. The fact that Mr. Tall, Dark, and Menacing smelled good just seemed wrong.

He scanned her face. Trying to decide how to proceed? "What's your earliest memory?"

Disturbing dreams. "Memories? I thought you'd want money. I don't have much, by the way. Let's not play this stupid game."

"You don't want to answer me? All right. I can wait. I've got all afternoon. How about you?"

"Afternoon?" She blinked at him, then cut her stare over to the long windows on the other side of the room. Sure enough, behind the closed shutters, golden sunlight seeped in between the slats and under the frame.

"It's almost noon," he provided, easing back and releasing her wrists.

How had she lost nearly twelve hours? Horror spread through her, cold and thick. "Please let me go. I have a rehearsal at two. I *have* to be there. Next week, I'm supposed to audition for a part in Dallas for one of Texas Ballet Theater's upcoming shows."

"Then I suggest you talk fast," he growled. "Your earliest memory?"

Bailey couldn't believe that he'd abducted her to ask the first thing she could remember. Did he know how crazy he sounded? But if it would satisfy his weird curiosity so he'd release her . . . "Falling on the playground and losing a tooth."

"How old were you?"

"Five, I think. What does this have to do with anything?"

"Who was with you?"

Why did it matter? "I don't remember."

He stared at her with eyes narrowed, dissecting her. She didn't think he believed her.

"Look," she began. "I hope you find whoever you're looking for, but I'm not her. I really am Bailey Benson from Houston, just like the records state. I'm preparing nonstop for the biggest audition of my career. I'm also expecting company tonight, and he's really special, so—"

"Blane?"

When he ground out her friend's name, she froze. "How did you know that?"

"I was in your house for a few hours last night. You really should lock your doors and windows better." As she gaped at him, he sent her a little smirk. "By the way, I secured your house as much as I could before we left. You need better locks and a security system going forward."

Bailey wanted to ask why he even mentioned it, but that wasn't the most important question of the day. "So you were the one in my room, hovering over me in the dark?"

She remembered that heavy presence, just before she'd felt the prick of a needle in her neck.

"Yes. Why did you have a reaction to Viktor Aslanov's picture on TV?"

"Who?"

"The infamous scientist. He was murdered. They showed his photo in the montage during Callindra Howe's interview."

Bailey couldn't answer her captor's question. She'd seen Aslanov's image before. Every time, it upset her in a way she couldn't explain. "I don't know. Why did you take me from my house in the middle of the night?" Another terrible thought occurred to her. "Are you going to rape me?"

The big man reared back. "The idea of forcing a woman makes my skin crawl. Besides, I was mostly raised by a single mother and I have two sisters. They'd all have my balls if I even tried."

"A-are you going to kill me?"

He tossed his hands in the air. "Were you listening earlier when I mentioned that I'm trying to save you from winding up six feet under?"

"And what? I'm just supposed to believe you?" She gaped at him. "If you're such a stand-up guy, why are you drugging an innocent woman—you did drug me, right?"

"Sedated. It wasn't like I spiked your drink at a bar to take advantage of you."

No, he'd just injected her with some unknown substance that left her unconscious for half a day. Because that was so much more virtuous. "What exactly do you want from me, Mr. . . . What's your name?"

"Not relevant. The only thing that matters is that my goal is to prevent you from winding up like this." He shoved the screen of an iPhone in her face, and from corner to corner it was filled with one of the most gruesome images she'd ever seen.

Bailey screamed. "Oh . . . What the hell?"

Someone had punctured a young woman's rib cage multiple times with something that made symmetrical, seeping holes. They'd cut off her ears, ripped out teeth, snipped off toes. God, she couldn't look anymore. Why would anyone do that to another human being?

"She's not the first victim. In fact, she's the fifth. They should find number six soon, sadly. I was just hours too late to save her, but you . . ." He swallowed as he pocketed the phone again. "I refuse to let that happen to you."

"Why would you think anyone would want to hurt me? How do I know that's not your handiwork?"

"You mean besides the fact that I've already told you I'm busting my ass to save you? If I wanted to torture you to a slow death, why would I show you my intentions first so you'd fight me more?"

"I don't know! If you're a deranged killer, you're not exactly logical."

He shook his head, looking as if he were grappling for patience. "Let's just say that I work for a government agency and that I'm the one wearing the white hat in this scenario. I generally try to avoid bodies, unless they belong to bad guys. Ballerinas don't usually fall into the 'most wanted' category."

"Then explain this to me. You drugged me—"

"Sedated," he corrected.

"Whatever. You take me from my house and life without first uttering a word to me. If you're the good guy here, why didn't you just try to talk to me and explain the situation?"

"Let's role-play this scenario. I walk up to your door and knock. You answer like I'm a pesky salesman or someone trying to change your religion. You ignore me. I doubt highly you invite me into your house so we can have an in-depth conversation about dead bodies."

Okay, he had a point. "So you just abducted me? You didn't even try the logical approach."

He sighed. "We'll continue the scenario. After you slam the door in my face, then the real killer either breaks in or draws you out, and next thing I know, I'm looking at another gruesome crime scene photo. You don't like my methods. I get that. But I'm not going to apologize for wanting you alive."

"What's the rationale for trying to convince me I'm someone other than who I am?"

"A little thing called the truth." He sighed and shook his head. "Sorry. I know you're confused. This situation is difficult and stressful. It doesn't bring out the best in either of us. I'm not trying to be harsh or behave like an ass. We're up against someone sick, and time isn't on our side. So when you challenge me, I get flippant and sarcastic. This isn't how I wanted our discussion to go. I know I'm asking you for a lot of trust. I wish this was easier and we had more time to debate, but we don't."

The apology disarmed her, and Bailey wasn't sure what to make of him. Yeah, he'd behaved a little like an ass, but what if anything he said was true? What if someone *was* coming for her?

"If I listen to you and I can prove that I'm who I claim to be, will you let me go?"

"As soon as I can figure out who's responsible for all the bodies and stop them, sure."

"Why are *you* doing this? Why aren't the police involved?"

"The bodies aren't in any one town or area. And when it involves something that's a potential threat to national security, it's way beyond local police."

"National security?" Now she knew he had to be off-kilter. "How do you think I can possibly threaten the country?"

"Not you, others. I can't say more now. I'm still waiting to confirm who's behind all this."

"That's convenient," she drawled.

"Look, I've been chasing these people from D.C. to Miami. The latest body today was in Mobile. We'll hear about one in Oklahoma shortly."

Whoever he was, he really believed what he was saying. In fact, he was downright passionate about it. That didn't make him less crazy, but if her only avenue out of here so far was to prove that she was Bailey Benson and no one else, then she'd do that.

"I don't know exactly what proof you need that I am who I claim to be. I have a birth certificate and a Social Security—"

"You do, and they were all courtesy of your adoption and Uncle Sam."

"No, you're wrong. I—"

"Well, the woman I'm looking for isn't any of the girls already dead. If the bastards responsible for these murders had found who they're seeking, they wouldn't still be looking. By the way, all the victims were your age, give or take a few months. They were all adopted somewhere around December 1998. They—"

"That's what I'm trying to tell you. I wasn't adopted."

"Are you sure? That's why I asked about your earliest memory."

"And I told you."

"You don't remember anything at all before losing that tooth? *Anything?*"

Not anything real. "Do you?"

"I don't have a nut job or two hunting me, so what I remember is irrelevant."

"How do you know this isn't the work of some serial killer?"

"Whoever this handiwork belongs to, I'll bet he trained once with the CIA or some other government agency. He knows what he's doing, but he leaves telltale marks. Same guy, same M.O. And he always tears apart the vic's residence, as if he's looking for something. That's not common behavior for a serial killer. So let's get back to your earliest memory. Is there something you're not telling me?"

His questioning made Bailey feel as if he was trying to lead her to a specific answer. In the interest of saving time and frustration, she cut to the chase. "What is it I'm supposed to remember?"

He peered at her, those hazel-green eyes studying her, as if trying to pry her brain open and see all the thoughts inside. "Let's try this on for size. Do you have any memory of a really cold day in the middle of farmland? Of walking the side of the road in the snow, covered in blood? Of being spotted by a couple in a blue sedan driving down the road?"

Bailey's heart stopped. He'd described a snippet of her dreams, but . . . they were just a product of her imagination. Her mother had assured her of that over and over. Her father had been adamant about it, in fact. She'd stopped mentioning the dreams to anyone years ago.

So how did this stranger know?

"What is it? You went pale. You're remembering an event?"

She shook her head automatically. It had to be a coincidence. A good guess. Something that made sense. This didn't.

"Yeah, you're remembering. Try to focus. Jesus, I've been looking for you." He leaned closer again, his face anxious. "Keep going. What next?"

In her dream, nothing. She never made it past the sedan and the couple stopping for her. "This can't be . . . It's just a dream I've had a time or two." More like a thousand times or two.

"What if it's not a dream, but a memory?"

"No. Then I would remember it. It doesn't snow in Houston. I've never been to a farm like that. I've never seen that couple in my life."

"Really think about it. If it's a dream, and you've remembered it even after you woke, it had an impact on you. A big one. There's a reason for that."

He leaned in even more, and his male scent curled in her nose again. Bailey wished she could say that he came across as creepy or stalkerish. But no, he just looked hot. Older than her, yes, maybe by eight or ten years, but when she looked at him, she realized that all the guys she'd been dating and eyeing were boys. This one? He was a *man*.

That sounded all kinds of stupid and wrong, but seriously . . . He had a rugged appeal that was impossible not to notice.

Bailey frowned. How long did it take for a girl to fall in lust with her captor? Should she be checking her sanity, her IQ, or both?

"Do you remember anything in the dream before the couple in the car? Before you left those red footprints in the snow?"

She frowned. "How do you know there's anything in the dream before that?"

"Because I know the history of this event. I know what really happened before that little girl fled that house and walked down the side of the road in shock until Good Samaritans found her and took her to the local sheriff. Tell me what's in your dream. We'll see if they match up."

And give him anything that he could use to claim that he was right? That she was this missing girl? "Why don't you tell me what you think happened?"

"The murder of four people. Here." He turned away and grabbed a file she hadn't noticed sitting on a nearby dresser. He thumbed through some of the contents until he came to what he wanted. Photos. He took a few in hand and prowled back in her direction. "Any of these look familiar?"

When he shoved the first picture under her gaze, she looked at the little white house, all alone in a big pasture, and a jolt of shock sizzled through her. It was the house in her nightmares. It wasn't dusted with snow in this photo, as it was in her dream. But the same slightly dingy façade. Same white door with the brass knob. Same two windows on either side of the door. Same little detached garage behind the house and a bit to the left.

Bailey felt the blood drain from her face.

"You see that in your dream?"

"I-I . . ." How was that possible? "Maybe it's a coincidence or I'm psychic or I saw it on the news. I don't remember a murder. I would have recalled something that horrifying."

"Maybe not. If you're the girl who lived there and survived the massacre—and I think you are—you were barely five when it happened. You may have blocked it out. It's not uncommon for the human mind to 'forget' things that are too traumatic to process."

She heard what he was saying, and in his shoes she'd probably think that she was the missing girl, too. But it just didn't compute. She had a good memory. How could she possibly have let a quadruple homicide slip her mind? Her parents had been insistent that the dreams were simply products of her imagination and that she'd never been in danger. Even her psychologist had comforted her with the idea that her nightmares were probably nothing more than a representation of her fears. Which made sense to her. Every time she had the dream, she woke in a terrified shudder and often stayed up for hours. She even had a collection of comedies queued up on Netflix to help her forget.

"I grant you the coincidences are really weird, but me being that girl . . . it doesn't add up."

"Потому, что она вмешается вы."

Because it scares you.

"Of course it does," Bailey answered automatically.

Then she gasped. What the hell had just happened? He hadn't spoken in English. In fact, she didn't remember ever having heard that language. Yet . . . she knew exactly what he'd said.

"Because you know I'm right. And you understand Russian." His smile turned savage.

"Lucky guess." She felt herself paling, struggling to comprehend.

"Bullshit. You're the woman I've been looking for. Do you want to know your real name?"

This could *not* be happening. "Bailey Benson. I have no idea how you figured out what was in my dreams. I can't imagine why you chose me to taunt or mess with or whatever. But I am not going to believe the mad ravings of some guy who—call it what you want—*drugged* me, dragged me from my bed, and tied me to his. And now you're telling me that the parents who gave birth to me aren't my parents at all and that I survived a massacre. No."

"Why would I lie? Why would I risk going to fucking prison to save you if I didn't absolutely believe what I'm saying?"

"I don't know. I don't know *you*. I don't understand any of this. I need to get out of here."

"Do you remember the picture on my phone? You want to look like that?" he challenged, pulling his mobile from his pocket. "If you don't remember how grisly it was, I can show you again."

No. God, no. Bailey shut her eyes. "I don't need to see it."

"Maybe you do if you're going to try to bury your head in the sand and pretend that I'm some random loon."

He had to be. She didn't have a better explanation, but abducting a woman from her bed proved that he couldn't be dipping both oars, right? Believing she was some other woman who knew Russian and had totally different parents until they were butchered when she was five . . . Hell no.

He sighed and sat on the edge of the bed again. When he lifted a hand to her, Bailey flinched, tried to shrink back, but he only pushed the hair from her face and cupped her cheek.

"Don't touch me," she spit out, her heart pounding.

Immediately, he eased back. "I'm not trying to scare you, just give you comfort."

"You want to comfort me? Leave me the hell alone. Let me go."

A long moment passed. He hesitated, seeming to ponder the situation and giving her another one of those piercing stares that made her shiver. Finally, he stood.

"I can give you half of what you want. I'll leave you for a bit and give you some time to think. But I can't let you go. You're here until I can figure out how to keep you safe. Too many people have died for this cause already, and I'll be damned if I'm going to let them add you to the list. You hungry?"

Honestly, she was. And her stubborn pride wanted to refuse to take food from him. The other part of her knew that if she wanted to have the strength later to escape, she couldn't cut off her nose to spite her face.

"Yes."

"Your medical records say you're allergic to peanuts. Anything else? Foods you don't like."

How had he learned that? Bailey didn't want to ask. She just shook her head.

"Fine. I'll have someone bring you something shortly."

So they weren't alone? Maybe someone else would show up and take pity on her, realize that she didn't belong here and—

"I see the wheels turning in that pretty head. No one here will help you. They all know the stakes and won't let you escape. There's no way out of here anyhow." He stalked over to the big floor-to-ceiling windows and opened the shutters. Sunlight streamed in . . . and bars covered the windows.

She wasn't escaping easily.

Her captor fished in his pocket and extracted a key. He leaned over her, their faces too close as he braced his hands on the headboard and peered into her eyes. Breathing turned difficult. Her heart thumped hard against her chest.

"I know you think I'm crazy," he whispered. "Give me time to change your mind."

When he reached out and uncuffed her wrists, Bailey didn't dare refute him. Slowly, he helped her lower her arms to her sides, massaging as the blood rushed back. His touch zipped through her, hot and electric. Powerfully frightening. God, what was wrong with her?

Bailey recoiled. She'd always had bad taste in men, but she refused to stoop so low as to admit her attraction to him. "I got it. Don't—" She tried to scramble away from him. "Don't touch me."

He lifted his hands up in a gesture of surrender and stepped up, off the bed. "I only meant to help, but . . . The bathroom is through that door." He pointed somewhere behind her and to her left. "Before you get excited, the window in there is covered by bars, too. Otherwise, you're free to roam this room. I'll bring you some books and magazines in a bit."

With a pivot, he turned his back to her. She couldn't stay here and wait for him to convince her of his lunacy.

Instinct kicked in. This might be her best chance to escape.

Bailey eased off the bed and crept to one of the shelves near the window, grabbed a heavy wooden statue from its shelf, then tiptoed behind him.

As soon as he unlocked the door and opened it, she rose up on her tiptoes and lifted her arm soundlessly. Normally, she'd never be able to hit anyone. But this was life-or-death.

He whirled suddenly and gripped her wrist in his unyielding hold. She couldn't move as his eyes burned into hers.

"Sweetheart, I've worked as an undercover agent fighting some of the most dangerous people in the world longer than you've been legal. Did you really think you were going to surprise me?"

His mocking question made her feel small, helpless. She hated him for that. "Let me go."

He grabbed the wooden block from her hand, then released her. "Nice try. By the way, the name your biological parents gave you when you were born was Tatiana. You were Viktor Aslanov's youngest daughter."

Then he was gone, the door secured with a sturdy click behind him. Bailey stared, gaped, rooted in place. Could any of what he claimed actually be true?

Chapter Four

THE moment Joaquin let himself out the bedroom door, Mitchell Thorpe, Dominion's owner, stood, blocking the hall with one sharp brow raised. His stare censured. Despite the man's impeccable suit, Joaquin was pretty sure Thorpe could be a badass. Since he'd had a really long few days without a lot of sleep—and no peace whatsoever—he didn't need the other man's shit.

"I appreciate that you're in a difficult position." Thorpe adjusted a cuff link. "As soon as I heard screaming coming from my bedroom, I called Logan. He explained your situation a bit more in depth. I allowed you to come here because the Edgington brothers vouched for you and I was given to understand that you were protecting the potential target of a killer, not abducting a woman. Club Dominion maintains a strictly consensual environment. You can't keep that woman here against her will."

Joaquin swallowed, fighting frustration and dread. "I get that you don't want anyone shining a light on this place or trying to shut you down, but—"

"I have enough of those problems already. Both the evangelists and the asexual lobbying to end my club are apparently either not acquainted with orgasm or afraid of it, so . . ."

A hundred tactics ran through Joaquin's head. He finally settled on the truth. "She's in shock. I'd hoped that once I jogged her memory a little, she'd remember the past. Even though she admitted she has nightmares about the night her family was murdered, she's adamant that she's not Tatiana Aslanov. I need time. If I let her loose now, it won't be long before whoever is doing the hideous work for these bastards will catch her. Did Logan tell you how they're torturing these women?"

"You want to keep her safe. It's admirable. But I can't have her here against her will." His stance softened slightly. "Are you sure she's Aslanov's daughter?"

"I've got the right woman. She even dreams about the house in the snow and the couple who found her wandering the side of the road. I need a few days to convince her and find out what she knows." Thorpe still looked skeptical. "What if these bastards were still after Callie?"

"Why does everyone use Callie against me?" Thorpe's expression thundered with anger. "Leave my submissive out of this."

Joaquin tossed up his hands. "She was ass deep in this mess for nearly a decade. You know just as well as I do that if they'd gotten their hands on her, they would have tortured—"

"If you finish that sentence, you won't have any teeth left." Thorpe looked dead serious. "Callie has suffered long enough. Sean and I are doing our best to make her happy now. We will do whatever it takes to keep her as far away from this as possible."

Time to step back. This tactic was simply pissing Thorpe off, and Joaquin needed the man's cooperation. "Fine. Sorry. If you'll let me, I'd like to talk to both Sean and Callie. I think they have information that could save Tatiana's life."

"I'll ask Sean if he'll talk to you. That's up to him, and will depend, at least in part, on what the FBI wants to keep strictly in-house. Callie . . . Sean and I will have to decide that together. The TV interviews Callie gives are never in depth. They're a matter of survival, since they keep her too public for anyone to kill. But a direct probe about who chased her and why might be too much for her. It's barely been three months. And with the stress of the wedding . . ."

"You agreed yesterday."

"Before you added kidnapping into this mess."

Joaquin didn't like Thorpe's answer, but he understood it. "I know she went through years of hell. I wouldn't ask her to tread this ground again unless I believed the information could help save lives. You and Sean can be beside her every moment."

"I'll consider it. I'd like to talk to Tatiana." Thorpe phrased it like a request, but it wasn't.

Joaquin hedged. "She's probably showering now and she needs some food first."

He didn't understand the protective instinct that suddenly filled him. No, it wasn't quite something protective that nagged at him. Instead, it was almost . . . possessive. That made even less sense. From everything he'd heard, Thorpe was devoted to Callie, so he wasn't likely to proposition anyone else. Besides, Joaquin barely knew Aslanov's daughter. She was just someone he had to keep alive, nothing more.

But he enjoyed the thought of covering her fragile body with his own and filling her with his cock. In fact, parts south stiffened and rose at the idea. He held in a curse.

Thorpe paused. "I'll make sure she gets food. While she's eating, she and I will chat. I'll keep it friendly."

Despite those assurances, Joaquin still wanted to say no. But Thorpe held him by the balls. If he wanted to keep Tatiana someplace secure and talk to the people who could tell him about the group responsible for these murders and their motive, then he had to play by the club owner's rules. It fucking grated on him.

"She's afraid."

"I'm sure." Thorpe looked at him like he was an idiot for stating the obvious.

Despite all the praise the Edgington brothers had heaped on Dominion's owner, Joaquin wasn't sure he liked Thorpe at all.

"You took her from her bed and brought her in here unconscious," the club owner pointed out. "I don't approve."

I wasn't asking for your opinion, Mr. Stick Up Your Ass. "I didn't have better options."

"Well, now you have forty-eight hours to make your . . . guest consent to being here or I'll take matters into my own hands."

Joaquin gritted his teeth and watched Thorpe walk away. He stalked down the hall in the opposite direction.

Now what the fuck was he supposed to do? He could study the evidence again, but he'd done that a thousand times. Without fresh eyes or clues, he was no closer to knowing exactly who had killed Nate or why. Small mercy they hadn't tortured him terribly. And if he didn't want to see the woman in Thorpe's room reduced to a bleeding heap of flesh, he needed to bite his tongue. He also needed to figure out how the hell he was going to convince Tatiana to consent to being here in the next two days. He'd given her his evidence. He didn't have a lot of other avenues left.

So he found the bar instead. With the club closed, he didn't see anyone except a muscle-bound guy with a square face, a cleft chin, and a fuck-off attitude. The guy took up the space behind the bar on a step stool, looking at a security camera behind a plastic dome in the ceiling.

"You work here, man?"

The big guy didn't look at him, just directed a screwdriver at the camera's protective bubble. "Yep. I'm Axel, head of security. If I'd gotten a vote, I wouldn't have let you come in here with an unconscious woman who hadn't consented to be here with you."

Get in line. "You'll be happy to know that Thorpe doesn't approve either."

"I have zero tolerance for bullies and even less for rapists."

"Whoa, I'm a federal agent protecting someone who hasn't figured out she's in danger yet." And why was he explaining himself to this guy? Because Axel kept this place safe. *Damn it.* "Is it possible to get a beer around here?"

"We don't serve much booze. Things like restraints, wax, and fire play don't mix well with intoxication."

Joaquin's temper ignited. He rattled Axel's step stool. "I'm trying to save a woman's life. Not rape her. Not get drunk. Why the fuck am I the enemy?"

Finally, Axel looked his way, his blue eyes sharp. "Why should I give a shit about your little feelings? You're a stranger to her, restraining her to a bed against her will. Not only that, if this place gets shut down, I don't have a job and fet folk in Dallas won't have a safe place to play."

He didn't know much about the fet community or their tribulations in finding a protected environment. He didn't want to put anyone out, but he couldn't sacrifice Tatiana's safety, either. "I'm going to convince her that she wants to be here, okay?"

"Make it fast." And with that, Axel was done talking.

Whatever. Maybe a beer wasn't a great idea anyway.

But without something to drink or anything to do except wait, he was going to climb the damn walls. Back down the hall he stalked. How the hell could he become someone Tatiana trusted in the next two days? The only two possibilities he saw: He had to become her friend . . . or her lover.

Joaquin wrestled with his conscience, then buried it. If she wouldn't see reason, he'd have to influence her in whatever way he could. He wasn't out to break her heart, just make sure she lived. And if he got to touch her . . . The situation seemed like a win-win to him.

He smiled and started to plan.

* * *

BAILEY looked up to find an imposing man striding through the door to the bedroom, carrying a tray. He wasn't the same one who'd tried to convince her that she was the Russian scientist's daughter.

This one was more refined, a bit older, but he still had an edge of danger that made her take a half step back.

"Sit." With a jerk of his head, he gestured toward a desk against the far wall.

It looked more decorative than anything. She'd already tried searching inside it for anything useful, especially a way to reach the outside world. She'd settle for Morse code at this point. But she could find nothing. The drawers were locked, and twelve years of ballet and a penchant for science hadn't given her the skills of a petty thief.

Since this man gave off an air that warned her against messing with him, she did as he bid. Besides, Bailey could smell food even across the room, and she was starved.

As soon as she sat, he set the tray in front of her and disappeared through the bathroom.

"That's roast chicken with fingerling potatoes and asparagus," he called across the room, then emerged a moment later carrying a robe. "You can wear this for now if you're cold."

She hadn't been earlier, but after her shower, she'd been unable to find a hair dryer and the strands of her wet hair now brushed all over her back, wetting her nightshirt. She didn't have any other clothes with her. But no complaints. She hadn't expected to find a new toothbrush, a razor, a comb, scented body lotion—a whole array of toiletries.

"Thank you." She didn't take her eyes off the man as he pulled up a nearby chair and regarded her with concerned eyes an unusual shade of gray.

"You're welcome. My girlfriend isn't exactly your size, but she's far closer than anything I could offer you."

He was nearly as tall as the last man who had walked through that door and not any less built. Anything of his, she'd swim in.

"So . . ." he went on. "I'll bring you something of hers shortly. I wanted to feed you first." He looked at her untouched plate and frowned. "Go ahead."

Bailey picked up her fork. The man seemed imposing, but not menacing. Still . . .

"Who are you? No offense, but I don't trust you or your weirdo of a buddy."

"I'm Thorpe."

His name sounded familiar. She wasn't sure exactly why. Then again, everything with her right now was off-kilter. Maybe she was hallucinating.

He wore a ghost of a smile. "And that weirdo isn't exactly my buddy. Joaquin is a friend of a friend, more like. I don't know him well, so I can't precisely set you at ease there. I've already told him that I don't like you being here against your will. That aside, our mutual friends are very highly decorated soldiers and the best men. If they say you're in danger, then you are, and I would caution you against making yourself an easy target for killers."

She didn't have any reason to believe him. For all she knew, Thorpe and Joaquin—the name fit his rugged, macho kind of vibe—had a good cop/bad cop thing going on. It might all be an act, and the pair of them might be playing her. But her gut told her no.

Spearing some asparagus, she popped it in her mouth. She had to believe that they wouldn't talk until her ears bled about keeping her alive, only to then poison her. "I'm not eager to be an easy target. But Joaquin didn't say a word to me before shoving a needle in my neck and dragging me here."

Thorpe's lips pursed in disapproval. "We've exchanged words about his methods. He knows I'm not happy. This place is mine, and I made it clear that while he's under my roof, he'll be playing by my rules. I'll make you a promise, too. Nothing will happen to you that you don't want."

"I don't want to be here at all."

"I understand. Give him two days to work this case and see if he can solve the problem so you can walk out of here without a threat hanging over your head."

"I can't put my life on hold for two days."

"I'm sorry. I know this is difficult."

But Thorpe wasn't going to change his mind or help her escape. "I have a rehearsal today. I never miss them. Then my friend Blane is coming over tonight, and I'll need to let him know I won't be there."

"That's not my decision. I'll speculate that Joaquin won't give you a phone so you can tell the world where to find you, but you're welcome to ask him."

"How could I tell anyone where I am when I don't even know?" she pointed out. "How do I make you understand? Blane will report me missing if I don't show up or tell him I'm somewhere safe."

"And maybe that's for the best." Thorpe stood. "These killers are watching. If you disappear, maybe they'll hesitate or make a mistake. You don't want to give them any reason to pay Blane a visit and try to extract information from him, do you?"

After that photo Joaquin had shown her on his phone? "No!"

"That's what I thought. Now I'll leave you in peace."

She recoiled from the urbane man. As *GQ* as he looked, she sensed there was far more under his surface and that she'd just been manipulated.

"Wait!" Bailey bit her lip until he turned to face her with an inquiring brow. She got the distinct impression he wasn't used to taking orders from anyone. "Why should I trust you?"

A little smile broke across his face. "Let me put it to you this way: I have no reason to lie and everything to lose if I don't keep my promise. You may not believe me yet, and that's fine, but you will be safe."

* * *

ABOUT twenty minutes after Thorpe's departure, Bailey heard a click of the door again and spun around to see Joaquin enter, a plastic grocery sack in hand. God, it was stupid, but she almost gaped at him. It felt ridiculously schoolgirl of her, but he'd showered and shaved, and the absence of stubble showed off every sharp angle of his jaw and chin. He wore another pair of jeans and another tight T-shirt that showed off his muscled physique. The fact that he was physically gorgeous wasn't enough to interest her, though. Her reaction now was about the totally new warmth in his eyes.

"Hi." He entered, setting the bag down on a nearby bookcase and locking the door behind him.

"Hi." She didn't know what else to say.

"I'm sorry about earlier, if I scared you. *If.*" He snorted. "I'm sure I did. Whether you believe me or not, I don't want to see you wind up like the others."

"So it's okay to abduct me?"

"Strictly speaking, no. But I figured better kidnapped than tortured and murdered. The lesser of two evils." He shrugged. "Not a perfect choice, but I didn't have many other options in the few hours I had before this sick bastard came for you."

And she supposed that pointing out once more that he could have talked to her first would again fall on deaf ears. Besides . . . would she really have listened? She'd probably have written him off as a psycho.

"That government agency you work for condone kidnapping, Joaquin?" She couldn't resist taunting him a little.

He did a double take, then frowned. "So Thorpe told you my name? Fine."

After jerking something from his pocket, he flipped open a little leather case to reveal a badge of sorts and an ID that stated his name was Joaquin Muñoz and he worked for the NSA. Bailey stared. Even though he could have forged it, the document looked pretty official. Maybe it shouldn't have, but seeing his credentials made her believe that he probably wasn't a completely crazed weirdo—just mostly.

She glanced again at him. Manly. A little exotic. Interesting. And there she went into stupid-ass territory again.

"You get enough to eat?" He gestured toward her half-empty tray.

Bailey nodded, glad to have a reason to look anywhere but at him. "I don't know where Thorpe got the food, but it was good."

"He told me he was the master of takeout." Joaquin grinned.

She smiled in return, then caught herself. Wiping the expression off her face, she crossed her arms over her chest. "I need to call Blane and tell him I won't be home tonight. He'll be worried."

"Thorpe told me you two talked about this. I agree with him. You disappearing will throw this killer off guard. Maybe he'll slip up. Maybe he'll act out. I need to find some way to figure out who's responsible and be able to prove it. Blane will be safer if he knows nothing."

Before she could respond, the phone in his pocket buzzed. He pulled it free and read. For a moment, Bailey considered grabbing it from his hand and calling 911, but he'd take it from her before she could get the call out. He'd even dismantled the lock on the bathroom door—she'd checked—so she couldn't hope to outrun him there and keep emergency dispatchers on the phone long enough to trace the signal.

Holding in a sigh, she decided to wait for a better opportunity. At least he didn't seem menacing anymore. In fact, he almost looked . . . friendly. Because Thorpe had duped her into trusting them? Bailey didn't want to be stupid, but what if someone really was after her? What if she truly was safer here?

Suddenly, Joaquin cursed, a low, ugly growl. Then he stared at the ceiling as if grasping for patience. When he looked her way again, his expression had gone bleak.

"What is it?" The words slipped out. She shouldn't be concerned about him, but he looked genuinely upset. It simply wasn't in her nature to stand back and watch people suffer.

"Remember the missing girl in Oklahoma I told you about?" When she nodded, Joaquin shoved his phone under her face. "Here she is."

Bailey stole a quick glance, then looked away. The photo was every bit as stomach-turning as the last one he'd shown her—maybe more. The woman wasn't a brunette this time, but a blonde. She'd bled more before she died. Her face looked permanently contorted in pain.

Everything about the sight made Bailey's stomach recoil and fear zip through her. Maybe she'd been too trusting? How did she really know Joaquin was telling the truth about the who, where, and when or this victim?

"Is there a news item about this murder? Anything to read?"

He sent her a crafty stare as if he saw right through her question, then gave her a decisive nod. "I'm sure there is. I'll find it. Because then you'll know that I was here with you and couldn't possibly have committed this murder."

Bailey wanted proof and waited while he flipped through his phone until he came to a local news station from Oklahoma City. The grisly discovery was front page news.

She scanned the story. The coroner estimated the time of death somewhere between nine and eleven that morning. If authorities could have found this girl just a bit sooner . . . But given the picture Joaquin had shown her, this killer had been working his personal brand of gross on her for hours.

Since Bailey wasn't sure if she was still in Houston or elsewhere, she couldn't state absolutely that Joaquin hadn't driven to Oklahoma City, committed this crime, then come back to her. On the other hand, even if he had moved her somewhere near the scene of the crime, he would still have had to come back here, clean up, have a conversation with Thorpe, and appear in front of her looking perfectly calm. It seemed unlikely. She also didn't buy that Joaquin would abduct her, bring her somewhere pretty swanky, feed and promise to protect her if all he intended to do was slice and dice her.

"It's terrible," she murmured.

"I didn't do this." His tone looked every bit as adamant as his expression.

"Trust me. I'd prefer to believe you."

"There's no way I could have killed this girl by even nine a.m., driven the three hours from Norman to Dallas, showered, and appeared here beside you *before* noon. It's not physically possible."

"So we're in Dallas?" She latched onto the little fact with hope. It wasn't much, but it was something.

"Yeah."

"How do I know that's not just a story to make me trust you?"

"Are you kidding?"

Was *he*? "I didn't know you yesterday at this time, and the first time we met, it's because you abducted me. And I'm supposed to simply trust you? Really?"

"I don't know whether to applaud or paddle you."

"Paddle?" She shot him an incredulous stare. "Like I'm a bad little girl and you're going to put me in my place?"

The whole time she spoke, he punched something into his phone. Into the silence afterward, he didn't say a word. Finally, he lifted his head. "No, like you're a stubborn woman who I wish would see reason, and if softening up your ass would do that . . ." He shrugged. "It would be my pleasure."

Bailey blushed. The idea of him spanking her made her both furious and a bit shivery, which was strange. Then again, everything right now was.

"Not happening."

He gave her a smug smile that said they'd see what happened, before he held his phone under her gaze again. "Here."

She looked down at his screen. It was an app that located an iPhone. He'd used it to trace his own. The map showed them smack in the middle of Dallas.

"Do you believe me now?"

Bailey didn't want to give him the satisfaction. He confronted her, confounded her. He'd taken her, threatened her. And yet . . . everything he said about the murders, their location—it all seemed to be true. It could be a hoax, yes. At this point, it would be a really elaborate one. Why would anyone bother?

But that didn't mean he was right about everything. She wasn't a dead Russian scientist's daughter.

"If you didn't come here to show me a picture of another body, why did you come?"

"To check on you. To bring you those clothes Thorpe promised." He stalked across the room and retrieved the bag he'd brought when he first entered, then he thrust it into her hands. "To see if you needed any goddamn comfort."

Bailey took the bag and peeked inside. Clothes, just like he'd claimed. The frustration in his tone made her feel a little guilty, which was probably stupid. But if he was right and someone else might mistake her for Tatiana Aslanov and kill her, then he'd risked his ass to help her. She bit her lip.

"Thanks," she muttered.

"Go see if that fits. If not, I'll find something else."

Would he try to attack her while she was in the bathroom changing or was she just sounding paranoid? If he hadn't violated her while she'd been tied up and passed out, why would he try to assault her now?

"Sure."

With a last glance over her shoulder at him, she peered up into his craggy face. God, he really was so masculine. She'd never been one of those girls who got off on having a guy who was a lot bigger than her. She'd always wrinkled her nose at bodybuilder types. Sure, she didn't mind tilting her head back a bit to kiss a guy, but . . . She shook her head. So she was thinking of kissing Joaquin now? After she'd just worried he might attack her? Where the hell was her head?

She sighed and eased into the bathroom, shutting the door even though it no longer locked. She tore into the sack. A new pair of panties with the tags on them. They were a little big, but not bad. Same with the jeans. The bra, however, was a joke. Thorpe's girlfriend had clearly been more gifted in the boob department than she was. If she wore it, that bit of lace would only bunch under the T-shirt he'd included. She shoved the pretty white undergarment back in the sack and donned the blue cotton shirt. Like everything else, it was a little big, but hey, it would conceal the fact she wasn't wearing a bra.

Shoving her nightshirt in the sack as well, she opened the door and found Joaquin waiting. His stare fell on her, intent, evaluating. Heat transformed his green eyes and sucked her in. Their gazes locked. Under the too-big shirt, she felt her nipples bead.

She swallowed. "Everything fits well enough."

No way was she going to tell him about the bra.

Slowly, he nodded, scanning her body. "Your feet cold? You need socks?"

If he was a murderous freak, would he care? "Please."

"I'll hunt you up some." He inched closer, as if he feared spooking her. Then he stretched out his hand. "Come sit with me. Can we talk about what's going on again? I'll bark less."

Bailey really didn't want to. But if this truly was happening to her, it looked serious. And the only way she would be able to leave Joaquin's captivity was to listen and do her best to cooperate.

Sucking in a breath, she hesitated, then put her hand in his. Electricity pinged up her arm. She wouldn't have thought it possible, but he focused even more intently on her. Her heart stuttered. The connection was surprisingly intense. Her head spun as he led her to the bed.

When he wrapped his hands around her waist and lifted her to the mattress, she stiffened.

Before she could protest, he turned away to grab the chair from the desk and drag it in front of her. He plopped down and hoisted one foot on the bed frame, his big legs spread. "Tell me about the rest of your dream. Where does it start for you?"

She jerked her stare away from the faded denim between his thighs. "Always the same. I look down and find that my pink shirt is red for some weird reason. I know I need to leave the house. I'm not sure why but I'm convinced that I must be quiet. There's something all over the walls. Paint . . . or blood. I don't know. Anyway, I walk into the hall and head toward the door at the end, but the red stuff is around my feet, and I almost slip on it. It's warm. Then when I reach the door, I realize it's all over my hands. I start to panic. The wind blows the door open, then I'm outside." She shrugged. "You know the rest."

"You don't see anyone else?"

"No."

"Dead or alive?"

"No," she reiterated.

He crossed his arms over his chest, stared at her for an unnerving moment, then rose and left the room. Bailey stared at the closed door with a frown. What had she said or done? Was he coming back?

Why was the thought that he might not upsetting?

Before she could puzzle that out, he returned with the folder of photos he'd brought earlier. He rifled through it until he came to one. Instead of simply sitting and handing it to her, Joaquin approached with caution. With care.

"I want you to look at this and tell me if anyone in this photo looks familiar to you."

"If it will help . . ." She nodded.

Joaquin turned the photo in her direction and put it in her hands. When she looked down at the family, her immediate response felt like a punch to the gut. She couldn't breathe. Felt faint. "Who are these people?"

As soon as the words left her mouth, she recognized Viktor Aslanov. The slight woman beside him with the graceful hands must be his wife. Bailey felt as if she'd seen that face before. On the news, maybe? Three children surrounded them. The oldest, a boy with dark hair. He looked about six. Beside him, a little girl with light brown hair smiled, flashing a row of straight baby teeth. In front sat a toddler who looked maybe two. She had a shock of platinum hair and something in common with her father—bright blue eyes.

"Are you trying to tell me you think the youngest one is me?" she asked Joaquin, surprised to find that her voice shook.

"Yeah. This picture was taken about three years before the Aslanovs died. A family member in Russia provided it to authorities shortly after the murders. The little one there . . . The shape of the eyes is the same as yours."

True. Bailey wanted to argue that the hair color wasn't the same, but hers had been much lighter in the pictures her parents had taken of her as a young girl. It had become progressively darker between about seven and puberty. She chewed on her lip.

"Does the toddler look familiar? Did your parents have any pictures of you at that age?"

"No. Our house burned down when I was—"

"Five?" he asked with a knowing stare.

She opened her mouth to answer, then slowly closed it as she exhaled. "Yeah."

"Convenient, don't you think? All your baby pictures were mysteriously lost? They didn't ever send your snapshots to grandparents, aunts, uncles—anyone who could send copies back?"

"My mother said that she was estranged from her family, so she considered herself an orphan. My father was an only child whose own parents had passed away before I was born."

"Not saying it's impossible, just asking you to entertain the idea that they might not have been completely honest." He stood and leaned over the photo, then pointed to Aslanov's wife. "You look a lot like her."

She'd noticed that and hadn't wanted to even think it.

"Same build. Same hair color. Same lush mouth."

Joaquin had noticed her mouth? Bailey's gaze bounced up from the picture to his face. The hot stare was back. She licked her lips, and he followed her motion. He didn't move or change expression, but she sensed his every muscle tightening. Suddenly, she had a hard time breathing.

God, she couldn't be attracted to him, not after he'd taken her from her home without her consent. Not when her life was so up in the air. Not when she didn't know for sure who she was.

Bailey jerked her stare back down to the woman. "What do you know about her?"

"Not much. I did some asking around this morning and got a few answers. Aleksandra Aslanov had been a ballerina for the Bolshoi before the fall of the USSR. She was lovely and lauded. She met Viktor after a performance. He was smitten. He came from an influential family, and she'd barely danced her way out of poverty. They married quickly. Based on timing, I'd say she was pregnant.

"Around the time the USSR collapsed, Aleksandra gave birth to a son and they left the country. In the vacuum of power, Viktor had no more funding, and he knew there was more money in the West. At first, the U.S. resisted letting him in because of his controversial theories and experiments. He eventually convinced the U.S. government that he'd only conducted his radical experiments at Soviet edict. Of course, everyone discovered later that wasn't true, but by then, he and his small family had moved to that farm in rural Indiana—not too many people asked questions out in the middle of nowhere—and they'd added two more children to their family."

"So . . . he went to work for Callindra Howe's father, trying to cure cancer. Aslanov stumbled onto something that later got him killed. At least that's what they said on the news." She frowned. "But why?"

"There are gaps in the story, yes. That's another reason I'm here. Thorpe, whom you met earlier, knows others who have more information. I just haven't seen these people yet."

Bailey frowned. Maybe Joaquin was simply stalling or full of crap. Maybe he was trying to lull her into a false sense of security.

Heaven forbid if he was telling the truth.

Panic crept through her system. She couldn't imagine a scenario in which everything she'd known had been a lie, everyone she'd loved had really begun as a stranger.

Gathering her knees up to her chest, she wrapped her arms around them and resisted the urge to rock. "I can't help you."

Joaquin stood and leaned over her, dropping a big, dark hand on her shoulder. "Tatiana?"

She sent him an angry glare, shaking her head. Tears filled her eyes, stinging like acid. "That's *not* my name."

He stroked her arm softly, and in a distant corner of her mind she marveled at how tender such a big man could be. "If you don't want me to call you that, I won't. I just want you to consider that if you're not Tatiana Aslanov, there are an awful lot of coincidences here."

She clutched her knees tighter. He wasn't saying anything she hadn't already thought, but somehow, hearing it out loud scared her more. "Even if I am her, I still can't help you. If that's me, that whole part of my life . . . it isn't even a memory. It's just blank. There's nothing."

Caressing his way back up her arm, he lifted her chin with a gentle finger. "I know I'm asking for a lot. You would have been very young. But I don't have anything else. I'll work with you the best I can, but I've got to press ahead. If I don't, others may die. You'll be in danger. You'll never have your life back. And I'd never forgive myself if something happened to you. Can we agree to keep exploring who you might be and what you might know?"

"I'm scared," she whispered.

It was probably stupid to admit that to him, but she didn't have anyone else now. If she could believe Thorpe—he wasn't necessarily in her corner, but he didn't like Joaquin's methods. On the other hand, if her captor was being honest about trying to stop these terrible murders, then . . . well, he wasn't hurting her. Upsetting her, yes. But were his actions really awful? She didn't want women dying, especially in such ghastly ways. Maybe he was actually kind of noble.

She did not just think that. No, she had. Damn it. Because she wanted to believe nothing bad would happen to her? Or because she was actually identifying with her captor. Both probably. She was sounding dangerously Stockholm syndromish. Fabulous.

"I know, baby girl." His voice deepened, roughened.

That probably should have come across as patronizing. Instead, the words sounded like an endearment sliding off his tongue. His timbre made her tremble.

"Come here." He didn't give her time to deliberate, just wrapped his arms around her and lifted her against his chest.

Bailey's first instinct was to struggle for escape. Then she realized that Joaquin wasn't holding her tightly. She could step away at any time she wanted.

Joaquin pressed her cheek against his chest, and she felt his big arms cross over her back, heard his heartbeat thud in her ear. He surrounded her, strong, masculine, and . . . seemingly so safe. What was wrong with her? She fought the feeling. Breathed in, out, tried to clear her head.

But no, it was still there. Why? Because her instinct knew that Joaquin wasn't dangerous? Or because somewhere deep down she knew he was the first person in her life to give her the truth?

"Look at me." His voice turned deeper still.

Bailey heard the low, coaxing note, knew she should resist it. But she didn't want to.

Slowly, she lifted her head from his chest as he thrust his hands in her hair and tugged just enough so that she had nowhere to look but into his eyes. Catching her breath was suddenly hard, thinking even more difficult.

"Joaquin . . ." She wasn't even sure what she was asking for.

He scanned her face, seeming to drink her in. His eyes went dark, hot. His grasp on her hair tightened. "Right here."

Then he began to lower his mouth to hers.

Chapter Five

A JANGLING at the bedroom door startled Bailey. She yanked away from Joaquin just before his lips touched hers, then jerked her gaze to the knob as she dragged in a breath. The door opened and Thorpe stood in the opening, staring at the two of them. His expression told her that he knew exactly what he'd interrupted.

As heat climbed up her face, Bailey turned away, unable to look at either of them. With the spell broken and Joaquin's solid form and musky scent not clouding her thoughts, she felt so vulnerable, stupid. Out of her element. If she wasn't careful, she'd end up being a victim of some kind—probably of a broken heart. Joaquin was way too good at seduction.

"Sean and Callie are back. I've spoken with both of them. They'll talk to you. For the record, I'd rather leave Callie out of this, but Sean wants to exchange information. I'll show you where they are. If you'll follow—"

"No need for that, Mitchell. We're here," said a feminine voice.

Mitchell. Mitchell . . . Thorpe? That name—she remembered where she'd heard it now. He was Callindra Howe's former boss. Which meant that Callie must be . . .

Bailey whirled around to see faces she'd seen on TV at least a dozen times. Callindra entered with a welcoming smile, her dark hair streaming over her shoulders, carrying an Hermès handbag that probably cost as much as Bailey's entire gross earnings last year. She recognized the shoes as Chanel. Coupled with a gorgeous shimmery blue blouse, bling jeans, and perfectly red lips, the heiress looked positively stunning.

Then another man sent her a sidelong glance that chastised as he stepped in front of her. "Lovely, what did we talk about before Thorpe and I let you come in here?"

Sean Mackenzie, Callindra's fiancé. Holy cow, the former FBI agent was every bit as good-looking as he appeared on TV. But Bailey found herself truly drawn to the expression Sean sent the other woman. Somehow, that one dominant look promised both hell and hot sex—later. But under that his eyes danced with affection.

What would it be like to have any man look at her like that?

"Pet?" Thorpe drawled with a raised brow.

"You told me to stay out of the conversation until someone asked me a direct question. I didn't say anything to her. I just smiled. The poor girl looks nervous."

"So much for you maintaining a low profile . . ." Sean sighed.

"C-Callindra Howe?" Bailey blinked. The woman was, like, a celebrity.

"Just Callie." She peeked around Mackenzie's broad shoulder. Then with an impish grin, she looked Thorpe's way.

"A minx, I tell you." Mackenzie shook his head.

"Always," Thorpe agreed, then sent Callie a disapproving stare. "What am I going to do with you?"

Her grin broadened as she sent him a come-hither stare. "I have ideas."

Bailey blinked and barely kept her mouth closed. Did Mackenzie realize his fiancée was flirting with another guy, one who'd stated earlier that he had a girlfriend?

Sean turned and brushed a lingering kiss on Callie's rosy lips, holding her close. "So do I. Now greet Thorpe, then we'll get started."

She kissed her groom-to-be again, then headed over to Thorpe, who welcomed her with open arms—and a scorching kiss. Bailey nearly gasped in shock.

"I have ideas, too, pet," he muttered. "You may not like them, so be ready."

"Mitchell, I haven't seen you all day. I missed you," she murmured in a pretty pout. "But Sean and I finished the last of the wedding stuff. We're ready for Saturday."

"No surprise party for my birthday?" The question sounded more like a threat.

Callie's pout deepened. "I wanted to, but Sean put his foot down."

"Excellent." He kissed her forehead. "Now turn around. There's someone you should meet."

Tucking her hand in Thorpe's, she reached for Sean's, too. The three of them stood linked. Together. Bailey suddenly understood that Callie was in love with them both. It was all over her face. They loved her just as madly—and seemed to not only accept that fact, but to share her.

A bolt of envy pierced Bailey. Other than her one short-lived romance as a senior in high school that had resulted in a prom date and the loss of her virginity, she'd never experienced much in the way of romance. Being cooped up in a dance studio with a bunch of other aspiring ballerinas and a few guys who'd been mostly fighting the urge to come out of the closet hadn't been great for her love life.

Thorpe urged Callie forward. "This is Bailey Benson and Joaquin Muñoz. They arrived early this morning from Houston. Logan sent them."

"I'm Callie Howe." The heiress held out her hand politely, and they both shook it.

"Soon to be Mackenzie." Sean corrected with a grin, then shook their hands, too.

The gorgeous brunette cocked her head to one side, giving Thorpe a puzzled glance. "New members?"

Of what? Bailey wanted to ask.

Before she could, Joaquin shook his head. "Logan's brother is married to my little sister. I'm working on a case. The guys suggested that I talk to Mackenzie. And especially to you, Callie."

"Why don't we all sit?" Thorpe suggested. "It's not going to be a quick conversation."

"Thanks. I appreciate this." Joaquin pulled two chairs toward a window seat. He took the one closest to the door.

Thorpe settled on one end of the bench under the shuttered glass, Sean on the other. With a happy smile, Callie settled herself in the middle. Sean wrapped an arm around her shoulders, and she rested her head against him. Thorpe dropped his hand on her thigh possessively, making her smile widen just a bit more.

The trio's openness about their relationship surprised Bailey, but they looked utterly at peace. Meant to be. They'd probably known it at first sight and just fallen madly in love. Callie had obviously been much smarter in her romantic life, and Bailey chastised herself again for letting Joaquin nearly kiss her. He wanted to protect her—if he was telling the truth. Big if. But he hadn't sought her out looking for eternal love. She shouldn't be stupid enough to allow herself to feel any emotion for a man capable of abducting a woman and possessing frightening information about a string of mutilated bodies.

"So if Logan sent you to talk to me, this must have something to do with whoever killed my family," Callie murmured, her smile dimming. "Are those two dirtbags from LOSS back from Mexico and on my tail again?"

"LOSS?" Joaquin leaned forward in the chair beside her.

Nice to know she wasn't the only one already confused.

Sean sighed. "The League of Secessionist Soldiers. We've managed to keep this paramilitary separatist group's involvement in this case out of the news, so they probably sound unfamiliar."

"They must be the well-funded fuck-all-crazies Logan mentioned." Joaquin sighed.

"They are," Thorpe confirmed. "Convinced the country needs to be dissolved so that we can all form our own sects based on blood, race, and religion—the purer the better."

"Bigots, in other words," Joaquin spat.

"The gun-toting kind." Thorpe's lips lifted in a smile, but it wasn't a pleasant expression.

"Precisely. As you're probably aware, Callie's father paid a Russian scientist for his research."

"Viktor Aslanov. I know," Joaquin cut in, looking tense, anxious.

Bailey tensed. Did she really want to know all this?

"When Daniel Howe discovered that his money had funded research he never intended, he demanded Aslanov turn it all over to him. But the Russian—"

"Had already sold it to LOSS. But why would a separatist group want Aslanov's research?"

"Well," Sean drawled. "To defeat a military with the size and sophistication of the U.S. forces, they need a leg up. They're never going to outspend or out-train Uncle Sam. So why not genetically alter your own soldiers to make them stronger, faster, and smarter?"

"That's insane." Bailey stared at them all. "That won't work . . . will it?"

Thorpe shrugged. "Since we've never seen the actual research, we don't know what exactly Aslanov sold them. We've read guesstimates and heard rumors. We can speculate, but . . ."

"We tend to think that they found whatever work Aslanov had already given them valuable because they'd purchased another phase of research from him." Mackenzie paused. "When Aslanov didn't deliver, they wiped him and most of his family out, then came after Callie's father after they pieced it all together a few years later. But Howe had burned everything the scientist gave him. So the radical idiots shot him and Callie's younger sister."

Bailey sucked in a breath. The people Joaquin swore were after her had killed a man and a child in cold blood, as well as tortured multiple women to death. They wouldn't have any compunction about killing her brutally, too. Maybe she was better off here . . . with Joaquin.

"Daniel Howe left notes about the documents he received from Aslanov, but I'm not sure we'll ever know the exact contents of the research," Sean finished. "For nearly a decade, they came after Callie. We assume they hoped she knew something. Or maybe they simply wanted the last witness to her family's murder out of the way. Luckily, Callie was resourceful and she eluded them."

When he flashed a smile at Callie, the woman's stare caressed him with total devotion. Thorpe's hand tightened on her, and she glanced back at her former boss with a secretive smile, fingering a gorgeous aquamarine circled by diamonds nestled in the hollow of her throat.

"Two of the members of LOSS chased her until Callie went public. Then her profile was too high for them to kill. We received intelligence that they slinked across the border into Mexico to hide out. That's all we know. We're digging deeper into their organization now."

"Do we know of any other people or groups who sought Aslanov's genetic voodoo?" Joaquin asked, clearly mulling over everything they'd heard.

Sean shook his head. "As far as we can tell, no one else knew of the scientist's work. We're not even entirely sure how Aslanov and LOSS hooked up. We do know that with the first round of research LOSS bought, they conducted some human tests."

"Somewhere in South America?" Joaquin ventured.

"We think in Peru or western Brazil, but that's not confirmed."

"Between some other coincidences and the fact that they're clearly willing to kill entire families," Joaquin began, "I'm starting to believe we're dealing with the same bad guys. And one thing I can tell you: They haven't given up."

"I didn't imagine they had." But Sean had hoped. Bailey saw that at a glance.

"Thorpe introduced her as Bailey Benson." Joaquin gestured her way. "That's how the world knows her. I think she's actually Tatiana Aslanov."

Callie's eyes bulged. She cast a glance at Sean, who gripped her hand. Thorpe set a bracing palm at her back.

"The Russian's youngest daughter, the one who disappeared?" Sean asked.

"It's his theory. I have no memory of that at all," Bailey rushed to clarify.

"But she would have been awfully young. She knows Russian and isn't sure why," Joaquin pointed out. "She had a visceral reaction to seeing Viktor Aslanov's face on television. She's a ballerina like her mother, but has a deep aptitude for science like her father. Most telling, she has dreams about the house where the murders took place and the exact scene in which Tatiana was found, right down to the details."

"It could be a coincidence," Bailey argued, but even to her own ears, that sounded unlikely.

"You were adopted at the age of five, just like Tatiana," he argued. "And you have her eyes."

"Blue eyes are common, and my parents never said I was adopted."

"Did they say you weren't?" he countered.

Bailey couldn't stop fighting for herself, her identity. The situation was frustrating and bizarre. Worse, Joaquin had uncovered more coincidences that made her uncomfortable. But she still couldn't imagine how she could truly be someone other than the person she'd known herself to be for the last twenty-one years. She couldn't wrap her head around that.

Sean leaned forward, his eyes gentle. "I know this must be hard to accept."

"Impossible." Bailey shook her head. "Accepting that your whole life has been a lie—"

"Not your whole life," Joaquin cut in, taking her by the chin and turning her to face him. "You're still the same girl who danced her first pointe at twelve. The girl who won the science fair in seventh grade. You're still the same person who grew up, made friends, had crushes, experienced life and loss and love. Just because your name might be different, that doesn't change who you are."

Oddly, his words made her cry. Or maybe the mountain of fear and confusion had finally collapsed in on her. She heard his logic and knew that a name shouldn't wipe out who she was or what she'd experienced and achieved. But it felt like more than a name. His beliefs called her whole identity into question.

"That's easy to say because it's not *you*," she tossed back. "J-just go on with your story."

Joaquin locked his jaw. In frustration, yes. But Bailey couldn't fail to see concern before he turned to the others.

Her stomach flipped over as she listened to Joaquin explain the bodies of women cropping up across the country, explained their similarities—age, background, coloring. As she listened again, Bailey closed her eyes, wondering how this could be happening. Less than twenty-four hours ago, she'd been a just another Houston woman prepping for an audition and vaguely contemplating where her life would lead.

Now she was in Dallas with a dark, dangerous man she barely knew, wondering exactly who she was and if she'd make it out of this ordeal alive.

"So they're after you?" Sean concluded at the end of Joaquin's story, leveling a heavy stare at her. The affectionate fiancé had been replaced by a cold agent.

"That's what Joaquin thinks."

"Yes," he answered Sean.

"Did you see any evidence of anyone else pursuing you before yesterday?"

"No."

"Were you watching for that?" Joaquin challenged.

"Why would I? I never imagined anyone would be after me. I was an ordinary woman living an ordinary life. I just did my thing."

"If you're Tatiana Aslanov and LOSS is onto you, that's not the case anymore." Sean tried to soften his warning with a compassionate stare. "Even if you're not the missing girl, they believe you might be. So you're still very much in danger."

His words reverberated through her system, echoing the worry in her head. Bailey sat back in her chair and blinked. Confusion, anxiety, horror—it all hovered just under a blanket of smothering shock. Everything was coming at her so fast . . .

She jumped out of her chair and paced away, not caring that Joaquin stared after her. She didn't even want to think about how surreal all this was again. But that part was becoming harder and harder to ignore.

Heels clicked across the floor. Bailey tensed just before someone laid a gentle hand on her shoulder. She whirled to see Callie standing beside her.

"I know this is difficult. They're so focused on the who, when, why, what, and how to crush the danger that they forget we can be overwhelmed and scared."

Bailey nodded. The woman appeared so collected. Not just that, but whole—both inside and out. Looking at her, no one would ever guess that she'd run for her life for almost ten years, that as a teenager she'd been hunted from state to state, identity to identity. But Callie had overcome and found her future.

Whether she was Tatiana Aslanov or not, if anyone believed she was, they would hunt her. She had to focus on that now. Hopefully, the rest would sort itself out.

Pressing her lips together to try to keep her composure, Bailey blinked away more tears. "When you were running from these killers, did you ever have anything that felt like a normal life?"

Callie opened her mouth, then closed it. She shook her head. "I'd love to make you feel better, but I would rather prepare you for reality. No. I was always looking over my shoulder." With a squeeze of her arm, the woman went on. "We can hide you here for a while. Sean, Thorpe, and Axel will move mountains to keep you safe." She glanced back at the three men, now in deep discussion about LOSS and how to keep them off Bailey's tail. "I think Joaquin would do the same and more."

"I-I don't even know him. We were 'introduced' when he stuck a needle in my neck to drug me and bring me here."

"He did it to keep you safe," Callie pointed out. "That's a tough way to meet, and I'm sure it doesn't inspire confidence. But if it makes you feel any better, the men he knows, Logan and Hunter Edgington, they're protectors through and through. They saved my friend, London, from someone trying to kill her. They're both former SEALs. You don't know them or me, but I swear if they have anything to do with Joaquin, then you're in no danger from that man. Besides, I see the way he looks at you . . ."

Bailey glanced past Callie and found Joaquin's stare drilling into her. Protective. Hot. Full of unspoken intent. As their gazes locked, it impacted her somewhere in the middle of her chest, then boomed uncomfortably lower. Taking a breath got difficult. As she fell into his green eyes, a wave of dizziness floated through her head.

She jerked her gaze free. God, she sounded like an idiot swooning over a good-looking man. He was a dangerous stranger dragging her into dangerous crap.

"I'm focused on staying alive," she told Callie. "But hearing that I might not be who I believed . . . That's a lot to accept."

"Of course it is! My situation was different because I voluntarily changed identities, but the result was the same. Lots of new towns, new lives, new . . . everything." Callie shrugged. "The important thing is stopping these guys so you can be you again, whoever that ends up being."

Digesting those words, Bailey chewed on her lip. Callie understood what she was going through probably better than anyone else;

she'd cut through all the emotion and gone straight for the heart of the matter. She'd given what sounded like good advice.

"Yeah. Me." Whoever that was. "If I'm that girl, I don't know anything."

"At least not that you remember now." Callie sent her a soft expression of sympathy. "Give yourself a break. Everything is happening quickly. You can't expect to just snap your fingers and accept that homegrown terrorists are out to get you, that your family may not have been your biological relations at all, and that people you have virtually no memory of may have given birth to you."

"You got that right." She didn't see the humor in this situation, but she tried to smile. It was either that or cry again. Besides, Callie understanding her plight was somehow really reassuring.

Bailey hadn't experienced a lot of empathy growing up. Her father had often been distant, her mother flighty. Sometimes, she'd felt like a stranger in her home and wondered why she was so different than her parents, why they had nothing in common.

Maybe now she knew.

"It's equally hard, I imagine, to know that you lost a biological family you don't even remember to the same violence hunting you now. I remember my dad and my sister really well, obviously. But to have them gone in an instant and still have to elude killers in the middle of my shock and sadness, to find safety . . . It took me a long time to feel as if I'd grieved properly. Longer still before I finally believed I could start looking forward, rather than back."

"I can imagine." And Bailey had a terrible suspicion that her own life could be one giant mirror of Callie's years on the run if she couldn't direct these dangerous killers away from her. But how?

"Don't forget, though. You have an advantage," Callie added. "I had no one for years, not until I came to Dallas and met Thorpe."

The woman turned to glance at her former boss and . . . whatever else the man was to her. He met her gaze with a reassuring nod before turning back to the men's conversation.

A flicker of regret crossed Callie's face. "Even when I came to Thorpe, I didn't tell him who I was. I didn't trust anyone. Eventually, he figured it out, but I'll always wonder if my life would have been . . . I don't know, easier? Fuller? Less terrifying, maybe, if I'd opened up sooner. Sean came along about four years later. Same story. They had to pry everything out of me."

"And now you're with them both?" Bailey blurted the question. "I'm sorry. It's none of my business."

"It's fine." Callie grinned with a little wince mixed in. "Our relationship isn't conventional, but it works for us. Thorpe and I tend to butt heads. Sean is the calming influence we both need."

"The referee?"

"Something like that. I love them both so much and I'll be forever grateful that they fought to save me." Callie leveled her with a serious stare. "Joaquin is fighting to save you. I'm not suggesting you should fall in love with him or anything, but you have someone on your side already. Be grateful. It can make a huge difference."

"Ultimately, I have to get myself out of this mess."

"You do, but fighting this alone is over your head, just like it was over mine. We're talking about terrorists and killers. Me trying to do everything without help cost me a lot of years of misery, not to mention that I'm damn lucky to be alive. Sometimes, helping yourself is figuring out who might stand beside you and make your world a safer place." Callie glanced at Joaquin.

Bailey mulled the woman's words, then glanced at her captor. Or was he her savior? She really didn't know anymore.

Suddenly, Sean rose. "I'll see what I can find." Then he looked Callie's way. "I'll be right back, lovely."

She smiled. "I'll be here."

"Why don't you go eat something?" He frowned at her, concern settling over his face.

"I will." When he sent her a skeptical glare, Callie grinned. "I promise."

With a squeeze of Bailey's hand, she strolled back to Thorpe and settled beside him. He curled her against his side and held her close.

"You're still not eating, pet?" Thorpe asked gently, but he didn't sound pleased.

"I've just been so busy."

He leveled her with a demanding stare that said he refused to let the subject go.

"All right. I'm going." She gave a long-suffering sigh and rose.

Thorpe swatted her ass. "A meal, Callie. Not an apple. Not a cup of yogurt. I left you several choices in the fridge. Warm one up."

The gorgeous brunette looked like she really wanted to protest, but she didn't. "Yes, Sir."

At the reverence in Callie's tone, another pang of envy pained Bailey. The heiress had found her place in this world, people she belonged with and to, men who watched over her. Looking back on her childhood, Bailey realized that she had shared a name and a house with her parents . . . but no real bond. And she hadn't connected with any boyfriends, never felt the sort of love flowing between these three. So she'd focused on her dance and tried to use it as an outlet for her yearning.

But none of that mattered now. Someone wanted to kill her because she might be a long-lost Russian child. Until she could shake them, she couldn't figure out who she was, where she belonged, and who she belonged with.

As Callie let herself out of the room, Bailey made her way back to her seat and sank onto the cushion, feeling more alone than ever.

"You okay?" Joaquin asked.

He didn't have to care at all. She resisted softening toward him for asking.

"I'm all right. Where did Sean go?"

"To see what other information he might be able to dig up to assist you," Thorpe offered. "He's still consulting with the FBI on this case. They might have some background that will help. If nothing else, he'll get the murder of these women on their radar so they can start investigating possible tie-ins."

A good thing. Even if she never came within sneezing distance of danger, these madmen needed to be stopped so no one else faced this fear or endured the dead women's horror again.

To Thorpe, she just nodded.

He frowned at her. "I'm working some angles from here, too. Joaquin and I have been talking. I've sent Axel, my head of security, down to Houston."

"He'll see if anyone is looking for you and make sure that no one messes with your boyfriend because they're looking for you."

Joaquin must mean Blane. Bailey opened her mouth to explain that he was just a friend, then stopped. The man who'd taken her from her house had tried to kiss her. Worse, she'd nearly let him. If he believed that she was taken . . . well, she didn't really expect him to keep his distance because of it. After all, a guy willing to pluck a sleeping woman from her bed might not have a lot of scruples, but at least she could use Blane as an excuse if Joaquin tried to kiss her again. It wasn't much, but it was all she had now. And she needed a boundary between them. She had enough on her plate trying to decipher her real identity and hide from killers. But that wasn't all. Joaquin oozed this sex vibe that told her he'd been around the block. She, on the other hand, was still taking baby steps down the driveway. He'd chew her up and spit her out. The last thing she needed was to get emotionally tangled with someone like him.

"Thanks," she said to Thorpe. "Blane will appreciate that."

"You're welcome."

Sean opened the door a minute later with a piece of paper in hand. With a purposeful stride, he headed in her direction. "Joaquin said you don't remember anything before you were five. And that you only dream about being picked up bloody on the side of the road. Is that right?"

Where was he going with this? "Yes."

"Do you have a vivid image of the little girl in the dream?"

"No." Bailey frowned, trying to remember the nightmare in detail. "Parts are fuzzy, but I don't see the girl's face. I *am* the girl, so I see a shirt, a hand, a pair of bare feet. Nothing else."

He glanced down at the paper he carried. She saw now that the back looked glossy. It was photo paper. He glanced between the page in his hand and her a few times, then whistled. "I used my FBI contacts to get this from the sealed police files in Crawford County, Indiana. Not many have ever laid eyes on this picture. Take a look, Joaquin."

The other man took it from Sean's hand. After the merest glance, he swore. "What color shirt are you wearing in the dream?"

Dread sliced through Bailey. "We've been over this."

"Remind me."

She clamped her lips shut and leaned toward Joaquin, trying to peek at the photo, but he turned it facedown on his lap.

"I want to see," she demanded.

"Answer the question first. What color is the shirt?"

Why did she get the feeling that answering would open a Pandora's box of crap? That it would rain a bunch of shit down on her head? Even if it did, she couldn't afford not to face it. "P-pink."

"Is it clean or dirty in your nightmares?"

"It's stained with blood."

"Tell me this isn't you." Joaquin shoved the photo in her direction. "Look me in the eye and tell me you think this is some other little girl."

With shaking fingers, Bailey took the eight-by-ten and forced herself to look at it.

In the image, there sat a little girl staring at a wall in what looked to be a police station. Her eyes appeared vacant, her face whiter than pale. A paramedic hovered beside her, draping a gray industrial blanket around her shoulders in an attempt to keep her warm. Underneath it, she wore a pink pajama top smeared with blood. The face . . . she couldn't deny that it was hers.

With a cry, Bailey dropped the picture from her numb fingers.

Chapter Six

JOAQUIN jumped to his feet and rushed to Bailey. Shit, she looked ghostly white. Her pupils had gone nearly as wide as those of her child self in the photo.

He knelt and grabbed her shoulders. "Tatia—" No, she didn't want him to call her that. "Bailey?"

No answer. She looked through him. His gut clenched.

"Baby girl," he crooned. She'd responded when he'd called her that before, liked it. He didn't really want to stop and think about the fact that he enjoyed saying it to her.

"T-that girl . . . it's me."

Her four small words should probably have filled him with triumph or thrill or something other than this sick, roiling churn. He tried to reassure her with a soft voice. "I know."

"I . . . I don't understand." She finally blinked at him, and tears swam in her big blue eyes. Disillusion broke across her face. She looked so fragile, it tore at his fucking heart.

"I know it's a lot to take in." He caressed her arms. "I'm so sorry."

"We'll leave you two for now," Sean murmured, turning to Thorpe.

The club owner nodded. "Let us know if you need anything. Take care of her."

A subtle warning. Joaquin barely heard it as Bailey began to sob. He brought her to her feet and pulled her close. She fell limp against him, her legs barely supporting her. Now what?

Hell, he didn't do crying women. He didn't even do emotion. What he needed was a manual, training, or backup—something. But Sean and Thorpe were already shutting the door behind them.

As she clutched at his shirt and cast a begging blue stare at him, Joaquin knew he was on his own. He'd stirred the shit pot to avenge Nate, so he had to deal. Still, he panicked a little at the thought. When was the last time he'd been this close to a woman unless he was fucking a one-night stand? Hmm . . . Never.

"They lied to me," Bailey cried into his shirt, then abruptly pulled away, turning her back to him and wrapping her arms around herself.

"Your adoptive parents?" He watched her cross the room and fought the urge to follow. What was wrong with him? He should be happy that she wasn't sobbing on him anymore. Instead, guilt flayed him raw.

Bailey nodded, her light brown hair brushing the length of her narrow back, the ends curling toward her waist. She was so damn tiny, and he'd heaped a shit ton of problems on her shoulders. He had to be careful or he'd break her. Somewhere, his logical brain asked why the hell she mattered. Joaquin wanted to say it was because, as Tatiana Aslanov, she might know something useful. But he wasn't good at bullshitting himself.

Oh, fuck. Wanting to sleep with her he understood. But this crappy remorse cocktail with its anxiety chaser swirling through his veins? It wasn't easy lust. He'd wanted to kiss her earlier—no mistake. In fact, he'd wanted to rip Thorpe's head off for interrupting them because he'd been aching to strip off that too-big T-shirt and get his mouth all over her pretty hard nipples while he worked his way into her pussy.

Right now, he wanted to kick his own ass for crushing the world as she'd always known it. Doing so was safer for her. She'd be better equipped to elude danger if she understood it. But in less than a few hours, he'd ripped away the veneer of her existence to expose its secret underbelly. She couldn't take more now.

And for some fucking reason he didn't understand, he wanted to fix everything in her life so she had no reason to do anything except smile.

"Of course!" she shouted back. "Whoever they really were. They lied to me about everything. Who I am, where I came from . . ." She clenched her fists and turned on him with a little red nose and trembling lips. "They made me think I was crazy. By the time I was seven, I was seeing a shrink for my 'delusions.' And all that time, they spoon-fed me my school lessons, made me home-cooked meals, drove me to dance class, and placated me about spats with friends or boys who didn't like me. It was all just a lie. So if they weren't really parents, what were they? Babysitters? Bodyguards? Brainwashers?"

In the face of her furious hurt, remorse smacked him again. He probably could have handled her more gently. *What could be kinder than barking questions, digging through her memories, and shoving pictures at her until you ripped apart her identity, dumbass?*

Joaquin dragged in a deep breath. "I wasn't able to get a lot of information about your identity before I took you. Since then, I've been trying to fill in the blanks. Some of the info is coming faster than other bits, so I don't have a complete picture yet. I've got a few people working on it."

"But you think they were FBI agents?"

"That's my best guess."

"Tell me what you know," she demanded through clenched teeth.

He understood the anger. It was bolstering her, and without it she feared falling apart. "They obviously raised you and kept you safe. I'm sure that was their number one job. Any memories of your past or hints that you remembered a life before them would need to be squelched. Not because they wanted to hurt you. Tatiana Aslanov disappearing kept you safe and gave you an opportunity to grow up normally. You probably resent the hell out of them right now, but most likely, those two agents accepted a thirteen-year assignment, knowing they might never see field action again. They had to shed their previous lives, abandon their own family. They had to become mom and dad to a stranger until you turned legal. They might not have been perfect, but they did their job. It was a shitload better than you growing up in some government detention facility."

"I-I . . ." She gasped in an agitated breath, fighting her temper. "You're probably right about them making sacrifices to bring me up in a safe environment. They did that well. On the other hand, they made me believe we were a family, then they allowed themselves to 'die' shortly after I turned eighteen. They abandoned me. And you're defending that?"

"No." *Crap.* "They may not have had a choice. I was just trying to make you see the other side of the coin. I doubt it was easy for them, either."

"Obviously, they haven't missed me much, since neither of them has attempted to make contact with me in about three years."

"I'm sure they would have been prohibited from doing that."

"Which tells me they value their jobs more than the girl they raised as their daughter. And what about you? You're with another government agency, so you're here to . . . what? Be my lover? Does Uncle Sam think you need to crawl between my legs in order to watch over me?"

Joaquin ground his jaw. She was hitting low, and the logical part of him understood that she was hurt, so she was lashing out at the messenger because she didn't have anyone else. But that didn't stop his temper from getting swept up in her cyclone of emotion. "I'm not here on anyone's orders. In fact, I'll probably be fired for pursuing this case because Tatiana Aslanov isn't on my boss's radar. When it became obvious the agency intended to do nothing, I couldn't leave you to that horrific death. So here we are. But let me clue you in, baby girl. Uncle Sam doesn't tell me who to fuck. I can't fake an erection, even for the sake of God and country. That kiss we almost shared? That was me wanting you because just being in the same room with you makes me want to strip off everything you're wearing and impale you with every inch I've got."

When he eased closer to Bailey, she squared her shoulders and raised her chin. "Don't come near me."

That defiance made him wish again that he were a spanking kind of guy. He'd really like to melt that starch in her spine. If she wasn't going to let him comfort her, he'd be more than happy to adjust her attitude with a good smack or ten on her ass, then follow it up with a thorough fucking. A nice handful of orgasms would do them both a world of good.

"I am so done with people lying to me," she ground out.

That pissed him off. "You think I'm lying to you? About which part? Your parents being agents? That I'm sorry? Or that my cock is aching to fill your little pussy until you dig your nails into my back and wail out in pleasure?"

Her face turned pink. "You're not sorry about any of this. I'm also not buying your sudden desire bullshit."

"I will be more than happy to prove you wrong right now." He reached for the button of his jeans. "I'm ready if you are."

In some distant corner of his brain, Joaquin realized that combating her hurt with challenge wasn't going over well. On the other hand, something about arguing with her while he'd been imagining her underneath him hadn't gotten his blood just flowing, but boiling. If fucking her would, in any way, prove to her that he wasn't lying, he was beyond down with getting busy. If she let him, he'd give it to her hard and wicked—repeatedly.

"No!" She managed to look indignant, but her cheeks had gone rosy. The pulse at her neck was pounding. Her nipples poked at her borrowed shirt angrily.

He put his hands on his hips. If she looked down, she'd see his straining zipper. "Do you still think I'm lying?"

"I'm done with this conversation."

"If you're telling yourself you don't want me at all, then you're the one lying."

"Pfft. You might know facts about me on paper, but you don't know *me*."

"So if I touched your pussy right now, you wouldn't be wet?"

He'd always liked a good challenge. It was probably one of the reasons he loved his job. But facing off with her this way made his blood sing, too.

"No." She shook her head a bit too emphatically. "And you're not touching me to find out. Leave me alone."

"You're worried that I'd find you juicy. You're afraid to admit that I turn you on." He stalked closer, his footfalls heavy, his eyes narrowing in on her.

"Stay back," she warned—but her eyes said something else entirely.

"Tell me you're not attracted to me." He reached out, his strike fast as a snake's, and gripped her arms. He dragged her closer, fitting her lithe little body against him and holding in a groan when she brushed over his cock. "Tell me you want me to stop. Remember, you don't like liars. I don't, either."

She didn't say a word, struggled a bit for show. Mostly, she parted her lips and panted. Her cheeks heated an even deeper rose. Her chest heaved. Never once did she look away from him. "I'm involved with someone else."

"If you think whatever you've got going with Blane is going to stop me . . ." He didn't bother to finish his sentence; he just laughed.

"So you're not listening to me say 'no'? You're not respecting my feelings for another guy?"

"Let's just say I'm proving my sincerity to you." He tightened his grip. When she gasped and her stare fell to his lips, triumph raced through his veins. "I'm also testing you. That pretty mouth of yours might lie to me, but your kisses won't."

Joaquin didn't give her a chance to protest again. Normally, he would have. Women 101 was never to proceed without express consent, but this thick air of tension electrifying his blood and seizing his lungs was something entirely new and intoxicating. Their fight seemed to be helping Bailey forget her shock and sadness, not to mention the fact that it revved her, too. She wasn't immune to him—not by a long shot. Thank fuck.

Thrusting a fist in her hair, he pinned her in place and lowered his head. His mouth crashed over hers. The collision impacted his entire system, like a bomb detonating inside him, like a battering ram flattening his inhibitions. As he groaned into the kiss, he couldn't stop himself from shoving her against the nearest wall, forcing her lips apart, and thrusting his way deep.

Bailey didn't fight him at all. In fact, she threw her arms around his neck and opened to him, drawing him in and kissing him as if she might disintegrate without his touch. One of her legs wrapped around his hip.

In his book, her response was a screaming "hell yes." And it supercharged his need with the potency of rocket fuel.

Joaquin dragged in a harsh breath, then sank even more into the tangle of lips. He curled his arms around her and lifted her up, pressing her body harder into the wall and taking handfuls of her ass into his palms.

Jesus, he was going up in flames. How long would it take him to get her naked and screaming his name? As she whimpered and grabbed his face to kiss him even harder, he hoped it wouldn't be more than thirty seconds. Otherwise, he would spontaneously combust.

The kiss had no end. He could breathe inside her. He could feel on top of her. Every time her heart beat, every time she took a breath, every time she grabbed him a little tighter, it felt right. Yeah, she wanted this as much as he did. Each cell in his body celebrated.

As he captured her against him and turned for the bed, he

changed the angle of their kiss, sucked in a desperate gulp of air, and smelled her arousal in the room. God, she was sweetly pungent, potent. He wanted her right fucking now.

He bent, and her back hit the mattress. As Joaquin climbed between her thighs, he covered her slender body with his own and trapped her mouth under his again. She wrapped her legs even tighter around him and lifted her cunt right against his aching erection.

With a grunt, he gripped one hip and did his level best to forge them together. Damn it, he had to get their clothes off, had to bury himself as deep inside her as he could, but he didn't want to leave her mouth long enough to undress.

His free hand snaked under her shirt and found her braless. He enveloped the sweet mound of her breast with its impossibly hard nipple. Her moan for more half demanded and half pleaded, sending his desire soaring even higher. He couldn't remember wanting any woman even half this much. Holy hell, she was going to be one incredible pleasure to fuck.

But if he followed through with all the sizzle and passion searing between them, would she feel as if he'd taken advantage of her emotional state? Would she hate him tomorrow?

Joaquin forced himself to tear away from Bailey's mouth. Struggling for every panting breath, he stared down at her dilated eyes and swollen lips, seeking the answer. He almost couldn't stop himself from kissing her again, taking her under him, and—

A phone he'd tucked away in his back pocket rang. The chime was unfamiliar, a bit like classical music, only less lilting and more provocative.

"What the hell?" he cursed and reached for the device, ready to throw it across the room for breaking the breathless mood between them.

Bailey's blue eyes widened with distress. He'd been kissing her just moments ago, and she'd been like the headiest siren seducing him to a burning hell he would have been all too happy to endure. So how was it possible that seconds later her face could turn so wrenchingly innocent?

"Blane," she gasped, then reached for her phone.

The sound of the other man's name on her lips pissed him off way more than it should. "How do you know that's him?"

The chime sounded again, and she grew more urgent to have the phone, stretching even harder toward his pocket. Joaquin kept the mobile out of her reach.

"That's his ringtone," she insisted. "He's looking for me."

"He's going to keep looking. If necessary, Axel will throw him off your track. You can't talk to anyone from your old life now, not until I figure out how to make you safe."

Okay, so that wasn't precisely true. Mostly, but . . . Bailey talking about her boyfriend while he still lay on top of her stuck in Joaquin's craw. Not that he was jealous. Well, maybe he was. But he really didn't need some Lothario punk messing up his investigation. And all right, he couldn't stand the thought of this bastard near Bailey. Joaquin couldn't imagine any way she would have kissed him with that much need if Blane had been giving it to her good and wringing the multiple orgasms from her that she deserved.

"Give me my phone!" She struggled to push him off and get the device.

That wasn't acceptable. He pinned her to the mattress. "No. I already told you that."

"I want my phone. Blane will just worry and—"

"Do you find the 'N' or the 'O' confusing, Bailey? Or is it the two letters together that baffles you?"

"It's my phone. You have no authority over me."

Her assertion made something inside him stop dead cold. "You want to test me on that?"

The chiming of the mobile stopped.

"Argh!" she grunted, pushing at his shoulders. "You big thug, get the hell off me. I can't breathe."

If she was screaming at him, she was breathing just fine. But her rejection stung.

With a curse, he zipped to his feet and held out his hand to assist her off the bed.

Bailey stared like she didn't quite trust his gesture and made her own way upright. That chafed him raw, too. He *really* wanted to paddle her ass red until . . . what? She stopped defying him. Yeah, that would be a nice start. Until she lost the attitude? That would suit him, too. Most of all, he wanted to do it until he felt her melt against him again.

Damn it, he had to get his brain out of his dick and focus.

He pulled the phone from his back pocket and stared at the screen. Blane had left a voicemail. How thoughtful.

Joaquin ground his teeth together. Why was he letting a twerp he'd never met bug him? Oh, because the other guy had once had the pleasure of spending time in Bailey's pussy.

Not anymore.

Yeah, being with Bailey would be dangerous for Blane and all that bullshit. But Joaquin wasn't forfeiting his chance to experience the pretty little ballerina in his bed just because some other guy had been there first.

"I'll be back." He turned and stomped toward the door.

"Don't you leave and take my phone."

Joaquin ignored her and kept walking.

"You're going to listen to my voicemail, aren't you?"

He gave her credit for being smart. "Yep."

Not only did he need to know if this guy was going to be a problem to work around, it was time to find out just how deep her relationship with this prick went.

Her footfalls across the floor were his only warning before she grabbed his arm and pulled him back around. "Stop making me question my sanity, then ignoring me. I might be small, but I'm not some wimpy little pushover—"

"I'm warning you right now. Unless you want to be flat on your back again, this time naked and stuffed full of my cock, don't touch me."

It took a moment for his words to register. Finally, her eyes widened, and she uncurled her fingers slowly from him, then lifted both palms beside her head as if he'd barked at her to put her hands up. It would almost be funny if her rebuff weren't so irritating. How had this girl twisted his balls up in knots with one damn kiss? He'd kind of been an ass about it, too. Being on edge in more than one way wasn't good for his mood.

"Sorry," he mumbled, rubbing at his tired eyes. "I'm out of line."

"So you'll give me my phone and let me talk to Blane?"

Why didn't she just stab him in the guts? Faster and more straightforward than this verbal torture. He was already more addicted to Bailey than he wanted to admit—than he could even believe—but that didn't change a damn thing. "No."

Before she could argue with him again, forcing him to listen to her whine for her boyfriend, Joaquin yanked the door open and slammed it behind him. Quickly, he locked it.

Flopping back against the surface, he closed his eyes and sighed. What the fuck had happened in there? He'd gone in to convince her that she was Tatiana Aslanov and nearly ended up fucking her. Worse, now his body seemed cued into her, like she was the itch he hadn't scratched and he was going to suffer a terrible set of hives until he did. No, it was more. Deeper. He hated this confusing feelings shit.

Distance between him and Bailey would be good. The door wasn't enough of a barrier between them. He couldn't afford to separate himself from her by a few miles, so he'd settle for a few hours, a few drinks, a few work-related problems. He'd check in with Hunter, Jack, and the others to see what new information they'd gleaned about her adoptive parents. Yeah, that would work. And this fucking boyfriend stood between them, too. Couldn't forget about that.

Joaquin marched down the hall until he came to the smaller bedroom he'd crashed in last night. As soon as he entered the little space, he hunted through Bailey's phone until he found the button that played her voicemails. He listened to Blane's message once, twice. Then he couldn't decide whether to be furious or thrilled as fuck.

He clasped her mobile in his hand, gripping it so tightly it flickered. With a curse, he shoved it back in his pocket, took a deep breath, and counted to ten.

If he were smart, he'd wait on this confrontation. With a bad mixture of desire and anger juicing his veins, he wasn't feeling like he had two brain cells to rub together. He wanted to blame her because he desired her so badly, but that would make him an absolute douche. He was a grown man able to take responsibility for his penis. Honestly, he had no one to blame for this antsy, overheated mood but himself. He'd wanted to avenge Nate, so he'd pursued this case. He'd been determined to learn Bailey's real identity, so he'd stripped away the façade of her life and exposed the truth underneath. He'd allowed his need for her to burn past his good sense, so he'd kissed her. No, he'd all but fucked her mouth with his own. And now . . .

"Shit!" He stalked back to the bedroom Bailey occupied, unlocked the door, and let himself in. He wasn't at all quiet as he banged it shut behind him.

Bailey snapped her gaze his way. She sent him a wary stare but didn't back down. Why did that make his dick hard all over again?

"What?" she snapped.

"He's your boyfriend?" Joaquin challenged.

"My sex life is none of your business. What happened earlier between us shouldn't have. Don't try to coax my cooperation again by doing your level best to nail me. I was stupid enough to fall for it once, but never again."

Every time she opened her mouth to defy him, he clawed an inch closer to taking her over his knee. He ground his teeth together and drew in a bracing breath, looking for some self-control.

"Answer. The. Question," he snarled.

She crossed her arms over her chest and leveled him with a glare. "My relationship with Blane has nothing to do with your case."

Damn it, she was right. Whatever bad attitude had crawled up his ass needed to crawl right back out . . . but he couldn't seem to make that happen.

"I heard the voicemail he left." Joaquin held up the phone. "Blane would be far more interested in being my boyfriend than yours. Why did you lie to me?"

She hesitated. "I just let you draw the wrong conclusion."

"Bullshit. You *lied*."

"I didn't. I said I was involved with someone. I simply didn't say it was in a dance capacity."

He rolled his eyes. "Why the misdirection, then? You thought if I believed you were taken I'd keep my hands off you?"

"Something like that," she admitted.

Joaquin scoffed. "Did it feel that simple when I kissed you? Did any part of that feel like I wasn't dying to touch you?"

She couldn't quite meet his gaze. With head bowed and light brown curls swirling around her shoulders, she looked fragile, confused, and a little contrite. "No. It felt like you wanted me, but that doesn't make sense in my head."

You aren't alone.

"I don't know what to think," she went on, almost pleading for some sanity.

The anger drained from him. "Bailey, I've heaped a lot on your shoulders today. I'm sorry. I shouldn't have picked a fight with you." He frowned, genuinely confused. "Or did you pick one with me?"

"Probably both." She smiled a bit ruefully.

"Yeah. Whatever . . . I didn't mean for things to be this way."

Her expression fell. "I'm scared, Joaquin. I'm scared of where my life is now. I'm scared of who's after me." She hesitated, looking so delicate once more. "I'm scared of you."

Hell if that didn't make him feel like a heel. "Baby girl, I would never hurt you. I know we didn't have the most auspicious meeting. I came on strong today. I've been an ass. I don't have an excuse, just an apology."

She lifted one delicate shoulder in a half shrug. "I tore into you, too. I just . . . I'm overwhelmed. There's so much happening, and I don't have anyone to blame except you."

He nodded, taking a careful step forward. Touch her? Don't touch her? Finally, he settled for cupping her slender arm, but he wanted so much more. "It's fine. I'm a big boy. I can take it. Put everything on my shoulders."

Instead, Bailey closed her eyes and seemed to withdraw into herself. "Even if you'd let me make a phone call, I hardly have anyone to talk to but you."

His first thought was that she must be exaggerating. Then he paused. Parents gone. No siblings. Who else did she have in her life? "Tell me about your relationship with Blane."

"He's my best friend. I jokingly refer to him as my gay husband. He's an incredible dance partner. He's helping me prepare for the upcoming audition. He guides me through some of the catfights and ugly politics of a professional dance company. I listen to the trials and tribulations of his rocky love life. He pushes me to open myself more so that when I dance, people see my soul."

"What the hell does that mean?" Joaquin blurted. He didn't like the idea that Blane used her as a sounding board, then turned around and criticized her.

"No, he's right. What separates a technically beautiful dancer from a spellbinding one is their ability to emote with their body. Technically, I'm great. Everyone says it. I have a hard time coming out of my shell. I want to. I mean to. Blane is . . ." She smiled, clearly in awe. "When he dances, you just feel all his life experience. His joy, his heartbreak, his struggles. He's wide open for the audience, and they drink him in. He can move people to tears. He's trying to help me be more like that."

"How?" Had he misjudged Blane? Maybe the guy swung both ways and wanted to give Bailey more "life experience." If he did, Joaquin would be happy to knock his nuts back against his spine.

"He encourages me to take a chance here and there. He tries to help me find ways to laugh or cry or . . ." She shrugged. "Get mad, fall in love. Care about something other than the perfect pointe. I'm not sure I'm a very good student. I know he's right, but I just don't know how to actually follow his advice."

This wasn't his area of expertise. Emotions were something he usually avoided at all costs. They got people killed in action. But Joaquin couldn't not try to help her. "What about when your adoptive parents passed away? Didn't you feel something then? Or after your first boyfriend or . . . " He grasped at straws. "What about after you had the dreams?"

"I feel plenty," she corrected. "I *think* I'm releasing myself through dance, but everyone who sees me says I look like I'm just on the cusp of opening myself and giving something beautiful through performance before I pull back behind my walls. I'm not even aware of it." She shook her head. "Sorry. But that's what Blane and I do together. When we rehearse, he pushes me to my limits and tries to make me reveal my soul."

Well, he wasn't any expert, but he didn't see how Blane talking and demonstrating would be productive. Something had to motivate her to tear down her barricades and share herself. She was keeping her feelings in for a reason. Fear? Self-consciousness? Could be anything. "I have faith in you. You'll find it."

Of course, until he figured out how to stop the crazies at LOSS from chasing after her, she wouldn't be dancing for anyone. But one glance at her and Joaquin knew she'd been born for it. Her soul would wither without it.

He still wanted to avenge Nate, but he needed to fix this for her, too. How and why she'd become important he wasn't sure. He wasn't going to examine it, just admit that she was now a priority. He would make it better for her, period.

She sent him a tremulous smile, her pillowy mouth curling up. "Thank you. You know it's really twisted that you abducted me, and yet I've had more meaningful conversation with you than I had with my last three boyfriends put together. File me under Patty Hearst."

Joaquin laughed. Bailey was unpredictable—and he kind of liked that about her. The last colleague he'd tried to date? Snorefest. He'd known what she'd do next way before it had even crossed her mind. But this little ballerina seemed constantly full of surprises.

"Maybe it would help if you think of me not as a kidnapper, but as someone who just wants you to live to dance another day."

Her eyes lit up. "I like that. Thanks."

"You're welcome." He tucked his hands into the pockets of his jeans before he grabbed her again and kissed her breathless.

She took a half step toward him like she might want the same thing. Joaquin sucked in a harsh breath. If he touched her now, he'd lose his damn mind and peel her clothes off. As good as fucking her senseless sounded, she was too raw. She needed to process the revelation of her identity. He didn't need to give her something more to deal with.

But even with perfectly sound logic rolling through his head, Joaquin reached down to cup her face as she lifted it to him. Hell, he could drown in her eyes. She retained an innate sweetness he could almost taste on his tongue . . .

Christ, listen to him. Next he'd be drinking red wine and reciting poetry while taking long walks on the beach. What was up with that?

Still, he really didn't give a shit how stupid he sounded as long as he got to taste Bailey again.

He leaned in, closer, dropping his lips near hers. His cock

stiffened. His heart pounded. His breathing turned sharp. Just another inch until he had her mouth under his again . . .

A knock at the door startled him, and he jerked upright to find Thorpe barging inside again. He swore. Jesus, this guy had the worst timing ever. Hell of a bad trait for a Dungeon Master.

"What?" Joaquin barked, stepping close to Bailey. Shielding her as if he had to protect her from Thorpe? Where was his head? Well, besides in her panties . . .

"Just had a call from Axel." Thorpe sounded grim.

Joaquin looked over his shoulder at Bailey, but she met his gaze head-on. Despite all the bad news she'd already had today, she hadn't totally fallen apart. The woman was made of stern stuff.

"You ready to hear this?" he asked, double-checking.

"If it has anything to do with the people looking for me, then yes. I need to get back to my life so I can figure out what that's meant to be."

It was on the tip of his tongue to tell her that she didn't have to wade to a conclusion all alone, but he stopped himself. After this case was over, probably in the next day or two, it was unlikely he'd ever see her again. He might not be a peach, but he refused to make promises he couldn't keep.

"Good," Thorpe said into the silence, shutting the door behind him. "Here's what I've got. You have an elderly neighbor on your west?"

Bailey stepped up beside him and nodded. "Mrs. Lester. She's kind of a busybody, but she means well. Why?"

"Magically, Axel charmed her into talking."

"No, she likes to talk."

"Maybe that's it, because Axel doesn't have a charming side. Anyway, she's been watching your place all day. Seems she got suspicious when men started showing up at your house. She said that you having so much male company was out of character."

She didn't deny it. "Except Blane. She's used to seeing him."

"Apparently, Mrs. Lester saw you snooping around yesterday, Joaquin. She got pretty indignant when she didn't see you leave and assumed you'd spent the night." Thorpe chuckled.

He didn't see the humor. "Who else dropped by?"

"When Blane showed up looking for Bailey today, Mrs. Lester realized he had no idea where she'd gone, so she went from annoyed to alarmed."

"Mrs. Lester likes to bake cookies for Blane. She says he reminds her of her son. Poor thing has no notion that he can't keep his dance regimen and eat those cookies."

"After Blane left, she kept watching your place. Then it got interesting . . ." He grimaced. "A soldier she'd never seen before knocked on the door. She said she saw him walk around the house and peek in the windows. She was about to call the police until he knocked on her door and explained that he's your uncle Robbie, home for a surprise visit."

"I don't know a soldier, and I don't have an uncle Robbie." Horror spread across her face.

"That's what I thought. Axel asked her to describe your 'uncle's' uniform. What she said was bang on with what Callie had seen before. They sound exactly like the uniforms the nut jobs of LOSS wear."

So their speculations had been right. Someone who'd tried to dig up Aslanov's research and silence Callie had turned their attention to the scientist's long-lost daughter. That didn't particularly make Joaquin feel better. "Thanks for the confirmation, man. It's what we expected. Did anyone send a sketch artist to Mrs. Lester so we can try to ID this guy?"

"Already on it," Thorpe said. "We should have something by tomorrow."

"It doesn't exactly set me at ease that someone snooped around my house." Bailey's voice sounded a little thin, thready. Afraid.

"It gets worse." Thorpe whipped out his phone and opened his text messages. A small collection from Axel contained pictures of the inside of Bailey's little quirky, historic-charm house. It had been trashed—every room, every surface, every nook and cranny. All of it turned upside down and inside out. A broken chair, papers scattered, dishes in shards.

She opened her mouth, but no sound came out. The silent devastation all over her face was like a mule kick to the gut. "Why?"

"All of the previous victims' houses have been thoroughly searched. They're looking for whatever they can find about the victim and her ties to Aslanov's research. And since you weren't home, I'm sure they poked around for e-mails or travel arrangements—anything to indicate where you might be. You're next on their list." Without thought, Joaquin wrapped his arm around her.

"But they don't know I'm Tatiana Aslanov."

"None of the other women they've slaughtered were, and that didn't stop them."

Bailey began quaking against him. "Did Mrs. Lester see who did this?"

"We're speculating 'Uncle Robbie' is the culprit, but she didn't see him enter the house, so not definitively," Thorpe murmured, shaking his head. "Sorry."

"Whoever it was also didn't leave behind any prints to identify him. The police checked. They only found yours and Joaquin's." Another damn dead end.

Chances were that "Uncle Robbie" was also the killer or his right-hand man. Either way, he was a person of great interest, worth hunting down and grilling. They had to figure out who the hell he was.

Joaquin took Bailey's face in his hands. "Look at me. I won't let them hurt you, baby girl. I'll figure out how to stop them."

"We will," she insisted. "If these bastards are ruining my life, I'm going to help put a stop to them."

Gumption and guts—she had both. He liked that about her. But he wasn't about to have her in more danger than she already was. "I've got it."

"The best thing you can do is stay here and keep your profile low," Thorpe advised. "It kept Callie alive for four years."

Bailey didn't look happy with that advice, since she pursed her lips together stubbornly, but she didn't argue. Yet. But despite her fear, Joaquin wasn't sure how long he could keep Bailey from jumping into the battle to fight for her tomorrows.

Chapter Seven

BAILEY paced the bedroom. Joaquin kept walking in and out with Sean and Thorpe. They'd ask questions, then leave again. That didn't do anything to cure her nerves. Then Axel arrived from Houston to show her the pictures of her devastated house in person. The images freaked her out all over again. Just knowing that someone who wanted to kill her had been in her home made her tremble with fear.

But her volcanic attraction to Joaquin scared her almost as much. Every time she turned around he was there, hovering, his hazel eyes dark with concern and desire. Though he hadn't touched her in hours, he made her yearn. She could still feel his lips shoving hers wide apart, his tongue surging deep, his hot fingers curling around her breast, his body heavy as he covered her own and ground his cock against her needy flesh. God, he was big all over.

It was official. She'd gone crazy, lusting dangerously after a guy she'd known less than twenty-four hours, one who had ripped her entire world apart. On the other hand, he was the first person in her life to be truly honest about everything—her identity, the killers on the loose, the lengths they'd go to in order to capture her . . . the fact that he wanted her.

Pacing, Bailey swallowed and cast her nervous gaze to the door again. Would he come back to this bedroom tonight and want to finish what they'd started earlier? If so, what would she do? She'd never experienced anything like him. Their sparring sent her head buzzing, her blood humming. She wanted more.

Bailey glanced at the clock on the nightstand. Nearly eleven o'clock. Most likely, she'd be alone tonight. That should make her happy, and she was perversely pissed off that it didn't.

Behind her, the latch clicked suddenly. The door opened. Bailey whirled around, her heart pounding. Instead of Joaquin in the opening, she was a bit let down to find Callie. The heiress wore a lovely red corset-looking top that had her breasts nearly spilling over and a skirt so short it bordered indecent. She had the sort of soft curves Bailey had always wished for. But a glance down at her own chest confirmed that the Boob Fairy had passed her by.

"Hi," Callie said softly. "Want some company?"

It beat the hell out of wondering what to do next. "Sure. Come on in."

"Sean and Thorpe caught me up on everything that's happened in the last few hours." Callie came closer, surprisingly graceful on stilettos. "I've been through it myself, so I really do understand. If you need an ear . . . I'm here."

"Thank you. I—" *Have no idea what to say.* Besides murderous bad guys, Bailey had nothing on her mind except Joaquin. She really couldn't expect the woman to help her sort out her confusion about how she felt. "It is what it is."

Callie shrugged. "That's one way of looking at it. But now that you know who's after you and why, would you rather be anywhere but here?"

Zing. The brunette didn't mess around or mince words. "No. It might chafe me to be away from home, dance, and my friends, but here is safe."

"It is. I'm living proof of that. I'm sure you're worried about the men chasing you."

"I'd be an idiot not to be."

"True, but you can't do anything about them right now," Callie pointed out. "Sean, Thorpe, and Axel have this place on lockdown. I don't know Joaquin well, but he seems as paranoid—excuse me, cautious"—she rolled her eyes with a hint of humor— "as the rest of them."

"Pretty much," she admitted. "It's not Joaquin's fault that LOSS wants information they think I have. I don't, but I doubt they'd ever believe that."

"Nope. They'd torture you until they felt sure you'd coughed up whatever you knew, then they'd end you."

Bailey shuddered. "I know. I saw the pictures."

"Sorry. I didn't mean to make you focus on that crap. You hungry?"

"No. Joaquin keeps bringing me meals that would be a lot for even him to eat, then frowning at me for not inhaling the whole feast."

Callie laughed. "Sean and Thorpe probably had a hand in that. They're convinced I don't eat enough to keep a flea alive, too. The pair of them are always trying to tempt me with some savory or sweet dish. But I have my ways of distracting them."

At her wink, Bailey wasn't sure whether to gasp or giggle. "Neither looks like they'd be easily led around by their guy parts."

"Not often," Callie admitted. "Sean compromises a little. And under Thorpe's hard-ass exterior, there's a softie only I get to see."

Her blue eyes, rimmed in charcoal, twinkled. A smile curled her rosy lips. But it wasn't Callie's makeup or anything she wore that made her beautiful; it was her joy. The woman glowed with it. Not only did Callie have a man who knew and loved her through and through, she was doubly lucky to have two. That sparkling rock on her finger was a symbol of Sean's claim, and she seemed every bit as smitten with the FBI agent as she was with her former boss. Bailey didn't know a lot about that relationship, but she'd bet the bling around Callie's neck was Thorpe's collar.

"How about . . ." Callie tilted her head to one side, studying her. "You've had a hell of a day. Want to get out of this room for a bit?"

That sounded like heaven. Being cooped up in this one space for twelve hours, she was getting a case of cabin fever. But . . . "Is it safe?"

"Sure. We won't leave the place or anything. Maybe just grab a glass of wine?"

Even better. She rarely allowed herself an alcoholic treat. The extra calories showed when she wore only a leotard. But right now, as she wondered when—or if—she'd ever resume her normal life to put on spandex or dance for a crowd again, booze sounded fabulous.

"Please," Bailey all but begged. "I'm so keyed up."

"I totally understand that. Follow me." Callie led her out the door and down a long hall.

Odd, but it didn't look like any house Bailey had ever seen. More industrial, perhaps. But maybe that was the stained concrete floors and long hallway. Then again, some people liked that sort of thing.

She glanced around, waiting for Joaquin to jump out of a corner or one of the other guys to follow them. "They're really going to turn me loose without an armed escort?"

The woman's heels clicked down the hall as she cast a surprised glance over her shoulder. "You're with me. Besides, there are security cameras all over this club. They'll be watching and they'll know immediately if something is wrong."

"Club?" Though Bailey kept walking, everything inside her froze. She could only think of one club Sean, Callie, and Thorpe would all spend time in.

Callie opened a portal that led to another hall, this one with doors lining the left of the corridor. Each of the portals was closed and the lights overhead turned down low. "You didn't know?"

"Are you saying we're—"

"Pet?" A male voice farther down the hall and beyond an open door drawled.

Callie dashed to the portal. "Yes, Sir?"

Bailey came up behind her to find Thorpe sitting in what looked like his office, behind an enormous desk. Sean lounged opposite in a plush chair, holding a tumbler of Scotch.

"Where are you taking Joaquin's guest, lovely?" her fiancé asked with a nonchalance Bailey didn't believe at all.

"Did you have Joaquin's permission to remove her from her room?" Thorpe sent her a smile that looked a lot like a challenge.

"She wants some fresh air. I promised her a glass of wine. She's had a terrible day."

They both looked to Bailey for confirmation, their gazes a silent demand. She wondered how the hell Callie didn't stammer or falter under the weight of those two intent stares.

"I'm just really nervous, worried . . ." Bailey didn't know how else to describe the restless edge of fear biting into her.

Sean nodded, then sipped at his drink, as if weighing his words. "You know, Bailey, that bad things await you outside these walls. You wouldn't use my lovely's good heart to try to escape now, would you?"

Ouch. He might look like the more easygoing of the two, but Bailey was beginning to think that looks could be deceiving.

"No. I have no interest in playing hide-and-go-seek with ruthless psychopaths bent on my destruction. I swear."

The two men exchanged a look before Thorpe nodded in permission, then addressed Callie again. "I'll be letting Axel know you're on the floor. Don't dawdle and don't mingle. Keep Bailey behind the bar and away from prying eyes. No one needs to see her."

"Absolutely," Callie promised. "The last thing I want is someone recognizing her and showing up to ruin my wedding."

At that, Sean smiled. "I don't care if the ceiling is coming down and there are twenty terrorists chasing us. You're not wriggling away from the altar until you're my wife."

"I'd hold the ceiling up and shoot them myself." Callie grinned.

The men laughed, then Thorpe called back to them. "Ten minutes. You two come back by then or—"

"I have a clear picture of the 'or,' Sir. You've made that crystal over the last few months."

He smiled smugly. "Excellent."

As Callie turned away with a giggle, Bailey just blinked. She still was a little stunned by their unusual relationship.

"Who else knows? About the three of you, I mean?" Bailey murmured as they walked away. She'd heard whispers in the press, but never imagined it was more than innuendo or rumor.

Callie shrugged. "We don't flaunt our relationship. Of course, we don't go far to hide it, either. Sean likes public displays of affection, so when we're all out, he's more likely to hold my hand or kiss me. Thorpe is very private. He usually smiles at me in public. Sometimes he puts an arm around me or kisses my forehead. That can be construed in a lot of ways."

Wow. It sounded complicated to Bailey, but she had enough to worry about in her own life without tangling her brain up in the bride-to-be's.

At the end of the latest hall, Callie stopped before another door and pushed it open as if it weighed a ton. As she held it, Bailey slipped under her arm and into an open area. The space was dark and loud—and obviously public.

"Are we seriously in Club Dominion?" she shouted over what sounded suspiciously like people striking flesh, followed by moaning.

Callie nodded. "Where did you think we were?"

"At your house or . . ."

Over the din of the music, Callie laughed. "No. The house isn't nearly as secure as this place. Besides, Sean and Thorpe wanted to keep an eye on you and Joaquin. There's no place better for observation than here." Reaching back, she grabbed Bailey's hand. "Look down so your face is hidden."

Bailey didn't question that suggestion. She jerked her gaze down and followed as the other woman led her along a shadowed walkway. Then they headed through a flap that swung back and forth on a hinge. Out of the corner of her eye, she spotted a bar. People stood behind it, drinking mostly water bottles or cans of soda. The slaps of leather and the sounds of both pleasure and pain sounded louder now. The reality clicked with Bailey then.

"Holy cow . . ."

Callie spun her away from the bar and the crowd of people beyond, putting them at their backs. "You okay?"

Define "okay." Bailey's heart pounded. Joaquin had brought her to a BDSM club where people . . . did whatever it was they did to spice up their sex lives? Oh, shit. He had. They were surrounded by sex. God, she could even smell it in the air.

"Any particular wine you like?"

"Um . . ." Her brain wouldn't work. Bailey desperately wanted to turn around and see what she'd always been wretchedly curious about. "Anything white."

"Sure." She sounded amused.

Vaguely, Bailey heard Callie uncork a bottle, followed by the clinking of a glass and the splash of liquid. Instead of paying attention, she kept trying to peek over her shoulder at everyone and everything behind her. Surely, no one here would be a crazy foot soldier for LOSS. She had no ties to Dominion or to Dallas. Why would anyone think to look for her here? It made her feel brave enough to turn to get a better look.

A big man wearing all leather had a woman in a G-string folded over his lap. He landed slow whacks of his palm onto her bright-red butt. After each, she bit her lip, then her lips moved as she apparently counted. Beyond those two, a vaguely familiar man toyed with a gorgeous woman's nipples, then clamped them with dangling jewels that were almost as gaudy as the wedding ring on her finger. A forty-something woman dressed in wickedly tall thigh-high boots dragged two young men around by leashes. Bailey stared, not sure she even blinked.

"Is this all new for you?" Callie murmured, handing her a glass.

A million replies raced through her head, but she could only wrap her brain around one. "Yeah."

The other woman laughed. "I thought so. We've got a few minutes left. Want to observe from somewhere you can't be seen?"

Bailey bit her lip. She shouldn't. She didn't need more curiosity about BDSM or sex right now. She didn't need to wonder why Joaquin had brought her here. She especially didn't need that pang of desire cramping low in her belly.

"Please." She sipped at her wine, not really aware of the taste, other than the fact that it landed light and fruity on her tongue.

"You got it. We just can't be too late. I'll risk five minutes, though. It's worth the spanking."

Bailey looked at the man smacking the woman's ass, then back to Callie. "You like that?"

She gave a secretive smile. "Given by the right man in the right way, it's an incredible pleasure."

Frowning, Bailey looked at the heiress. She supposed it made sense. Callie had lived here for four years. She was in love with Thorpe, a man who gave even someone with Bailey's limited knowledge an obvious Dom vibe. She supposed Sean must have a similar bent because, while seemingly quieter on the outside, he'd also given off an air of authority.

Kind of like Joaquin.

Bailey almost dropped her wine.

At the last minute, Callie shoved a hand under the stemless glass for the save. "Something wrong?"

She didn't even know how to answer, couldn't even manage a shake of her head.

Callie led her up some stairs and unlocked a door, and they entered another masculine domain with a sofa, a few chairs, and a huge observation window overlooking the entire main floor of the . . . What did one call a place like this?

"Spit it out, doll. You've got questions." Callie nodded at her.

Bailey blew out a big breath. A million. Then she realized that the other woman wasn't holding a glass. "Where's your wine?"

Wrinkling her nose, she held up a water bottle. "I feel so dehydrated. Been running all day. I just need water. Besides, I have to fit into my dress on Saturday."

With a nod, Bailey turned back to the windows and caught sight of the familiar man who'd moved from attaching body jewelry to his bound wife to giving her a soft, almost lazy flogging.

Bailey watched ecstasy cross the woman's face. Obviously, she was enjoying every slow strike of the strips of cloth or leather or . . . whatever it was. Every time, the man caressed her skin with the flogger, his wife's body twitched or bucked. Bailey found herself tensing, holding her breath, anticipating his next smack.

"Who is that?" she asked Callie absently. "He looks so familiar."

"You've probably seen him on the news. That's Jason—"

"Denning. And that's his new wife?"

"Yes. I've known Jason for years. I never thought he had the capacity to actually fall in love. Nice to know I'm wrong. And oh, you never saw him here."

"Sure." Bailey shrugged. It made sense that privacy was a big issue at a place like this.

The man she'd first seen was finally done spanking the woman previously perched over his lap. Now he held her in his arms. The sight struck Bailey on a visceral level. The tenderness he now showed her after the almost ruthless way he had spanked her made no sense—and yet Bailey responded with something far beyond curiosity.

Damn it, she was actually wet. Worse, she felt almost envious.

"I don't understand." She pointed to the pair cuddling together on the bench.

Callie just smiled. "Most likely, he was disciplining her. Now he's giving her aftercare. If he gave her a command she didn't heed or she failed to observe a rule, then it's his right as her Dom to punish her. Or it could be that the spanking was for their mutual fun. It's something they both wanted. You can see that."

Bailey could. The woman clung to her Dom, with her head on his shoulder as he caressed her back and whispered something in her ear. How could an ass smacking like that morph into something so tender?

"Sometimes, when you feel like your world is spinning out of control, it's so comforting to hand yourself over to a man you know will help you relieve your troubles. I'm sure that sounds old-fashioned or silly. I can, in fact, take care of myself. She can, too. You have to be strong to truly submit. But that . . ." Callie gestured to the pair. "What those two are sharing is priceless. I can't explain. It's not one-sided. He needs control and he needs to be needed. Believe me, they're giving something precious to one another."

Psychologically, Bailey had no idea how that worked, but she didn't doubt Callie. Another jab of envy, this time altogether different, stabbed at her. What would it be like to trust someone enough to give herself over and let him turn her inside out? Reduce her to her most vulnerable moment? Scrub her soul raw?

"It's . . . beautiful."

"Done right, with affection and trust, it is," Callie whispered, as if she found the moment sacred.

It felt that way to Bailey. She swallowed down more wine.

"We should go," the brunette said. "I'm going to get more than a friendly tap on the ass if I don't get you back and spend some time with the guys."

"Thorpe will really spank you?"

"I can almost guarantee it. But as the wedding has drawn closer, Sean and I are both on edge. Like we're worried something is going to come along and screw it up. He's been a bit paddle-happy lately, too."

And she didn't seem to mind one bit.

"Let's go," she offered as Callie headed toward the door.

"Do you want more wine before we head back into the secure area?"

Bailey hadn't finished the glass she had. "No, thanks."

The woman opened the door, and a big, burly guy with flat eyes and shoulders like the side of a mountain stood there with a look of annoyed expectation. Axel.

"Oops. I guess I forgot to tell my watchdog that we were coming up here. Darn. I think I'm in more trouble." A saucy smiled played at the corner of Callie's lips.

Bailey kind of wondered if she was crazy, then shook her head. Crazy like a fox maybe. If Callie got the sort of connection from her men after a spanking that she'd seen between the couple on the floor, Bailey imagined she'd be happy to disobey a little more often.

As the other woman started down the stairs, Bailey stopped her. "Why did Joaquin bring me here?"

"The way Thorpe explained it, he needed a safe place to bring you, but he also knew that Sean and I would have background that no one else would. Two birds, one stone."

That made sense. And it should have set her at ease that he apparently hadn't had kinky sex in mind when he cuffed her to someone else's bed. On the other hand, she felt oddly unwanted, almost rejected, that his motives hadn't been lascivious. Other than the hot kiss they'd shared, he hadn't pursued anything sexual before or since.

"Is Joaquin . . . Do you think he's like, um, Thorpe and Sean?"

She didn't know how to ask the question without sounding sexually interested. Heat flamed across her cheeks.

Callie stared over her shoulder. "Dominant? I don't know him well. But if I had to guess? Oh, honey. He's got all the earmarks. I don't know how much he actually knows about the lifestyle, but I'll bet if he spent even a few days here without having to worry about bad guys and dead bodies, your ass would be a fabulous shade of red."

"Mine?"

"Yours. He's watching you. And just a heads-up: You left your room without saying a word to him."

"But I'm with you," Bailey protested.

"A Dom, especially one who's borderline paranoid about your safety, isn't going to care if you'd been guarded by the entire Secret Service. He didn't know and he didn't make the arrangements. End of story." Callie shrugged. "But maybe I'm reading Joaquin wrong and he doesn't roll that way. We'll find out."

Maybe they would, and the possibilities Callie raised made her pulse flutter and her sex clench. Hell, why did that man excite her? And why did the thought that he would want to strike his palm to her bare ass in the name of discipline rev her up?

Because in the last twenty-four hours, she'd gone absolutely mental.

Following Callie down the stairs, she found her stomach knotting as Axel grunted and gestured them ahead. He guarded their flank as he shepherded them back to the secure area of the club.

Callie looked a little nervous as she glanced over her shoulder at the hulk. "How bad is it?"

Axel grunted. "Don't expect to sit at your wedding."

She winced and shoved open the door leading to the hallway that held Thorpe's office. In the doorway, he glanced at his watch, then raised a dark brow. Perched on the edge of Thorpe's desk, Sean polished off the last of his drink, then shook his head, tsking. Joaquin stood just behind them both, looking positively furious. Bailey swallowed.

"Do you need a new watch, lovely?" Sean asked, his voice silky.

"No," she answered softly, head bowed.

Bailey knew how the woman felt. When she risked a glance at

Joaquin again, she fought the odd urge to apologize, look down . . . something.

He came at her on angry footfalls. "Are you fucking crazy?"

"Of course not."

Joaquin took hold of her half-full glass and sniffed. "Wine?"

"I thought it would relax me." She took it back from him and downed the rest with challenge in her eyes.

"Did you drink any?" Sean asked Callie sharply.

"No." The heiress shook her head and held up her bottle. "Water. See?"

That clearly surprised Thorpe. "You passed up wine. Are you feeling all right?"

"Mitchell . . ." She sent him a saucy scowl.

Joaquin ignored the trio and rounded on Bailey. "If you wanted something to drink, you could have asked me instead of going into a public area of the club where anyone could have seen you."

Bailey didn't want to get Callie in trouble. "We got a glass, then she took me to a secure observation room. I'm fine."

"I had Axel watching them," Thorpe supplied.

Joaquin still didn't look happy.

"You never told me I couldn't leave the room with your friends," she argued.

Her statement made Joaquin look like he wanted to grind his teeth into dust. "Do you remember the pictures of the bodies on my phone? Do you really want to chance that happening to you? Because if Axel could drive up from Houston and arrive here a few hours ago, I guarantee that anyone else who got the idea that you might be here could have reached Dallas by now, too."

He made perfectly good points. Bailey felt a bit guilty that he'd gone to so much trouble to save her and she'd succumbed to a little cabin fever and the desire for some vino. Seeing him somewhere between angry and disappointed dug at her in a way she didn't understand. She had a hard time meeting his gaze. "Sorry."

"Did anyone see you?"

"I don't think so. We kept to the shadows before we left the most public area and went to an observation room. It was up high. The windows were tinted. No one could see."

"But you weren't supposed to stray far from Axel's side," Thorpe pointed out, looking at Callie like her ass was grass and he was the lawnmower.

Not that Bailey worried about her new friend. The woman would probably enjoy her punishment. What would it be like if Joaquin did the same to her? The idea made her shiver.

Callie objected. "She just wanted to see—"

"Do you really want to take up this argument?" Sean prodded.

She hesitated, then shook her head. "No. She was curious and . . . I wasn't thinking."

"Let's go." Thorpe stepped away from the desk.

Sean fell in beside him, motioning Callie closer with a sweep of his fingers. She followed them silently toward the door.

"If you need anything around the club tonight, Axel will be here until four a.m. If you want food or drink, our receptionist, Sweet Pea, will help you," Thorpe instructed. "We'll be back tomorrow morning, but you have our numbers if there's an emergency."

"I do." Joaquin nodded. "Thanks." Then he looked Bailey's way. "I'll deal with this situation."

* * *

AS he took her by the arm, Bailey looked like she wanted to protest. Before she could engage in anything so unwise, Thorpe and Sean swept Callie out of the room and down the hall. The brunette turned to Sean and said something, looking as if she was trying to argue her case. Her fiancé shook his head. Her Dom smacked her ass.

Now, there was a good idea . . .

Joaquin turned his attention back to Bailey. "Come with me."

She didn't say anything. For once, she was surprisingly quiet as he led her back to the bedroom she'd been staying in. He shut the door behind them, locked it. The sound made a soft *snick* in the otherwise silent room. He took the empty glass from her hand, managing not to succumb to the urge to slam it on the nearby dresser.

"Explain what the hell you were thinking." He was willing to hear it, not that he expected to like it.

"I already did." She shrugged, but didn't quite meet his gaze. "It's been one devil of a day. You've turned my whole world upside down. I barely know who I am right now. I just wanted out of this room for a few minutes. I wanted wine. I wanted a moment's peace. That's it."

Joaquin tapped his toe, feeling antsy. While he understood her desire for some fresh air and some liquid fortification, with this much danger lurking, he didn't like it. At all. She'd put herself in goddamn danger without thinking. He repressed the urge to fidget. No other woman had ever made him this itchy or had crawled under his skin so quickly. Why her?

"You wanted?" He didn't mean to bite out the words, but they slipped free.

If he'd followed even half of his urges simply because he'd wanted, she'd have a red ass, a sore pussy, and be wearing a smile of satisfaction. And damn it, he had to stop thinking like that.

"So you just thought, the murderous freak who likes to butcher women . . . 'Ah, fuck him'?" he challenged. "Because you're what? Smarter? Stronger? Or you're just playing the odds?"

Bailey looked chagrined for a moment, then her anger kicked in. It showed in the tightening of her soft lips and delicate shoulders. She drew in a deep breath, but somehow only looked angrier for it.

"Why do you care?" she spit at him. "I only matter because I was born Tatiana Aslanov, and you think I can help your cause, whatever that is exactly. Otherwise, you wouldn't have given a damn about me. You would have passed me on the street without looking at me twice if I'd been anyone else."

Joaquin stared at her for a moment, his shock climbing. He'd spent just enough time at Dominion, observing Callie and her Doms, to understand a bit about how the relationship flowed. He'd heard of BDSM before, but never seen it in action until the past twenty-four hours. He'd be lying if he said it didn't fascinate him. And he'd realized quickly that when Callie put on her "bratty pants," Sean and Thorpe came down all over her.

Bailey was sounding pretty bratty about now.

He'd also seen a man spanking his sub tonight when he'd gone looking for Bailey in a panic. Axel had explained the reasoning behind the discipline to him. A short explanation, yes. But he got the part about the submission and the endorphins mixing together to send her into a subspace that would calm her mind and emotions.

Casting a considering glance to Bailey, he pondered his next move. What if she needed this and didn't know it? Hell, he'd never spanked a woman in his life, but the way he felt like a damn volcano right now, he had to get his palm on her bare ass or he was going to blow.

"Come here." He pointed to the ground right in front of him.

She bristled. "I'm close enough."

He found himself sucking in a breath, squaring his shoulders, tightening his jaw. "Get the fuck over here. It's not a request."

Now she looked a little nervous. But her mouth still kept running. "Or what?"

Amazing that she'd managed to take her brattiness to another level. From what little he'd gleaned in the last day or so, if he had any intention of giving this shit a whirl, he had to shut her attitude down now, establish boundaries and control—quick.

"Fine. We'll bypass the 'or what' conversation and I'll just show you."

As he stomped toward her, she tried to back away, but the desk stopped her. Before she could get around it and inch to the door, Joaquin grabbed her by the wrist and hauled her toward the bed.

"I've had enough, Bailey. You don't run out of here. You don't show yourself in public. You don't put yourself at risk. You don't question why I care." He just did. Not that he could explain it even to himself. "You want some peace? I'll give it to you."

He jerked her against his body, her back to his chest. Bailey gasped. He went stone hard, all the blood rushing to his cock at the feel of her against him, at the thought that within mere heartbeats, he'd have her ass under his palm. The moment couldn't come fast enough.

With his free hand, he jerked at the button and zipper of her borrowed jeans. They were a size too big, just like the panties underneath, so getting everything off her hips and shoving it all down her thighs was far easier than he expected. She yelped in surprise.

Joaquin ignored it as he lunged to the bed and planted himself on the edge, then dragged her facedown over his lap, doing his best to settle her squirming. Holy fuck, she had a gorgeous ass. Pale, firm, as delicate as the rest of her.

"What are you doing?" she shrieked. "What the—"

He interrupted her tirade by smacking the flat of his palm directly to her left cheek. Shit, her skin was so soft. The slap rang in his ears, then reverberated in his brain—the sound playing over and over in his head. His blood heated, came to a rolling boil. His cock got even harder. Something inside him stood tall, grew to a mountainous swell with some need to take her, touch her, control her, dominate her. Own her.

As he lifted his palm away, he saw the red imprint of his handiwork. The sight fascinated him. Glowing. Pretty. Perfect. He cupped her cheek, rubbed it, kneaded a little.

"What is wrong with you?" she cried. "Are you out of your mind?"

Probably. Shockingly, he didn't give a shit in that moment.

Instead of answering her, he repeated the process, raising his arm high, then brought it down with resounding force on her right cheek. The crack of his hand on her butt, the little jerk of her body, followed by a cry . . . *Yeah. Fuck yeah.* He'd always supposed that a spanking could be erotic, but he'd never guessed how much. This was flipping his switch in a way he'd never experienced. Arousal burned so hot, it actually stung his veins. All he could think about was doing it again and again and again until she screamed, until her head quieted, until she begged him to fuck her.

That was it. The urge to work inside her pussy was strong, but he knew immediately that just getting her under him once or twice wasn't going to cut it. He had to claim this territory as his own. His to kiss, to punish, to fondle, to arouse . . . to take. Jesus, the urge was killing him.

He swallowed and raised his hand again, already looking for another place to land his palm and turn her skin red. In the back of his head, he knew she'd questioned him. From his observation earlier, he'd figured out that neither submission nor endorphins happened in the blink of an eye, so if it took more than a few of his spankings for this to register properly with her, that was more than fine by him.

By the time that logic had wended through his brain, he found the perfect spot to land his next strike—high on her left cheek, a bit farther from her hip. He eyed that spot like a target, aiming for a bull's-eye. With a *whoosh*, he lowered his arm. The blow hit exactly where he wanted. Instantly, the sound of his skin on hers filled his ears. More of the amazing, arousing sensations filled him. Shit, being with her made him feel eight feet tall. A brighter shade of red bloomed across her ass, and he rubbed it again, fascinated.

"No!" she gasped. "Stop it! You can't do this."

Her little voice tugged at him, sounding so confused and scared, deflated all the arousal and confidence he'd been building. Like a pin into a balloon, it popped, burst.

"Please . . ." she cried out.

Joaquin flinched.

"Shit. Oh hell." He tried to hold her against him, soothe her. Guilt gouged out a mountain of regret inside him. "I'm sorry."

She shoved away from him, looking at him with accusing eyes as she yanked her clothes back into place. "Don't touch me."

He shook his head. What the fuck kind of monster was he, to smack her ass and enjoy it so much? Maybe he hadn't done it right. Or he'd misunderstood what he'd seen earlier. It was entirely possible that he'd liked the idea of spanking her so much he'd projected his desires on Bailey. Whatever. She obviously didn't want this.

As her whole body twitched with the sound of her sobs, he ached to reach for her again and offer shelter. But she wanted nothing to do with him.

He backed away, then turned for the door. "I really am sorry."

With a curse, he forced himself to walk away from her. As he shut the door behind him and locked it again, breathing hard, his gut soured more. Every footfall seemed to weigh a hundred pounds more than the last. Something in his chest actually hurt.

As he slammed into his little cubicle of a room, he marched to the bed, sat down, and thrust his head in his hands. Jesus, had undercover missions and years of cloak-and-dagger shit, coupled with so much fucking death, finally warped him?

Chapter Eight

THE following morning, Joaquin was pacing outside Thorpe's office, just waiting. Over a mostly sleepless night, he'd made some decisions. He didn't relish them, but last night's spanking debacle more than suggested that he'd come unhinged somewhere along the way and needed to get his shit straight before he messed up Bailey's life any more.

Finally, Thorpe sauntered down the hall, heading for his office. He and Sean walked side by side, heads turned in conversation. Suddenly, they stopped. Callie, trailing behind and digging through her purse, smiled up at them both. They each took a turn bestowing a kiss on her red, glossy lips before she headed deeper into the club with a jaunty wave. She stopped short when she spied him. Joaquin winced. He probably looked like shit. It was how he felt.

"Is Bailey still in her room? Can I see her?"

"Yeah," he choked out. "I managed to scramble together a bagel and some fruit for her. Would you mind taking it to her?"

Callie cocked her head. "Sure. You don't want to?"

"It's better if I don't."

She raised her brows in question, but didn't comment. "All right."

As she doubled back to the little kitchen area, Thorpe glowered. "What's wrong?"

"Did something happen with Bailey's would-be killers?" Sean asked.

No, they'd been quiet for hours now, and he didn't like it. But at this point, he'd just add that to his shit list and move on.

"Nothing. This is . . . personal. Can we go in and shut the door?" Joaquin gestured to Thorpe's office. He knew he'd better fess up to last night's fiasco. Maybe damage control now would save his ass later.

"Sure."

Dominion's owner looked relaxed enough, but Joaquin sensed his sudden tension. As he made his way to a chair in the office that oozed with sleek sophistication, Sean closed the door. The echo resounded in the otherwise silent room. Joaquin heard the mental tick-tock in his head as the seconds slipped away. Their expectant looks weren't getting any less tense. Might as well cough the truth up before Bailey told Thorpe a tearful tale and the man threw him out or otherwise intervened.

"When Bailey and I arrived, you told me that everything at Dominion was consensual, that she had to be here of her own free will within forty-eight hours. I fucked up last night and I wanted to tell you that I'll make it right."

Sitting now, Thorpe drilled him with a glare. "How exactly did you fuck up? Explain."

The man's disapproving tone made Joaquin tense. "I was alone with Bailey last night and I lost my head. I—"

"You didn't force the lass, did you?" Sean asked sharply.

"Are you asking if I raped her? No," he barely managed not to shout, then searched for calm and a delicate way to explain. But he'd always been short on diplomacy and long on brute force. "I . . . I understand that you two are Callie's Doms. I know your members here practice BDSM. I get it in principle."

"But . . ." Thorpe prodded.

"I misread Bailey's signals." He shook his head, that crappy shame sludge slogging through his veins. "I was angry and I spanked her."

The club owner rose to his feet, his brows drawn down in a glower. "You punished her while you didn't have control of yourself and your temper?"

That voice more than suggested his answer better be no.

"I had control of myself," Joaquin insisted. "I was pissed off, but I wasn't a raving lunatic. The second she said no, I stopped."

Sean sent Thorpe a stare, and the man sat again. "You didn't have a safe word in place?"

Joaquin didn't know exactly what that meant, but he could guess in context that it would be some word Bailey could say that would stop what he'd been doing. "I wasn't aware that I should have one. None of this was exactly planned."

"Next time, agree on a safe word, something she can easily say but normally wouldn't during play or sex. If nothing else, go with a traffic light. Red for stop, green for—"

"There won't be any 'go' between us. I'm pretty sure I shit in that mess kit." He sighed. The thought of scaring her bugged him every bit as much as the idea of never touching her again.

"Why would you say that?" Sean asked. "You should never hit a sub in anger, that's true, but I'm sure if you talked—"

"I . . ." Joaquin shrugged. "I don't have any experience with this stuff. I thought she might be submissive, but when she pleaded with me to stop, I realized she must not be. While I was really digging it, she obviously didn't feel the same."

The guys exchanged a look before Thorpe frowned at him. "Not submissive?"

"She begged me to let her go like I was . . . torturing her. What else was I supposed to think?"

"She's submissive," Sean supplied.

"Absolutely." Thorpe nodded.

Great. So it was him Bailey objected to. Well, they had met because he'd drugged and abducted her. *Gee, wonder why she doesn't want you to beat her ass, too?*

"Well, either way, if she wants to submit to someone, it won't be me." He stood and rubbed his palms down his jeans. "I'll talk to her this morning, promise not to touch her again, and get her to consent to remain here for her own safety until we can sort out these killers from LOSS."

"What exactly did she say when you spanked her?" Thorpe wanted to dissect the situation. Why the hell wouldn't he just leave it be? He'd explained and apologized. Revisiting this humiliation wasn't exactly at the top of his bucket list.

"She said, 'No. Stop. You can't do this.' The usual kind of stuff that means 'get your fucking hands off me.' I'm sorry. I got lost in my own head. Seeing the red my hand had left on her ass did something to me. I—"

"Felt somewhere between a hundred feet tall and invincible?" Sean supplied with a grin.

Joaquin hadn't expected either of them to just get it. "Yeah."

"Dom space," they said together.

"You were into that place in your head where the act of topping your sub made you feel powerful and needed and like you had found not just a niche, but something you require. Does that sound about right?" Thorpe crossed his arms over his chest.

"Exactly." Joaquin couldn't believe it. The guy had pretty much reached into his mind and read it word for word.

"You definitely roll dominant."

That didn't do him a lot of good if Bailey wasn't willing to submit to him. And he really couldn't blame her.

Sean leaned forward in his seat, elbows on knees, and spoke softly. "She needs time, man. You didn't meet under the best of circumstances. She's in danger. She doesn't know you. But there's no way she isn't interested in what you could give her."

Thorpe nodded. "Bailey may not realize yet that she's submissive. Your biggest issue, though, is trust. It may take a bit more time for you to get inside her walls so that she can let go with you. There's a good chance the spanking shocked more than repelled her. Did you see if she was wet?"

"I wasn't going to shove my fingers up her cunt when she was already crying at me to leave her alone," Joaquin pointed out. He wished they'd stop with the third degree already.

"I understand," Sean assured. "Consider that maybe her logic was telling her that she shouldn't like 'abuse' from her captor. In the right circumstances, with enough trust between you, I can almost guarantee that girl likes a spanking."

Joaquin studied the pair of them, their words turning and tumbling in his head. Was there any chance they were right? Sure, he'd found his Dom space, and that had been awesome. Addicting. Life altering. But what had Bailey been feeling? She'd liked their kisses. Even when they'd been rough and he'd pressed her up against the wall, she hadn't objected one whit. In fact, she hadn't seemed anything but turned on when they'd been arguing just before he'd taken her across his lap. Maybe . . . she just wasn't ready to trust him, and who could blame her?

Oh, hell. What did it matter? He'd brought her here to protect her, not start a relationship or explore his Dominant side with her. This chapter of their lives was probably better put behind them. In a few days, he hoped to have these freaks from LOSS pinned, driven back, or roped up—something. He and Bailey would go their separate ways. End of story.

Except something inside him didn't like that ending.

Joaquin frowned. This wanting more than a romp from a female was a first; he absolutely didn't know what to do. Normally, he was decisive. He delved into a situation, fixed it, then stole back out. No harm, no foul, no worrying about how anyone felt. But the idea of doing that again made his gut tighten in objection. That fucking wasn't happening. He wasn't really sure why it mattered. It just did.

Who did he have in his life? He sat back in his chair. His best friend had been gone a couple of weeks. He'd barely had time to bury Nate or be astounded by the fact that, when they'd finally tracked down his next of kin, they discovered that he hadn't spoken to any of them in almost a decade. They hadn't seemed shocked at the news of his death, and barely saddened. Is that how Joaquin wanted his mother or sisters to react when some asshole's bullet found him?

It shouldn't matter. It never had before . . . but somehow it did now. And he wanted it to matter to Bailey, too.

Wait! How did spanking the woman and her liking it, or not, have anything to do with his connection to his family? Jesus, he was losing it.

"Thanks for the pep talk, but it's a moot point. I doubt I'll be spanking her again. She's made herself clear, and I need her consent to stay here way more than I need her okay to paddle her. I just wanted to be aboveboard and tell you what happened."

"Was she breathing hard?" Thorpe ignored his speech and asked.

"Yeah. She was scared."

"Maybe . . ." The club owner shrugged. "Maybe not."

"Were her cheeks flushed? Her nipples hard? See any of the usual arousal signs?" Sean asked.

Honestly, he hadn't thought to look as soon as she'd begged him to stop touching her. "Just drop it. It's done."

"If that's what you want, sure." Thorpe sent him a cavalier glance that said if he didn't pursue this, he was an idiot. "The truth is, I think you need this in your life. I suspect she needs this even more. She feels scared and everything is beyond her control. The opportunity to be with someone who can make her feel protected and will assume the responsibility for her onto his shoulders is something she craves, I'll bet. But you can't know for sure unless you two communicate."

Yeah, communicating wasn't exactly his bag. Joaquin often forgot that something went down better if he sugarcoated it. He winced as he imagined himself suggesting to Bailey that she'd obviously liked him beating her ass and that he didn't appreciate her making him feel like a douche about it. Hell, that would make him sound like some sort of creepy misogynist rape-happy prick. No thanks.

"Point taken. Now I need to check in on her." Because that sounded like as much fun as gouging his eyes out with a screwdriver.

Joaquin headed for the door, but Thorpe's voice stopped him short. "Talk to her. Or I will."

He whipped around and leveled the Dungeon Master with a pissed-off glare. Being under this roof kept Bailey safe, but it was starting to come at a steep price.

"Don't meddle in my life," he warned. "I did you the courtesy of informing you. I didn't ask for your advice."

"It wasn't advice. It wasn't a suggestion, either. You have until lunch to talk to her or I will take her aside and ask her some very personal questions until I get to the bottom of this."

"Why the fuck would you do that? I said I wouldn't touch her again."

Thorpe sat back, raised a brow. "Don't make that promise. Based on the way you look at her, I don't think you can keep it. Besides, I won't have her upset about anything more than the assholes hunting her down. I especially won't have her worried enough to call the police."

"Use your head." Sean's voice might be a bit softer, but the message wasn't. "What happens if these thugs track you down? What happens if you have to flee with Bailey suddenly . . . only she doesn't trust you enough to take your outstretched hand? Could that hesitation cost both of you your lives? Do you want to take that chance?"

* * *

BAILEY was sitting on the bed, towel drying her hair, when she heard a knock. She tensed, but rose to answer the door. Then remembered that Joaquin had locked it last night after he'd spanked her and run. *Son of a bitch.*

Cautiously, she approached the door. If he'd come back to berate her or rev her up and flee again, he would find that she didn't have much to say. Making sure the borrowed robe covered the essentials, she leaned against the solid portal. "Who is it?"

"Callie. I've got your breakfast."

So Joaquin wouldn't even feed her now? Because he was worried? Embarrassed? Ashamed? It shouldn't matter, but Bailey still wished she knew the answer.

"Come in," she told the other woman.

A moment later, Callie unlocked the door, holding a plate in one hand, with a paper shopping bag dangling from the other.

After she shoved the keys in yet another designer bag, the woman looked up with a smile. "A bagel and some fruit?"

As Bailey took the plate, she frowned. She was hungry, and now probably wasn't the time to mention her usual high-protein, low-sugar nutrition. "Thank you."

"And some more clothes. I shopped for you a bit. I hope that's okay."

Anything Callie brought her would be better than the nothing she'd come with. Not to mention the fact that the woman had great taste.

"Absolutely." She took the bag from Callie's outstretched hand. Inside lay some yoga pants, workout shirts, a few new thongs and bras—all in the right sizes—and a pair of flip-flops. How had Callie known the sort of wardrobe she preferred? "This is perfect. Thank you."

"You're welcome. I know when I've been stranded in an unfamiliar place with virtually no clothes, it always made me feel better to have something comfortable to put on my back. There's also a little bit of skin care and makeup in there. I guessed on what you might like . . ."

Bailey peeked in the bottom of the sack again and saw that everything remaining came in a lovely little box with the interlocking back-to-back Cs of Chanel. These items weren't necessities, but downright indulgences.

"You didn't have to go to this much trouble, but I really appreciate you."

Callie smiled, her eyes warm with understanding. "I've been in your shoes more times than I care to remember. Not that I was abducted, I mean. But unfamiliar surroundings, unfamiliar people, unfamiliar situation. I didn't have any money or time for more than the bare necessities. And I didn't have any friends. I could have used a few."

Bailey couldn't imagine anyone not liking the heiress. Then again, Callie's life on the run hadn't allowed her to form many bonds.

Impulsively, she hugged the other woman. "I need one now, so I really appreciate you."

"It's my pleasure. Did you sleep last night?"

"Finally. It took a while. I—" Bailey stopped. The other woman probably didn't want to hear about her spanking dilemma with Joaquin. "Just a lot on my mind."

"Sure. Totally understand." Callie cocked her head and studied her. "Mind if I ask . . . was it about being Tatiana Aslanov or about Joaquin?"

So much for trying to keep a casual front. "Honestly, both. And there's not much I can do about either."

"Was Joaquin mad?"

"Yeah. Weren't Sean and Thorpe?" Then a terrible thought occurred to Bailey. "Did I get you in trouble? I know you like a bit of it, but . . ."

Callie laughed, a light sound that lilted with happiness. "Let's just say that a little disobedience can come with a lot of rewards. It's called 'funishment' for a reason. Besides, I already know I'm in for more tonight."

"Why do you think that?" What was going on around here?

"I've got something up my sleeve. Just wait." She winked before her expression turned more serious. "You want to talk about what happened with Joaquin?"

He spanked me and I liked it. I wanted it. I hated myself for it. "No." Then she realized that sounded rude. "Sorry. It's just—"

"No apology necessary. I'm here if you change your mind."

"Thanks." Bailey gathered her courage. During her sleepless hours last night, one fact had occurred to her, and she was dying to question Callie. "I actually wanted to ask you more about the Aslanovs. I don't remember anything. I apparently understand Russian and their faces all looked familiar, but . . . the memories just aren't there."

"You were young. And if you were in the house when they died, as everyone suspects, it was traumatic. Others might wish you could remember, but I know why you can't. It's asking a lot of a little girl."

Bailey nodded, relieved again by Callie's compassion. "What were they like, my biological family? Did you know them?"

Regret crossed her kind, oval face. "I never met Viktor's wife and children. I really only saw him a handful of times, the last being when I was about ten. I remember his thick accent. I remember . . ." She smiled. "His bushy mustache and beard. He joked with my sister and me once that he was in training to be the next Santa Claus when his hair went white. Everyone said he was brilliant, even my dad—and he wasn't a man prone to throwing that word around lightly."

The man Callie described just didn't sound anything like the scientist who performed such unethical experiments as to alter human genetics. "I don't know what kind of man he was."

Callie shrugged. "I don't think he tried to discover all those genetic anomalies, at least according to the notes my father left behind, which he based on your father's research before he burned it. I think he really did set out to try to find the genes that caused cancer and stop them from eating away at people. I don't think he meant to exploit anyone or anything. He needed money, and with three small children . . ."

In order to feed her and her siblings, her father had elected to do something unethical and sell his accidental discoveries to homegrown terrorists.

"Do you know if he understood the kind of people he was dealing with?"

"I don't know if he did at first. Eventually, he figured it out. According to my father's notes, he was terrified of them. At one point, he pleaded with my father to lend him some money." Callie shrugged. "I've often wondered if Dad regretted refusing him when he heard about your family's deaths. Or when they broke into my house and killed mine."

"You have to believe he did. Just like I have to believe that mine wished he'd made different decisions. But we'll never know for sure."

"We won't, but I've consoled myself with the idea that things happen for a reason. I couldn't figure out at the time what possible purpose their murder could serve. But maybe it was part of fate's larger scheme to keep DNA-changing information from the hands of people who would abuse it. And I know that if my life had turned out differently that I would never have met Thorpe and Sean."

True. Bailey chewed on her lip. What different path had losing her biological family served in her life? She'd grown up in Houston, not rural Indiana. She had been raised an only child, and it saddened her to think that she could have otherwise had siblings. Maybe her biological parents would have raised her to appreciate her Russian heritage. Would she have had dance in her life? All good questions with no answers. One thing she knew for sure: If the rest of the Aslanovs had lived, she would never have met Joaquin.

Why did that idea disturb her?

"Thanks. I appreciate you sharing what you know."

"My pleasure. Why don't you eat your breakfast and change. I'll give you some privacy."

Bailey really didn't want Callie to go, but with a wedding in a few days, she couldn't expect a busy bride to hang out with her. But she still had one question she wished she didn't. "Have you seen Joaquin?"

"Yes, just before I came in. He was heading behind closed doors with Thorpe and Sean for what looked to be a heavy conversation."

She wanted to ask how he looked or if he seemed upset, then she realized how junior high that sounded. The truth was, she'd panicked when he'd touched her because she had liked it too much and she hadn't had the guts to admit it. She had let him blurt out apologies and leave, thinking the worst. But what else could she have said to him? *Please, Guy I Barely Know, spank me hard?*

"Thanks."

Callie nodded. "I'll check in with you later."

As soon as the woman left, Bailey meandered into the bathroom to change her clothes and brush her hair. She kind of wished that Joaquin had brought her flat iron along when he'd taken her from her house, but alas, he probably hadn't given her beauty regimen a single thought. Trying to work with her natural waves wasn't something she did happily or often, and she made a mental note to ask Callie about some sort of hot implement in the future.

After doing what little she could with her hair, Bailey pondered snooping through the bedroom again to figure out what exactly some of the sex toys in the nightstand did or flipping on the TV. She was about to open a drawer when she heard another knock at the door, this one firm, decisive.

Joaquin. Somehow, she knew he'd returned.

Bailey dragged in a nervous breath, anticipation and dread swirling in her belly. "Come in."

Sure enough, the door flung open, and he filled the frame—all six-plus feet of him with broad shoulders straining a white V-neck T-shirt, showing off a chest as hard as concrete. He kissed like a man who knew how to make a woman melt. He spanked like a Dom who had a point to make. He was insistent. Sure of himself. He was nothing like any of the boys she knew. Damn it, if that didn't excite her.

"Good morning. I have to talk to you about last night."

She crossed her arms. That conversation would be totally embarrassing. "Can't we just forget it?"

"No." He stepped in and shut the door behind him, locking it. "I upset you. That wasn't my intention. I've never hit a woman in my life. I've never spanked one, either. You . . ." He shook his head. "Never mind. I don't have an excuse. I pushed you. I scared you. I hurt you. I'm sorry. That won't happen again."

Guilt pummeled her. He might have pushed her, but he hadn't done anything she hadn't enjoyed. "You didn't scare me. Or hurt me."

His entire body froze. "Then what did I do to you?"

"Nothing, really." *Just stirred up my blood and made me ache for you.* She couldn't bring herself to meet his gaze. Even now, the lie sat heavy on her conscience. "I'm fine."

Joaquin closed the remaining distance between them and grabbed her chin. "Look at me. Since I didn't hurt you, did my actions offend you?"

"No," she breathed, unable to look anywhere except into his eyes. Why did she feel as if she could get lost here, as if he would always catch her and hold her upright even as he kept her off balance. "You shocked me."

He nodded as if that was a given. "It shocked me, too. Especially that I liked it."

Wow, that was honest. She opened her mouth to say she had, too, but the words just wouldn't come.

"What about you?" he demanded.

Bailey blew out a breath. How was she supposed to answer him? *You made me wet enough last night to masturbate?* "I . . . didn't hate it."

His grip on her chin tightened a fraction. He frowned, his gaze deepening as if he wanted to pick her thoughts apart. "Were you at all aroused?"

Why couldn't he be like so many of the people she'd met during her years of dance, polite and indirect, folks who rarely pinned her down to force out an uncomfortable reply? Even Blane often let her off the hook.

She swallowed, trying to escape Joaquin's hold and his gaze. He allowed neither.

"Let go," she murmured, aware that she had no real power in this situation.

"Not until you answer me. And if you won't, we'll repeat last night until I figure it out."

Against her will, her breath caught. The memory of his hand on her ass made her heart pump, her insides flare with heat.

Joaquin stared, not missing a thing. He scanned her flushed cheeks. His gaze fell to the pulse hammering at her neck. Then that burning stare dropped to her breasts, zeroing in on their tingling tips poking desperately at the fabric of her shirt.

He knew. That knowledge flared in his hazel eyes, which looked even more green as the sunlight streamed into the room and across his face. She had nowhere to run or hide to escape his insistence.

Squeezing her eyes shut, Bailey berated herself. She owed him the truth. But hell if it wasn't embarrassing to admit that she found the guy who'd taken her from her home and spanked her against her will hot.

"Bailey?" he prodded. "I haven't been less than honest with you."

"I know." But she still couldn't look at him.

"Open your eyes," he demanded, waiting until she'd complied. "Did you find my spanking arousing? Because if you need me to confess first, I'll be perfectly happy to tell you that it turned me on like nothing else to see my hand on your pale skin. The redness I left behind after every blow—the marks I'd given you—made me beyond ready to finish stripping you down and fuck you. Does that make it easier for you to tell me the truth?"

She felt her jaw drop, even as desire stung her. "You can't say that."

"Why?" His free hand lifted to her waist, skimmed up her rib cage—and kept climbing.

Every muscle in her body grew taut. Bailey couldn't breathe. Would he dare to just— She had her answer a moment later when he cradled her breast in his hand and feathered his thumb across her beaded nipple.

Her breath caught on a gasp.

"You're aroused." He didn't even ask, just stated fact.

Oddly, Bailey was a bit relieved. "It doesn't make sense."

"Maybe not." He shrugged. "But there it is. I want you. You want me."

"I'm not ready for sex." She shook her head.

Holy crap, did he think that barely twenty-four hours after he'd kidnapped her, she was going to just spread her legs and welcome him inside her body? She'd always been shy about that sort of thing. She'd had one fumbling lover back in high school. Intercourse had always been something she could take or leave. But already she knew Joaquin would be nothing like that.

He nodded. "I respect that. I understand it. It shouldn't even be the first thing on our agenda right now."

God, he'd finally thrown her a bone, and she was taking it. "Exactly."

Joaquin leaned closer, and she could smell his woodsy, musky scent. It made her weak-kneed and somewhat dizzy, especially when he murmured in her ear. "But it doesn't mean I'm not thinking it. It seems impossible for me to concentrate on much else when I'm around you."

His words were like a touch right over her most sensitive spot. How could one sentence make her pussy throb? "We still have to figure out exactly who's after me and how we're going to stop them."

"I've got a team working on that. I'm hoping we can run the sketch of 'Uncle Robbie' through some federal databases today and see if we get any hits. Until then, we need to deal with one another. I need you to be honest."

"As it pertains to the fruit loop looking for me, I will. But I don't see why I should have to confess whether or not you turned me on."

"Well, if I wanted to force-feed you some reality, I might remind you that in life-or-death situations, our ability to trust in one another's honesty might well determine whether we live to see another day." He shrugged. "But I'm willing to admit that it's about more. I like you. I want you. I intend to take you to bed. Not before you're ready," he assured her. "But I'll make damn sure we get there."

Who the hell did he think he was? "Do you push every woman you meet this hard?"

"No. It's something about you. We share a high-voltage, almost chemical attraction. I'm not denying it." He thumbed her nipple again. "Why are you?"

As a fresh flare of tingles filled her, Bailey jerked away. "I didn't come here to screw, so get that out of your head."

Joaquin dropped his hand and stepped back. Immediately, she missed the warmth of his touch. Her body ached. Her nipples tightened in distress at his loss.

His jaw firmed, and he didn't look pleased. "I didn't come here to screw, either. I came here to save your life and figure out who wants Tatiana Aslanov enough to leave a string of dead bodies. We're still waiting on information from our investigation so we can solve the case. Until then, I don't have much else to focus on beyond how much I want you."

He'd been nothing but starkly honest. She'd been evading his questions and refusing to be completely honest. "Joaquin, can you understand this last day has been a lot for me to take in? I don't know what's going on half the time. I don't know you. I don't know my surroundings. I barely understand what happens inside these walls."

Some of the steel left his stance. He stepped close again and held an arm out to her, motioning her to step into his embrace. Bailey needed his comfort and understanding too badly to refuse. Callie had been a lovely balm to her, a kindred spirit, not to mention a kind soul. But the other woman's comfort didn't soothe her the way Joaquin's did.

Bailey stepped into his embrace and wrapped her arms around him. With a little sigh, she closed her eyes and rested her cheek on his chest, listening to his heartbeat. To others, it might seem stupid to look to him for comfort, but Joaquin was so solid—a protector. He'd risked so much to save her. While he'd been open with both himself and his desires, she had freaked out and clammed up. The realization made her feel more than a little ashamed.

He stroked a large hand down her hair. "I know this has been a lot for you. If there'd been more time, I would have convinced you more gently that you were a target and that you needed to come away with me for your safety. I regret that I scared you initially and that I didn't stop to think about how difficult this must be for you. I'm sure being even remotely turned on by the guy who dragged you from your bed in the middle of the night seems foolish. You may even be berating yourself."

"Totally," she confessed, holding him tighter. He understood. After she'd been less than honest with him, he had still given her compassion. And she'd needed it in the worst way.

He skimmed her cheek with his fingers, then cupped her chin, forcing her to look up. "I know. But honesty really is important between us."

Bailey chewed on her bottom lip. She'd come from a world of art, where the perception was far more important than the reality. No one in the audience during a performance saw the blistered feet, felt the shin splints, knew the punishment a dancer's knees or ankles took. They simply enjoyed the choreographed elegance. Even the childhood she remembered had been something of a performance, apparently acted out by two agents she hadn't truly known. She was so grateful to him for being honest.

Bailey felt more ashamed than ever. "I liked what you did to me last night and I didn't understand. I've never experienced anything like that. I panicked. I felt stupid and ashamed for wanting more. I'm sorry if I made you feel bad about what happened."

He cradled her face in his hands. "Thank you. I needed the truth."

Joaquin paused, then looked into her eyes. She couldn't miss the desire there, but his expression held more. A yearning to hold her. A need to protect. A possessiveness he couldn't quite hide. Against her will and her logic, excitement invaded her belly and settled with an ache a bit lower.

Then he bent his head. Bailey felt her body go taut, her excitement turn to thrill. Her lashes fluttered shut and she turned her face up, anticipating his kiss. Maybe it wasn't smart. Maybe someone would write a term paper in Freshman Psych about her someday as a case study in Stockholm syndrome. Right now, all she knew was that Joaquin felt like the most solid part of her life and she couldn't wait for his mouth to cover hers.

Instead, he brushed his lips over her forehead and pulled away. Bailey tried not to be disappointed.

"I've got to call Hunter and some of the other guys working this investigation. A few things before I go. Thorpe made it clear to me when I brought you here that he would only allow us to stay if you consented to be here. We have until tomorrow at noon to convince him that I'm not forcing you to be here against your will."

Of course he wasn't. Bailey had seen a picture of what awaited her back home. No thanks. "I'll talk to him."

He nodded once. "That would set him at ease."

She gave him a little grin. "And get him off your back?"

"That, too," he admitted. "Thorpe has stressed that Dominion is a completely consensual environment. I understand that and I respect it. I wouldn't want any woman doing anything sexual against her will. I refuse to even have the question between us. So until I'm absolutely sure you're willing, I won't touch you again."

His words made her go cold. Was he serious? "What do you mean?"

"How was I unclear?" He studied her, his broad shoulders towering, his whole mien daunting.

She thrust her hands onto her hips. "Weren't you the one vowing to get me into bed five minutes ago?"

"Yes. And I meant it. Whatever this attraction is between us isn't going away. I'm not giving up until I feel you under me, your sweet pussy gripping my cock. But I'm not going to give it to you—or anything else—until you ask me for it."

Chapter Nine

LATER that evening, Joaquin paced Dominion's hallways. The afternoon had been too quiet, way too full of time to wish like hell that something would break in this case. But nothing yet. Bailey's house hadn't turned up any unfamiliar prints. The sketch hadn't been released so far. Sean had offered to see if anyone could get a pinpoint on LOSS's location and recent activities. The investigative standstill skewered Joaquin's nerves.

Then there was Bailey herself. He'd brought her lunch, his stomach twisting with nerves. He'd fought criminals, tangled with a hurricane, and hunted terrorists for almost a decade. Why should a woman who barely came up to his shoulders turn him inside out?

Because he'd put the ball in her court and swore he wouldn't touch her until she asked him to. That didn't stop desire from clawing his insides. And if she never asked him? Joaquin didn't want to imagine never feeling her delicate body against him, their hearts pounding together as he claimed her lips and—

Not a helpful train of thought. Moving on . . .

A solid rap on his door had him whirling toward the sound. "Yeah?"

The door opened, and Sean stuck his head inside. "Can you join us for a few minutes? Bailey is with my bride. We could use your help."

Joaquin had no idea what this was about, but anything to stop pacing the same twelve-by-twelve area would be a blessing. "Sure."

He followed Sean down the hall, past Thorpe's empty office, then out of the secure area and into the public dungeon space. Immediately, his blood boiled. Was the place open? Probably, since he could hear voices. Goddamn it, Bailey had shown her face and risked herself again. What for this time? Knowing that spanking her was off the table really chafed.

But as he drew closer, light from the dungeon spilled into the hallway. Someone turned on a catchy pop tune, then the scraping of metal against the floor filled his ears. When he and Sean turned the corner and Joaquin entered the room, he stopped.

The only people inside were Callie, Bailey, and Axel. The pretty brunette climbed on top of a ladder and Bailey handed a bright blue streamer up to her. In fact, the whole room was filled with multicolored paper swagged from the corners of the ceiling, tables laden with food, and lots of balloons. To one side, a multi-tiered cake with plastic handcuffs sported a big number "40" in black icing.

"Italian cream?" Axel asked, pointing at the cake.

Callie nodded. "His favorite."

"What the hell is this?" Joaquin barked.

Everyone in the room turned. Callie frowned.

"A birthday party." Sean leaned in. "We needed one more tall person to finish hanging streamers and we're running out of time. He'll be here in fifteen minutes."

"Who?" Annoyance jabbed Joaquin. He didn't know anyone here and didn't give a shit about milestones right now unless it saved Bailey's life. The distraction from his purpose bothered him.

"Thorpe." Callie stared at him, her expression daring him to say a word or refuse.

Since the man had given him a safe place to stash Bailey, he didn't. Forcing himself to relax, he nodded. "Sure. It's his fortieth birthday?"

"Today."

"On April Fool's Day?" Were they kidding?

"Isn't it funny?" Sean was obviously having a good laugh from the situation.

"He ordered me not to give him a surprise party, but who doesn't play a practical joke every April first?" Callie flashed him a mischievous smile.

Joaquin couldn't remember the last time he'd celebrated a birthday with anyone, much less his own. Years and years ago. Hell, he'd turned thirty roaming a south Texas swamp, wearing night vision goggles and dodging bullets. He hadn't remembered that he'd turned another year older until two days later. If he hadn't been on a mission, who would he have spent his evening with? Joaquin mentally listed his friends. It took about two seconds. None of them were the birthday party type. Even Nate, the only person he'd been close to in years, might have offered him a beer at most. They would have spent the evening talking shop.

As Joaquin studied the room, he felt almost . . . envious. Thorpe was surrounded by people who loved him. That had never mattered much to Joaquin, but now he wondered what he'd been missing.

"Here you go." Sean clapped him on the back, then handed him a roll of white streamers and some tape. "In the far corner. It looks like Callie and Axel have this side covered."

Within three minutes, he and Sean had hung the last of the decorations from the ceiling. Callie checked the cake again, arranging the plates and forks, then glanced through the snacks and drinks on the nearby table. Axel brought out a bag of ice from the kitchen, and Bailey helped him dump it into a freezer behind the bar.

The atmosphere was festive, full of anticipation. Joaquin frowned, feeling out of place.

"I think that's everything." Callie looked around the room in satisfaction. "I wish everyone would hurry up and get here."

"Everyone?" he questioned.

Sean's phone dinged with a text message.

"Is it him?" Callie asked.

"No," he murmured, reading his phone. "The Edgingtons. They'll be here in less than five."

"Hunter and Logan?" Joaquin asked.

"And their wives."

"My sister is coming?" He looked around the room. Beyond the tables and the decorations, the play equipment still stood—a spanking bench, that big cross thing, a padded table. Whips, floggers, crops, and other shit he couldn't identify hung all over the wall. "She doesn't belong here."

Callie slanted him a wry glance. "Her membership says she does."

"The Santiago brothers and their wife aren't far behind them."

"Good." Callie pressed trembling hands to her stomach. "I'll get all my questions answered."

Sean smiled up at her and bent to press a soft kiss to her lips. "That you will, lovely."

"Does the room look all right?" she asked anxiously.

With a sardonic glance, Sean looked around. "I'm sure it's far more than Thorpe expected."

That made Callie grin, and for a moment they looked at each other as if no one else existed. Joaquin could actually feel the love between them, enclosing them together in something so excruciatingly personal it nearly gave him hives. He'd never encountered anything like it.

Watching them filled him with discomfort, yet he couldn't look away. Coming home to someone who was the center of his world . . . What would that be like? His father had died when Joaquin was young, and his mother had remarried an absolute prick. He'd been relieved to hear that she'd divorced him.

Joaquin glanced across the room at Bailey, who stood in shadow behind the bar, watching Sean and Callie with a naked longing on her face that stabbed him in the gut. *Fuck.* Even if she ever found the courage to ask him for so much as a peck again, a smart man would turn her down.

So far, when it came to Bailey, he hadn't proven himself to be terribly bright.

A moment later, chatter filled the foyer area around the corner. A woman with a high-pitched Betty Boop voice said hello—the woman everyone called Sweet Pea. Greetings ensued, and Joaquin winced when he heard his sister a moment later. He still wasn't quite sure what to say to her. *Hi, I hope you're having a nice life*? The thought not only made him uncomfortable, but sent guilt rolling through his stomach. She reminded him of all the shit he didn't want to remember.

Joaquin crossed the room to Bailey. "Let's go."

She looked up at him with big blue eyes, silently pleading. "I don't want to go back to that room. I'm bored and I'm not used to being cooped up." She raised her chin. "I want to meet your sister."

Hideous idea. He could only guess what Kata would tell her. "No one can know you were here."

"There will be fewer than twenty people at this party. You know most everyone attending," Callie reasoned. "Bailey helped me a lot today. I'd love to have her here." She looked a little uncertain. "I don't have many friends coming. The Edgington wives don't seem to like me."

"They don't know you well. Give them time," Sean scolded her, then turned to Joaquin. "I promise, no one coming would dare to breathe a word of Bailey's presence. As you can imagine, we're a pretty tight-lipped community."

Joaquin looked around the room again, at all the trappings of

BDSM. So Sean probably told the truth. That didn't mean Joaquin liked any of it—risking Bailey, seeing family.

He gritted his teeth, but before he could grab Bailey and drag her from the room, Kata came barreling around the corner, carrying a gift bag and wearing a black dress that hugged her swollen belly. She was beginning to waddle.

"You didn't say good-bye." Kata came at him, hands on her hips. "Again."

"It was kind of a life-or-death situation," he protested.

She scowled. Obviously, she didn't like it, but she understood. "Did you find the woman you needed to protect?"

He turned to look for Bailey, who stepped forward, the light above making the golden tone of her blond-brown hair glitter. "I'm Bailey Benson. You're Joaquin's sister?"

"When he remembers that he has family, yes." She sent him a snappy stare, then directed something kinder Bailey's way, hand outstretched. "I'm Kata. Nice to meet you."

Bailey shook her hand, looking so petite next to his sister, who was both taller and very pregnant. "Nice to meet you, too. You have the same eyes."

"So our mother always says. Did you know she's remarried, by the way?" Kata asked him.

No, he hadn't had a clue. His mother sent cards to a P.O. box he almost never opened. Sometimes, she left voicemails on his cell phone, but work had given him a different phone and number. Since he didn't have a personal life, he rarely ever looked at his personal phone.

His ignorance must have shown, since his sister kept talking. "Yeah, she married Hunter and Logan's dad, Caleb, this past September."

Whoa. "Seriously? She married your husband's father?"

"Yep, and they're very happy. If you tuned in every once in a while, you would have known." She gave him an acid smile, then turned to Bailey. "Do you need anything? Are you all right?" His sister sent him a knowing glare. "Is my big brother treating you well?"

A flush zoomed up Bailey's fair complexion and her stare trailed away. "I-I'm fine."

"Oh, hell," Kata muttered with an incredulous stare. "He tried to get you into bed, didn't he?"

Joaquin wasn't sure whether to bark at his sister that it was none of her business or ask her how the fuck she knew. Hunter saved him the trouble.

His brother-in-law set his big hands on Kata's shoulders and spoke calmly. "Ease up, honey. It's a birthday party. Thorpe will be here any minute. Let's play nice. You can snap at Joaquin later."

Like hell. "Thanks, buddy."

Hunter sent him a jaunty smile. "Don't mention it. I have great respect for her hormones. You should, too."

Kata elbowed her husband, then sighed. "Fine. I'm going to put Thorpe's present down and get some punch. Where's Tara . . ."

Joaquin's sister glanced around the room until she found a little redhead next to Logan. They were speaking to Callie. Even from a distance, he could see that the conversation was stilted, and Logan was doing his best to smooth things over.

"Is something wrong between them?" Bailey asked.

"Tara has always thought that Callie wanted her man," Kata said, "but I told her Callie has always been stuck on Thorpe. I was right. I'll see what I can do over there. Why don't you come with me so I can warn you away from my brother?"

Before his sister took more than a couple of steps, Callie broke out in a smile. Tara returned the expression, and the two hugged. Sean hovered behind his bride, looking pleased. The two men shook hands. Logan said something, and everyone laughed. Kata and Bailey joined in, Hunter just behind them.

Joaquin's sister introduced Bailey to the group. Tara smiled warmly and conversation ensued. Logan dropped a hand on the petite ballerina's shoulder and asked her a question or two. She nodded and murmured a short answer, looking a bit shy. And so goddamn beautiful she made Joaquin's cock stand hard. But it was more because he also didn't like the Edgington brothers hovering around her. Joaquin's head told him they were married. The rest of him didn't care because he didn't want anyone else's hands on her.

Jack Cole and his redheaded wife breezed in a moment later, the man guiding her with a hand at her back. He turned and dropped his head to whisper something in her ear. She lifted a hand and let it glide across her belly. Her gauzy, flowy blouse almost hid a baby bump. After setting another wrapped gift on the little table, Jack's hand joined hers over the emerging mound.

Joaquin grimaced. What the hell was the appeal of chaining yourself to a desk to come home to the same woman every night, who'd eventually nag about what you didn't do to help around the house while raising snotty rug rats who would someday become defiant teenagers? He'd always wondered that. But now?

He glanced at Bailey. Something vicious kicked him in the chest . . . then gripped him lower. What the hell?

"Hey, man." He watched Logan approach Jack with a slap on the shoulder. "Morgan, how are you feeling?"

Jack shook Logan's hand as Morgan smiled. "Really good. This pregnancy is much easier than the last."

"She's getting the hang of hormone overload," Jack quipped.

Morgan batted his shoulder, then turned her attention to Logan. "How are those precious little baby girls of yours?"

Logan rubbed the back of his neck. "Sleepless. Tara needs to stop worrying and relax. Mandy and Macy are spending the night with Grandpa Caleb and Carlotta, so . . ."

"So it's on in the dungeon tonight, huh?" Jack grinned. "Don't do anything I wouldn't do."

"That leaves the field wide open," Morgan teased.

"We might not be able to engage in impact play now, but orgasm deprivation is not off the table, *mon couer.*" Jack's smile wasn't pleasant.

Logan cleared his throat and coughed into his hand, obviously smothering a laugh. "Who's holding down the fort tonight? Deke?"

"No." Jack wrapped his arm around Morgan as his face turned more serious. "They stopped Kimber's labor, but she's on strict bed-rest for at least the next week. Stone agreed to watch Oracle and alert me if anything goes down. He's getting some help from Tyler and Xander's buddy Decker McConnell."

Joaquin shouldn't be surprised that a man like Jack wouldn't leave the private security company he owned with Deke completely untended. In fact, he was relieved. Stone had proven damn useful. Maybe he'd turn something else up.

"Thanks for the update. I'll swing by and see my sister tomorrow," Logan promised.

"She'd like that," Morgan assured him with a smile.

Joaquin just stared. If Kata had gone into early labor—or any labor at all—he would never have known. That shouldn't bother him. After all, Hunter could more than take care of her. But Nate's death had made one fact brutally clear: Life could be cut unexpectedly short at any moment. Kata was one of the few people on the planet he knew would be there for him, if he'd let her.

"We're not late, are we?" A big Latin-looking man in a slick suit sauntered in with a grin, holding hands with a very pregnant blonde.

Behind her, another man with dark hair and designer duds held her other hand. In his left, he clutched a prettily wrapped bottle. His more serious face looked carved with lines of experience, but when he smiled, his happiness projected all over the room. "If we are, it's Xander's fault. My younger brother takes more time to do his hair than me and our wife put together." When the blonde between them laughed, he prodded her. "Come on, back me up on this."

Xander sent her a scowl.

"Javier, I love you. I'm pleading the fifth."

"Tell the truth," he demanded. The silent *or I'll punish you* hovered in the air.

"You don't have to do anything he says, *belleza*," Xander assured her smugly.

She withdrew her hands from theirs and frowned primly. "You guys know the rule. Work your squabbles out before you bring them to me. There's only one way I'm ever in the middle of you two."

At her broad grin, Javier dropped a hand to her distended belly. "We remember."

"Let's reenact that tonight." Xander nuzzled her neck.

The blonde giggled, then headed toward Callie, shaking her head. The two women embraced, and the petite brunette asked if they could speak privately soon. When the other woman agreed, Callie turned and introduced Bailey.

The blonde's name was London. She wore the hugest wedding rock Joaquin had ever seen, along with a truly happy glow. The older brother set their gift down, then the two men each grabbed a bottle of water and watched their wife with indulgent grins.

Joaquin stood in a corner, now alone, watching the interactions around him. Chatter drifted through the room. Smiles abounded. Friends stood beside one another. Spouses offered a soft caress, held each other's hand. A jovial air hung in the room. These people were happy not just to be celebrating a friend's birthday, but to be all together as well.

Bonds and encumbering responsibilities like these had always annoyed him, felt foreign and constricting. Did these people know something about life that he didn't?

A glance at Bailey proved she fit right in, easily conversing with London and Callie. Tara and Kata joined them a moment later. Jack finally released Morgan's hand and she drifted into the circle of women. Not long after that, all the men clustered near the door, talking shop and ribbing one another. Joaquin stood alone. Normally, he preferred that. Today, he felt oddly . . . left out.

He frowned. It didn't matter. In a few days, he'd never see most of these people again.

Sean approached him, beer in hand. "You all right?"

He wondered why the man cared. "Fine."

"You look pissed off."

Confused. "Thorpe's a great guy and all, but I'm supposed to be saving Bailey's life, not hanging streamers and partying the night away in a dungeon."

Waiting for play I won't be having with a woman I have no business wanting.

Hell, his thoughts made him sound pitiful.

"You got another one of those?" He nodded down at Sean's beer.

The former FBI agent pointed to Axel behind the bar. "He'll hook you up. Before you get one, did you talk to Bailey about last night?"

It chafed him to answer to anyone, but he knew Thorpe and Sean had him by the balls. "Yep. We're square."

"Good. You know things might get . . . heated tonight."

Joaquin barely managed not to wince. "Bailey and I will be gone before then."

Sean just smiled, as if to tell Joaquin that he was out of his mind. "Whatever you say."

Suddenly, Sean pulled his phone from his pocket. The little screen lit up, and he shushed the crowd. When all fell silent, he hit the button to answer. "Hey, Thorpe. You on your way back?"

Whatever the other man said made a secretive smile cross Sean's face. Callie sent him a questioning look, and the man's grin only grew. His merry blue eyes danced with mischief.

Callie turned to Bailey and London with a whisper. "Uh-oh."

Tara tried to hold in a smile. "That looks like trouble for you."

"It would be like Thorpe to decide that his birthday present is to find a new way to torture me in the dungeon."

Bailey stole a glance Joaquin's way. When she caught him looking back, she jerked her stare toward Sean. "I think your other man might be in on that."

"That wouldn't surprise me at all." Callie winked at her fiancé.

"Great," Sean said into the phone. "See you back here in a few."

The second he hung up, Sean shoved the phone back in his pocket, and Callie hustled over. "How long?"

"Less than five."

She nodded. "We're ready. I kept it small, so that helped."

Sean cocked his head. "Thorpe will still want to light up your ass for this."

"The only people I asked over were those who could legitimately be helping Joaquin with his case. If their wives came and fun ensued . . ." She shrugged as if the matter was out of her hands.

"Nice try. But that's still going to get you in trouble, lovely."

"I didn't invite the whole dungeon." She mock pouted.

"Yet. That shindig you have planned once the three of us come back from our honeymoon?"

She bit her lip. Her starkly vulnerable expression surprised Joaquin. The woman seemed so confident, so the insecurity on her face took him aback.

If Callie, who had two men so obviously madly in love with her, could feel unsure, what must Bailey be feeling?

"I'm hoping his birthday present will be exactly what he wants."

Sean pulled her close. "Oh, lovely. We've talked about this. It will. Have faith."

Callie drew in a deep breath and nodded. "I do."

"Don't forget those words before Saturday." He tapped the end of her nose.

She laughed. They kissed.

Joaquin stared. Envy pierced him, which made absolutely zero fucking sense. He had no idea what Thorpe's gift might be, but he knew those three were going to be ridiculously happy. Joaquin was pretty sure he'd die alone. For the first time ever, that bugged the shit out of him.

Well, wasn't he a bright ray of sunshine?

"Kill the lights," Sean barked at Axel behind the bar.

The big slab of muscle nodded, and the windowless room went pitch-black a moment later. Joaquin heard Bailey's little gasp of surprise and fought the oddest urge to go to her side and comfort her. She was a grown woman, and the dark wouldn't hurt her. Nor would anyone currently in it. Somehow, logic didn't diminish the need.

He moved through the blackness, heading to her most recent location. There she was, right where he'd left her. Joaquin knew her by her scent. He wrapped an arm around her, bringing her body against his own. Being near her instantly soothed him.

She tensed, struggled to escape.

"It's all right," Joaquin assured her with a whisper. "It's just me."

Then he winced. That would probably make her fight harder.

Instead, Bailey relaxed, almost melting into him. That unconscious show of trust made everything seem oddly right in his world.

Earlier today, he'd listened well and hard to Thorpe and Sean talk about what it meant to be Dominant, his responsibilities to a sub, the dos and don'ts of BDSM. The more they talked, the more he wanted what they described. He saw now that he'd largely sought control of his partners. He'd fantasized about bondage off and on since his teen years, but restrained the desire to nothing more than holding a partner down to the bed. Ropes and cuffs weren't casual hook-up conversations. He'd never stayed with any one female long enough to "explore." But Bailey's sweet submissive nature, coupled with her quiet strength, flipped some switch in him. No turning off his desire to be on top of her in every way he could fathom.

He caressed her arm, gentling and soothing her, as the door to the club opened, then shut. The click of a man's loafers resounded on the concrete. The man entering the room sighed.

"Why is it dark in here? Where the devil is everyone?" He tapped the wall, presumably fumbling around for a light switch.

Suddenly, a bright glow flooded the room.

"Surprise!" everyone else in the room shouted.

Thorpe stood there, looking utterly taken aback. He blinked, looked at the crowd, the decorations, at Sean . . . then his stare landed on Callie.

"Pet," he drawled. "I appreciate the thought, but we discussed this."

His pissed-off Dom voice sounded like he'd sharpened it on the edge of a straight razor.

Joaquin noted that, under his grip, Bailey tensed. Yeah, she would hate disappointing anyone.

"April Fool's . . ." Callie smiled, but reached to clasp Sean's hand for moral support.

Thorpe didn't say anything for a taut moment. "My unfortunate birthday has somehow led you to believe that my wishes were a joke?"

The stunning brunette looked uneasy. "It's kind of a big deal, Mitchell. Please be happy. This weekend will be so focused on Sean and me with the wedding."

"As it should be."

"I didn't want your big day to go by uncelebrated."

Thorpe turned that penetrating stare on Sean. "You're in on this?"

"Guilty." Sean shrugged. "We've been planning this occasion for a couple of months."

The dungeon owner almost managed to appear impatient and displeased, but a smile lurked under it all and gave him away. "So you encouraged this?"

"C'mon, man. She's right; it is a big deal." Sean shrugged. "You can handle being the center of attention for one evening."

He crossed his arms over his chest, looking unmoved. "Just remember that paybacks are a bitch." Then he turned to Callie. "And you, my sweet little pet . . . prepare to have a red ass. Every one of my forty birthday spankings will be for you tonight."

Bailey stiffened and edged away. Joaquin let her go, lamenting her loss. She trusted him to keep her safe but not to touch her. He'd really fucked up and didn't know how to change that.

"I figured." And Callie didn't look too distressed about it.

Now Thorpe appeared downright eager, and Joaquin totally understood. Bailey stood barely two feet away from him. As he raked his stare down her back, his gaze settled on her pert ass. He hardened, then cursed. That gap between them might as well be two continents because he didn't know when—or even if—she'd ever let him touch her again.

And he had no one to blame but himself.

"But first . . ." Callie bustled across the room and grabbed a margarita rimmed with salt from Axel and put it in Thorpe's hand. She held up a bottle of water of her own. "A toast to the birthday boy. You're a great friend, protector, partner, and person. I got so very lucky when I walked through Dominion's door. I don't know if I'd be alive without you. I certainly know I wouldn't be this free or happy. I hope this is your best birthday so far."

"Here! Here!" Sean raised his own brew. "We might not have gotten off to the best start"—Sean grinned, and everyone in the room chuckled— "but there's no man I'd rather share my days and my wife with. *Salud*."

The man was surrounded by the family he'd chosen, by respect, devotion. Love. Joaquin listened with increasing discomfort. Blowing out a breath, he realized he had no idea what any of that felt like. In that moment, he wanted to.

He glanced again at Bailey, who looked at all the proceedings with longing on her face. To a girl who had been orphaned twice in her life, no doubt the lure of attachments and people who cared would be attractive. Logically, he knew why she didn't want to have anything to do with him. Hooking up with the guy who kidnapped her when she was running for her life wasn't the best move. But did she also shy away from him because she knew on some instinctual level that he wasn't the kind of man who could give her what she sought?

Gritting his teeth, Joaquin jerked his gaze to Thorpe again, who looked suspiciously moved as he pulled Callie against him with a hard kiss. "This is probably one of the most amazing things you've ever done for me. I'm touched." Then he scowled. "But I'm still going to spank you."

She groaned, and Sean slapped him on the back. "We've got a few gifts for you first."

Tara and Kata both grabbed their presents off a nearby table. London and Morgan followed with theirs and a few from others who'd been unable to attend. The birthday boy opened bottles of finely aged booze, cuff links, driving gloves, and a handmade deer-skin flogger.

Finally, when the table was empty, Callie swallowed nervously. "Sean and I have two gifts for you."

Axel disappeared, then returned a moment later with a big blow-up doll that looked like a drag queen in tacky lingerie. Painted on the plastic abdomen with red lettering were the words "poke me."

The entire room dissolved in uproarious laughter. Even Joaquin grinned, because there was no way someone as sophisticated and obviously adored as Thorpe would ever resort to sex with an inanimate object, especially such an ugly one. Joaquin's smile became a laugh when he even tried to picture it.

"Going for double or nothing on those spankings, pet?" Thorpe drawled.

"Oh, I gotta have a picture of this." Logan jumped closer, camera in hand.

Before Thorpe could protest, Sean shoved the doll beside his friend, working it right against Thorpe's body. Logan snapped a photo, howling at the image in his viewer.

Thorpe muttered a good-natured threat Sean's way. Callie stepped between them, and they both put their arms around her. He dropped a kiss on her lips. "You're in so much trouble, sweet brat."

"But I'm *your* sweet brat," she quipped.

"That you are. You're lucky I love you so much. Otherwise you wouldn't sit for a month. As it is, I'm not sure you've recovered from last night, but I don't mind adding a little more soreness to that backside so you don't forget me on Saturday."

"I never could forget you, Sir." She turned, suddenly serious. "Ever. I know I never will. Your second gift?"

"Ah, yes." He nodded. "What have you cooked up now?"

"We," she corrected. "All three of us."

Joaquin stared, a thought prodding him.

Thorpe froze, looking as if he had the same suspicion, as Callie handed him a box. "Open it."

The man didn't move a muscle for a moment, just stared at the outpouring of love from her blue eyes, then flipped his gaze to Sean, who nodded, clearly holding his joy in.

Tearing into the gift, Thorpe tossed the bow and paper aside, then ripped the box open. Inside lay a tiny little garment in pristine white with black lettering inside a big red heart.

"I love Daddy," he muttered, everything except shock sliding off his face. Then he jerked an urgent, searching stare to Callie. "You're pregnant?"

She took his hand and led it to her flat stomach with a soft nod. "Seven weeks. I think when the three of us slipped away to the beach . . ." She looked really uncertain now, her eyes tearing up. "I hope this makes you happy. All I've ever wanted was to fill your heart and—"

Thorpe crushed her against his chest, halting her speech. He cupped her face, his stare searching. "In forty years, I've never been this happy. You're the best thing that's ever happened to me." He reached out to clap Sean's shoulder. "Both of you. Thank you. A baby is the best gift you could have given me."

As he kissed Callie passionately, Joaquin wondered whose baby she carried. Did she even know? Even if she didn't, none of them looked as if they cared. They were just happy to be together and soon to be a family.

A glance at Bailey proved that she'd welled up, happy tears that wished them joy—while quietly revealing how desperately she wanted a family of her own. A thought blindsided Joaquin: What if he planted life inside her? He blew out a breath. Hell of a thought . . . but for some reason, he wasn't rejecting it outright.

Hunter sidled up to him, staring as Thorpe and Sean shook hands while cradling Callie between them. "That even tugs at me a little."

Joaquin refused to admit the scene had affected him, too. "Maybe you can find something at the drugstore to take for that."

"You want to be an asshole? Fine. My concern is my wife. She's about to have a baby and she wants to be closer to her family. She wants our son to have an uncle besides Logan." Hunter looked at his younger brother, who poked his finger into the gaping mouth hole of Thorpe's blow-up doll with a howl, and shook his head. "Right now, I understand why. Jeez, he's acting like an idiot."

Hard to disagree with that. "What's your point?"

"I understand missions and being out of pocket and feeling somewhere between detached and on edge. But that's not a real life. Yeah, national security is important, but you need a personal stake, too, or none of this shit really means anything. Kata wants you around, but I won't let you continue to hurt her. If you want to visit when you're available and be a stand-up brother, I'm all for it. That would make my wife happy. And your mom would sure love to hear from you. Since she's my stepmom now, I feel more than a little protective. But if you want to continue isolating yourself and being a prick, go the fuck away. And stay there this time."

Chapter Ten

AN hour later, Bailey hovered in a corner of the dungeon and watched everything around her with wide eyes.

London looked far too pregnant to breathe, much less engage in any sort of dungeon play, so her husbands had simply curled up with her on a sofa across the room. Xander massaged her shoulders while Javier rubbed her feet and slightly swollen ankles. They punctuated the pampering with kisses. Unfortunately, Morgan had been exhausted after a busy week with a kicking fetus and a toddler, not to mention a little queasy, so Jack had taken her home. Thorpe had already bestowed forty of the sexiest possible swipes of his hand across Callie's backside and fed her cake from his fork. After some very passionate kisses and Sean sneaking a hand up her skirt, the three of them had disappeared, supposedly to work on replenishing the snacks. *Right . . .*

Kata, faced with the same challenges as London, spent the evening curled up on Hunter's lap in an overstuffed chair, watching Sweet Pea kneel at Axel's feet. He looked like a mountain beside the dungeon's petite receptionist.

He peeled off his tee and ordered her out of her retro shirtwaist dress and berry-pink bra. Once she'd complied, he affixed nipple clamps to her pert breasts and engaged her in a kinky game of Simon Says, rewarding her when she followed his specific, exacting commands. If she failed, he punished her by eliminating sensations and praise. Sweat sheened on their skin. Axel watched the girl with absolute concentration as he walked slow circles around her, just waiting for his next opportunity. She concentrated, breath held and desperate to please.

Their game turned Bailey on, but the other scene going on a few feet away held her in thrall.

Logan had stripped Tara down to a sturdy nursing bra and her tiny thong. He kissed her mouth softly, then worshipped her with a brush of his lips over her collarbones and breasts before inching down to caress the handful of reddish stretch marks bisecting her stomach.

"Don't, Logan." She squirmed to get away as his tongue traced the lines low on her belly.

He grabbed her wrists. "We're going to cover this again, huh? I'm not perfect, you know. I have scars."

"That's different," she murmured, avoiding his gaze.

"Look at me." He waited until she complied. "It's totally different. Your stretch marks are a beautiful badge of honor to me. I have two perfect daughters because of you. So don't be self-conscious. And don't make me paddle you again."

When he bent to kiss her marks once more, Tara winced and squirmed. "I just don't feel—"

"You *are* beautiful, as much as you've always been," he vowed. "And I warned you. Now you're in trouble. Again. This is one argument you'll never win, Cherry."

He grabbed a sputtering Tara and flung himself in a nearby chair, then spread her facedown across his lap. His big hand sailed down to smack her backside. She yelped, jerked, tensed. A bright red handprint appeared on her pale skin. Without missing a beat, Logan did it again.

Bailey stared, jaw hanging open. Was everyone going to let this man hit his wife simply because she'd had a self-conscious moment? She understood that her self-debasement wasn't healthy and why it displeased him, but . . .

Clutching her spiked punch in hand, she sneaked a glance around the room to find the others either watching with interest, like Joaquin, or not paying attention at all. No way would she stand by idly while Tara endured.

Bailey stood and headed over to stop them. Someone had to.

Kata shoved up from Hunter's lap and waddled in her direction, cutting her off. "Don't."

"Are you crazy?" Bailey knew what that spanking felt like. Slightly painful, primal. Disturbing. Hot.

"Never been around BDSM?"

"I've read a book or two. I pretty much get it." She gestured to Tara. "But it's obvious—"

"So the answer is no. Your head tells you that what you're seeing is wrong, but some other part of you responds?"

Bailey whipped her gaze around to Joaquin's sister. "How did you know?" The words slipped out. Horror spread through her. She closed her mouth, then sighed. "It looks abusive."

"That's how I felt when I first found the lifestyle." Kata smiled. "I knew almost nothing about it until I met Hunter. I was both attracted and terrified. Everything he did to me seemed like something I should hate and protest. But when I almost lost him, I got honest with myself. I loved everything about it." She cast a glance over her shoulder. "Look at them now."

Bailey followed suit and somehow witnessed a whole different scene. Logan still spanked Tara's ass at a brisk, almost blistering pace, but everything else had changed. The woman was no longer tense, but had melted into him, muscles lax, skin flushed. Her cries rang with passion, rather than weeping with pain. Heck, the two of them even seemed to breathe together, seemingly symbiotic, connected by his desire to touch her and her need to feel his concern.

Bailey let loose the breath she'd been holding. "What I'm seeing . . . it doesn't make sense."

"It does if you're in Tara's shoes."

"I have been, but—" She looked Joaquin's way, then realized what she was saying to the man's sister and winced. "Sorry."

"My brother spanked you?"

Kata sounded downright fascinated. Wasn't she weirded out by that knowledge? Then again, if she watched her brother-in-law discipline his wife, maybe they were all beyond that.

"Yeah," Bailey admitted softly. "But I stopped him in the middle."

Kata sneaked a glance at Joaquin. "He's interested, you know?"

"In me?" Kata and Callie both thought that. Why hadn't they figured out that men like him, locked in life-and-death struggles, didn't want silly little ballet dancers. "Not really. I'm important to his case, but—"

"You're important to him as a woman," she assured her. "Look, I'll be honest. I haven't seen much of my brother in years. When we were kids, our dad passed away after getting caught in a domestic dispute in the line of duty. He took a bullet to the chest. Doctors tried to perform surgery to repair the damage to his heart, but he bled out too fast.

"After that, Joaquin began to disconnect from everyone around him. Sometimes, it feels like I lost more than one family member that day. He didn't attend my high school or college graduations. Hunter and I eloped, but Joaquin only attended our family ceremony for an hour. He didn't even know that our mother had married Hunter's father last fall. To see him interested in *anyone* is heartening."

It was probably stupid, but a pang hit Bailey's heart. He'd lost someone he must have loved dearly at a young age. How solitary had he been since? How much had he been hurting because of it?

Bailey wished she could help Kata—and Joaquin—because she

knew what it felt like to be without family. She knew the pain of holidays spent around a Christmas tree by herself, about passing the milestones of life and not having the people she loved to share them with. Just like she knew that Kata was subtly asking her to help heal Joaquin. It hurt even more to shake her head.

"He's trying to solve a case. He might want to sleep with me. I'm available and not a total troll. But he's not trying to make any sort of emotional connection with me."

"Why did he spank you?" she demanded.

"I made him mad."

"Because . . . ?"

"He thought I'd risked myself too much by going into the public area of Dominion one night. I was with Callie and no one saw me, but—"

"He was worried about you," Kata argued with a smile. "He didn't want you to get hurt. That tells me he cares."

Bailey hated to burst her bubble. "He didn't want to lose the only person who might be able to help him understand why people are dying."

Kata wagged a finger in her face. "If he didn't care at all, he'd have locked you in a room and ignored you completely until he wanted to question you. Instead, he tossed you over his lap and put a bare hand to your bare ass, am I right?"

"Yeah." So what was her point?

"That's a very personal way to punish someone. He wanted to discipline you himself. He wanted to feel you as he did. A lot of Doms would have chosen isolation as a punishment, especially since it would keep you safe. Instead, he put his hands on you. You're here at this party, talking to his sister. And he's watching you right now . . . It grosses me out a little that I can see how much he wants you, but I'll take that any day over his indifference."

Bailey swallowed down a knot of lust. She didn't want to want him. And she didn't want to be responsible for Joaquin's emotional state or whatever Kata was suggesting.

"My wife is very smart. And very right," Hunter murmured, approaching in her blind spot and wrapping an arm around Kata's waist.

Bailey whirled, then took a half step back to include him in the conversation. The look on Hunter's face didn't hold the slightest hint of teasing. He genuinely believed, as Kata and Callie did, that Joaquin wanted her as something more than a witness.

"I would have only administered a spanking in that situation if I had some visceral need to feel a sub's reaction to my discipline."

Why would a Dom need that? Her brow wrinkled with confusion. Kata smiled.

"In other words, Joaquin would have only punished you that way if he wanted to see and feel for himself that he'd gotten through to you," Hunter explained. "Drinking in your pain and pleasure, experiencing you lowering your walls and surrendering to him, would help him believe that you wouldn't foolishly risk yourself again. Isolating you would have been easy, probably even effective. But it would have given him absolutely no assurance that you understood. If he didn't care, that wouldn't matter."

Hunter's words slapped Bailey. Kata had said the same thing, more or less. For some reason, maybe because Hunter was a man interpreting a man's actions, everything he said made more sense. Carried more weight.

Bailey lifted her fingers to her throat, her head racing. Joaquin didn't just want to take her to bed, but she mattered in some inexplicable way? But if the only way he could show caring was to spank her, she should resist—no matter how sexy he seemed.

As she cast her gaze across the room, she saw that Logan had pulled Tara against him, chest to chest as he cradled her on his lap. She sobbed and he held her tight, crooning in her ear. But the woman didn't look at all angry. Instead, she appeared somewhere between grateful and ecstatic.

Bailey thought back to the scene she'd witnessed in the dungeon with Callie the other night. That woman had worn a shockingly similar expression. Their tenderness looked so achingly poignant.

No way Bailey could deny that she wanted someone to care for her. No, not just someone. She cast a clandestine glance at Joaquin, only to find him watching her with a laser-focused stare. He watched her every gesture and nuance. No doubt, he'd be asking her questions later about what she'd seen and how it made her feel. She didn't know what to say.

Kata let out a sigh of relief. "Thank goodness Logan finally helped Tara cry."

"Yeah," Hunter added grimly.

"She's been bottled up since giving birth," Kata explained. "She's trying to be supermom and superwife. She's gone back to work in the last few weeks and isn't getting enough sleep. She's so worried about letting everyone else down. Logan has been trying to get her to open up, release her stress, and lean on him more."

"That ought to do the trick." Hunter smiled.

"You mean . . . he spanked her for *her* benefit?" Now Bailey was really confused.

"I doubt Logan was complaining," Hunter drawled. "But yes. He had to get past her walls and reach the woman underneath. Now that she's opened up, they'll be able to better communicate and work everything out. Otherwise, Tara was only going to keep getting more brittle until she shattered."

Bailey stole another glance at the couple and knew Hunter was right. In a weird way, she saw the logic. If Tara didn't have her guard up anymore, Logan could dig down to the real problem and fix it. She could no longer say she was "fine."

Biting her lip, Bailey wondered . . . Had Joaquin been trying to reach her?

"I can tell by looking at them now that Logan loves his wife. Of course he'd want to help her," Bailey argued. "If Joaquin wants to put me in a state where I'm compelled to let my guard down, it's only to help me remember the past I've apparently forgotten. He needs that information."

"He does, but discipline is to teach you a lesson, not to jog your memory. While you're still in danger, will you leave your appointed safe zone again without talking to him first?"

Her first impulse was to remind Hunter that she was a grown woman and would do whatever she wanted, but the demand in his expression made her think twice. "Probably not."

"Mission accomplished," he quipped.

But Logan spanking Tara had looked both emotional *and* sexual. So had the scene in the dungeon a few days ago. When Joaquin had smacked her backside, Bailey had experienced the event on a deep level that, yes, had also been sexual.

She opened her mouth to ask if she'd misunderstood Joaquin's spanking, then closed it. He'd gotten his point across to her. And if his reaction had been anything to go by, it had aroused him, too. What did that mean?

Hunter whispered something in Kata's ear, and she gave him a come-hither glance. In the background, Logan lifted Tara and locked lips with her in a way that left Bailey no doubt what he wanted. He strode toward the back of the club, flung open a door, and let it slam behind them.

In a corner, Axel now cuddled Sweet Pea, whose face looked exhausted but peaceful. Oddly, their embrace seemed comforting, not erotic. The little receptionist, now back in her bright dress, gave the slab of a man a grateful smile. He stroked her hair, murmuring something to her that made her nod, her eyes shine. What they shared was so different, but still so poignantly connected.

Finally, Sean, Callie, and Thorpe emerged from the kitchen again, carrying a few more sodas and bottles of water. The pretty brunette adjusted her skirt. Her cheeks looked flushed. She wore a supremely satisfied expression echoed by her two men.

Envy pierced Bailey. She wanted what all of them had—comfort, belonging, connection. Love. Her parents hadn't been her parents at all, but had raised her for a paycheck, then left without a qualm. She'd never had any grand love affair except with dance. She'd never had true connection with anyone, even when she thought she had. It devastated her to realize that she'd always been alone.

Loneliness sat like a crushing weight on her chest. But even more feelings she could barely identify battered her. She tried to process everything she'd witnessed at Dominion, not even sure why merely glancing at Joaquin wrenched her. No, she knew. Because she wanted him far more than she should. Bailey wished she could write her feelings off as just wanting *someone* in her life. But she knew that desire well. This was more intense—and totally focused on him.

He made her yearn in a way she didn't understand. It wasn't letting up. No idea why. He hadn't exactly been a peach to her. He'd challenged her on every level. Scared her. Pissed her off. Made her question her identity and her entire life.

But he alone also evoked this something that made her fear she couldn't do without him.

Bailey looked away. She was so screwed. If he wasn't connecting with his own family, then hoping to share what the others at Dominion had with him was the stupidest insanity.

Her future stretched out in front of her, one without Joaquin. And she still had no family, so few friends. It made her sad all over again.

Crap, even the thought was going to make her cry. Great time for a pity party . . .

"I think I'm done for the night. It was great to meet you," she said earnestly to Kata and Hunter. "Best of luck with your beautiful baby boy."

The pair exchanged a glance before Kata put a hand on her shoulder. "Are you sure? I wish you'd stay. I'd love more female company."

Her offer was sweet, but Bailey couldn't handle being Kata's charity case. "I'm just really tired. Maybe I'll see you again someday."

Before they could protest, she smiled, then turned away to skirt the room. She headed for Thorpe, who stood with Xander and Javier beside the sofa. London had curled up on the cushions, now fast asleep.

In between their good-natured ribbing about pending parenthood, she tapped Thorpe on the shoulder. He excused himself from the other men.

"Happy birthday," she murmured. "Callie wanted to celebrate you so badly. I hope you're not angry with her."

His face softened, and Bailey had the feeling very few people ever saw the unguarded side of this imposing man. "Thank you. Don't worry about Callie. Every day, she makes me happier than I was the day before. I'll treasure her forever for that."

His gaze traveled across the room to rest on the woman and her fiancé, holding hands and talking in a quiet corner. Sean toyed with the ring on her finger, then played with the collar at her throat. She smiled up at him as they exchanged the most naked glances of love. Thorpe looked on, his expression nothing short of peaceful and proud.

Wondering if Callie had any idea how lucky she was to be so adored, Bailey teared up again. "Good night."

Thorpe's gaze jerked back to her. "What's wrong?"

Bailey didn't bother saying nothing; he'd never believe her. "I just want to be alone."

"Is Joaquin still keeping you here against your will? I'll intervene if you need me to."

"No. Thanks, but he's convinced me I'm safer here." At least physically. Her heart was probably in a whole heap of trouble. "You've got your hands full with a wedding on the horizon and a baby coming. Don't worry about me."

"Don't ask me for something impossible. I know he'll keep you safe from the crazies chasing you. I counseled him about disciplining you in anger. If it happens again, you tell me immediately. I'll fix it."

"I'm fine," she insisted. "Really." Well, except for the terrible realization that she had no one, the man she ached for would probably never want more from her than a screw, and once this surreal danger had passed she would still be alone. "Night."

As she turned away, he grabbed her arm, his grip gentle but not allowing escape. "Do you need help, Bailey? A hug? An ear? Tell me."

He slipped into big brother mode so easily and compassionately. She hated turning him down.

"No." She sniffled. "I'm the, um . . . work-it-out-in-my-head type."

He let out a deep breath, obviously not liking her answer, but he released her. "All right. If that changes, I expect you to come to me. You're under my roof. That makes you my responsibility. I won't have you any more upset than this situation already entails."

It was so kind of him. She tried not to cry more. "I appreciate that. I hope the rest of your birthday is great. I already know you're going to have an incredible life with the people you love. Congratulations."

Bailey drew in a shaky breath as she turned away—only to find Joaquin's stare all over her. She jerked her gaze to the back of the room and made a beeline for the hallway that held her room. Before she could escape, he fell into step beside her.

"You're crying."

What did he want her to say? That some ridiculous part of her craved closeness with him? He wouldn't understand. Hell, she didn't. Better to leave it be. "PMS."

"Don't lie to me," he snarled.

"I'm tired. Can't I just want to be alone? You know it's been a trying few days."

His insistence faded. Grim understanding took its place. "I've put you through a lot. Tell me how I can help you."

"I don't need your pity." God, the thought of it would make her cry even more.

His hazel eyes narrowed. "That's not what I'm offering you."

Bailey wasn't sure she believed him. She was too confused to sort it out right now. The door to the room she slept in was mere feet in front of her. A few more steps and she'd be behind it. Then she'd be able to think—and breathe air not tinged with his scent. She wouldn't have to feel him all around her and be too aware of what she was missing.

How crazy was it that she was lonely, yet running away from people who'd offered to spend time with her? One glance at Joaquin and she knew why: She wanted quality, not quantity. She didn't know Kata or Thorpe. They meant well, but . . . she couldn't settle anymore for the superficial exchanges that, except for Blane, comprised all her friendships. She needed something real, deep, abiding. True.

What a shame she'd never get it from Joaquin.

"If you want to do something for me, go spend time with your sister. She needs you."

His lips pursed. He didn't look pleased. "Did she or Hunter say something to upset you?"

"No, but you shouldn't take your family for granted. Take it from someone who has spent the last three holidays alone." She grabbed hold of the doorknob and wrenched it, trying to shove the door open.

As he grabbed her hand and stilled her, Joaquin's towering presence behind her filled her with trembling need.

"You're shaking."

No kidding. Bailey sighed, certain that if he didn't stop pressing his concern on her, she'd fall apart. She had to stop tripping his guilt trigger. Or the next time he showed caring, she might have a weak moment. "It doesn't matter. You brought me here to keep me alive. I still am. Leave it there."

He whirled her to face him and wedged a finger under her chin until she looked at him. He sucked in an agitated breath. "That isn't going to fly with me, baby girl. I'll give you an hour alone. After that, I'll be back. Then we're going to talk. That's nonnegotiable."

* * *

JOAQUIN could barely breathe past his anger by the time Bailey made it into her room and he strode back down the hall to the party. He replayed what he'd seen, knew who she'd been talking to when her upset had started. He wasn't eager to talk to his sister. But by God, he would do whatever he must to figure out what the hell had hurt Bailey.

He came at Kata like a freight train, not stopping until he was nearly in her face. "What did you say to Bailey that upset her?"

Kata reared back with a shrug. "Nothing."

"At the very least, you said something to her about me neglecting the family."

Even as the words slipped out, Joaquin knew the orphan in Bailey would see that as somewhere between an awful waste and a terrible sin.

"I didn't put it like that. I just said that I didn't see you much these days. Shortly after that, she got upset. I tried to talk to her, but . . . I don't expect her to confide in me. She barely knows me."

Obviously, Bailey had declined to confide in Thorpe, too. Joaquin couldn't deny that she'd also shut him out completely when he'd followed her to her door. Damn it. He must look like a heartless asshole to her.

He stared at the far wall, dragging in an agitated breath, then looked at his watch. Fifty-eight minutes until he could go back to her room. Even if he could see her now, what would he say?

"You should go talk to her," Kata suggested. "I think she could use it."

"I tried," he bit out.

"My wife is just trying to help. Stop browbeating her," Hunter cut in with a dangerous edge to his voice. "She doesn't need you climbing down her throat and upsetting her, especially when she's nearly eight months pregnant. So why don't you stop being a douche and step back?"

Joaquin sliced his gaze over to Kata. She wasn't looking at either one of them. Clearly, she didn't want to contradict her husband, but her expression told him that was mostly because she couldn't disagree.

He dragged in another breath and looked down at her belly, which Hunter rubbed protectively. Cursing under his breath, Joaquin winced. He couldn't blame his brother-in-law. In Hunter's shoes, he'd tell himself to back the fuck off, too.

Scrubbing a hand down his face, he sighed. "Sorry, Kata. Bailey has endured a lot in two days and it's not over. I know there's no way to avoid causing her pain entirely. I just . . ."

How did he put into words something he really didn't grasp himself?

"You wanted to spare her whatever you could. I get it. She matters to you," Kata said softly.

Joaquin frowned. How had his sister come to that conclusion? For that matter, how had he come to care about Bailey so quickly?

"Something like that," he grumbled.

"She thinks she's nothing more than a case to you. If that's true, you need to make that clear and keep your hands off her."

His little sister telling him how to run his life wasn't exactly improving his mood, and he looked at Hunter for backup, only to realize that the man was strictly in his wife's corner. *Well, shit.* But wasn't that as it should be?

Hunter's phone beeped, and he pulled it from his pocket, read a text, then shoved it back in his jeans. "Stone is here. He's got intel."

Tonight? "He drove out here from Lafayette? I thought he was watching Oracle."

His brother-in-law nodded. "He said it was urgent. Jack is on his way back, and they can always call Tyler for backup if shit hits the fan in the interim. I'm going to ask Thorpe if we can use his office."

A moment later, Hunter and the club owner exchanged some words. Sean joined in. Less than thirty seconds later, Thorpe took Callie's hand and kissed her forehead while Hunter and Sean headed back in Joaquin's direction.

"You two wait in Thorpe's office. I'll bring Stone back," the groom offered.

They both nodded, and Joaquin held in a grimace. If Stone was traveling a few hundred miles just to fill him in, none of the news could be good.

He settled in a chair facing Thorpe's desk. Hunter hung back near the door. It didn't take long for Sean to arrive with Stone. Sean seated himself in Thorpe's big chair that Joaquin thought looked more like a throne, while the tech guy Jack employed plopped into the other chair facing the desk.

Joaquin turned to look at the guy beside him. "Thanks for coming out here. Lay it on me."

A lot of men would hesitate before imparting bad news. Not Stone. "The police sketch of the guy who broke into Bailey's house is done. I'm sure they intended to call you tomorrow, but I was trolling through their case files and thought *what the hell?* I printed it out. Here." He passed a piece of paper Joaquin's way. "Look familiar?"

"No," Joaquin said after a glance. But he wasn't the one who needed to remember seeing this face in the past.

"May I?" Sean held out his hand.

Joaquin passed it over and watched the other man study the drawing of the balding man with the unremarkable face and the unfamiliar military coat. Sean dissected it visually with a scowl.

"It might be one of the guys who pursued Callie, Thorpe, and me through Vegas last November. I didn't get a good look at him. It was a car chase, after all. But he definitely looks familiar."

"Fucking fabulous." Joaquin resisted the urge to punch a wall. The damn stress was mounting, as were the connections between Bailey and the bastards who had caused Callie a decade of woe.

They'd likely killed Callie's family, given the fact that they'd tried to do her in as well. Were these the same assholes who had killed Bailey's birth parents and the other Aslanov kids?

"I want to show this to Callie, see if he looks familiar to her. I think you should show it to Bailey, too."

Joaquin didn't love that idea, but he agreed. "I'd planned on it."

"Good. I'd also like to run this through the bureau to see if we get any hits on facial recognition software or if he matches up to any known dissidents on file."

"Ahead of you," Stone said. "He's been identified as Joseph McKeevy. He's a known, longtime member of LOSS. He's a real asswipe, by all accounts. He's a known felon with a couple of armed robbery charges on his rap sheet. But he has a special affinity for crimes against women. He was convicted as a minor for raping a friend of his younger sister's. After a few years in juvie, they released him, but he turned out to be a repeat offender. He was the prime suspect in a string of torture/rape/murder cases near his hometown of Springfield, Missouri. He disappeared into Mexico for a while. We think he spent time in Juárez, contributing to the body count of women assaulted and snuffed out before being buried in the desert. He sneaked back into the country a few years ago. I'm guessing LOSS has given him the green light to continue his sick ways in the name of breaking up the USA. Great group of folks."

"Any open warrants on him?" Joaquin asked.

"Please . . ." Stone rolled his eyes. "He's been wanted for years. LOSS has managed to shuffle him around and hide him well. If I had to guess, I'd say they take good care of their number one assassin. Getting our hands on him won't be easy."

"Any idea where he is now? Still in Houston?"

"This morning, a traffic cam saw him leaving the city, getting onto 45 northbound."

Toward Dallas. Joaquin felt as if Stone had punched him in the chest. His heart stuttered. He couldn't breathe. Why would McKeevy be heading to Dallas? His worst fear was that this sick fuck was on the loose and looking for Bailey, with the idea of making her his next victim.

Everything in Joaquin's body rebelled. He'd do whatever he must to keep her safe. Yeah, he wanted to nail the asshole who'd killed Nate. But his gut told him that ambition wasn't just about avenging his friend. If anything happened to Bailey . . . God, he couldn't even think it.

"I'll be right back." Sean disappeared with the sketch.

"Can you give us a minute?" Stone said to Hunter, who shrugged, then followed Sean.

"Now what?" Joaquin asked the moment he and Stone were alone in Thorpe's office.

The muscled tech guy shrugged without a hint of apology. "That meeting I told you about, the one to determine whether you'd been fired for misappropriating government resources to work your personal case?"

Joaquin froze. "Yeah?"

"You came out on the losing end of that. Sorry, man."

He'd been fired. *Fuck. Seriously?* But Stone's expression didn't give him any hope the news had been a joke.

Work had been his life for the last decade. He couldn't remember a time in his adult life when he hadn't been preparing for a case or working undercover on one. He'd shoved aside anything that looked like a personal life to immerse himself in law enforcement. After one "misstep" to solve a friend's murder and keep women from dying, he'd been tossed out.

He sighed, feeling his entire body sag. No idea what the hell to do with his life now. "I wish the news had been better, but thanks for giving it to me straight."

Stone shrugged his beefy shoulders. "That's how I'd want it, too. What will you do next?"

No idea. Really, he had nothing. Yeah, he had no place of employment anymore, but he also had no responsibilities to live up to. His apartment was a shithole, mostly because he was never there enough to care what it looked like. Every place he'd ever had he had viewed as temporary. He certainly didn't have a wife or girlfriend who'd care if he couldn't afford to take her out on Saturday night. No kids to feed and clothe and take to the doctor. He'd been socking away more than half his income for a decade. He could afford to live for years without working again. In the past, not having a caseload would have bugged the shit out of his sense of purpose. Now? Well, it gave him more time to make whoever had killed Nate pay. And to keep Bailey safe.

"Solve this case. Put some well-deserving assholes behind bars. Then . . . I'll figure it out." Finding a new job was another problem to be handled in the future. The danger to Bailey stared him in the face now. No contest what was more important.

Behind him, the door to the office opened again, and Sean strode in like a man with purpose, Hunter right on his heels. They both looked agitated.

"We may have another development," Sean said as he rounded the desk and sat again.

Callie drifted into the office, looking somewhere between worried and absolutely furious. "That bastard is going to screw up our wedding, isn't he?"

What the hell was Callie talking about? Joaquin turned to peer at her with a questioning glance.

"Lovely . . ." Sean stood again and reached out a hand to her.

With a sigh, Callie went to him and put her palm in his. The man pulled her close, then settled back into Thorpe's chair, guiding her down into his lap.

"I've worked really hard to plan this event," she pointed out.

"You should be more worried about why he's trying to crash it."

"Who?" Joaquin butted in. "Someone I need to know about?"

Sean tossed the police sketch back his way. "McKeevy. We've made every vendor working the wedding submit bio information for every employee and contractor scheduled to be at the event. Looks like he was hired last week to be one of the photographer's assistants when the other one mysteriously vanished. He's going by the name Timothy Smith."

"That's really fucking creative," Stone drawled.

The assassin's assumed name was the least of Joaquin's worries, especially when Sean set a picture on the desk—an eerie match for the police sketch. "Callie had this in her files. I think he's a dead ringer."

Agreed. "You think he has any idea Bailey is here at Dominion? Or do you suspect he's planning some nefarious shit at your wedding?"

"Could be either." And Sean looked absolutely livid about that.

"I eluded these people for years. I think it's far more likely he's got vengeance on his mind and wants to hurt me," Callie said. "How could he possibly know Bailey's whereabouts?"

"We've been very careful about that," Sean added.

"Except the night the girls went to the front of the club while the members were playing. Do we have a list of who was there that night?"

"Yeah. I'll have Axel pull that. In the meantime, show this sketch to Bailey. Maybe she saw this guy prowling around her house or her dance company before you intervened. And it's a long shot, but maybe, if he was involved in her family's death in any way, his face will trigger her memories."

Joaquin took the sketch from Sean, wishing like hell he could spare Bailey all this danger and drama and upheaval. Right now, he'd rather not show her the face of a dangerous killer, then ask her questions about her distant past. She'd been so fragile tonight. It wasn't that he couldn't afford to break her; the investigator in him should have sensed her weakness and pounced for blood. But the man in his skin now couldn't bear to hurt her anymore.

Unfortunately, he didn't have any other option if he wanted to keep her safe.

"I'm on it. I'll let you know what she says. Anything else?"

Sean shook his head.

"Not from me." Stone stood. "I'm heading down the street. I know a stripper who will give me a decent blow job for fifty bucks. She doesn't usually work on Tuesdays. See you around."

As he disappeared, Sean made his way to the door with Callie in tow, holding back a laugh, then looked at Hunter. "Great coworker you've got."

"Tell me about it." Hunter scoffed. "Jack hires really brilliant former operatives, but some have the personality of a bleeding hemorrhoid."

"The way your brother tells it, yours isn't much better," Sean teased.

"Yeah? Logan can kiss my ass, too."

The two men laughed before Sean stuck out his hand to Hunter. "Thanks for coming to help make Thorpe's day special. I think Callie and I are going to round up the old man so he and I can tuck our lovely into bed."

She smiled as if nothing would make her happier.

Hunter shook his hand. "Thanks for the invite. I'm going to take my wife and find a hotel. It's too late to drive back tonight."

"Here." Sean fished into his pocket and tugged out a set of keys. "Crash at the house. There are six bedrooms. Thorpe, Callie, and I won't be far behind you. If you see your brother, tell him that he and Tara are welcome there, too. Xander, London, and Javier are going to stay."

"You sure?"

"What are friends for?"

Hunter pocketed the keys. "Thanks."

"We'll be back in the morning," Sean said to Joaquin. "If you need anything—"

"I have your number."

"Good. See you tomorrow."

Sean and Callie left then, presumably to find Thorpe so they could cuddle up for the night. Joaquin felt a bit of envy. What would it be like to have a house to share with loved ones? To invite friends to crash there for a night? To spread out and call some place home?

"Do me a favor?" Hunter said now that the two of them were alone.

"What?"

"I know you have to see Bailey tonight and run that sketch by her. Go easy."

"You're just full of 'helpful' advice tonight." His brother-in-law's attitude crawled up his back. "Obviously, you think I'm an unfeeling bastard. Why don't you do me a favor? Give it a rest until you know who you're dealing with."

Hunter looked equally annoyed as he crossed his arms over his chest. "I'm pretty sure I already know, and I wouldn't have gone with unfeeling bastard. But since you did, it'll work. It pretty much describes how you've behaved."

"You don't understand the situ—"

"I do. Look, you lost a parent. It hurt. I get it. I lost my mom, too, and it—"

"Hold that fucking speech right there." Joaquin's anger climbed ten notches. He never talked about his dad—and he refused to start now. "I'm talking about Bailey. My father's death isn't relevant to that."

"According to Kata, it's relevant to everything. But I guess you have your head that far up your ass because you like the smell. Whatever, man." Hunter shrugged. "Bailey is not my responsibility, and I know Thorpe is already up in your business about her. Trust me when I tell you I'll encourage him to stay there."

"First, you warn me away from my own sister, and now you're trying to tell me what to say to . . ." What was Bailey to him? More than his captive. But she wasn't his girlfriend. Or his lover. He wanted to do more than protect her. He'd never even considered forever, yet he couldn't imagine letting her go. "Bailey?"

"I'm not trying to give you a hard time, just give you a hard truth.

She wants you. She's attached to you. You've already put her through a lot. If you're just going to fuck-and-run, back off now. You'll crush her if you don't."

Hunter didn't wait for his reply, just left the room. Joaquin stared into the open, empty hall, guilt a hot, stinging sludge in his veins. Would his father be proud of him today? The thought came out of nowhere, but Joaquin didn't even have to think about the answer.

No.

Eduardo Muñoz had worked hard. He'd even given his life for his job, but he'd been a family man through and through. He'd loved his wife and adored his children. Every day, he'd let them know how much he cared. Joaquin remembered the special father-son summer days they'd shared. His father could have chosen to do anything with that time—beer with buddies, patrolling a crime-ridden neighborhood—but he'd chosen to spend it with his son. Dad would never have approved of Joaquin's workaholic ways. Eduardo would have approved of the way he'd pushed all family and friends aside even less.

Joaquin hated Hunter in that moment for making him realize it.

With a curse, he grabbed the sketch and photo from Thorpe's desk and exited the room, taking a sharp left down the hall to Bailey's room. He glanced at his watch. Nearly an hour had passed. Perfect timing.

As he neared the door, he drew in a deep breath to calm his anger and center himself. Hunter was right about Bailey, too. The girl didn't need more shit, and Joaquin had no doubt more would come her way before the case was closed. He refused to cause her more pain than necessary.

Time to decide . . . fish or cut bait? Pursue her and try his hand at something beyond sex or strictly protect her and keep his distance.

Joaquin knew what his gut was telling him as he neared her bedroom door. As he raised his fist to knock, he heard wrenching sobs inside. Fuck knocking. He had to get to her now. It was his responsibility to give her what she needed and make her world right.

Chapter Eleven

THE door to her bedroom rattled suddenly. Bailey sat up as Joaquin barreled inside, holding a piece of paper, his face troubled.

She wiped her tears from her eyes and cheeks, wishing she could hide her red nose and swollen eyes. "What?"

He set the piece of paper on the dresser just inside the door and headed unerringly in her direction. "Baby girl . . ."

His pity hurt. Joaquin wasn't an uncomplicated man. He wasn't simple to understand—or get along with. But he'd risked everything to keep her safe, no denying that. He'd let her decide if she wanted to make the next move in their odd dance when she knew damn well he hated not having control. The way he looked at her right now, as if he would part the seas and scorch the earth just to reach her, made Bailey's heart catch.

So, so dangerous . . .

He sat beside her, cupping her cheeks, his intent expression telling her that no one else in the world mattered right now. "Talk to me."

And say what? "Nothing to discuss."

"Bailey, I know you feel alone, but you're not."

Lord, he'd figured her out so easily. She probably ought to be embarrassed, but she simply felt too sad to care.

He peered down into her eyes, as if trying to crawl inside her head and read her every thought. His hazel eyes looked so green beside that thick fringe of his black lashes. They were almost too beautiful for a man that rugged. Normally, she fell into his glittering gaze all too easily. Tonight, the compassion in those depths was too hard to take.

"I have Blane. When all this is over and I can go home, I'll make it up to him."

He scowled. "Fuck Blane."

"If I could grow a foot taller, shoulders like a lumberjack, a beard, and different plumbing, maybe he'd be interested. But since that's impossible . . ."

A lopsided smile crossed Joaquin's face. "I'm glad it is. And don't try to distract me. I meant that you're not alone because I'm here."

Bailey had suspected he meant that, but she wasn't sure she believed him. After all, he wanted information from her that—if she even had it—sat locked deep in her memories. He'd been pretty patient, too. That had to be running out. Besides, if he wasn't going to engage with his own family, she doubted he'd suddenly want to get involved with her on any deep level.

She tried to squirm away. If she didn't, the lure of his comfort would be too much to resist. She'd throw herself against him and sob on his shoulder. He'd only feel more sorry for her. Her eyes would only swell up more. None of that appealed.

Joaquin held tight.

"Don't worry. I'm good," she assured him, then leaned over to the nightstand and reached for the box of tissues she'd brought from the bathroom earlier. He didn't let go. "Your sister seems nice."

"You're changing the subject again." His tone sounded like a warning.

"Joaquin . . ." Bailey searched for the right words, something to make him shut up without having to spill every worry and feeling.

"Just leave it. I'm tired and frazzled. There were a lot of strangers there tonight. That's usually uncomfortable for me."

He gave her a considering stare. "Did you feel out of place?"

"A little. I barely knew anyone. I'm introverted, so conversation with people I don't know can be tough."

"If you wanted to leave sooner, all you had to do was say so. I thought you were excited to be at the party."

"I was at first. Then . . ."

Being an outsider in a room filled with overwhelming love had gotten to her. Crap, she had to stop this little boo-hoo fest.

"Go on."

"I don't know. Callie said the party would be small, but it didn't feel that way."

"Yeah, you might have to take her concept of a 'little' gathering with a grain of salt. Her wedding is intimate, but her 'small' reception ballooned to two hundred people." He tucked a strand of hair behind her ear. "You're feeling better now that you're back in this room?"

"Yeah." Just more depressed than she wanted to admit. She was alive and had a better chance at staying that way because of Joaquin. She had to stop thinking of the loved ones she didn't have and pull herself out of this funk.

He still wore a concerned frown. "Can I get you anything? You hungry?"

She shook her head. "I've been in a shame spiral since eating the bagel Callie brought me for breakfast. I never wolf down that many carbs. I'm so far off my exercise regimen."

"Don't worry about that, baby girl." He stroked her face again. "You look perfect to me."

Bailey couldn't stop melting. If only he'd quit touching her and staring at her like she mattered to him, maybe she could. He wasn't coming on to her. His touch didn't feel sexual. The fact that he wasn't trying to nail her but simply asking why she'd been crying got to her more.

"You don't have to babysit me. Go back to the party."

Joaquin shook his head as if he knew better. "I'm not leaving you alone. I saw how you looked at everyone, like you wished you were part of the group."

New tears stung her aching eyes. Why couldn't he just leave it alone? "Please don't feel sorry for me."

"I don't. But I know you find it hard to be without family."

Bailey tried to downplay the truth. "I know being with yours isn't your thing. Most of us seek connections to the people who have similar experiences and values. Believing that someone has my back is huge to me."

"I know what you're saying." He sent her a soft smile that made her heart turn over.

"I'm sorry to hear about your dad. Your sister said you were just a kid. How old?"

"Almost thirteen, so it was a long time ago."

"Kata said it hit you hard. Is that why you don't see your family much now?"

"Bailey." He took her chin in hand and snagged her stare with his. "I'm fine. I wasn't the one in tears tonight."

But he stood apart from the people who would love him for a reason. "Just because you don't cry doesn't mean you aren't hurting."

He released her and let loose a long sigh. "But when you're crying, it definitely means you are. I put you in this shitty mess. I haven't been easy on you. I'm sorry. Let me help."

A couple of protestations ran through her head. He'd taken on the responsibility for her safety, not her emotional state. She didn't want to burden him. Bailey wasn't quite certain why her mood even mattered to him. Studying Joaquin, she tried to unravel the mystery. He said he wasn't giving her pity. Maybe he was bored? Lonely? Horny?

"I felt alone tonight," she admitted. "But that's not uncommon. I haven't been really close to anyone . . ." She sorted through her memories, then realized whatever she thought she'd shared with her adoptive parents had been a lie. "Maybe ever. Joaquin, let the people who care about you into your life. Your job is important, but it isn't everything."

"Especially since I found out tonight that I've been fired." He tried to shoot her a self-deprecating smile.

She gasped in horror. "That's awful. I'm so sorry. Because of this case?"

"It doesn't matter. I wouldn't change what I've done. I'd still come find you."

Not that she'd asked him to hunt her down and abduct her, but Bailey still felt vaguely guilty. "I'm sorry that saving me cost you your job. You were only trying to do the right thing and prevent me and other women from dying."

He shrugged. "We're both out of place now. Maybe . . . it's time for me to think about a life beyond work. I haven't in over a decade. Longer, really. I got my first job at sixteen to help my mom make ends meet."

"Because your dad was gone and it was hard for her on one income?"

He froze, then nodded slowly. "She married a real asswipe not long after that, but he put a roof over our heads. I didn't like or trust him, so I kept working. When my father was still alive, he would tell me all the time that if he wasn't home, I was the man of the house. At his funeral, I realized I'd assumed that position permanently."

Bailey's heart reached out to his. He'd been just a kid. "How did that make you feel?"

"The weight of my responsibility was daunting. My mom went back to work within a few days of his death, so I found myself cooking and doing laundry. My sisters helped, of course. There's only twenty-one months between me and Kata, with our middle sister, Mari, wedged between. But I became the father figure, disciplinarian, referee, and caretaker."

"At twelve?"

He shrugged, looking pensive, and Bailey wished she could read his thoughts. "I was a month shy of thirteen."

"I would have thought that experience would make you and your sisters really tight."

After a considering frown, he shook his head. "Looking back, I took care of my family, worried about them, did my best with them. Mari was a gifted student, so she was often buried in homework and study groups. I think school was her escape from the hurt of Dad's absence. Kata was just always so damn independent. Constantly gone, hanging with girlfriends, flirting with boys. I spent a few of her teenage years sure that she was going to make me prematurely gray. But she turned out all right. Once they were grown, I wanted to start living for me."

"Growing up, you missed your dad a lot, didn't you?"

Joaquin nodded. "Besides having to be a man before I actually was one, I missed his humor and wisdom. He always seemed to know exactly what to say to make me realize the error of my ways while making me laugh."

"Your sisters would probably like to talk to you about him. I'm sure they miss him, too."

He didn't even have to open his mouth. Bailey already knew that, not only did he avoid talking to his sisters, he probably didn't talk to anyone about his dad. So why was he talking to her? He'd come to console her when he needed some cheering up himself.

Could he possibly be interested in her as more than a potential mattress tango partner?

"They've both got husbands now. Mari has two boys. Kata is having one soon. They have normal jobs, community ties, connections with friends. We've got nothing in common anymore."

"Except that you're a family. Do you know what I'd give to have one of those?"

He squeezed her hands. "Bailey, I'm sure your birth parents

would be very proud of who you've become. Accomplished, self-supporting, smart, gorgeous, kind."

She teared up. "It kills me that I don't remember them. When I see pictures of Viktor Aslanov, it's like a punch in the stomach. It was a shock to find out that I look like my mother. I know next to nothing about her or my siblings. That hurts. What would my life have been like if my birth father had never sold his research to LOSS? I'll never know."

He took her hand in his and squeezed. "No. Fate had other plans, baby girl."

"I had what I thought was a really normal upbringing. My adoptive parents guided me and took care of me." She teared up again and turned away. "It's just hard to sit here and question whether any of what they said and did for me over the years was duty or love."

Joaquin slid his cheek over her palm and turned her back to face him. "There's no way they didn't care about you." He brushed his thumb over her lower lip. "You're impossible to resist."

Bailey's stomach dropped out from under her. She blinked up at him, losing herself in his eyes. Her heart thudded. For a man who had barely spoken to his family in years, who'd deflected all but the most impersonal contact since puberty, he was opening himself for her.

She took in a trembling breath. "Joaquin . . ."

Honestly, she wasn't sure if she was protesting his touch or inviting him closer. She didn't know if he genuinely cared about her, but the hope that he did lingered in her heart, whispering to her, encouraging her to reach out for him.

Her head disagreed. Callie's and Kata's opinions aside, his primary interest in her was still his case. Even if he'd lost his job, this man wasn't suddenly going to wrap his arms around her and want to spend forever with her. She was pretty sure that even a night in his bed would just prove to her that she was in over her head.

Before she could make up her mind, regret crossed his face and he backed away. The opportunity evaporated. Disappointment took its place, though she supposed keeping distance between them was for the best.

"Are you too tired to look at something?" he asked, his tone far less personal. "It's for the case."

Bailey hated that her hesitation might have stifled his urge to share his feelings for the first time in two decades. Even if he wasn't invested in her, she wanted to help him end the murders so they could both move on. "Not at all."

"Thanks." He lifted himself away from the bed and made his way back to the dresser, then returned, paper in hand. He thrust it in her direction.

It was a sketch of a man. "Who is that?"

"Does he look familiar at all?"

Bailey studied it for a minute longer. "Maybe. If it was an actual photo, I might—"

"Like this?" He put another image in front of her, this one a four-by-six color photo of a bald man with a graying fringe around his head. A round face and flat blue eyes dominated the picture. For some reason she couldn't fathom, the sight of him filled her with terror.

"Yes," she breathed. Her voice shook.

"Where?" He grabbed her shoulders.

She searched her memories and came up empty-handed. "I don't know."

"Recently?"

Bailey thought back to all the people she'd met associated with the dance company, everyone from benefactors to building employees. Nothing. No one she remembered from her crappy waitressing job matched that face. The memory of him seemed fuzzy, distant.

"No."

"Think about this. Focus. If you can picture his face, can you place where you might have seen him?"

She tried. He hadn't been a teacher or neighbor or pastor. No friend or coworker of her dad's.

But she knew she'd seen him somewhere in the past.

"I'm sorry. Who is he?"

"His name is McKeevy. Does that sound familiar?"

She'd never heard of him. "No. Should it?"

Joaquin shrugged. "He's the top assassin for LOSS. We think he's trying to crash Callie's wedding this weekend."

Bailey gasped. "And kill her. What are Sean and Thorpe going to do? They can't let him anywhere near her. Even the sight of him made my heartbeat surge. Fear is pressing in on my chest. I associated his face with danger before you told me anything about him. They have to protect Callie."

"They will." He discarded the picture and the sketch on the nightstand, then clasped her shoulders. "I'll put the picture away for now. Take a deep breath. Relax." He waited until she'd complied. "Any chance you saw him when you were very young?"

Filtering back through her memories, she knew he hadn't come from her recent past. "Probably. It's the only thing that adds up."

"But you can't place him?" When she shook her head, Joaquin caressed her shoulders with his thumbs, a gentle comforting. "All right. Put it in the back of your head for now. Maybe something will occur to you. But don't be scared. You're safe with me. I'll keep you that way."

Bailey believed him. As long as Joaquin watched over her and stayed one step ahead of the crazies of LOSS, she'd be alive. But would she have a life? "I'd love to, but I don't think I have that luxury. Maybe you should leave the photo here with me tonight so I can study it."

He hesitated, and his expression told her he didn't love the idea. In the end, his logic prevailed. "All right."

"Sean and Thorpe must be so worried about Callie."

"I'm sure, but they'd move mountains to keep her from harm's way."

"They've done it before," Bailey agreed.

"I'd do the same for you."

She swallowed down a lump. "You don't have to say that. I'm going to cooperate, so buttering me up isn't necessary."

"Is that what you think I'm doing?" Thunder crashed across his expression, his dark brows sliding over his eyes that lit with anger like lightning.

"Your case hinges on me. It seems like common sense—"

"Baby girl, when it comes to you, I got off the 'common sense' bus a while ago. If I hadn't, I'd still be interrogating you day and night. Sleep and food would be on the back burner. In fact, I'd be facilitating your exhaustion to see if it would loosen your tongue or if I could trip you up in inconsistencies. In short, I'd be doing everything I could to leave you unsettled and off balance in the hopes it could help my case."

Instead, he was putting her comfort and mental well-being first. "None of that would make me remember the past any faster."

"You might be surprised."

She reared back. "You've employed those tactics before?"

"I've done things that would make you recoil in horror. I did them without blinking. Getting answers was my job. I did it. I moved on." He sighed. "Then came you."

"You said I had nothing to do with your job."

"You never did. I wasn't working this case for anyone but me and the people who've been slaughtered. I don't really give a shit that the U.S. government fired me. It gives me more time and energy to keep you safe. There's another job out there. But there's only one you."

Oh, goodness. He knew exactly what to say to make her believe that she mattered, to make it okay to want him. Bailey already knew Joaquin was more than she could handle. Her one experience in the back of a limo on prom night hadn't prepared her for all his masculine aggression. He scared her even as he turned her on more than she'd imagined possible.

Bailey swallowed. Guard her heart or throw her body into the fire? What good in life had come from protecting her feelings? So, Ryan Fuller, the butthead who had taken her virginity, hadn't really cared about her. She'd been more humiliated than hurt. She'd recovered. Joaquin might not be Prince Charming, but all the testosterone he exuded made it hard to refuse him. To be honest, she liked him more than a little. When it came to doing right, his moral compass seemed to be set to true north. His methods might be unorthodox, but he sought justice, even above his own career and personal relationships. Bailey had to admit she found that wildly attractive.

Besides, having a killer hunt her brought home the fact that tomorrow wasn't a given. Or was she just rationalizing because she wanted Joaquin so badly?

"Really, you don't have to say that to make me cooperate with your investigation."

He dragged her closer. "Damn it, we've been over this. You know better." His fingers tightened. "And if you can't remember, let me remind you. Tell me to kiss you."

Joaquin hovered now, so close his breath warmed her lips. His stare delved into hers, demanding, urgent. But his touch remained gentle. He checked himself for her. In fact, he'd revealed one of his deepest pains and shared it with her. That had to mean something.

Bailey pulled herself from his drowning stare, her gaze skating over the hollows of his cheeks and the firm angles of his chin. His lips, full and so close, waited for her.

God, she was probably going to regret this.

"Kiss me," she panted.

Not even a single beat of her heart passed before he tumbled her back to the bed. The second her back hit the mattress, his fingers dug into her hair, fisting tightly at her nape. He angled her head to his liking and devoured her lips. His chest eclipsed hers. His hips wedged between her thighs, making himself at home.

Bailey couldn't lie to herself and say she didn't like it. As he drove his tongue deep and took command of the kiss, all her self-control and will to resist disappeared. He didn't ease inside or test his welcome. No, he crushed her lips with his own and took complete command.

He tasted like a heady swirl of man, beer, and desire. The stubble of his way-past-five-o'clock shadow scraped gently as he grabbed her wrists and shoved them over her head. As soon as he transferred his grip to one hand, he took deeper possession of her mouth, his tongue surrounding hers, laving, seducing. He gripped her hip, his fingers holding her tight.

Under him, Bailey arched restlessly. His onslaught was everything she remembered—unrelenting and insistent—but more. Hungrier. Somewhere between another swooping kiss and a long groan, she tasted his hot persuasion. Less than twenty-fours had passed since he'd last seized her mouth, but his touch vowed it had been a lifetime to him.

Her head spun. Her heart soared. Her only anchor in this dizzying desire was Joaquin. She couldn't throw her arms around him, so she wrapped her legs around his hips and ground against his thick erection. He prodded her sex, sending an electric impulse skittering between her legs.

The appreciation in his moan inflamed her more. He knew precisely how to enthrall her, and he used his knowledge without hesitation. Bailey floated in a thick morass of need she'd only believed possible in books or movies. It scattered logic. It set her body aflame.

She whimpered and opened her mouth wider. Joaquin claimed the space instantly. Her whole world narrowed to him alone as she caressed his tongue with her own, still pushing her hard nipples into his chest and gyrating on his cock between her legs.

He tore his lips from hers, breathing heavily. Searching her stare, he cupped her nape again, and aligned her under his mouth for his next conquering kiss.

"Tell me to take off your shirt," he murmured first.

She craved the touch of his fingers on her bare skin. "Touch me."

"I want to so fucking bad, I'm about to crawl out of my skin. But you're going to have to tell me that you want me to rip that little shirt off your body and expose those pretty nipples before I lay a finger on you. Full consent or nothing."

Bailey couldn't catch her breath. Her blood heated, raced, churned. As he dragged his lips up her neck and skimmed across her jaw to hover just above her mouth, she knew she'd say almost anything to feel him inside her.

"Take my shirt off," she gasped. "I want you to see me."

Joaquin didn't hesitate. He didn't bother with buttons or dragging the garment over her head. He released her wrists, fisted the silky soft fabric just above her breasts, and yanked. It gave easily, rending under his strength.

Cool air splashed her skin. The hot flame of his stare negated the chill. Her nipples beaded under her bra. The way he looked at her, like he'd die if he didn't take her, made Bailey reach for him.

The second she wrapped her hand around his shoulder, she wished he'd lose his shirt. Everything under the cotton felt steely, unyielding. She was no stranger to men with good physiques. Dancers were always well developed. The strength and discipline necessary to execute lifts made for cut chests, bulging shoulders, and tight abs. But Joaquin excited her more. He hadn't developed his muscles by wearing spandex and lifting women who weighed less than a hundred pounds. He'd earned his on the streets, in battle, trying to make the world a safer place.

"Take this off." She tugged at his sleeve.

He raised a black brow at her but didn't move.

"Please . . ." She wheedled, kissing her way up his chin, brushing the corner of his lips.

"If we're both undressing, you understand it's very likely I'm going to fuck you."

"I haven't said yes," she reminded him with a sly smile.

Joaquin propped his elbow on the mattress beside her head, his face hovering over hers. "I wouldn't stop until I found a way to make you scream your consent. You think about that, then let me know if you want me to start stripping down."

The girl inside her knew she ought to heed his words. Some devil inside her prodded her.

"Making me scream sounds pretty ambitious. It may not be something you're able to do."

He froze. "If you have any intention of putting a stop to this, don't tease me. Because I'll be so fucking happy to prove you wrong."

His words only whipped her into a darker frenzy. Bailey had little doubt he could do exactly as he threatened. And the idea made her sizzle. "Please take off your shirt."

A slow smile spread across his face. "You're in so much trouble, baby girl. I'm going to enjoy the hell out of this—and make sure you do, too. I won't rest until I've wrung every ounce of pleasure from your body."

"Promise?"

At her taunt, he gave her a low laugh, then raised himself up enough to straddle her. He didn't make a production of removing his shirt, just reached behind his head, gathered it in his fist, yanked, and flung it across the room.

Bailey gasped. Each inch of him rippled and bunched with every movement. Dark satin skin stretched across hard flesh. A light dusting of hair over his chest led to a treasure trail that zipped down the line bisecting his chiseled abdomen. Honestly, if she had conjured up a fantasy man, he'd have looked a heck of a lot like Joaquin.

"Your turn," he said thickly, sliding a finger under her bra strap. "Tell me to take it off."

She swallowed down nerves. As a ballet dancer, she wasn't exactly the most gifted in the breast department. Small boobs worked great in a leotard, and she never had to worry about curves messing up her lines. It was even a bonus when she wanted to wear something backless or strapless because she didn't have to worry about finding the right garment to support girls she lacked. But staring a potential lover in the face . . . A man as downright manly as Joaquin probably expected ample breasts. He'd probably had some beautiful ones in his past.

"I'd rather see you lose the rest of your clothes."

"Maybe so, but I might not be motivated to lose my pants until I see your nipples. Give me permission to strip you out of that bra."

His gaze looked fixated on her breasts. The undergarment didn't hide much. He had to be able to see that, well, there wasn't that much to see. Her legs and her butt were way better.

"You seem like the kind of guy who always gets what he wants. I'm in the mood to make you wait." She gave him a mock sigh. "But after bagels and booze and other stuff I almost never eat, these jeans are awfully tight."

As she toyed with the button just below her waist, he watched. "Are they? We can't have you uncomfortable. You want to lose those or do you want help?"

If she dropped these jeans, the chances they'd actually have sex increased exponentially. Bailey doubted very highly that he'd be okay with making love to her with her breasts still covered. On the other hand, maybe she could occupy him in other ways before she had to expose her nonexistent chest.

"Why don't you help me?" She dropped her fingers to her zipper and let it fall with a quiet hiss.

Joaquin gripped the denim, looking at her like he couldn't wait to tear into her. Her heart skipped. Blood rushed to all the places it only should when aroused. Lord, she was probably in way over her head. So why was she baiting the beast? Because he made her feel desired and sexy, and she wanted him every bit as on edge as she felt.

"I can't resist a damsel in distress." He tugged on the fabric around her hips.

As she held on to the lacy waistband of her nude panties, he made quick work of her jeans, jerking them down her thighs, past her knees, then shoving them beyond her feet. He tossed them across the room, too—in the opposite direction he'd thrown her shirt.

As he looked down at her now, his eyes darkened, glittered with lust. He gripped her hips, his hands so big that his thumbs almost met on top of her mons. Bailey's breath caught. He nearly touched her *there*, and as electric as her body pinged now, she couldn't imagine how turned on she'd be when he actually did.

"Pretty panties, but useless. I want to see that beautiful pussy underneath."

Joaquin had more than a way with words in bed. He'd probably done this a few hundred times. Bailey felt herself both falling under his spell and mentally flailing. How did she answer him?

"I took something else off. Now it's your turn. Your jeans would look better on the floor."

Where had that voice come from? She'd sounded almost seductive.

He gave her a hard stare. "Somewhere along the way, you've gotten the idea that sex with me is an egalitarian activity. Let me assure you otherwise."

"You think you're going to run this show?"

"There's no *think* about it, baby girl. Since you and I have come here, I've had more than a conversation or two with Thorpe and Sean. I've realized a few things about myself."

Callie's assurances that Joaquin had all the earmarks of a Dom rushed back to her. "Oh."

"That bother you? Because if it does, we need to stop now and have a long talk."

She could stop this train wreck with a little white lie. No exposing her small breasts or her needy soul to a man who'd probably crush her in a single night.

Even knowing he would probably hurt her sooner or later, Bailey just shook her head. "It turns me on."

Relief slid across his face. "Good. I can tell that wasn't easy for you to admit."

"When I was a senior in high school, someone dared me to swallow straight Tabasco sauce. That was easier."

He laughed. "You're an unpredictable little thing. I like it. I was expecting you to be refined. Totally polite in bed. The real you is way sexier."

Joaquin pressed their chests together. Bare abdomens met as he kissed his way up her neck and consumed her lips again. At his first touch, he sent her reeling. That dizzying slide into desire dragged her under even deeper, to a place where focus and restraint burned away. She grabbed his steely shoulders and clung as she opened to him completely.

Just as he penetrated her mouth, he dragged his fingers up her rib cage and paused under her breast. Her nipple beaded painfully in anticipation. He raised his head, fixed utterly on her.

"Tell me to touch you," he barked.

He wanted to be in control, but he'd promised her that he wouldn't do anything until she gave him a green light. For a moment, Bailey felt a sense of power that balanced the scales a bit. It probably wouldn't last long; she fully believed he'd take all her control, then leave her whimpering and panting and totally sated.

"I'm not sure I'm ready," she admitted softly.

He downshifted immediately, skimming his palm back down to her waist. "When was your last lover?"

So far in the past, she was embarrassed to admit it. "A few years ago."

"Years?" Joaquin let out a stunned breath, then caressed the side of her face. "Don't be nervous. I love everything I've seen so far. I have no doubt you'll make me sweat when I see the rest. Can you trust me on that?"

When he put it like that? Bailey nodded.

"Good. We're supposed to have a safe word. It's something you can say to stop the action if I play too hard with you, but you can also use it if you're feeling uncomfortable or self-conscious. Would that help you?"

"Totally. Thanks."

"How about . . . if we stay with traffic lights. You say 'red,' and I'll stop touching you entirely until we talk it out. Now, will you remove that damn scrap of lace over your nipples before I lose my ever-loving mind?"

So masculine, so determined. And so something the female in her couldn't resist. Bailey did her best to shelve her worries. "Do it for me?"

"Oh, fuck yeah. Sit up." He tugged her upright and rose above her, crouched over her body, their chests nearly brushing.

His fingers prowled into her hair again, tightening slowly until he tugged, forcing her to arch her neck just under his lips. His breathing picked up speed as he swooped down and covered her lips again, diving in and tasting every recess.

Now that he had her where he wanted her, the hand he'd anchored in her hair skated down her back, making her tingle. His other hand curled around her shoulder until both met at the back of her bra strap.

Vaguely, she realized he must possess a lot of core strength to hold this position above her without leaning on her or bracing himself on the mattress below. But as soon as the thought formed, he'd unhooked the two little wire fasteners across her back and she was free.

Joaquin didn't bother taking the bra off. He inched back, pushed the cups up, then lunged down, latching onto her left nipple and sucking it as deep as he could.

The contact was a lightning strike to her clit.

His fingers bit into her spine. He sucked in a breath as he all but inhaled her breast past his lips. The suction jumbled her thoughts and blew her mind.

Bailey tunneled her fingers in his thick hair and pulled him closer. She surrounded her fingers with the thickness and gasped. Breathing became irrelevant when he switched to the other nipple, took a playful bite with his teeth, and swept it into the hot oven of his mouth.

Quickly, she realized that the nip of his teeth both made her tingle and prepared her sensitive flesh to take more sensation. She let loose a ragged moan. Her one attempt at sex in yards of taffeta in the back of a moving vehicle hadn't at all prepared her for Joaquin.

"These are . . ." He shoved her back against the pillows and braced his forearms up her back. His fingers curled around the front of her shoulders, positioning her exactly how he wanted her before he returned to the first nipple. "So fucking incredible. They're even harder than they were a minute ago. I'm not going to let up on these for a long while."

And he meant that, taking Bailey along for the ride until her nipples throbbed, fire laced her veins, and her sex ached.

"Joaquin!" She sounded like she was begging because she was.

"Tell me what you need, baby girl."

Bailey didn't know. Harder. More. Something . . . She couldn't get a word out, just panted and fisted his hair.

He gave her a guttural growl. "Give me an answer."

"I don't know. I need . . ."

"Want me to give you what you need?" he asked as he transferred his lips to her other nipple again, this time pinching the first in a relentless press.

She yelped, yet it felt so good. She wasn't just drowning in pleasure; it was a riptide with a vicious undertow taking her farther and farther down.

"Yes. Please. Now."

"I'm going to make this so fucking good." The sharp edge of his teeth scraped her nipple again. "After I make you suffer a little."

Suffer? She hadn't asked for that. "What?"

"You told me earlier that you were in the mood to make me wait. I feel exactly the same."

Before she could protest again, he dragged her bra strap down her arm, grabbed her hand, and shoved it over her head. Edging up her body, he grabbed something just above her. A second later, she felt soft but sturdy fabric grip her wrist. A clicking sound resounded in her ears.

"Cuffs?" The thought both terrified her and made her swoon.

"I want you totally at my mercy."

Somehow, she doubted he'd have much. He'd overwhelmed her in nothing flat. She couldn't wait for more.

"Say yes to me." His hazel eyes bore into her, commanding her every bit as much as his dark voice.

"Yes," she whispered.

Before she could even blink, he yanked the other strap down her free arm, then slung the lacy garment over one of the bedposts. She lay before him in nothing more than a small, sheer pair of panties and a nervous smile as he restrained her other wrist to the bed with a sure click.

Bailey's heart leapt into her throat. Was she ready for this? Could she really handle him? Joaquin played like a fantasy in her head, but reality . . .

"Relax," he murmured. "I'm going to be all over you. There won't be an inch on your body that I haven't touched when we're done. But I won't hurt you."

Physically, she wasn't worried. Emotionally? Was she that girl who couldn't sleep with a guy without caring more than a little? Prom hadn't counted really. She'd had a huge crush on Ryan and she'd been slightly tipsy. Buying into the fantasy that they were some dream, meant-to-be couple while she'd been trussed up in white and he'd worn a tuxedo had been awfully easy. Giving herself to Joaquin was something she'd chosen while stone-cold sober. Not for a moment did she imagine they had a future. Tonight, she could give in to the pleasure, give herself a reason to smile when winter turned the skies cold, and enjoy being touched by a man who knew his way around a woman. It was sex, pure and simple.

"I know."

His gaze caressed her, reassuring and rewarding at once. Then his stare skittered down her body, caressing every trembling swell and every shadowy dip. He lingered on the stab of her nipples, still straight and swollen, all but begging. Joaquin dragged his fingertips down her skin in a light caress designed to make her shiver. Into his touch, she arched.

He cupped her breast, his palm swallowing her flesh. With a slow slide, he brushed his thumb over the tip. Bailey's breath hitched. Her whole body tensed.

"Sensitive nipples. I love that. Boobs are great, but the point of them is the nipples—literally. I can't wait to torture these and drench your little panties. Unless . . . Are you already wet, baby girl?"

With an inquiring brow raised at her, his fingers began the inevitable slide down her belly. The dim lighting had hidden the fact that he'd aroused the hell out of her—until now. All he had to do was get his fingers over that silk and he'd know how much he turned her on.

"Wait!"

He paused, his palm hovering just over her navel. "If you're scared or upset, we'll figure it out. If you're hiding from me, that's not going to fly. Do we have a problem?"

"I-I . . ." She blew out a breath. Bailey didn't understand the panic washing through her. Wasn't the point for him to arouse her so she could get wet and they could have sex? "No. Not a problem."

"Perfect. Tell me to feel your panties."

The low rumble of his voice, coupled with his mesmerizing gaze, compelled her. Letting him know that he'd aroused her gave him power. But she'd had underwhelming sex once. Now she wanted to be turned inside out.

Bailey swallowed, gathering her courage. "Feel them. T-touch me."

Something in his expression gentled for an instant before his eyes narrowed and the predator in him came out to play. His fingertips made contact with her overheated skin again. She jolted at his touch. Every time he put a hand anywhere on her, she felt him all through her body. Why? How could he do that to her?

None of that mattered as his touch slid down, down, easing over the lace waistband of her panties, then inched even lower. Finally, he grazed the silken fabric, now thoroughly drenched by her arousal.

He applied more pressure with a low, appreciative moan. "That's wet. So sweet. I can't wait to put my mouth right here . . ." He rubbed a little circle over her clit. "And you're hard, too. You're ready to come, aren't you?"

Bailey arched into his touch, hoping to deepen the pressure.

Instead, he eased off. "Answer the question."

With a mindless whimper, she pulled at the cuffs, tried to lift her hips—anything. He withdrew completely. "Bailey?"

"Yes. I want to."

"Tell me in a complete sentence."

"You're making me wait," she accused.

He nodded. "Just like I'm making sure I know exactly what you're willing to let me do."

If she hadn't been so turned on, Bailey knew she'd be mortified. But just the promise of his fingers dancing over her sensitive bundle of nerves again was all she needed to push past her embarrassment. "Please make me come."

"Such sweet begging. I'll definitely consider it. Soon."

His words barely registered before he rolled on top of her and captured her mouth in a demanding press, spreading her lips wide with his own, without patience or apology. With the kiss, he seemed to take her entire body. She felt suspended by a thickening line of desire. It held her afloat, against him, breath held, waiting . . .

Bailey lost herself in the skillful slide of his lips, the urgent surge of his tongue. She curled her fingers into fists, wishing she could touch him, bring him closer—something that would ease the ache now throbbing deep behind her clit.

Joaquin tore his mouth away, breathing heavily as he stared down into her eyes. "I don't know why the fuck you get to me this way. I wasn't meant to touch you. I never took you from your life with the intent to hustle you into bed."

To most, she would probably have no reason to believe him. But she did.

"I never thought I'd trust you," she admitted. "Then you were honest with me."

He grimaced. "I was harsh. I'm sorry about that."

"Make it better?" she asked breathlessly.

"It's on."

The words had barely cleared his mouth before he clasped his lips around her nipple. Easing to her side, he didn't let go, just drew her in more deeply. She groaned through the suction, her legs shifting restlessly, parting.

Joaquin didn't have to be tempted or coaxed. He glided his fingers unerringly back to her clit as he nibbled at the hard crest of her breast again. The double-punch stole her breath. Her sex gushed with moisture, more than ready to ease his path deep inside her.

The teasing circles of his fingers didn't speed up. He didn't press harder. Instead, his touch was a never ending taunt, a burning pleasure that built toward an incendiary explosion. The little catches of her breath seemed to excite him more. The erection he pressed to her thigh only grew thicker, harder. Damn, she wanted that.

Under his touch, the throbbing rushed up, crowding her senses. A surge of euphoria momentarily robbed her sanity. Bailey cried out.

"That feel good?"

"That was great." Far better than anything she'd ever given herself. It definitely surpassed anything Ryan Fuller had given her on prom night.

"Was?"

She hesitated. "Yeah. The orgasm is over."

Joaquin sent her a wolfish laugh. "That wasn't an orgasm."

"Of course it was." It had to be. The edge of the pleasure now wasn't quite as sharp as it had been. What else could it have been?

"Is that what you think?" He lifted his fingers from her needy bud.

Instantly, demand slammed her as desire returned full force. She gasped and looked up at him with wide eyes.

"Exactly," he growled. "Why would you think you'd had an orgasm?"

"I-I've never . . ." God, how embarrassing to realize that he knew more about her body than she did.

"Never? Was your last lover totally inept?"

Pretty much. She hadn't known it at the time, but they'd been the blind leading the blind, so the confusion made sense. "Inexperienced."

He kissed the side of her breast. "Oh, the things I'm going to do to you."

The thought made her feel faint. Already, he'd done far more than she'd ever experienced. And if he gave her more pleasure than she was acquainted with, well, then . . . wow.

"Can we hurry?"

"Oh, impatient. I don't know, baby girl. You were prepared to make me wait."

But she'd waited her whole life. Joaquin alone had been honest about her identity. Now he was showing her genuine pleasure between a man and a woman. "I was wrong."

"You were." He nodded. "You can make it up to me by asking me to remove your panties."

Bailey ached to shove them down herself, but with her hands tethered to the bed that was impossible. "Take my panties off. Please. Now."

"Hmm." He rubbed the firm square of his jaw, pretending deep thought. "That was more impatience than sincerity."

"I mean it. I need it." She was begging and she didn't care anymore. Pride was nothing in the face of this ache. Bailey hated that he'd been able to undo her so easily, but honestly, had she expected to keep up with him? No.

"I'm teasing," he assured her, then took hold of the lace around her waist and slowly began dragging the scrap of fabric down.

The chilly air hit her hip bones before he paused just above her mound. Her entire body tensed as she waited, wanted. But he dragged it out, making her guess if he would continue, when he'd decide. Finally, he tugged the silky bit down and pushed them to her knees before anchoring a foot in the crotch. He kicked down to finish the job.

Bailey didn't watch that, just saw his gaze zero in on her swollen sex. She felt his stare like an actual touch. Everything sensitive between her legs surged and leapt, pouting and anticipating.

He dragged a knuckle down her slick, smooth lips. "You're bare."

"I have to wax. My costumes are sometimes thin and pale. Revealing. I'm sorry if you're disappointed—"

"Fuck no." That finger of his skated over her wet flesh again, making her stomach knot, her desire ratchet up. "I love it. Spread your legs."

"Why?" Her voice shook. The idea both terrified and aroused her.

"Because I asked you to. If I can't see your pussy, I can't look at it and think about all the dirty, perfect ways I'm going to eat it."

Bailey literally couldn't breathe.

"I . . ." The rest of the sentence wouldn't materialize. She probably looked like an idiot with her jaw hanging open. And yes, she knew that men did that to women every day, but not her.

"Is that a yes?" He laved her nipple, his hazel eyes drilling into hers, darkening and heating as he did.

"Yes." The sound came out more like a panting breath than a word.

"Good. Soon. First, I want to really make you come and watch your face." He dipped his head again and affixed his mouth to the other nipple, sucking rhythmically as his finger zipped back down her belly and stopped just above her aching sex. "Spread your legs. I won't ask again."

Bailey didn't hesitate. If she'd never had a real orgasm, then she wanted one. And she wanted Joaquin to give it to her. If he was going to drown and overwhelm her anyway, she might as well go big or go home.

He chuckled. "That's perfect, baby girl. I like you eager for my touch. I want to make you just as eager to fuck."

"Do you talk like this to every woman?"

Joaquin cocked his head, clearly considering. "I usually don't say anything. Somehow I can't not talk to you. Not sure what's up with that. Does it bother you?"

She shook her head. "I love it."

"I can't promise it will last once we're really busy, but . . . yeah. I like rattling you with a few words. Did you know you blush? Your skin is so fair, you flush rosy all over. That turns me on."

Heat crawled up her cheeks, and she laughed. "Like this?"

"Exactly." He pressed a kiss to her lips, to her jaw, then trailed his lips all around her nipples. Before she could protest, his fingers dipped into her furrow again, skimmed directly over her clit.

Bailey gaped and tightened, whimpering when he didn't stop.

He inserted a finger inside her next, his thumb still strumming the little bead of nerves above. "Jesus, Bailey . . . You're tight and sweltering. I can't wait to get my cock inside you."

She didn't answer, couldn't even find her voice or her brain. She finally stopped fighting the inevitable and gave herself over to the explosive pleasure he wrung from her.

As he added another finger inside her, Joaquin prodded a spot deep, then worked her clit in smaller circles, teasing more than pressing. Always making her ache and wait. But the need built and escalated, clawing at her until her head swam. Until her belly tightened and her thighs trembled. Until she held her breath in desperate need of his next stroke.

The crescendo of ecstasy just kept soaring. Dizziness assailed her. Desire screamed inside her just waiting for one more touch . . .

"You're so fucking sexy. *Now* you're going to come. Do it . . . for me."

Chapter Twelve

JOAQUIN gritted his teeth, watching that sexy flush make Bailey's entire body turn rosy. He'd wondered for a seeming eternity how she'd look and sound as she came. He sucked her nipple back into his mouth and tugged as his fingers prodded the spots that had her hitching breath becoming gasps. She cried out—a high-pitched, panicked sound fraught with need and the loss of control. Her eyes went wide, her stare crashing into his and begging. She went straight to his cock.

Holy fuck, she was going to unravel him.

With her next wail, she clamped around his fingers, her clit turning to stone under his thumb. She pulsed and bucked, riding the wave of orgasm—the sort she'd never had in her life. Knowing he was the first man to show her that pleasure, imagining that he might be the only man to ever give it to her, drove him dangerously to the edge.

"Joaquin . . ." She mewled his name as her back arched.

He didn't let up, continuing to stimulate her all the way through the crest of the peak, then letting her down gently until she panted up at him, her blue eyes so full of wonder. Christ, his chest felt like it was going to burst. His heart filled with something he couldn't explain.

The rest of him swelled with pride because tonight he wasn't just a man, but *the* man she needed.

Where the fuck was all that coming from?

A long gasp for air later, a sweet sigh fell from her lips. A sated blush suffused her. Her body went limp, her eyes dreamy.

"That was an orgasm." She wore a loopy little smile.

"It was." He swallowed, trying to beat back the need to strip off his jeans and fuck her in the next ten seconds. But logically knowing she needed to recover and being able to give her the time? Not the same thing—and not easy.

"I want you so damn bad, Bailey." He gave her clit a gentle prod that made her twist up and whimper. When she spread her legs a little wider, silently asking him for more, Joaquin knew he had her again. Now she would be all his.

"Yes . . ." She shifted restlessly, still drunk from the stimulation and the release of dopamine, hormones, and endorphins.

"Tell me to fuck you." His growled words came out rough. It was all he could manage. He probably should have told her that he wanted to make love to her. But where Bailey was concerned, he couldn't seem to find patience or restraint. He wasn't even sure he'd know his own damn name again until he'd filled her with his cock and found the oblivion of release.

His choppy breathing only turned more ragged as he waited for her answer. She blinked and tried to focus. Her lips parted, glossy, swollen, red. Then she thrust her hips up at him.

Jesus, she was going to kill him if he didn't get inside her soon.

"Fuck me, Joaquin."

He should probably warn her that this wasn't going to be romantic, gentle, or easy. He should probably take a deep breath and slow way down. But his fingers fell to his fly and his brain hit autopilot. He ripped at his snap, jerked down his zipper, and shoved everything aside, as he situated himself between her legs. All he could see was the nirvana of her pussy. All he could feel was the thick need coursing through his veins. Nothing had ever been this urgent. No woman had ever made him more rabid for satisfaction.

Joaquin gripped her hips and fitted himself against her opening. Just the touch of his sensitive head to her sweltering, wet flesh jetted an electric arc down his spine. He tossed back his head and groaned, pushing forward. He couldn't get into her fast enough, couldn't fuck her deep enough.

It didn't take long to notice that she was goddamn tight. He growled as he tried to pry his way in only to come up short.

"Baby girl," he whispered against her lips. "Take a deep breath."

Once she had, he captured her mouth, consuming her in a demanding kiss. As he did, Joaquin arched forward. Her body gave way to him one agonizing inch at a time. Instantly, he took the space she ceded to him.

His head slipped inside her sweltering heat, then the sensitive spot underneath. His eyes rolled into the back of his head. He didn't want to break the kiss, but a groan slipped free. Under him, she sucked in a shocked breath, but she spread wider for him.

The feel of her was everything he'd imagined. Hell, she was more potent than a wet dream. Joaquin shoved a bit deeper, praying like hell that he wasn't hurting her. It had been a while for her, and her last boyfriend had obviously been a fidiot in bed. But damn it, submerging inside her was proving more difficult than breaking into Fort Knox.

He nipped at her bottom lip with his teeth. "Breathe again. That's it. Inhale. Yeah . . . Now let it out."

As she did, her body loosened. He thrust the rest of the way inside. Her swollen pussy enveloped him, a snug clasp that robbed him of equilibrium and the ability to give a shit about anything but plowing into her and making her come again.

Joaquin withdrew, and the shudder of sensation rattled down his spine. He groaned, cursed, gripped her tighter. Holy hell, she was going to fucking decimate his self-control.

He cupped her chin and took her lips again, needing to be inside her in every way. His tongue plunged deep in rhythm with his cock. Under him, she shook and arched, writhed and flushed again.

He had to make her come once more. God knew how long he was going to last in this sugary-snug pussy.

Fitting one hand under her ass, he tilted her and slid down a fraction. When he braced on his knees and shoved up again, the head of his cock dragged over her most sensitive spot inside. He pressed onto her clit. She mewled, her fists clenching, her legs lifting to cradle his hips. Fuck, he'd never seen any woman sexier.

He sank deeper, prodding the end of her passage. Her cry of bliss was almost as much reward as the ecstasy zipping through his body.

"I'm . . ." She couldn't catch her breath. "I'm going to—"

"Come, baby girl. Yeah. Fuck. Do it."

Her back twisted and her face contorted. He kept pushing into her, the pace slow and punishing, scraping her insides with every thrust. She screamed like a wild thing, arms tugging at her cuffs and rattling the headboard. Those strong muscles in her thighs squeezed him, as did the clasp of her pussy. Pleasure didn't just sizzle and burn. It turned nuclear, boiled his veins, charred his restraint, and wiped away his ability to give a crap about anything except sharing this orgasm with her. Next time—and there would be one—he'd go slow and find a way not to pound into her with every ounce of his strength. He'd love her a lot more gently. Right now?

"Fuck!" His balls felt heavy and tight as tingling sparked. The telltale escalation of sensation spiked to something stratospheric. Joaquin squeezed her tight, wondering how he could prevent himself from losing his fucking mind. When he blew, he already knew it wouldn't be like any previous climax.

He'd rather forfeit his next fifty years than give up his next thirty seconds with Bailey.

As soon as the thought hit his brain, along with the tangy-sweet whiff of her pussy and the womanly scent of something floral and exotic, he lost it.

The pressure inside him gave way to sexual agony. A scream claimed his throat, scrubbing it raw. He planted even deeper inside her, picking up the pace, thickening, then releasing with a blast of ecstasy.

In that moment, he realized that he'd lost his head so thoroughly that a condom had never crossed his mind. That alone stunned him beyond words. He'd never, ever forgotten to glove up. But that wasn't all. He'd also given Bailey far more than his seed. Something in his chest twisted and clawed, yanking at him, beating at him. He looked down at her, her softly parted lips, the wonder in her blue eyes, the jut of her juicy nipples.

Mine, mine, mine . . .

Yeah, all his. Attachments had never been his thing, and he wondered if this need to clasp her to him forever would pass.

As he poured himself into her in a shocking, seemingly endless orgasm, he sincerely doubted it.

* * *

BAILEY listened to the sounds of Joaquin in the shower, her head racing. After withdrawing from her slowly and uncuffing her, he'd left her body a mass of head-to-toe tingles. She'd climbed out of bed and darted to the shower. Her tears had just started to flow when he opened the bathroom door and charged into the room.

In fact, he'd ducked into the shower with her uninvited.

"What's wrong?" he asked, wrapping his arms around her.

Joaquin stood too close. Emotionally, she felt as if he'd scraped her raw. Having him in her personal space now just slammed her psyche with a frightening vulnerability all over again.

She pushed back, but he didn't give an inch.

"Bailey . . ." he warned.

"Nothing." She didn't know how else to answer him. "Tonight—the party, the picture, the sex—it was too much."

His face softened. "If I came at you too hard, I'm sorry."

The contrition there told her that he meant it. "It was just intense. I wasn't expecting that."

"I wasn't either," he admitted. "I meant to be gentler."

Bailey shook her head. "That wasn't what you needed. I don't think it was what I needed either. It sure wasn't anything like my last time."

He clenched his teeth. "Wipe him from your memory bank."

Was he jealous? As crazy as that sounded, it was the only conclusion she could come up with.

"Don't worry," she assured him. "He's the reason my first time was my last."

"Are you kidding me?"

Joaquin sounded shocked. She supposed that, at her age, he'd already had sex a zillion times. She just hadn't seen what the big deal was until him.

Bailey pushed him away. "I can shower alone. You don't have to help me."

"I'm sorry. That came out wrong." He reached for her again, wrapping his hands around her waist and drawing her closer. "I'm just surprised."

That stung. She shoved him back. "You're surprised I don't sleep around?"

"No. That's not what I meant. Forget it. You're rattled and upset. My brain is still fogged over with pleasure. I'm not leaving you." He reached for the soap as if the matter was closed.

She was both annoyed and relieved. Jeez, she sounded contrary. "You're used to getting your way."

"Not always, but I fight when I know I'm right."

Like this case. Like saving her life. Like not leaving her alone to sort through her feelings now?

Rubbing the scented bar between his hands, he lathered up, then set the soap back in the dish. "Turn around."

"I can wash myself."

"I know." He sighed. "Can you just stop being stubborn for a second and let me take care of you? I drove into you like a Mack truck. I just want to make sure you're okay so I can feel a little less guilty."

When he put it like that . . . She nodded and spun around, presenting him her back and moving her hair over her shoulder, out of his way.

His hands glided over her back, starting at her shoulder blades, then skimming down her rib cage. He embraced her waist, enveloping her in his strong grip. Shuffling closer, he kissed the sensitive spot where her neck and shoulder met. He breathed over her skin and nipped at her lobe as he eased his soapy palms over her hips, then pressed against her body.

"You're so fucking beautiful," he murmured.

She shivered as he nipped his way across her neck to settle against her other ear.

"Thank you for trusting me with your body, for putting your life in my hands."

As his palm worked inward, over her stomach, then began gliding lower, Bailey tensed. His fingers worked past the swollen lips of her sex to graze her sensitive clit.

She gasped and grabbed his wrist, closing her eyes. "Stop. As soon as I got in the shower, I realized we forgot a condom."

"I'm clean," he swore. "If you want me to prove it, I will."

"Unless you're sterile, that's not the only issue."

"Whatever happens, we'll work it out."

She whirled on him. "Your own family, the people you grew up with, never see you. Why would you bother with some girl stupid enough to let you kidnap her and knock her up? You wouldn't. I bet that if I told you I was pregnant tomorrow, you'd run in horror. I'll take half the blame for this mistake, but do me a favor. Don't touch me anymore."

Because the thought of getting close to Joaquin—maybe falling in love with him—only to have him bail on her was more than she could take.

Bailey pushed her way past him, heading for the shower door. He grabbed her arm. "That's not going to happen. The lack of a condom tonight was my mistake. I take responsibility entirely. If you get preg—"

"Stop it. Just . . . don't. You took my whole life from me and you can't respect my one wish, to leave me alone?"

Joaquin cocked his head, looking dark and sure of himself. "If I thought staying away from you would solve anything or make you happier, I'd give it one hell of a try. But in your head, everyone important in your life has left you, so I don't think you want me to repeat the pattern, no matter how much you protest otherwise."

Bailey couldn't look at him. Damn him for seeing through her again and being so right. She trembled, on the verge of tears once more. She hated the way he'd crawled under her skin.

She jerked from his grip. "Can you at least give me five minutes to myself?"

"Five," he growled. "Don't leave the room or get into trouble. And don't think I don't give a shit. I've been fighting for you since I laid eyes on you. I won't stop."

She grabbed a towel and left the bathroom then. After throwing on the cotton nightie Callie had brought her, Bailey crawled between the sheets. She lay staring at the wall, wondering what the hell had happened tonight. Joaquin had reached her as a woman on every level. She'd opened herself to him—and she didn't know how to stop. Worse, by the time she'd sorted through the tangle of her thoughts, her five minutes was up.

The shower cut off. The glass door opened. A minute of silence later, he emerged with a towel around his waist, skin bronzed and slick, big body tense, hazel eyes watchful.

His wet hair was slicked back from his face. Rivulets of water ran down his bulging chest. He stood in the doorway, taking up all the space. Without meaning to, he sucked the air from the room. Bailey's mouth went dry. If she stared at him anymore and let herself dwell on the shocking pleasure he'd given her, she was liable to do something stupid, like throw herself at him again.

"Good night." She forced herself to roll over and turn her back to him.

He'd leave the room soon enough, go back to his and give her some breathing space.

A moment later, she heard rustling cloth, then felt the mattress dip behind her. She swiveled around to watch him—stark naked—climb into bed beside her. "What are you doing?"

"Sleeping beside you. Tell me it's okay to hold you."

"You never ask, do you?"

A corner of his mouth climbed up in a crooked smile. "Not if I can help it."

Bailey wanted to be angry with him, but it wasn't his fault if he made love like a god. Afterward, he'd tried to pry from her whatever had obviously upset her, so that didn't exactly make him a bad guy, either. If he scared her emotionally, that was more her fault than his. His relationship with his family, while head-scratching to her, was none of her business.

"You can hold me." She gave in with a sigh.

Joaquin scooted over to her side of the bed and wrapped his arm around her. He nuzzled her neck. His erection prodded her back. He felt so good—sexy, comforting, dominating, protective. Kind of perfect to her.

"You're . . ." She wriggled her butt against his cock.

"Hard?" he murmured in her ear. "You do that to me. I'm a grown man who can control it. Usually. But I won't touch you unless you ask me to."

That seemed to be a theme with him. A part of her was tempted to turn in his arms, throw her leg over his hip, and invite him inside her body again. Another part of her knew she still needed time to process tonight—and any future implications it might bring.

"Good night."

"I've never seen the benefit of spending the night next to anyone. You're making it pretty obvious." He kissed her neck, the lobe of her ear. "Night."

* * *

COLD seeped into her. Bailey shivered as she looked out over the little farm she called home. Fresh snow had fallen the night before, and everything seemed quiet. She hunched down in her pink pajamas, wondering how long Daddy wanted her to stay outside in her brother's fort. Where was Mommy? She'd had her bath. Wasn't it time for dinner?

She'd wanted to go back into the warmth of the house long ago, but her father had sent her outside and told her to stay here, no matter what. But screams from inside the house had sounded full of terror and pain. More loud noises had jarred her. The air around paralyzed her with fear, especially after the bald man kicked in the back door and ran inside. Since then, a man had been crying out in agony.

Bailey didn't know what to do.

"Please, don't," the voice she'd been hearing shook and pleaded. Her father. He sounded weak. In pain.

She started to climb out of the fort and run to him, then remembered her father's stern words.

Hide outside and be very quiet. Sing your song in your head. Stay there, no matter what.

She hesitated. A shiver wracked her. Inside her fuzzy socks, her toes had gone numb.

Finally, she heard the squeaking of the back door. The stranger who had entered the house earlier stepped outside, holding Daddy by the arm and dragging him along. Her father wasn't fighting, but tripping over his feet. In fact, he looked back at the fort. Blood stained his cheek. Their eyes met, and he pinned her in place with a grim stare.

When the stranger jerked on his arm again, he dragged Daddy to the car. She saw a trail of blood in the snow. Her father was hurt. Was that man taking him to a doctor? Where was Mommy? Her brother? Her sister?

The man shoved Daddy in a black car she'd never seen, then scanned the yard. Bailey ducked and peeked at him from the cracks between two pieces of corrugated metal. The stranger had mean, pale eyes. He looked angry.

Bailey bit her lip. What if he'd hurt Daddy?

Before she could decide what to do, the stranger flung himself in his car and drove off. She watched the black car get smaller and smaller as it bumped down the dirt road. Finally, it disappeared. She didn't understand what had happened.

Time seemed to last forever, and the cold finally forced her from her hiding spot. Unwinding from her crouched position, she inched out of the fort and tiptoed to the back door.

Inside, it was even more quiet. No TV, no laughter, no sounds of cooking.

She wandered from room to room, frowning at the red all over the walls, staining the floor of the hall. As she stepped into her parents' bedroom, she peeled off her socks, then . . .

Everything faded. Then suddenly, she was running for the back door with her shirt stained. Wind blew the portal wide, and she sprinted for the road in bare feet. Her teeth chattered until a nice couple in a blue sedan found her. Bailey climbed inside their warm car, rocking back and forth in confusion. She didn't know what to say.

Bailey woke with a gasp.

She sat up. Hand pressed to her chest, breathing hard. Her heart thundered.

The nightmare she'd had all her life had come back to haunt her again. This time, she'd seen visions that had never appeared before, like Viktor Aslanov. Never before had she acknowledged him in her dream as *Daddy*.

She'd also never seen the stranger who'd made Viktor bleed before dragging him away, which was clearly what her adult mind told her had happened. She knew the Russian had been tortured, then eventually killed, his body dumped on the side of a road.

But somehow, the stranger who had taken him away looked familiar.

"Bailey?" Joaquin sat up beside her. "Did you dream?"

She nodded absently, trying to piece it all together. A sick feeling assailed her. "Where is that photo?"

He wrapped an arm around her and eased her against his body. "Of McKeevy? On the nightstand. I'll get it."

"No." Lunging out of Joaquin's embrace, she stood and turned on the nightstand lamp. Just like in her dream, the air held a nip. Her feet felt frozen. Her hand shook as she reached for the photo.

Yes, she'd definitely seen those mean, pale eyes.

Bailey trembled harder. She started to sweat.

Joaquin leapt to her side. "What is it? Tell me."

"This man was in my dream. He never had been until tonight, but I saw him this time. He barged into our house and dragged Viktor away."

"Did he kill everyone else in the house first?"

"I don't know. Maybe." It was all so fuzzy to her.

"What did he say when he broke in?"

"I wasn't inside. In my dream, Viktor had sent me outside to hide in my brother's makeshift fort. He told me to stay there. But after this man dragged him away, I went back inside." Bailey shook her head, then blinked up at Joaquin. He represented protection and comfort now. She needed those. "I've never had that part of the dream before."

"Anything else new?"

"Not really." She frowned. "There's a bit of a blank spot in between me coming back to the house and me running outside again, this time all covered in blood. I can't see that part."

He wrapped her in his arms. "You've kept the memories locked away for years because they're traumatic. You're starting to remember. Maybe seeing McKeevy's face jarred something? You're sure it was him in your dream?"

"I'm sure. He was younger, a little less bald, but those cold eyes were the same."

Joaquin kissed the top of her head, and she let his heat seep into her. "You're shaking."

"The dream has always scared me." She looked up at him, big and strong, somehow her anchor in this crazy, upside-down world she now inhabited. "This time, I'm terrified."

"I know. Come back to bed." He tried to take the photo from her grip.

"No. I need to think about this."

She clutched the glossy picture of the man who had probably murdered her whole family. On the surface, he didn't look particularly evil or even remarkable. If she'd seen him in person now, she probably would have thought he was a teacher or bank teller—some occupation where he had to be polite. He wouldn't like putting on a nice face and would more than likely have cursed his students or customers in his head. But looking at him now, assassin fit.

"We know he left Houston and headed north. We don't know exactly where he is at the moment, but we're pretty sure where he will be on Saturday."

"Callie and Sean's wedding." Bailey was afraid for her new friend.

He nodded. "I need to call them, tell them about this development. We knew McKeevy was a member of LOSS and probably a threat. But to be ninety-nine percent sure he killed your family and that he broke into your house in Houston, too . . . that's a game changer."

"It's the middle of the night," she protested.

"I don't care. This thing is coming to a head. I don't know why he's chosen now, after all these years. But maybe, with some insight from Sean, I can figure it out."

Bailey touched a hand up to his big shoulder. "Wait."

She knew the minute he called the others, the danger would only become more real. She'd been living in a bubble these past few days. The last twenty-four hours had almost felt as if she'd started a whole new life. But her past had collided with her present. If she wanted a future, she had to bust out of her cocoon and meet this head-on.

Joaquin led her back to the bed and cuddled up beside her before he reached for his phone. "It's not quite four. I'll wait an hour, but no more. My gut tells me that time isn't on our side. McKeevy is on the hunt."

And because she knew what the sick killer had done to her father, seen what he had probably done to the victims Joaquin had been trying to save, she couldn't disagree. His offer of an hour of peace sounded like utter bliss. But he was right. The price of waiting now might be too steep.

"Never mind. Go ahead and call."

Joaquin nodded and dialed Thorpe. Fifteen minutes later, he, Callie, and Sean entered the club. Hunter and Logan were right behind him. Apparently, Axel had never left.

The group gathered in the main dungeon, still dressed in the trappings of Thorpe's party, as Joaquin explained Bailey's dream to the others. As soon as he mentioned the McKeevy connection, the room went dead silent.

"It's a dream," Hunter pointed out. "That doesn't mean it's true. Otherwise, Logan would have giant Tootsie Pops licking him while he sings One Direction songs."

"Hey!" Logan whapped his brother on the shoulder. "I would never sing shit from a British boy band."

"But we all know you'd be more than happy to be worshipped by lollipops," Thorpe drawled.

"Can we focus?" Joaquin growled. "Everything that's happened in Bailey's dream before now has been substantiated as fact."

"But isn't it possible the suggestion of this picture"—Thorpe held up the photo of McKeevy—"somehow made her incorporate him into the dream?"

"Anything is possible," Joaquin conceded with clenched teeth. "But—"

"The dream has always felt more like a memory," Bailey cut in. "And I've always known I was missing pieces. I still am. The whole middle just fades away from me. McKeevy being there, though, fits."

Joaquin nodded. "The torture is up McKeevy's alley."

"He didn't employ his gruesome routine on any Aslanov but Viktor," Sean pointed out. "The rest of the family was simply shot." He winced Bailey's way. "Sorry."

She shook her head. She mourned the loss of a family, but she didn't remember them.

"Maybe he was in a hurry. Maybe he got interrupted. Maybe . . . we don't know," Joaquin insisted. "It wouldn't be the first time the asshole dusted someone without taking them apart first."

Bailey frowned. What was he talking about? Who? She made a mental note to ask Joaquin later.

"The truth is, as soon as I saw the picture, I knew he was familiar and frightening. I had no doubt I'd seen him, then my dream supplied the answer," she told Sean. "I know this all sounds insane, but I'm telling the truth."

"It all fits," Joaquin insisted. "LOSS has been seeking Aslanov's research for about fifteen years. If they thought the scientist himself had kept a copy, they would have paid him a visit, threatened his family, and tortured him to extract its location. They also would have hunted Callie, hoping she knew something, before they eliminated that loose end. Only they could never find her until it was too late. That would have really pissed them off, especially McKeevy."

"I've been thinking . . . " Sean scrubbed a hand down his face, then looked at Callie. "I think we should postpone the wedding."

She shook her head, her dark ponytail brushing her shoulders. "Those bastards have defined my life for too long. I'm not letting them take my future away, too."

"Lovely . . ."

"We can protect her." Thorpe crossed his arms over his chest. "You'll be right beside her. I'll be right beside you."

"Tara and I are coming," Logan swore. "I'll help your guys secure the perimeter."

"Unless Kata goes into labor, we'll be there, too," Hunter assured Sean. "I'll do everything I can to keep Callie safe. Hell, most of the Oracle team will be in the pews, and you know Jack is a scary motherfucker when it comes to anyone threatening women. We'll lock the place down and use it as the perfect opportunity to catch McKeevy."

"Hell, I've got an idea on how to capture him before Callie even walks down the aisle. It won't even disrupt the wedding," Logan added.

"Please, Sean . . ." Callie reached out for her fiancé's hand.

He gripped it. "I don't like it."

"I want to be married to you now. And I'd like to wear my wedding dress before my baby bump makes that impossible."

"I'd rather have you alive than dead," he retorted.

"I doubt McKeevy would really try to off her in the middle of a high-profile event. I don't think LOSS wants that kind of attention," Hunter said.

Sean nodded. "That's probably true."

But he obviously wasn't sold on that thought.

"Besides, everything Callie once held secret is out in the open, along with the fact that her father destroyed his copy of the research. So maybe this is a recon mission or some other fishing expedition," Joaquin suggested and turned to Bailey. "Or maybe they've figured out that you're in Dallas with Callie. Maybe McKeevy is hoping you'll turn up at the wedding."

"And make yourself easy pickings," Axel added. "Because if he has to choose between offing Callie for revenge and torturing you to find Viktor Aslanov's research, guess what he'll take?"

The thought of seeing that man in person—even in a crowded church—made her stomach twist with anxiety until she thought she'd be sick. Being cornered alone with him . . . Utter panic filled her.

"I don't think we should stay here anymore," Joaquin said. "We know McKeevy broke into your house and trashed it, then left Houston, headed north toward Dallas. If he suspects at all that you're here, he'll stop at nothing to get to you."

Bailey didn't want to put anyone else at risk, especially people who felt a lot like friends.

Logan nodded. "In your place, I'd be shoving Bailey in a car and fucking flooring it to Timbuktu, if I could."

"Ditto." Hunter lifted a shoulder in a half shrug. "I don't see what offing Callie gets him at this point except a cheap revenge thrill. But Bailey . . . That's high stakes."

"You're truly the last living link to that research," Axel reminded her.

Thorpe and Sean exchanged a glance, then looked at Joaquin, who nodded. "We'll be leaving."

Bailey wanted to cry. How ironic that she'd come to Dominion terrified out of her mind and wishing to be anywhere else. In a couple of short days, she felt as if she'd grown closer to these people than she had to anyone else in years.

"Any ideas where you'll go?" Sean asked.

"No. But we'll figure it out."

"We know of a good houseboat just outside of Vegas." Thorpe winked at Callie.

"Mitchell! That was low-down." She huffed, trying not to smile. "And kind of wonderful."

"Only kind of?"

Sean looped an arm around her and kissed her temple.

"A lot," she confessed with a dreamy sigh.

Joaquin just shook his head. "I have some ideas on location. No matter what, we'll be out of your hair in the next two hours."

He stood and helped Bailey to her feet. She was loath to leave but didn't see any other way.

"Thanks for everything." He stuck out his hand to Thorpe, then to Sean. "Best of luck with your wedding and your future."

Sean gripped his hand. "When the danger is off, come back to see us."

"You two are welcome." Thorpe smiled and turned to Bailey, who fought the urge to cry. "Take care of yourself."

"Thank you—all three of you," she said from the bottom of her heart.

Callie rose, her blue eyes sad as she held out her arms. "Be careful. Stay safe."

Bailey nodded and hugged the woman, knowing she had no way to keep such a promise. She couldn't even be sure she'd have a chance to reconnect with these people. "I will. You'll make a beautiful bride and a great mother. Congratulations."

She wanted to say more, but Hunter shot Joaquin a pointed glance. "What should I tell your sister?"

"Nothing to say right now." He wrapped his hot fingers around Bailey's arm. "Let's go."

Chapter Thirteen

IT didn't take long to gather up their stuff. She and Joaquin had arrived at Dominion with next to nothing. Other than the few items Callie had given her, she was leaving empty-handed. Though she would have loved some of the comforts of home, Bailey knew McKeevy had destroyed much of it. Another reason to despise him. Besides Blane and dance, she wondered if she had anything worth going back to.

"Do you have everything packed?" Joaquin asked as he glanced around the room they'd shared last night, his stare lingering on the bed.

"There wasn't much."

"True." One look at her face, and he sighed. "Baby girl, don't worry. I'll protect you. Sean will continue working on this end to keep Callie safe with the help of Jack Cole and his guys."

She was scared, but probably not as much as she should be. Joaquin had already proven that he was smart and one step ahead of McKeevy. Her bigger regret was losing people she cared for.

Story of my life . . .

"I know."

He lifted a borrowed backpack filled with their stuff with one hand. With the other, he reached for hers. She appreciated his comfort. As hard as it was to leave all her new friends, being without this man would be far more devastating.

What would she do when he no longer had to bodyguard her and he left her to save someone else or seek his next mission? Bailey didn't want to think about that. She couldn't let a man she'd known a handful of days have her heart or the ability to crush her. She cared, yes. Maybe she was even falling in love. But she would carry on once he'd gone. Sadly, she already knew he would, just as she knew his departure would hurt like hell.

As the two of them left the bedroom behind and made their way down the empty hall, they passed through the dungeon. Someone had already cleaned up after the party. Even the garish blow-up doll had been deflated and lay in a plastic puddle on the bar, tacky lingerie piled on top. In the middle of the room, Logan scanned all around and finally picked up a woman's purse near the table where the gifts had rested.

He glanced up as they entered. "Good luck, you two. Kata really does miss you, man."

Beside her, Joaquin tensed. "Thanks. That purse a new look for you?"

Bailey blinked. He'd resorted to guy humor, rather than acknowledging the truth Logan had given him. His father's death must have been incredibly traumatic. Why hadn't he healed? Why couldn't he seem to engage with his own family?

God, her life was full of so many secrets, wrapped inside mysteries, all shoved into conundrums right now. Between that and lack of sleep, exhaustion weighed on her. The soreness between her legs was a potent reminder of the man beside her, too. Still, all she wanted to do was touch Joaquin again.

"Ha!" Logan shot back sourly. "Tara and I got a little carried away last night. She left her purse here and texted me to find it. But personally, I think gray and black are my colors." He held up the bag with a cheesy smile. "It's even got these nifty pockets so I can insert whatever weapons . . ." He tilted the purse sideways. Out spilled a small collection of baby toys, all tumbling to the ground in a clatter. A pair of pacifiers, a multicolored rattle, some cloth books with Velcro characters stuck on haphazardly, and a little ball that played music.

Bailey froze when she heard it. Her blood ran cold.

"What is that?" she asked, pointing.

Logan held up the toy, just now finishing its little ditty. "A ball."

"No, that song."

"'Hickory Dickory Dock.'" He reared back. "You've never heard it?"

"Her parents were Russian," Joaquin tossed back in a voice that warned Logan to back off.

"No, I've heard it. How does it go? Can you sing it?"

"Tell me what you're thinking." Joaquin set the backpack down and wrapped an arm around her in a silent show of support.

"It's something . . . A memory. I can't put my finger on it." She grappled for the memory and came up empty. She sighed in frustration. "I don't know. Please sing it."

Logan nodded. "Hickory Dickory Dock. The mouse ran up the clock. The clock struck one. The mouse ran down. Hickory Dickory Dock." He rubbed the back of his neck with a grimace. "It sounds less stupid when I'm singing it to infants."

Bailey shook her head. "Those aren't the words I learned."

"Maybe your parents sang it in Russian?" Joaquin suggested.

"No. It was . . . something about a fence, a big tree, a barn, and turning three times." Bits of the memory rolled through her mind.

Confusion crossed Logan's face. "I've never heard that version."

"Viktor Aslanov taught it to me."

"Who knows?" Joaquin hefted the backpack over his shoulder and guided her toward the door. "It's probably nothing. We'll be going now. Bye."

She stared at him. Why had he been so abrupt?

"Can I take that?" she asked Logan before Joaquin could pull her away. "I'll send it back as soon as I can."

"Sure." Logan handed her the little ball.

Bailey took the toy in hand. It felt spongy and soft, and she could see why babies would gravitate toward it. She shook it, but it remained silent.

"Bounce it." He tipped his chin in the direction of the table that had held the gifts last night.

She did, and it immediately played the tune again. The words Viktor had taught her jumbled in her head once more. But really, did some little kids' song her biological father had taught her years ago matter? Everything inside her wanted to say yes, but it sounded mental.

"I don't need this after all." Bailey extended the ball back to Logan. "I'm not going to take your daughters' toys."

"If it's jogging your memory, maybe you need this. Believe me, I've heard that sucker so much over the last few months, if it's gone for a long while, that won't be a loss."

She hesitated. "Your babies won't miss it?"

"Probably, but Tara and I also won't miss them each crying when the other has it. Really." Logan pushed the ball back in her direction. "Take it. If it will help at all, it's really a small sacrifice."

Every one of these people had been nothing but kind, protective, welcoming . . . Bailey wondered if she'd ever see them again. Damn it, she was going to cry.

Joaquin hustled her out the door and to a gray SUV before she did. The sun showed hints of cresting over the horizon soon, but everything around her felt still. She couldn't help but wonder if McKeevy was somewhere lurking in the dark, just waiting for his chance at her. Dominion had felt safe, as had its people. Now they were gone.

Inside the vehicle smelled of leather and Joaquin. He threw the backpack in the backseat, then climbed beside her and eased out of the lot, sans headlights. At this time of morning, almost no cars congested the streets. He waited until he'd cruised a few lonely blocks before flipping on the lights, punching the gas, and heading away from the club.

"Where are we going?" she asked quietly.

"I don't know." He looked tense, worried. "I have to think of some place safe, but with McKeevy and LOSS onto you, I think we have to start playing offense and try to access anything you can remember about the day your family died. Maybe that will help us. If he kept a copy of that research—"

"I don't know. If he did, I don't remember. I was barely five."

"But your memories are coming back. There's a chance we can extract more from your dreams. Anything you can remember might save you. Talk to me about that ball."

"The music is sparking something. I don't know what exactly. It's . . . fuzzy. Why didn't you want to tell Logan?"

"It's better for him if he doesn't know anything LOSS might want."

Bailey supposed that was true. She didn't want the people who had tried to help her at any additional risk. In fact, she prayed that, with her gone, Callie would have a perfect wedding.

With a sigh, Bailey squeezed the ball Logan had given her. She was almost loath to hear the song again, like it might open a Pandora's box of crap she didn't want to deal with. But the chime played in her head, taunting and compelling her. Besides, if information was power, she couldn't procrastinate in learning.

She tossed the ball against the dashboard, catching it as the rubbery orb bounced right back. It sang to her as she took it in her palm.

Hickory near the . . . something. The can't-remember hides on the something-or-other? The rest of the song just faded from her consciousness as she tried to recover the first two lines. Maybe if she could sing that much, the other lines would follow?

"Anything?"

"Not enough. It starts with hickory, just like in Logan's version. Then it veers off. Let me try again."

She bounced the ball against the dash one more time and let the melody play. "Hickory near the dock. The mouse hides on the . . . something. From the painted fence, jump three times."

"Then what?"

"That's all I remember."

Her inability to recall the song frustrated her. Not that she'd expected to bounce the ball a couple of times and the song would magically fill her brainpan. But the black spots in her dream, the fate of her family, really upset her—being unable to remember upset her. Why couldn't she just close her eyes and get it?

"Take a deep breath and relax."

Bailey did as Joaquin asked, but the more than vague edge of annoyance prevented her from actually unwinding. "Nothing."

"Hang on," he insisted. "Hand me the ball."

Sending him a sideways glance, she plopped the little sphere in his palm. He stopped at a light, then bounced the toy on the console between them. She shut her eyes again.

"Hickory near the dock. The mouse hides on the farm. From the painted fence, jump three steps left. Walk a straight line to the . . . something. Hickory near the dock." She sighed, her vexation climbing. "Is this even important?"

"Viktor Aslanov rewrote this rhyme for some reason."

"He was Russian. Maybe he didn't know the words."

"It's possible. But we've got nothing else. This sounds a little like he gave you directions to something."

"Or that's wishful thinking on your part. It's just . . . part of it doesn't want to come out of my memory bank."

"You haven't thought about this in forever. Try one more time." As he veered onto the highway heading north, he bounced the ball again, and Bailey did her best to listen.

Nothing new. She still couldn't remember where the rhyme said to walk the straight line to.

"Sorry." She shook her head.

"It's all right. We'll give it a break and work on it later. Maybe you should close your eyes and see if you can sleep."

She looked at him as if he'd lost his mind. "I'm pretty keyed up."

Joaquin shrugged, conceding the point. "And I could use some coffee."

"I don't drink it much, but that sounds good."

"Okay. Let's see how much of the rush hour traffic we can beat. When we get to the outskirts of Dallas, we'll stop."

"I've encountered plenty of stop-and-go crap in Houston. I'm for anything that bypasses the possibility of more. Why are we going north?"

"South isn't going to work," he tossed back. "No sense in going back to Houston."

"True." Especially since McKeevy knew where she lived. Her lease was up in less than two months. She'd been planning to sign again. Now she'd probably look for another place once she was safe.

If she was ever safe again.

"I'm trying to come up with a game plan. If we need to go east or west, I'll veer."

That made sense enough for now. "What do you mean by coming up with a good offense?"

"In a nutshell? Stop running. What LOSS wants isn't you, but what they think you might remember: where your father might have buried that research."

"Why do they want it so bad?"

"Could be a million reasons, but my best bet is exactly what Sean suggested: They're convinced they can genetically alter soldiers to kick the U.S. military's ass. Remember they want to secede from the Union."

"That sounds awfully . . . sci-fi."

"From what we can glean, your father's research was incredibly advanced. He was years—maybe even decades—ahead of his peers. It's also possible he was a hell of a snake-oil salesman and fed LOSS a bunch of mumbo jumbo about his capabilities, and they believed it."

"Seems like they'd want some proof." Why else would they give a scientist so much money? Bailey frowned.

"Yeah, I've thought that. Something has convinced them this information will solve all their ills, because they're awfully willing to kill for it. Maybe the bit of research they received early on convinced them they needed the rest. Who knows? Our problem is just keeping you alive. I think the key is finding whatever your father may have hidden."

"Do you know for certain he hid anything?"

"No," Joaquin admitted. "But a man flushing his life's work down the toilet willingly . . . I don't buy that."

Bailey shrugged. "But you're not upset about your job."

"I'm passionate about justice. I haven't given up on that. I'm just going down a different path for it."

And then what? she wondered, but didn't ask. Maybe she didn't want to know which of the four winds he'd follow out of her life once this danger had passed.

"So you're thinking we try to find whatever Viktor Aslanov might have salvaged. Where do we start?"

Joaquin hesitated. "I've been thinking about this. I think we have to go back to the scene of the crime."

"I don't know where he did his research."

"But we know where LOSS came looking for him and murdered his family. Maybe they had some hunch to hunt for the information there."

"Go back to that farm I see in my dreams?" The idea horrified . . . even as it made sickening sense.

"Yeah."

"I don't know where it is," she protested automatically.

"Sean can tell us."

He probably could, but . . . "LOSS has had something like fifteen years to search the place. If my biological father hid the research there, wouldn't they have found it? Wouldn't the place be occupied by someone else or torn down or something?"

"We'll find out. But if I'm going to spark your memory, I have to hope that something on the property will seem familiar. You could be looking at . . . anything and have a flashback of your past. The photo of McKeevy worked wonders."

Bailey couldn't argue with that, though she wished otherwise. "I'm scared."

"I don't blame you. I've never been able to face the house I grew up in. You lost your whole family and you don't know what this will stir up. You've been nothing but brave since I took you from Houston. Can you do it a bit longer? For me?"

His speech was part wheedling, part blackmail. Bailey sighed. But what choice did she have? If she wanted a life, she had to explore every possibility.

"Yes."

* * *

JOAQUIN called Sean as they headed north. Beside him, Bailey slept. They'd stopped for some fast-food breakfast and coffee. When they'd handed him a greasy bag at the drive-thru window, she'd wrinkled her nose; then she'd picked off all the cheese and nibbled delicately at the sandwich.

He smiled at the memory, then sent her a glance. No idea why he felt so . . . attached to her. Everyone else in life he'd been able to just walk away from. His mother had his sisters. His sisters had their husbands. None of them needed him.

But Bailey? She did.

It wasn't pity that kept him with her, though. Far from it. He didn't like being away from her, even felt weirdly off-kilter when she wasn't near. He liked to see her smile, got hard when she laughed. Seeing her so serene now filled him with peace. What the hell was up with that?

"You two all right?" Sean said by way of greeting once he answered.

"Fine. Thanks. Just driving," he said in low tones so he didn't wake Bailey. "Do you have the address of that farm she lived on with her parents?"

"You going there?"

"I don't know what else to do. But she makes a good point that LOSS has had years to comb the place."

"The feds, too. They took all kinds of equipment—sonar, X-ray, infrared cameras—and didn't find anything except a colony of mice by the barn."

"The one thing you didn't have was Bailey's memories."

"You got us there. It's worth a try."

Sean rattled off the address, then caught him up to speed on their plan to keep the wedding safe. Joaquin knew that Bailey really hated to miss it. Honestly, he kind of did, too. Sean and Callie deserved a good start to their marriage, and Joaquin had never seen a committed relationship with three people, but with Thorpe's iron will, Callie's devotion, and Sean's ability to negotiate truces, they'd have a great future.

Joaquin wondered what the hell he'd do with his life when this case was over. He had no job now. His shithole apartment didn't really qualify as a home. He'd drifted from his family, and the one close friend he'd had was dead. He was over thirty . . . and had nothing to show for it.

Jesus, listen to him. He had to pick up his whiny ass and move on. He'd find another job, another case, another shithole, maybe even more friends.

But not another Bailey.

The thought hit him right between the eyes.

"Hello?" Sean asked. "Can you hear me?"

"Yeah." Joaquin tuned back into the conversation. "Sorry. My cell skipped out for a minute. Can you repeat that?"

"Sure. Be careful. If we come across anything else, we'll keep you posted."

"Thanks, man."

"And you let us know how you're doing. Callie is worrying herself into a frenzy."

And wouldn't that touch Bailey's heart?

Joaquin felt his throat close up. "Thanks."

As they rang off, Joaquin thanked his lucky stars he'd bought his vehicle with a GPS program. He punched the address into the system and out spit directions. Only twelve hours and some change to go . . .

* * *

HOUR after hour rolled by in the car. Bailey stared out the window at the slowly changing scenery. The flat land seemed to simply stay flat. The foliage changed. The air turned colder. Spring may have mostly sprung in Texas, but up north, they hadn't quite gotten the memo.

After Little Rock, hints of civilization became fewer and farther between. The northeast corner of Arkansas still had snow. Missouri still looked miserably wintery, considering it was April. She still hadn't asked where exactly Joaquin was taking her.

In truth, she wasn't sure she wanted to know.

With every mile that passed, her stomach knotted tighter. Every cell in her body clenched with dread. What if seeing her childhood home sparked memories? What if it didn't? Or what if she remembered the bloodbath McKeevy had unleashed on her family? Bailey could only believe that she had escaped because her father had sent her outside to hide and LOSS hadn't paid that much attention to the number of children Aslanov had sired.

"You're too quiet," Joaquin said finally.

"I'm fine."

"Don't feed me that line of shit. You're worried."

"I am," she admitted. "What does that change?"

He sighed as they crossed into Illinois. "Are you hungry at least?"

"Are you going to feed me more fast food?" The idea made her stomach revolt.

"Probably. I'm trying to reach our destination before nightfall. No sense searching the property in the dark."

"We won't have much time before sunlight runs out anyway. You must be tired. You've been driving all day. And you can't have gotten much sleep last night."

"I don't regret that for a second. What about you?"

Heat rose up her cheeks. "I enjoyed it. I certainly understand the fuss about sex now."

Bailey would have thought that most men would preen when a girl praised their prowess. He frowned. "So I was good in bed but it didn't mean anything?"

"No, I . . ." Why did this man fluster her so easily? "I'm running for my life. And you won't stay around. Your sister made that really clear last night. So why does it matter?"

He just grunted. "We'll table this discussion until we figure everything else out, but I'm not done."

Great.

They stopped and had a sort of healthier lunch. Sub sandwiches with processed meat wasn't her definition of power food, but she loaded hers up with veggies and did the best she could. If she miraculously got to audition next week, she didn't want to be hugely out of shape. After that, they continued in relative silence, and she fiddled with the radio as each station played tunes then became static as the miles rolled on.

Late afternoon had almost spilled into evening when Joaquin turned the SUV down a dirt road. Her stomach clenched tight, and she wondered if she'd lose her lunch. Somehow, she knew the trek down this road wouldn't be more than a mile or so. It seemed to take forever, yet it wasn't long enough.

It didn't take long before he slowed. The GPS indicated their destination was on the left. Bailey pressed her hands to her stomach, looking at the seemingly innocuous, if neglected, farmhouse that had become a house of horrors in her nightmares.

The structure was still painted a white, though time and weather had peeled it in spots. The swing set she saw on one side of the house in her dreams had rusted out and looked like something ready for a Dumpster. The remnants of her brother's fort between the two trees tilted and gaped. If she hadn't known it had once stood there, she would have never guessed from its appearance now. A curtain sagged from the front window, which Bailey knew was in the kitchen. In fact, the drape was a print of little teacups and saucers. The roof had seen better days.

The whole place looked haunted.

"You're pale. Does anything look familiar?"

Sadness assailed her. Rage followed. LOSS had taken everything from her. Now that she sat here looking at the home, she remembered laughter. Her father had liked to tickle her in the mornings. Her mother had been teaching her and her sister to dance in the living room.

One organization's need to wedge the world into the order they sought had wiped out all she held dear in the blink of an eye.

"Everything." Her voice shook.

Joaquin bolted out of the car and ran around to open her door. "If you're too tired to do this today, we can come back tomorrow."

She shook her head. If she had to leave and live with a night of dread, knowing she'd return to this tragic spot . . . "We're here. Let's get this over with."

He looked as if he wanted to say something but refrained. Instead, he held out his hand and helped her to her feet. "You ready?"

No. "Why not?"

"Three days ago, you had no idea you'd been born Tatiana Aslanov. If memories are coming back, too, everything must be overwhelming."

She supposed that was logical, but the fact that he'd considered her feelings at all touched her. Far cry from the man who had awakened her while she'd been chained to a stranger's bed at Dominion.

"Yeah."

He tucked her hand in his. "I'll be beside you."

"Isn't anyone else living here?"

Joaquin grimaced, his hazel eyes reluctant. "No. Sean did some digging and found out it's been vacant all this time. Your father left the house and everything in it to your mother's sister, who still lives in Russia. Apparently, she's refused to sell it, hoping that someday you'd be found and might want it."

The fact that some relative she'd never met cared about her from halfway around the world touched her, but Bailey knew she could never spend another night in this place. "So you're saying she left a key somewhere?"

"The feds did. Sean told me how to access it."

He led her to the side of the house. On the back door, the one she'd darted out of in her dreams over and over again, a lockbox hung from the knob. With sure fingers, Joaquin punched in the code and the little tray opened, producing a key.

Joaquin took it between his fingers. "You want to do this?"

"No. Walking into the house is going to be hard enough. You go first, please."

God knew what it would look like. Had anyone scrubbed the walls or replaced the carpet after the murders? If the evidence still existed, would she be able to deal? Damn, she found it hard to breathe.

"Follow me. If you need to stop or take a break or talk about it—"

"I appreciate that. Can we just get it over with?"

Because if she waited too long, she would probably throw up.

He nodded, looking tense. No, worried. "However you want. I got you."

Funny how he liked to take away her control in bed and he assumed total responsibility when her safety was on the line, but with something this traumatic and emotional . . . he simply stayed by her side, so supportive. So compassionate.

"Thanks. I know this case has already cost you a lot, and you've done so much to keep me alive. Your sense of justice is amazing. What you've sacrificed to help me and try to save women you never knew is nothing short of incredible."

Joaquin waved her off and shifted his gaze around the side of the house. Finally, he stuck the key in the side door, but it didn't turn. "This must unlock the front."

"I guess." She shrugged.

Tugging gently on her hand, he led her to the front of the house. The lock gave him no resistance, and as Joaquin turned the old handle, the door squeaked open. Cold air from inside rushed her face, assaulting her. A shiver originated deep under her skin, all the way from the core of her being.

He pushed the door wider and stepped inside. As Bailey approached, stale air hit her nostrils, nearly making her knees buckle.

"I wonder how long it's been since anyone has stepped foot in here." He recoiled from the odor.

She wrinkled her nose and peered inside. "Smells like a long time."

The little living room still looked so much like the memories that suddenly rushed back to her. Chocolate-brown carpet that had seen better days still covered the floor. A plaid sofa in tones of blue that didn't match at all hunched against the wall. A small end table covered with a lacy scrap still sat beside it. A scarred coffee table the color of honey rested in front, still marred with the grooves from her brother's toy trucks. Everything looked caked with inches of dust.

Bailey wrapped her arms around her waist. The temperature

wasn't the only thing cold in here. The vibe of the place iced through her veins. The terror that had permeated the house that day still lingered and plagued.

She took a deep breath, trying to calm her fraying nerves. She'd never thought of herself as terribly brave, so being here tested her. Everything inside her wanted to flee. She couldn't and she knew it.

"You all right?" he asked, pulling her closer.

Thank goodness Joaquin stood by her side. No way she would have made it without him. He might not be the man who stayed forever, but she'd be grateful to him for standing beside her now.

"I-I'm trying."

"Ready to walk through the house? I'll leave the door open."

That might help with what she otherwise knew would be one of the most difficult things she'd ever endured in her life. She gave him a shaky nod.

A few more steps through the living room had them at the opening of the dining room. The pale fabric on the chairs still showed signs of stains from the children who had once eaten here. Her gaze lingered on the seat beside her mother's. It had been her own. The faint pinkish stain on the corner had once been red from a fruit punch spill. Her father had always plunked himself at the head of the table and quizzed her older siblings about homework.

Each memory seemed crystal clear now. How had she forgotten so much of her past for a moment, much less for years? Even more came rushing back. Her mother had often wrapped up her long hair and danced through the house when she'd thought her "baby" was napping. Bailey used to sneak out of her bed and watch. Her siblings had often liked to play hide-and-seek indoors, especially when it snowed. If their father was watching TV or studying his research notes, he'd sometimes lose his temper and bluster. But spats would always end in hugs, tickles, and giggles.

As Joaquin eased her from the dining room into the kitchen, she stopped. Faded linoleum countertops in a graying white sat on top of oak cabinets with old-fashioned scalloped trim. Some of the doors hung off the hinges now. Idly, she supposed that all the food had been cleared out or the stench would be unbearable. The white refrigerator still stood in the corner, no longer humming. The stove had been ancient fifteen years ago, and now looked like a relic.

Her memories of her mother were strongest here. She hadn't been much of a cook, according to her father, but he'd always appreciated her effort. Mama would toil for hours, trying to cook a special stew or soup, especially when winters turned cold. Daddy had often smiled at her effort, but looked as if he were choking on the result.

Bailey felt her lips lift in a little grin. So many good memories here. So many forgotten ones, like her brother's last birthday party and the cake that had somehow plopped onto the kitchen floor before anyone had taken a bite. Her last summer here, an old dog had wandered into their yard one day, sans identification tags. Her bother had named him X-Man. The big German shepherd mix hadn't lasted long before age took him, but Bailey remembered loving the big, protective canine and crying the day he died.

"You all right?" Joaquin asked softly beside her.

Tears welled, but she nodded. "So much is coming back to me. I don't know . . . This whole time in my life was blank. Now that I'm standing here, I remember everything."

He stroked a tender hand down her hair. "I'll stay with you. If anything scares you, just grab on to me. If you remember something about the case . . ."

"I'll let you know."

"Or if you want to talk about anything, I'm here."

Joaquin guided her out of the kitchen, through the little family room that overlooked the backyard. She recalled running out there in the sprinklers. Of course, everything was dormant now at the end of a long winter, the overgrown brown weeds nearly obscuring the back fence.

On the other side of the room, she caught sight of the part of the house she'd most dreaded—the hallway that led back to the bedrooms. As she stared into the opening, a lump of terror gathered in her belly. Whatever she didn't want to remember had happened on this side of the house.

"You ready?"

They were losing the light, so she had to be. Slowly, she nodded, feeling that lid to Pandora's box creaking open in her head.

He stepped through the opening into the hall first. The moment his athletic shoes hit the worn parquet floor, she pictured another man standing on that same surface. She closed her eyes and followed the memory. Her father had picked her up that afternoon and cuddled her, sung his version of the nursery rhyme with her, then made her promise never to forget it. Finally, he'd sent her outside through the back door at the end of this hall.

Bailey didn't want to open her eyes and look down that long strip of house that led to the portal, but there was nowhere else to look. Dark, musty, seemingly innocuous. But the moment she lifted her lids, a vision from the past assailed her. The walls splashed with red. The wooden floors slick with the warm, oozing liquid. Blood everywhere. She'd seen it after her father had been dragged away, after she'd come in from her brother's fort. Had the stranger simply come in and shot everyone?

She frowned. The memory seemed so close, but she couldn't access it. Something stood in her way . . .

"Do you need to pause here for a minute or do you want to move on?"

Bailey wanted to leave the house altogether, but that wasn't an option. She'd have no future if she didn't confront the past. "Let's move on."

The first bedroom on her right was her brother's. Tiptoeing to the opening, she found herself staring at the faded blue walls. A *Star Wars* poster had been ripped nearly in half, even as the edges clung to the wall. His bunk beds had been stripped of bedding. But she couldn't miss the huge red stain marring the mattress on the bottom bunk. And she couldn't escape the memory of her brother in his bed, lifeless, bleeding from a bullet to the head. He'd turned nine a few weeks earlier.

Bailey felt her body buckle. She pressed a hand to her chest. "Mikhail, my brother, was murdered in his room."

Who would do that to a child? Why?

She couldn't look anymore and jerked from the doorway. Joaquin was there to support her, wrapping his arms around her body, easing her head to his chest. He crooned nonsensical words. She didn't care that she couldn't understand what he said because his touch made it clear that he would stand with her no matter what. It didn't feel like he just wanted answers or to solve a case. Bailey would have sworn that he genuinely cared.

Flinging her arms around him, she sobbed quietly into his chest. He edged them away from the opening of the bedroom and leaned against the far wall, removing her another precious few inches from the tragedy.

For long minutes, he simply let her shock have its way. As she grieved, he lent her his strength and support. She sniffled, dreading what she'd find next, but a quick glance around proved that the sunlight was waning and their time was running low. She didn't think she'd find the mental muster to come back here tomorrow, so she had to tough it out for the rest of this wrenching house tour. Bailey had no idea if she'd remember anything of value, but she had to try.

"I'm fine." She pulled back.

He tightened his arms and braced a finger under her chin, lifting it. After a long scan of her face and a deep glance into her eyes, he blew out a breath. Obviously, he didn't like this, but he knew what had to be done. "Come with me."

Together, they made their way down the hall before pausing at the next door on the right—the room she had shared with her sister, Annika. The walls were no longer a sunny yellow. The grime on the windows and the setting sun made the darkening room look gloomy, shadow-filled. The child-size kitchen set and tea party equipment had all been taken away. The pale carpet still bore the scars of bloodstains splattered on the far side of the room. The closet door stood ajar, a terrible reminder.

As with the scene in Mikhail's room, Bailey remembered that horrific evening. Her older sister had tried to hide from her murderer in the closet, but he'd found her. So had Bailey, later, all huddled and crumpled in a corner of the dark little space. Some bastard had hunted her down and snuffed out her life. Annika's last moments must have been terrifying.

Bailey wondered why she had been spared when none of the others had.

"I have to get out of this room." She turned and bolted back into the hall.

Joaquin followed. "Was that your room?"

She nodded. "My sister and I, yes. I had the top bunk."

In fact, she'd remembered awakening that morning early and seeking out her mother, begging for pancakes.

Her mother.

Bailey's heart stopped as she headed toward the final room off the hallway. Her parents had shared that bedroom. She remembered sometimes hearing them arguing. Sometimes she'd heard moans and grunts, which she suspected now had been their lovemaking.

The cozy queen bed had been stripped bare, the mattress now a dingy white. The nightstands were devoid of the clock and jewelry that had always graced her mom's side of the bed. The bench near the window still had the needlepointed seat of flowers, but looked like a neglected antique.

Bailey inched closer but couldn't make herself enter the room—couldn't stop remembering her mother lying in a pool of blood, as if she'd come to check on the gunshots and Annika's screaming, then been gunned down herself.

More of that evening drifted back to her. Bailey recalled coming in from the cold and wandering down the hall, finding the carnage in each bedroom more horrifying than the last. Then she'd seen her mother, bloody and lifeless, on the floor. She remembered trying to shake her mother awake, somehow so terrified by the woman's open, sightless eyes. She'd screamed, thrown herself against her mother and hugged her tight, pleading for Mama to hug her, assure her that the world hadn't ended.

Into the dead silence, she'd fled the house in horror, wondering if the bad man would come for her next. When she'd darted back down the hall, she'd slipped in the blood and peeled off her socks before pushing out the back door, into the snow. The rest of the events fit her dream, all the way until the concerned couple in the blue sedan had discovered her. Then . . . nothing again before her life with Bob and Jane Benson.

"Baby girl?"

"My mom was killed right here." She pointed to a spot barely a foot away. "I found her body. I remember finding them all dead."

Joaquin pulled her close, and she could feel his ache of sympathy for her. "I'm here. Cry or get angry or . . . whatever you need."

What she really needed was to leave.

"There's nothing else to see in this house. I have to go."

"I'm with you. I've got you."

He led her to the yard, out to the blessedly fresh air. Standing in the yard, he cupped her face in his hands as the sun dipped lower toward the horizon. The golden rays made the olive planes of his face glow like rich bronze. The concern in his hazel eyes nearly brought her to her knees.

"I won't push you anymore if you can't do it," he murmured. "Tell me what you want."

"I'll be fine." She had to be. "Let's finish this."

He nodded. "Did your dad utilize the barn for any reason?"

"Like research?" She shook her head. "My mother cleaned it out so we could play there, but we kind of thought it was creepy. It was falling down even then, so we didn't use it much."

"So he didn't research in there?"

"Never. I can count on one hand the number of times I remember anyone even going in there."

He nodded grimly. "I need to look inside, just make sure there isn't some obvious place Viktor could have hidden his research. Granted, someone else should have found it by now if it were that simple, but I'll try anyway. Do you want to stay here or come with me?"

Bailey didn't want to be alone, but Joaquin needed to take advantage of the waning daylight. The remnants of her brother's fort, wedged between the two trees, tugged at her. She should check there while she still had sunlight. No idea when her father would have had time to stash something in this area that day. The timeline jumbled in her head a bit. She didn't remember her father being outside until McKeevy had shown up and dragged him out.

"Go ahead. I'm sure both the feds and LOSS have turned every inch of this whole farm upside down, but I'll try checking over here." She thumbed in the direction of the makeshift playhouse.

Joaquin looked reluctant to leave her, but he finally nodded. "Yell if you need anything."

She appreciated him more than she could express. "Thanks."

As he strode away to the barn behind the house, Bailey turned and blew out a deep breath before inching her way to the trees. Most of the metal pieces that her brother had tried to lean together or tape into something resembling fort walls were gone. Some had scattered across the yard. Some were nowhere to be seen.

She knelt between the trees, recalling that fateful day. Her father had sent her outside with the instructions to hide quietly, sing her song in her head, and stay out here. She remembered asking if they were playing a game. His smile had been strained as he'd nodded and answered that it was a very serious game. Could she be a big girl and play along?

She'd nodded happily, wishing her mom would have made more pancakes, not stew, for dinner. Then . . .

Bailey lowered herself to the ground and braced her back against the larger of the two trees, gathering her knees to her chest, as she'd done that afternoon. She closed her eyes and tried to remember anything else her father might have said to her. Anywhere he might have gone or hidden his research. Would it have been boxes of paper? Something smaller, electronic maybe? She really had no idea. She also had no memory of anything except her father kissing her, telling her that he loved her, then heading grimly into the house.

What she remembered next made her gasp. She choked, unable to breathe. Her thoughts raced. Her heart roared.

Bailey drew in a huge, jagged breath and screamed.

Chapter Fourteen

JOAQUIN heard the bloodcurdling cry from the side of the little farm. He pulled his SIG from the small of his back, clicked off the safety, then bolted to Bailey's side, panic charging through his veins.

He found her alone, curled up against a tree, trying to make herself as small as possible. She'd closed her eyes and opened her mouth wide. Tears streamed from the corners of her eyes and her body shook as if jolted by an electric shock.

Falling to his knees, he scooped her up into his arms and pulled her against him. "What is it? Tell me."

She shoved at him and scrambled to her feet. "Get me out of here." Across the yard she spotted his SUV and ran for it. "I need to go!"

He chased her down and lifted her against his chest. "Talk to me. Did someone show up just now? Startle you? Threaten you?"

"No."

So she battled her memory, not a flesh-and-blood foe—at least for the moment.

"Good. We have to lock up the house, then we'll go. Take a deep breath." As he opened the passenger door, he sank into the seat and cradled her against him. "I won't leave your side until you're relaxed. Just breathe."

Her tears fell harder. Concern stabbed him, slicing him down deep. How much more could she take in a short period of time? He'd ripped apart her entire world. Yes, to save her. Mostly to avenge Nate, to rail against the injustice of some asshat shooting the only friend he'd let himself have.

Now guilt ripped him a new one.

"I can't." She struggled to inhale, but kept tripping over her tears.

Her sobbing had destabilized her respiratory system. She looked too pale, her eyes too blue in her haunted face. He fucking had to help her.

Joaquin gripped her shoulders. "Baby girl, look at me. Right into my eyes. You have to take a deep breath. Yes . . ." He praised when she finally managed. "Now, let it out and tell me what scared you."

She hid her face in her hands, her shoulders shaking. She cried quietly now, but she still cried all the same. He fucking wished he could take this pain from her. If he'd never crashed into her life and had somehow managed to catch McKeevy and LOSS without destroying her world . . . But then he would never have met Bailey. She wouldn't have had the chance to completely change him the way she had.

Damn it, he was in love with her. Fine fucking time to realize it.

"Bailey?" he prodded softly.

She curled up into a tighter ball and shook her head. "Lock up the house. I'll get myself together."

He hated leaving her for even an instant, but he didn't see a choice.

"I'll be back in less than two minutes. Do you want me to give you my gun?"

Her eyes flew open, filled with terror. "No! Take it. I can't . . . Go."

With a grim nod, Joaquin tucked his gun away, then barreled to the house, where he ensured the back door was secure before he let himself out the front, locking it behind him and depositing the key inside the lockbox again. A glance back to the car proved that she hadn't moved, hadn't really found her way out of shock yet.

Charging back toward her, Joaquin couldn't deny he was happy to leave the house, too. It had an ominous vibe; the tragedy of three senseless deaths still scarred the surfaces and disturbed the air. He had to get Bailey away from this place.

By the time he made his way to her once more, she looked even more pale and troubled. He'd seen enough. "Let's go."

"Wait," she insisted. "I remembered something . . ."

Her body started shaking again. Sandwiched between the seat and the roof of the vehicle, Joaquin had no way to get to her so he flipped the lever that reclined the seat until she lay back nearly supine, then he leaned over her and cupped her cheek. "We don't have to talk about this here."

She nodded vigorously and miserably. "I know what happened to my family."

"You don't have to relive McKeevy coming into the house and shooting your loved ones. I understand."

"But he didn't." She took in a shuddering breath. "M-my father did."

"Viktor Aslanov killed your family? You're saying *he* shot them?"

"Yes. I remember everything now. He told me to hide outside quietly, sing my song in my head, and not come back inside. After that, he hugged me, told me he loved me, then went back inside. I heard gunshots, screaming, then more gunshots. Terrible silence followed. I was frozen. I didn't know what to do. I sat, rocking back and forth. Then McKeevy arrived, wearing some sort of blue military uniform. He busted into the house and yanked my father out, and shoved Viktor into his car. I never saw him again."

Another rough breath later, Joaquin couldn't stand that lost look in her eyes. "Ah, baby girl, I don't know what to say. You lived through hell."

"I lost everyone." She sounded bleak, so alone. New tears fell.

Joaquin knew what it felt like to lose. He remembered the awful night his mother had sat him down and told him that his father had been killed. The shock of it had been like a steel bar to the solar plexus. Numbness, denial, rage . . . He remembered every emotion, every step. He'd been nearly thirteen, old enough to understand the concept of death and the reasons behind his father's ultimate sacrifice. Bailey had been barely five and completely ill-equipped to comprehend death at all, much less that violent tragedy.

When he'd first laid eyes on her, he'd imagined she was a fragile little thing. Now he knew just how damn strong she truly was. He'd crumbled after his father's death, then cut himself off. Somehow, she'd managed to pick up, make a life, grow up a relatively happy kid. Even after losing the people she'd believed had given birth to her she had continued to persevere.

"Not everyone," he swore. "I'm here now. I'm not leaving."

She looked at him with wary eyes, like she didn't quite believe him. And why should she? After everything his sister had said and all he'd admitted, trusting his words would be tough. But he intended to prove himself.

What was he thinking here—something beyond comforting her in this moment? Did he want a girlfriend? A wife? Did he really want to be tied down to one woman?

No, but with Bailey, he didn't look at it as being tied down as much as connected to someone who made a difference in his life. She brought light. She made him feel again. He didn't think he could do without her.

"The thing is . . . Viktor Aslanov taught me that nursery rhyme we were puzzling through earlier. Only me. He told me to hide inside while he"—she took a moment to gather herself again, and he cupped her shoulder to lend support—"went inside and shot the rest of his family. Maybe he knew LOSS was sending someone for him."

Joaquin nodded. "He must have known he couldn't hide indefinitely with a wife and three children. He probably realized they would employ some terrible tactics to get the information they sought, so rather than making his family suffer or letting them use his loved ones' suffering to coerce him, he killed them as humanely as he knew how."

"It seems so surreal. Viktor Aslanov wasn't a violent man. He laughed. He loved. He . . ." Bailey dissolved into tears.

Joaquin felt helpless to ease her burden, and that frustrated him even more. "He was backed into a corner and he did what he thought he had to do, most likely. He probably died with a lot of regrets, but selling information to LOSS that he couldn't or wouldn't deliver had to be the biggest. His last day with all of you must have been so bittersweet."

"He sang that song to me over and over. He made me sing it with him. He told me never to forget it."

"It must mean something."

Bailey nodded, her eyes glassy. She looked so lost. He'd seen similar expressions on people who'd witnessed too much violence or the horrors of war. No wonder she'd had nightmares for so many years.

"I think it must. Sing whatever you can remember to me again."

She groped around for the ball and handed it to him. He bounced the spongy orb against the dashboard. As he caught it, he listened. Bailey closed her eyes, turned inward, and focused. Joaquin didn't interrupt her.

"Hickory in the park. The mouse hides in the dark. At the painted fence, jump three steps left. Follow the path to the sign near the dock." She shrugged. "That's it. I was confused before, but . . . that's it."

"It's a verbal map." He ducked from the SUV and looked around the farm. "I don't see a park, a painted fence, or a dock. If 'hickory' means a hickory tree, I'm not seeing one in this yard."

She scanned her surroundings. "I don't know where we were when he started teaching me the song. I'm exhausted. Maybe if I get some rest and think about it a bit more . . ."

Joaquin just hoped they had the time before McKeevy caught up to them or Bailey broke down. He knew she'd do her best, but the emotional stress she bore was more than almost anyone could take.

"Do you know of any bodies of water nearby that might have a park with a dock?"

She paused, then shook her head in silent misery. Bailey needed a good meal, a glass of wine, a good night's sleep—and for him to hold her. As much as he wanted to find all the answers now, she wasn't trained for missions.

"Let's go. We'll find a detailed map of the area online and see if something rings a bell."

Her shoulders slumped. "I feel like I'm letting you down."

"Oh, you're not, baby girl. Far from it. You pushed yourself today to remember so much. It must have been so difficult, but you kept fighting. I'm really proud of you." He cupped her cheek in his hand. "Let's go find you some real food and a bed to crash in. How does that sound?"

She blinked up at him, her blue stare clinging. "You'll stay with me?"

"Absolutely. Every moment you need me—and probably more than you want." He tucked her into the car, then shut her door and ran to the driver's side, slipping in beside her. "Just lie back and close your eyes. You deserve a break. Once you've rested, we'll come back to this and look at it with fresh eyes. Maybe we're missing something obvious or maybe another memory will jump out at you."

"Maybe." She sounded distant, tired.

Joaquin grabbed her hand and peeled away from the little house filled with hugely horrific memories. As he did, he dialed Sean, intending to let the man in on Bailey's revelations. The phone rang, and Joaquin glanced at the quaint farmhouse in the rearview mirror. He sincerely hoped she never had to come here again. If she did, it would definitely be too soon.

* * *

BAILEY stared out the window of the speeding SUV, watching the scenery slowly morph from rural to suburban. She really had no idea where Joaquin intended to take her. Did it matter?

Numbness dulled her senses, leaving behind only baffled disillusionment and shock. Why hadn't she realized before now that Viktor had killed his own wife and two older children? Had the FBI known and simply chosen to cover up that fact? Bailey wondered what other terrible truths lurked out there for her to recall or stumble onto.

"You want some dinner first? Or do you just want to sleep?"

Before they'd visited her childhood home, she'd been starving. Now she didn't think she could eat a bite.

"A shower."

She wanted to feel clean—not like the girl who'd been sired by a dad crazy or desperate enough to kill his family. That kind of heartbreak usually kicked off the evening news or splashed across the front page of a newspaper. When she'd heard similar endings before, Bailey had always believed the family must have had problems all along. Why hadn't someone seen the signs and found help? Why did people bury their heads in the sand instead? In her case, none of that was true—at least not to her recollection. And she ought to know. All she'd been doing today was resurrecting her long-lost memories. If there had been any strife or violence in her family prior, certainly she would have remembered that today.

"A shower. Sure. Let me put some gas in the car and find a place."

After a brief stop at a filling station, Joaquin ran in to pay cash and peered at his phone. A few moments later, he emerged with a couple of bottles of water in hand. "There's a decent place not far from here. You can clean up, then decide if you want food or sleep."

"You'll need something to eat," she pointed out. Worrying about him was so much easier than thinking about her terrible day.

"I can take care of that later." He reached for her hand. "Right now, I'm here for you to lean on. Whatever you need, okay?"

Bless him, he really had been her pillar today. He hadn't left her side once. Even more, he'd seemed to understand that she couldn't yet talk about what had happened. Bailey almost believed that when she needed an ear later, he'd still be there for her.

Welcome to delusion. Enjoy your stay!

"Thank you." She squeezed his hand. "You didn't exactly sign up for my drama and—"

"You didn't sign up for my abduction. Or for me to force you to acknowledge a whole new identity. Or take you to a BDSM club, introduce you to my sister, spank you . . ." He winced.

In spite of all the strain of the day, his self-deprecation made her smile. "Put that way, you sound like a real Prince Charming."

"I know, right? What can I say?" He shrugged. "I take the notion of sweeping a girl off her feet literally."

She sent him a faint smile. Joining in on his jokes felt far more comfortable than replaying the deaths of her family in her head over and over.

"Maybe you could try a little less hard next time?" she quipped.

"I'm usually a full-throttle guy, but I'll see what I can do."

They rode in silence the rest of the way to a budget chain hotel. Joaquin pulled into the parking lot and left to secure the room, keeping her hidden in the SUV. Bailey stayed behind the tinted windows, wishing she could close her eyes and make the horror of today disappear. Since returning to her childhood home, she'd had a nagging uneasiness she couldn't shake. She stayed alert for anyone around her who looked suspicious.

A family emerged from a minivan, looking road weary. Mom herded the three kids and all their toys toward the entrance while Dad grabbed the luggage.

From inside the hotel, a couple emerged. The woman glanced around clandestinely, then turned to the man. He kissed her passionately. When they broke apart, she looked at her watch and fished into her purse for her keys. She wore a wedding ring. He didn't. They headed toward separate cars. Bailey wondered if that woman's husband had any idea that she had a lover or if he'd been ignoring the signs of problems at home.

Another man in a hoodie parked near the front of the hotel and hopped out of a silver sedan, hands shoved in the jacket's front pockets. Was he the woman's cuckolded husband? Bailey wondered, as he scanned the parking lot. His gaze fell on her for a long, frightening moment. His flat eyes looked dead. Bailey shivered. But he quickly looked away, as if still seeking something or someone. She blew out a sigh of relief.

From inside, Joaquin walked through the double doors and headed to his SUV. "We're around back on the bottom floor. There's also a two-lane road that ends at the interstate, just in case."

She was glad he'd thought of such things. Honestly, all she'd been considering right now was a hot shower and a bar of soap so she could wipe away the grime of the day. Too bad it couldn't remove the stain on her soul.

"Thanks."

With a nod, he started the vehicle and put it in gear. She scanned the area for the man in the hoodie, but he was gone. He'd likely headed into the hotel. With a shrug, she glanced in the other direction and saw the married woman driving away. Her lover stood rooted in place beside his sporty coupe, watching her go. He looked ripped apart.

Bailey suspected she'd feel that way when Joaquin finally realized she'd become attached to him and he walked away.

Sadness dragged her down, even as the day's tumult still stirred her up. This odd jumble of emotions made her feel as if she overflowed with everything bad and wrong in life. She had a dark past, had lived through a lie of a childhood. Why couldn't she have one good thing right now?

Joaquin stopped the SUV in a corner of the lot, parking it as close to the back exit as he could. He handed her a key and picked up the backpack. "Room 192. You unlock the door and let me sweep the room before you go in."

She'd seen this tactic on TV and didn't understand how anyone might have broken into their hotel room, but if it made him feel safer to follow procedure, fine. In fact, given the feeling of uneasiness she couldn't shake, maybe caution was a good thing.

As she approached the door, she glanced around the parking lot, but didn't see anyone, so she shoved the key in the lock. The light turned green, and she heard a little click. Joaquin pushed on the door and extracted his gun from the small of his back, flipping off the safety. Bailey held her breath as he searched every corner, the closet, the bathroom, under the bed.

"The coast is clear." He motioned her inside.

She entered, letting the door shut behind her. He sloughed off the backpack and threw home the deadbolt.

"Take your shower. I'll find the phone book in this joint so I can hunt down something that resembles food."

With a nod, Bailey stumbled into the bathroom. It was utilitarian, but if it had hot water and shampoo, that was all she really needed.

After stripping down, she stood under the hot spray and let it melt her stress. Warmth cascaded over her scalp, through her tresses, rolled down her skin. She grabbed the little bar of soap and glided it over her body, then lathered her hair. In her mind, she did her best to wash away her biological father's terrible act of questionable mercy, the nightmares that had plagued her for years, the uncertainty of not knowing where tomorrow might lead her.

But instead of the choking emotions dissipating, more roared through her. She'd done her best to tamp them down and not fall apart in the car, but now? They rushed her like a tidal wave. All the hurt, confusion, disbelief, and sadness poured in. A trickling of tears sprang free. It became a steady drip, which then turned into a small stream. Finally, the dam of her self-control broke and her tears transformed into a downpour that squeezed her heart until she couldn't breathe or think or move. She couldn't do anything but crumple to the edge of the tub and sob.

Bailey had no idea how long she'd been sitting there, half under the spray of the shower, before Joaquin knocked.

"Baby girl?" he called through the door. "You okay? I've got a line on some good pizza."

She heard the words, wanted to tell him that she couldn't think about food now, but when she opened her mouth, the only thing she managed was to drag in a shuddering breath, then let loose an uncontrollable, heaving sob.

He didn't bother knocking again, just shoved the door wide open and burst into the room. Bailey tried to curl into herself. The sense of vulnerability nicked and sliced her until she felt as if she bled from every inch of her skin. She didn't want him to see her as a victim, a sad case, a tragic girl to pity.

But how else could he possibly see her right now?

Another sob wracked her. He bolted across the tiny bathroom in two big steps and straddled the side of the tub, then wrapped his arms around her and pulled her against his warm body.

"Bailey . . . Don't cry. Oh, baby girl." He cradled her tight. "I'm here."

"I'm b-broken." She managed to shove the words out between tears.

"Never," he swore. "You've had a tough day. I know a lot of men who wouldn't have made it through this shit half as well as you."

Maybe. Bailey didn't know if he spoke the truth, and her brain was too muddled to consider it. She stared at the water pelting the bottom of the tub. Joaquin's big, bare foot was drenched, as was the bottom half of one pant leg. She must be saturating his shirt with her wet skin and sopping hair. Still, he didn't show any signs of leaving her side or saving his clothing from a thorough soaking. He just held her and crooned.

"I can only imagine what you're going through. You've been carrying this secret for so long. To know that it's been locked inside must be terrible."

"I feel . . . I don't know how to put it." She shook her head. "Responsible? But I don't think, at five, I could have stopped what happened."

"No. If Viktor hadn't told you to hide, you would have died that day, too. Either he would have ended you as he did the others or McKeevy would have tortured you to see if you knew anything helpful before he killed you."

Everything he said was true, but that didn't make the words easier to take. "I wish I had been able to tell everyone sooner maybe. I don't know. Done something."

"That wouldn't have changed anything, either. What you wish is that you'd had more power in the situation, both then and now."

Bailey hadn't thought of it like that, but he was right. He understood exactly what she wanted. "Yes. I feel like I've done them a disservice by not speaking the truth sooner. And now I'm so angry with Viktor, LOSS, McKeevy . . ."

"And probably me. I've forced you into this."

"You were trying to save lives. I don't know where I'd be if you hadn't saved mine. Probably dead. And I would never have known the truth. Thank you for being my white knight."

He took her face in his hands and looked down at her as if he wanted to say something. But Bailey saw what she needed in his eyes—his strength, his comfort, his sense of right. For the first time, she knew what it was like to choose someone with her heart. She couldn't change either set of her parents or the way those relationships had ended. She'd drifted through a lot of friends, too. In retrospect,

Bailey figured that she'd cleaved onto Blane because he'd been funny, interesting, and so helpful with dance. But Joaquin . . . He filled her heart like no one ever had.

No denying that she loved him.

He might stay tomorrow—but probably not. She couldn't control that. All she could do was be with him now. He was a balm to her battered soul. He was the warmth that chased the chill from her heart. He made her feel alive, and she needed that so badly right now.

"Will you kiss me?" she breathed.

He pressed his lips to hers softly, lingering for just a moment before he pulled back.

Bailey wanted more. She wrapped her arms around his neck and opened her lips to him, plunging her tongue inside.

Joaquin tensed and pulled back. "Bailey, you need food and sleep."

"I don't."

"You're upset. I won't take advantage of you."

She loved his sense of right and wrong. It might be skewed to some people, but she understood. For him, the righteous end could justify the terrible means. He wasn't the kind of man to kidnap her lightly. Just like he wasn't the sort to take from her when he thought she couldn't spare anything to give.

"You're not. I'm asking you to fill me up with your touch, your affection. Replace all these bad memories with something good. Help me."

He frowned, his stare contemplative as he delved deep into her eyes. Finally, he rose and leaned over her, cutting off the shower. Then he helped her onto the bath mat and wrapped a towel around her, squeezing the water from her hair before it dripped on the floor.

Gently, he yanked on the strands falling down her back. "I don't have any condoms in the room. I picked some up today, but they're in the car. If this is what you really want, I'll go get them."

He should. She should let him.

"No." The word slipped out.

Bailey couldn't imagine letting him out of her sight. She couldn't be parted from him for even a moment. It wasn't logical. Then again, desperation wasn't. She needed to feel him in the most elemental way, man to woman, natural and real.

Nothing between them.

"I don't want you to wear one."

He hesitated. "Bailey, I don't think—"

She lunged up and melded her lips to his, her hands tearing into his jeans. She didn't want to think right now. She didn't want him to think, either. She simply wanted to feel. So what if she was reckless? Everything else in her life had gone to hell through no fault of her own. Just one moment with him. A pure connection no one could erase, something she'd never forget. Was that asking for too much?

He pulled back and gripped her wrists before she could lower his zipper. "I want you, too. So damn badly. When I sank deep inside you, the feel of you around me with no barriers was the most pleasure I've ever felt. I'd give anything to have that again. But if you got pregnant?"

Joaquin opened his mouth as if he had more to say, but she cut him off. "I know. I just don't care right now. My entire day has been surrounded by death. I have to feel alive. I don't want to feel latex. I need to feel *you*. You keep saying you'll be here for me. Do it. Please . . ."

His fingers tightened on her as he scanned her face. She saw the moment he chose to give in, and elation spiked, sizzling up her blood.

"Fuck," he muttered, then lifted her into his arms, carrying her out of the bathroom.

Seconds later, he dropped her to the mattress. Before she even stopped bouncing, he gripped her thighs and tugged, pulling her down to the edge of the bed and spreading her legs wide. With jerky movements, he tore off his T-shirt and knelt. Bailey barely had time to guess his intent before he fitted his lips over her pussy and swiped his tongue through her moist flesh, flattening his tongue over her clit.

She cried out at the instant jolt of sensation. But he didn't let up. Instead, Joaquin opened her wider and ate her like he was starved for the taste of her. All gusto, he knew exactly where and how to focus his tongue to make every nerve in her sex flare to life.

She looked down her body, watching his dark head work between her legs. As if he sensed her, he opened his eyes and snared her gaze. His mouth on her sex, his stare connected to hers—it had to be the most erotic thing she'd ever seen. A fresh flare of arousal lit up her system.

"Pinch your nipples. Let me see you do it," he demanded, nipping her thigh.

Bailey flushed. She'd never been one to touch her breasts during masturbation, but knowing he'd be looking at the way she manhandled the little nubs, hoping it would drive him mad . . . she couldn't wait.

Without hesitation, she gripped her nipples between thumb and forefinger and squeezed. The instant tingle shocked her, licking a line of fire down to her clit. Joaquin groaned and ratcheted up the heat by laving her little bud of nerves at a voracious, insatiable pace.

Under his touch, her chilled skin burned. Her tense body melted into the bed. Her empty heart filled. Joaquin could be dangerous, remote, difficult. But he wasn't irresponsible. If this man was willing to risk the sort of permanent connection with her that came from creating life, he must have feelings for her, too.

"That's it," he coached. "Harder. Make your nipples red. Make me die to take them in my mouth."

His words alone nearly made her whimper. She knew nothing but him and did as he'd bid, blinking down at him as he sucked her clit into his mouth and made her squirm with need.

A squeeze, a tug, a twist, she could feel her hard tips gathering blood and swelling as he nipped at her, the slight edge of his teeth grazing her most sensitive spot. She gasped and instinctively gripped the crests of her breasts harder. He pulled her flesh into his mouth again, this time giving her a little more bite. Her breath shuddered. When she twisted her nipples this time, the tiny bit of delicious soreness roused a whole new level of desire. How good would it feel if he sucked the tips into his hot mouth and worked them more? How hard would she come once he shoved his stiff length inside her and rode her to orgasm?

Once more, he trapped her clit between his teeth—not hard, but enough to make her yelp. As soon as the sting of pain dissolved, pleasure roared in. Her blood began to boil. Sensations gathered and knotted between her legs. She knew this feeling. He alone had given it to her before.

"Joaquin?"

"Hold on, baby girl. I'm not done tormenting you."

"But—"

"Who do you belong to right now?"

Bailey hesitated, trying to find her brain. He lowered his head and licked her, avoiding the one sensitive spot that would send her over the edge.

"Who?" he barked.

"You," she managed to breathe out.

"That's right. So you'll wait."

She twisted, trying to deal with her needy body and the relentless ache he'd created. Instinctually, she cupped her breasts and gave her nipples another vicious tug. Joaquin fingered her clit again and watched her, his eyes burning, vowing without a word to give her the kind of ecstasy that would blow her mind. As soon as he touched her, the orgasm loomed closer, taking over her body, an urgent swell of desire she wasn't sure she could delay.

She mewled and writhed, her legs falling open and begging him to fill her. He gripped her hips with biting fingers and devoured her with his greedy tongue again, quickly dismantling her self-control.

"So swollen. You want this." It wasn't a question. He knew it as fact.

"Yes. Please. Now."

Some vague part of her registered that she was pleading with him for sex. She sounded wanton and desperate—and she really didn't care. As long as he satisfied the ache, as long as he became one with her tonight and filled up all the dark, empty spaces in her body and heart, nothing else mattered.

He gave her a low, seductive groan. "I love the sound of you begging, baby girl. Now I'm ready to hear you scream."

Chapter Fifteen

BAILEY hadn't even processed his words before he rose to his feet, pushed her farther up the bed, tore open his fly, and shoved his pants down. His cock sprang free, thick and purple and ready. He took hold of her hips, bracing himself. With all his breath, he thrust forward and filled her, stretching her sensitive tissue, scraping every aching nerve. Her flesh tingled with both the pain and the pleasure of his sudden invasion. She gasped, dug her nails into his shoulder, and threw her head back.

"Look at me. Come!" he growled in her ear.

Their stares locked, and she lost herself in his hazel eyes as she splintered apart. Her heartbeat thumped against her ribs, roared in her ears. Every muscle in her body seized up. She stopped breathing, stopped thinking of everything except Joaquin. She cried out his name as she clamped down on his cock. A feral groan erupted from his lips as he pumped her furiously, prolonging the flare of ecstasy into something close to agony, so sharp and acute. Her keening cry filled the room, bounced off the walls, rang in her ears.

"Fuck, yes," he encouraged on a long growl.

Under him she bucked and lifted. The explosion of bliss unraveled her entirely. She closed her eyes, savoring the hard rush into climax.

"No, look at me." He reached up and tugged on her wet hair.

Obediently, she opened her eyes again. This time, the connection shifted something in her heart. It wasn't just love, but possession. Every instinct told her that Joaquin was claiming her as his for all time. Bailey willingly gave herself over. She'd never experienced a man so intense, so bent on justice . . . so perfect for her.

But from now on, he was hers, too. She'd fight for him. She'd die for him. He would complete her. He would be the one she built a new family with.

Maybe starting tonight.

The thought tripped another zip of need inside her, which he kindled with every demanding thrust into her body, sending her over the edge once more.

Pleasure drugged her veins. She softened like melted butter all around him. Her sigh of joy, coupled with her half-drunk smile, probably looked goofy. But in that moment, she couldn't have held her delight in for any reason. He made her sublimely happy.

Bailey had barely begun to relax when Joaquin withdrew and slammed her mouth with a hard kiss, dipping inside like a man starving for her taste. His urgency awakened hers again, and she kissed him back with all the passion only he roused.

"I need you. I have to . . . Damn it. Tell me if I'm too rough."

Without any idea what he sought, she let him have his way. Bailey trusted him. He might not be perfect. She might not agree with his methods all the time. But he'd never hurt her on purpose.

"Yes."

He sent her a primal snarl before he flipped her onto her belly and shoved his arm around her waist. With a tug, he pulled her onto her hands and knees, supporting her middle with the width of his steely forearm. A moment later, the head of his cock probed her entrance, found her wet flesh parting willingly for him, then thrust deep.

She screamed. In this position, her passage felt more narrow. He took up every ounce of space in her pussy—and then some.

"Did I hurt you?"

Was he kidding? "No." She could barely catch her breath, but who cared when he delivered that much pleasure? "It's amazing."

"You feel so fucking good," he groaned, reaching up to pluck at her sensitive nipples.

The touch shocked her system and replaced her sated heaven with the enslaving grip of desire again. How could he do this to her so quickly? So easily?

She hadn't even answered that question before he upped the stakes, leaning over her back and sliding his hand up her breast, over her collarbones, affixing his fingers around her chin. He tilted her head back and ground into her sex with short, deep strokes that sent off another violent wave of tingles.

"You're like the drug I can't get enough of. When I'm not inside you, all I can think about is fucking you. When I am, I don't think of anything but filling you completely and owning you."

His words made her shudder as he drove her into a spiral of panting, reckless desire. No denying that his possessive grip made her feel as if she was his completely. She'd never felt anything like it and knew down to her bones that only he could take her here.

Beneath his body, Bailey wriggled, gyrating with him. Together, they found a rhythm. A tilt of her hips as he pulled back dragged his steely length over all the nerves that made her gasp and claw the cheap comforter. She shoved back onto him as he plunged into her with a harsh grunt. Over and over and over, a seemingly endless rhythm. Bailey lost all sense of time, the world around them, even her next breath. All she needed was Joaquin. The way he dragged his sweat-slick chest over her back as he fucked his way even farther inside her with every thrust stunned her. She heard thunder in her ears, saw stars behind her eyes. Damn it, the heavens parted.

Her body jerked with anguished bliss, and she came apart again with a scream.

Joaquin cried out—the sound somewhere between shock and

sensual pain. He lost his rhythm. She lost her mind. Together, they soared into the euphoria of wrenching climax. A wet splash scalded her insides, and Bailey felt him coat her with his seed.

The thought of conceiving should have terrified her. Ballerinas who had babies usually kissed their careers good-bye. She'd worked her whole life to be the best. Already, she knew she stood a great chance of being chosen for more than a minor part at her audition next week—if she could, in fact, go.

Somehow, none of that seemed as important as having this man and the product of their love to share her life with.

Thoughts like that were so dangerous, but if he avoided being close to everyone, as Kata said, why was he here, risking the possibility that she might have his child? She had to hope that somewhere deep inside Joaquin's heart, he wanted more out of life now than to roam it in lonely solitude. She had to hope that he could love her, too.

* * *

AN hour later, they sat in bed, eating pizza. Joaquin grinned as he reached for another piece and bit off a huge chunk of cheese. "Favorite memory?"

Bailey thought for a moment, then giggled. "When I was about eight, my adoptive mom found a rescue dog named Beau. He was a little dachshund-terrier mix. He was definitely my dad's dog, always trying to be a man's man, despite how little he was.

"One time, my dad moved the barbeque under the overhang near the kitchen because it started raining. The house had two sliding glass doors to the yard, and one was just off the breakfast nook. So my dad was standing there grilling next to the glass doors, right? My mom loved cactus plants. She had a whole bunch of them along that glass door. Beau raised his front paws up onto the glass to be closer to my dad, but then he couldn't get down on his own. He ended up straddling the cactus. I was upstairs doing homework and my mom was in the laundry room. Next thing we know, we heard this huge yelp and came running. Beau was doing his best to stand on his tippy-toes over this big, round cactus plant, poor baby. It wouldn't be funny except . . . my dad had to use a pair of tweezers and get all the stickers out of the dog's underbelly and guy parts. He spent an hour consoling the dog, while trying not to howl with laughter." She frowned. "I think that's one of the few times I remember my adopted dad seeming like he was happy. It wasn't the best day of my life, but something that always makes me smile. What about you?"

His grin widened to a teeth-flashing smile. "When I was fifteen and had my first real girlfriend, we had this big date planned. She was a year older than me, and I won't lie: I was hoping to get lucky. I wanted to look good for this girl, so I washed everything I intended to wear that night. I also did a load of whites so I'd have clean underwear."

Bailey laughed out loud. "Eager, were you?"

"Stupidly so."

"Anyway, Kata had a new red shirt and wanted to play a prank on me, so she sneaked into the laundry room and slipped her shirt into that load, which I'd washed in hot water. Let me just also say that I'd decided that I should wash every pair of underwear I owned that day."

Bailey's jaw dropped. "So they all came out pink?"

"Oh, yeah. Like a weird, vivid tie-dyed pink. I wanted to kill her. Sometimes, I think it's a miracle she made it to adulthood."

"So did you get lucky that night?"

"No." And he still sounded sulky about it.

With an indulgent laugh, peace settled into Bailey. She and Joaquin talked not like people escaping a dangerous murderer together while hunting priceless information, but simply like lovers enjoying each other's company. Again, that sense of perfection and rightness seeped into her veins. Never in her life had she ever felt like she truly belonged anywhere or with anyone. But Bailey knew at a deep, visceral level that she belonged with this man. She wanted to tell him that—and admit she loved him. She didn't do it. Had she ever said those three words to someone as anything more than a passing joke?

If so, she didn't remember it.

"Worst memory?" she asked him, wondering if he'd open up.

He lowered his piece of pizza and turned his thoughts inward. "The death of my father was probably it for the longest time. I remember seeing him that morning before he left for work. He ruffled my head and told me that my sugary breakfast cereal would rot my teeth. He was drinking coffee, which I told him would rot his brain. It was one of our rituals. Hearing the news of his death that evening was hard, but surreal, you know? It really hit me the next morning when I poured my cereal that he'd never again tell me not to eat it. I shoved it all in the trash and went to my room and punched my pillow until my knuckles were bruised. But I never ate that cereal again."

Bailey's heart broke for the little boy who had idolized his fallen dad. In some ways, she'd been lucky to be too young to truly remember the family that had been taken from her. The memories she'd recovered earlier today had been the first to make her feel any connection to the Aslanovs. She'd realized that they'd truly loved one another. She'd experienced her first sense of loss for no longer having them in her life.

Joaquin remembered every moment of his heartache. She reached out to caress his shoulder and kiss the corner of his lips. He tasted faintly of pepperoni. She met his stare, certain that her expression would tell him that he'd become her moon and her stars.

Bailey held her breath, wondering if he'd try to disconnect. Was their intimacy now simply too much for him to handle? To her shock, he leaned in closer and layered his mouth over hers softly, lingering for a long minute.

"You're easy to talk to, even about my dad. You understand."

"I do. You loved him. The loss was difficult."

He shrugged. "You lost a lot more. Today seemed really hard on you. I'm so proud of you for pushing through. So many memories rushed back to you. Were you surprised?"

"Completely. But it was as if driving up to the little farmhouse unlocked some key in my head. The dreams I'd had for so long merged with the actual memories I'd hidden away. Suddenly, I had all the pieces of the puzzle. I didn't expect that."

"I think a lot of people would have just lost it at that point. But you didn't dissolve into tears, just soldiered on."

"I've got to. If I want a future, then I have to dig all this up. So . . . I guess we need to try to figure out where the rhyme Viktor taught me might be referring to. I wish he'd put something in the words themselves to give me a clue."

"What he gave you was already a lot for a five-year-old to remember. He had to have known that. Do you remember if he sang that rhyme to you all your life? Or do you remember when he taught it to you?"

Nipping at her lip, Bailey considered the question. "I remember he sang it a lot the night before all the bad stuff. That morning, too." She frowned, trying to sharpen fuzzy memories, but it was like looking at a series of snapshots or short home movies depicting various moments. "When we sang the song those last few hours, I already knew it. I remember being excited to show him how well I remembered it."

"So it wasn't completely new?" Joaquin leaned closer to her. As he propped his arm over his bent knee, the blanket barely covered his hair-dusted thighs and his cock pooling low in the space between his legs.

Bailey tried not to be distracted, but he was so gorgeous, so male, it was impossible.

"No." She managed to drag her thoughts into the conversation—mostly by jerking her stare down to the piece of cooling pizza in her hand.

"Do you remember if he took you anywhere before that? Do you remember a time when he might have shown you the dock or the painted fence? Or ever demonstrated how to find the 'mouse' he talked about?"

Wasn't that the question of a lifetime—literally? She blew out a breath and set her half-eaten slice of pie back in the box. Closing her eyes, she tried to think back, grab any memory that snagged her attention. They seemed awfully random. Mikhail putting a little toy truck down the toilet and clogging up the plumbing. Annika trying to help their mother cook and burning her hand on hot grease, requiring a trip to the emergency room. Her mother complaining about having to stay in a tent on a camping trip . . .

"That's it!" She sat up and blinked Joaquin's way in excitement. "We went camping. I don't know exactly when or where, but I remember my dad getting this idea that we needed a family vacation and packing everyone up in the car suddenly. My mother wasn't the sort to 'rough it,' but Viktor wouldn't hear of hotels on an outdoor excursion, so we bought a tent and took it from location to location. It wasn't ridiculously hot or cold, so I'm guessing it was either spring or fall." She tried to latch on to one of the memories swirling through her brain. "I think fall. I remember looking at big golden leaves at one of our campsites. Anyway, one morning, my dad took me fishing. I remember it now because my brother wanted to go and threw a hissy that my dad wouldn't take him."

"What else do you remember?"

She bit her lip. "We went to a lake, maybe." Bailey shook her head, wishing the details weren't so fuzzy. "We parked and got out. I remember being excited to be alone with my dad. That almost never happened. But then when he opened the back of the car, he didn't have any fishing equipment, just a shovel." The memory became sharper, and she sank into it, recalling more. "I was confused by that. When I asked, Viktor said he wanted to play a game instead." The last of the recollection buzzed through her brain, almost knocking the breath from her lungs. “He wanted to hide something and show me how to find it. Oh my goodness . . .”

“That’s it, baby girl.” Joaquin cupped her shoulders, seemingly to steady her, provide support. “Tell me everything you remember.”

“We’d been camping for a few days already. It seems like we were moving somewhere new every day. We’d drive for hours. My dad would say he was going for a walk by himself, then he’d come back and . . . It seemed like nothing happened until the day he said he wanted to fish. That morning, we didn’t pack up and drive somewhere else. Instead, Viktor woke me up early, and we drove away together. We didn’t travel long before he parked, then we walked. He helped me climb a fence that had been painted green, I think. People had carved their initials into it and someone had painted over it again. Viktor stopped there and started singing to me. He wanted me to sing with him. I remember jumping left three times from the fence post over and over until I fell down giggling.”

“Then what?”

“We trekked a dirt path. He pointed out a sign to me about no lifeguard being on duty, then he dug a hole in the dirt and . . .”

“And?” Joaquin quizzed.

“I don’t know. The memory just stops there. Viktor presumably buried something, but I don’t know what or where that scene might have taken place. I don’t even know if that’s really a memory of him hiding the research.”

He cupped her face. “One thing I suspect? He taught you the rhyme because he already had a plan and had decided to spare you. So he showed you exactly how to find his legacy when you were grown. That way, you could preserve it.”

“Why not my older brother or sister? He can’t have been sure I would remember any of this.”

“We’ll never know,” Joaquin said sadly. “It’s possible he couldn’t bring himself to shoot someone so young. Or maybe he thought

LOSS would never believe you'd know anything about his work and would leave you alone. I've looked at a few of the records. Your brother struggled in school."

"Russian was his first language. I don't think he spoke much English before he went to school. When I was little, my birth parents spoke mostly English. I remember my mother saying it would be better for us kids. But she hated the language." In fact, Bailey remembered her mother tsking in the kitchen at what a silly language it was.

"And your sister's aptitude was largely in dance, according to what I've seen."

"Yeah. Even at seven, her dance instructors oohed and aahed about her abilities. I went to the same dance school. They weren't nearly as excited about me."

"Looks like they were off base about that," Joaquin pointed out. "But your school records indicate you were the one who did best in English-language organized academic settings. Maybe that's why. Maybe he thought that someday, when you remembered his nursery rhyme and put everything together, you'd decipher his research or continue it."

Bailey shrugged. "And maybe we're crediting a very desperate man with a lot more rational thought than he actually had."

"Like I said earlier, we'll never know."

She shook her head. That made her sad all over again. "So now what? We know the rhyme wasn't referring to any location near the house."

"And that's why the FBI never found anything on the premises. They believe LOSS looked, too, because the crime scene was contaminated and the house trashed when the sheriff arrived. Sean said the FBI speculates that, after taking your father from the house, LOSS searched it from top to bottom. They believe that the sheriff arriving sooner than expected stopped the hunt, but after the murder scene had been cleared, they came back. Your aunt in Russia hired someone to clean it up and try to restore it as much as possible. The company reported that it had been 'vandalized.' But the walls lacked any sort of graffiti, as you'd expect if the culprits had been bored teenagers. They also didn't find any drug paraphernalia, like you might find with addicts."

"It's probably safe to say that LOSS didn't find anything there."

"Right." He sighed. "Do you remember anything you saw on this vacation with your family? Any landmarks?"

"So far, no. I'll keep trying. What will we do if we actually find the research? How does having it stop them from coming after me?"

"I think we have to take a page from Sean's book and be very visible and vocal about the fact that we've found what your father left and given it to the feds. Whatever we have to say to get these people off your back. I'm sure Sean and Callie will help."

She nodded. If they found her father's mysterious research that so many had killed and died for, Callie would absolutely try to help. Sean had worked this case when he'd been an FBI agent. He knew the stakes. He'd jump in, too. It felt good to have friends.

Bailey pondered the family camping trip, her past, her future . . . and the man in front of her, as she ate more pizza. Funny, she hadn't eaten this stuff in two years. It was better than she remembered. Or maybe it just seemed that way because she ate it wrapped in nothing but a sheet while in bed with the man she loved.

He polished off another piece, then wiped off his hands. "Feeling any better? Tired?"

"Strangely happy," she admitted. "I like being here with you." She felt herself blush, then smiled. "But I'm also scared. How long can we search for something I may never remember how to find? What if we can't find it? How long until someone catches up with us?"

Joaquin shoved the pizza box out of the way, then dragged her against him. "We'll figure that out if it happens."

"I can't expect you to give up your life for a month or six or—"

"I believe in you. You're smart. You've made tremendous progress already, just in the past two days. I have no doubt it will come back to you. Relax. Be patient with yourself."

Bailey tried to follow his advice. She closed her eyes, took a deep breath, and melted against him. Desperately, she tried to clear her head, scuttle her anxiety, and let the memories surface.

Nothing.

"You're still tense," he pointed out.

"I need answers now. Later might not help me. McKeevy will probably be trying to kill me later. So waiting isn't really an option."

"I'm going to protect you," he swore. "We're in this together."

"Why?" She stared into his hazel eyes, seeking an answer. "I don't mean to sound ungrateful. You've definitely saved my life and helped me piece together a lot of my past that I'd been unable to figure out on my own. I appreciate it, but . . ." She paused, looking for the right words to explain. "You didn't know me four days ago. Saving me cost you your job. I know you prefer to be alone, so this constantly babysitting me has to be a pain in your ass."

Joaquin pulled her into his lap and wrapped his arms around her. "You didn't cost me my job. I was pursuing this case even before I knew your name. I didn't have any plans to stop, no matter what it cost me. I . . ." He grimaced, then cursed under his breath.

"You weren't going to let more women die so horrifically, I know. Your selfless sense of justice is one of the things I really admire about you."

"Wanting justice served for those victims he tortured and killed because he sought Tatiana Aslanov wasn't really the reason I saved you. I had a friend." He sighed heavily. "His name was Nate, a private investigator, but we met in the police academy."

Bailey watched him struggle for his next words. Whatever he was trying to say caused him a great deal of pain. It creased his forehead and clouded his eyes.

"Tell me," she murmured.

"Kata wasn't wrong when she said that I pulled away from my family after my dad's death. I spent a lot of years wondering what the point of family and friends was. Eventually, you'd just have to endure the fucking terrible tragedy of losing them. In my head, the fewer people I gave a shit about, the less I'd have to hurt."

"But you have a mother and two sisters who love you. I'd give anything to have what you don't want."

"And I never considered it from that perspective until you. I'd convinced myself I was just fine, that I was keeping life simple, that my family had moved on without me. Nate was the first person I cared about since my father. We were pretty good buddies. We drank together, did our share of barhopping. We trained together, became beat officers together. I never really realized how much he meant to me until one of McKeevy's victims hired him. She feared she was being followed—and she was, by the long arm of LOSS. And as soon as Nate stumbled onto the truth, they broke into his house and double-tapped him in the head. After my shock wore off, an absolute cold fury set in. I'm not sure I've moved past that."

Bailey's heart went out to him. "How long has it been?"

"Less than a week."

She reared back and stared at him in stupefied shock. "I'm so sorry. You've been dealing with so much. The death, the danger . . . the long-lost orphan you had to babysit. You haven't had time to grieve."

"I don't think I really ever do." He sighed. "I just shove it down."

Bailey hadn't thought she could be shocked again, but Joaquin proved her wrong. "Did you ever cry for your father?"

"No. I wanted to a few times, but I stopped myself. I had to be the man of the house. My mom didn't need more children, much less a baby."

"Are you kidding me? Crying doesn't make you a baby. I sobbed for weeks after my adoptive parents supposedly died. I stopped going to college and barely went to rehearsal. Heck, I hardly left my house for what seemed like months. Does that make me a baby? And don't you dare tell me that it's okay for me to cry because I'm female."

His sheepish expression told her he'd been ready to respond with an answer like that. "I guess I've always seen emotions as a weakness. I'm all . . . up in the air about Nate's death. I couldn't go to his funeral because I was trying to keep you from being the next victim. It was a guilty relief. I also know Nate would have approved. He always sacrificed to do what he could for others. That's one thing I always admired about him."

"Was he married?"

"No. A loner like me."

A frown wrinkled her brow. "Why?"

He looked puzzled. "I don't know. He never told me his life story. We survived the academy together, drank, and chased skirts. I didn't let myself get close to anyone. We didn't talk or bond or become besties. We just . . . understood one another."

Bailey didn't think that sounded like much of a friendship, but who was she to judge? She only knew lots about Blane because he was an open book. He only knew stuff about her because he'd mercilessly pried it out of her. Maybe she'd shut a lot of people out in her life, too. But she wouldn't do it anymore, not when she could see a future and a family in front of her with this man, if she could just get behind his protective walls and convince him to let go of his grief.

"I'm sorry you lost him." She hugged him and rubbed her cheek to his, reveling in his scratchy-soft stubble. "I'm here if you ever want to talk about him or your dad, your sister or whatever. You've been here for me, especially today."

"You're not mad that I took you away from your life because of Nate? You don't feel as if I did it for revenge?"

Bailey shrugged. She could see how some people might interpret his actions that way, but she knew that under his anger at Nate's death, he was the sort of man who wanted to stop the murders. He really did want to save people. Now she just had to show him that he didn't have to stand apart as he did it.

She leaned forward and pressed a kiss to his lips. It felt good. Right. As she pulled away, she smiled at him. "You know, we're kind of good for one another. You helped me find the truth about myself. And I pried your secrets from you."

"Yeah, then you encourage me to cry," he quipped. "Great."

She winced. "I know that might not seem like a bonus to you. But really, you might not be able to move forward until you get it all out. I'll even be happy to dry your tears."

He rolled his eyes. "If you have to do that, I might as well hand over my man card."

"You'd never have to do that in my book. You are *plenty* of man."

Joaquin gave her a proud little grin, then it fell to a crooked scowl as he stared at the skin just under her chin. He swiped a finger across a tender spot. "I left a little bruise on you. Jesus, I'm sorry if I was too harsh. I get around you and I lose all my fucking finesse. Next time, if I hurt you, I expect you to say something."

Next time? He expected they'd be in bed together again? What if they found Viktor's research soon? Would that be the end of them? Or was he just as addicted as she was?

"Well, I know another way you could guarantee your man card with me."

He raised a dark brow at her. "What's that?"

"Why don't you show me again how much man you are?" Bailey tossed off her sheet and lay back on the bed, blinking up at him with a sultry glance.

Chapter Sixteen

JOAQUIN sucked in a breath, his entire body tensing. His cock certainly stood, loud and proud, ready to go again. He'd had her an hour ago, tops. He wasn't seventeen anymore. Yeah, he liked sex, but with the nature of his job, he'd gone without more often than not. So his obsession with Bailey made almost no sense . . . and he didn't really care. It felt good. He wanted more of her. He didn't want her feeling undesirable if he said no. *Right, like that would ever happen.*

Flinging his own sheet off, he revealed just how much she aroused him, stroking his length lazily with one hand. "This manly enough for you?"

She pretended to ponder him, but he heard her breath hitch and shallow, and he hid his smile. "I don't know. Seeing you isn't the same thing as feeling you. How do I know you'd be half as good for the second time tonight?"

He liked her hint of tease. "You know, you might have a point. You'd be far more convinced of my abilities if I did more than stroke my cock. Let's see . . . How would you like me to prove myself?"

Bailey pursed her lush mouth. "I have an idea or two."

"I have more ideas than that," he promised, abandoning his erection to stroke her nipple instead. "Wanna see?"

"Hmm, maybe." She looked up at him with those hungry blue eyes that damn near dismantled his self-control. Her hair spilled around her in a pale, golden-brown cloud, and he almost mounted and impaled her in a single breath. "I might have to hear them first."

"I'd rather surprise you. Will you trust me? Please."

She didn't hesitate. "Yes."

Joaquin was even more relieved to see that she immediately grasped the shift from playful to serious. He cupped her face. "I'd never hurt you."

"I know."

"I want to . . . explore with you." He wasn't sure how else to say that he wanted to try so much of what he'd seen at Dominion with her—and a million other things he hadn't yet dreamed up. If a way to give her pleasure existed, he wanted to be the man who gave it to her.

"You mean tonight, because we have hours to kill and TV is boring?"

"No, that's not what I mean." Joaquin gentled his expression. He'd felt a whole lot of determination to fuck her, but he understood why she needed to believe what they shared was far more. "You've got something I can't resist. I don't know what this is or where it's going, but I know I couldn't leave your side right now for anything. I wouldn't want to."

Tears welled in her eyes. Then she bestowed the most dazzling smile on him, so happy and radiant. "That's how I feel, too. Bet you never thought you'd wind up in something more than a fling when you took me from Houston."

He snorted. "Hell, I never thought I'd even have a fling from this situation. Sex was the last thing on my mind, until I saw you dance."

She frowned up at him. "When did you see that?"

"The night I abducted you. You danced around your living room and—"

"Oh my gosh! Where were you, peeking in my window?"

"Inside the armoire, with my knees crouched up around my ears."

"Holy crap, that's a small space."

"You're telling me. It only got smaller as my cock got harder."

Bailey didn't hide her laugh. "Really?"

"You think that's funny?" he challenged her.

"Maybe a little." But her eyes danced as if picturing him cramped up in a small space and fighting a hard-on amused the hell out of her.

"You know, I can't exactly prove my masculinity if you're giggling at me. That kind of disrespect deserves a little punishment, I think."

The smile slipped off her face. "Punishment?"

He nodded and sat on the edge of the bed, patting his thigh. "Put yourself over my lap, ass in the air, baby girl. I didn't get to finish my spanking last time we tried this. And you didn't give me an honest response."

She bit her lip and squirmed, pressing her thighs together. Now that Joaquin knew what to look for, he realized that she hadn't been frightened by him previously. She'd been shocked by her arousal. It had startled and possibly shamed her. This time would be different.

"Bailey . . ." He grabbed her chin gently. "Do it or say your safe word. It's 'red,' remember?"

She nodded. Her breathing turned choppy. "Yeah."

"You need to pick. If you're having trouble sorting through your thoughts, talk to me so we can come to an answer together."

Bailey licked her bottom lip, and Joaquin made a mental note to see what that mouth felt like wrapped around his cock soon. For now, he waited patiently, damn near holding his breath. This would be a good test to determine how much she really trusted him in bed.

Finally, she sat up, then crawled across the bed, approaching on his left. "Help me? I don't want to do it wrong."

"There's no wrong, but I'll always help you."

He took her by the waist and helped her across his lap. Once she was facedown, her ass directly in his line of vision, Joaquin lost himself in her scent, the warmth of her body across his bare legs, the spill of her silky hair toward the floor, and her pert butt so taut and small right in front of him. His hand would cover more than one cheek at a time. That fascinated him, as did the pale pink of her skin, her slender thighs parting restlessly, her erratic breathing.

"Joaquin?"

Petting a hand over her butt, then down a thigh, he silently comforted her. "Tell me, are you green right now?"

"Like traffic light green? Yes."

"Good. Let me have my way with you now. If it's too much, you know how to stop me." When she nodded, he tugged on her hair, gently lifting her head. "Did you mean to say something to me?"

"Yes."

He knew he should let go of her hair, but he liked the feel of it too much. Instead, he released the tension just slightly, then smoothed his left hand down the curve on her ass. "God, this is turning me the fuck on. Do you like having your hair pulled?"

"I do," she breathed out.

"Do you like being over my lap?"

"Yes." Her voice became something closer to a whimper.

That turned him the fuck on, too. He swallowed. "Do you want me to spank you?"

She paused, and the silence ticked on. "Um . . ."

"It's a yes-or-no question, Bailey. Just be honest."

"It's hard."

Joaquin could feel how badly she didn't want to answer him. "Because you're worried that saying no will disappoint or upset me? It won't. I came on too strong the first time. I didn't have your consent. We didn't have a safe word. I wasn't in control. I want to do this again, but the right way."

"I even liked it the first time," she finally admitted. "I told you I didn't because I was embarrassed. Who gets off on being smacked by the guy who kidnapped her? I didn't understand why I was that girl."

"There's always been a crazy chemistry between us, baby girl. It's feeling a lot like there always will be. We can't do this right if we're not honest. So you just have to tell me . . . green or red?"

She dragged in a shuddering breath. "Green. I want this. I want it a lot."

And Joaquin couldn't even begin to describe how thrilled he was that she enjoyed one of his kinks of choice. "You got it. I want this a lot, too."

Then he didn't bother saying anything more, just raised his arm and brought it down again, using the pull of gravity more than any real force. As he stared at her ass, a faint handprint appeared—then disappeared almost as quickly. He did the same thing to the other cheek with the same result. Hmm, he didn't want to truly hurt her, but this mild paddling wasn't floating his boat.

"Did that sting?"

"A little." But her tone said she'd really felt *very* little—and probably wanted more.

"Did you like it better this time or last? Remember, be honest."

"The last time."

"Me, too. I'll try again."

Quickly, he raised his arm again. This time, he lowered it with a whoosh he could almost hear. The sizzle of his hand striking her skin burned a hundred times hotter. The gasp of her little bite of pain got him a hundred times harder. The print of his hand on her pretty, pale ass looked a hundred times more vivid.

"*That's* what I'm talking about." Satisfaction poured through him. She looked fucking fine with his mark on her. "Bailey?"

"Yes." Her high-pitched reply told him he'd given her what she wanted, too. "Please more."

"My pleasure."

Joaquin let the blows fall, one after the other, in a savage but steady rhythm all over her upturned backside until it turned bright pink, then rosy, then vivid red. He stopped for a moment, tearing himself from the hazy fog of his desire. Every time he spanked her, his head swelled with the most amazing feeling, as if he was all-powerful and linked into this one woman. This time, he swore he could read her mind.

Just to be sure, he hesitated and listened to her choppy breathing, watched the flush of arousal crawl up her back. He tugged on her hair and turned her head to the side, leaning over until he looked into her eyes. Dazed, glassy, utterly aroused. With a smile, he dipped his fingers between her slender thighs and into the well of her pussy. Soaking wet. *Perfect.*

He tried to calm his own labored breathing, sucking in huge drafts of air and caressing her backside.

Bailey arched to his hand. "That . . . When you rub my skin like that, it's as if you're pressing the heat deeper into my flesh. It's sinking into my blood."

"You're aroused."

"Completely."

"Your pussy ache?"

"Totally."

The way she admitted it only notched up his arousal. "You want me to fuck you?"

"Right now."

If she hadn't sounded desperate and gasping for air, he might have told her that she didn't have the control here. But her voice indicated she dangled at the end of her fraying rope. Damn it to hell, he was at the end of his, too.

Joaquin lifted her up from his lap and guided her to face him before he eased one of her thighs over his lap. As she straddled him, he probed until he found her wet opening, then gripped her hips. He surged up on one violent thrust, shoving his way to the end of her passage.

Bailey gasped and blinked at him with a helpless stare. Her fingers curled into his shoulders, nails digging. "Joaquin . . ."

"More? Softer? What is it, baby girl?"

"More. Not softer. I felt you everywhere inside me. The tingles prickled up my thighs. The ache behind my clit is killing me."

"You want to come again?"

She nodded feverishly. "Please."

"We're going to do it together, so you'll need to wait for me."

She winced, as if she knew the waiting would be its own form of torture, but she swallowed her protest back. "All right."

"Good. I want to hear you, Bailey. If it feels good, sigh, scream, call my name. My goal is for you to run out of breath."

She opened her mouth to say something, but he cut her off with another plowing thrust. All she managed after that was a high-pitched cry that almost didn't sound human. Her walls tightened on him. With a lazy thumb, he slid a few circles over her clit, gratified when she repeated the sound, only this time it sounded like even more of a wail.

Her sound raged through his blood like a fever. Urgency jacked his system. His fingers bit tighter into her hips as he crashed up into her again. This time, she met him, slamming down for another slow, deep stroke. As he withdrew, the sensations were so acute. Peeling off his skin would affect him less. She danced like lightning through his body as they fell into a rhythm. He spiked up, she gyrated down. Together, they made a kind of bliss that sent his eyes rolling into the back of his head and a long, loud groan falling from his lips.

Tighter and tighter, her pussy clamped down on him, signaling her rise to orgasm. Even if he hadn't felt that, Joaquin would have known by the flush of her skin, the bite of her fingers in his scalp, the helpless begging in her blue eyes.

"I'm so close," she mewled.

"Good. So good, baby girl. Yes . . ." Joaquin could barely wrap his head around a coherent sentence right now. The pleasure steamrolled all thought. He couldn't breathe fast enough, couldn't get deep enough. He couldn't be with her enough to stop wanting her—ever. The thought seared across his brain and jolted down to his cock. "Now!"

Joaquin seized her lips, certain if he couldn't take her in every way possible at once that he'd lose his damn mind. He plunged his tongue in, danced around hers, and captured her screams as she let go.

Her hard, staccato pulses all around him launched him like a rocket. He surged inside her again, releasing a torrent of need and flooding her again, this time right against the opening of her womb. No doubt, they were playing a dangerous game—and he just didn't care. If he could be with her always, so much the better.

Their rhythm slowed, along with their heartbeats and breathing. She collapsed on him, clung, head on his shoulder, embracing him like he was the lone pillar holding up her life. Joaquin didn't want it any other way. He was in no hurry to withdraw, shower, and leave as he usually did with a lover. No, something primal inside him wanted to stay as long as he could and plant his seed deeper still until she was ready to take him again.

Something inside urged him to tell her that he loved her.

What would she say to that? Did he really know what love was? Maybe. Kind of. Who the fuck knew? All he could say was that Bailey hit him on the most profound level, and he couldn't imagine her not being in his life.

So how the hell was he going to manage when LOSS and McKeevy came calling? He refused to think about losing her. He hadn't been there to protect his father or Nate, but by God, he'd stay with Bailey every step of the way to keep her safe.

Gripping Bailey tighter, Joaquin kissed his way up her neck, down her jaw, back to her lips. "I can't do without you."

She froze, looking at him as if she understood the gravity of this moment, as if it bound her to him as much as he felt bound to her. "You don't have to, I swear."

* * *

THEY didn't sleep much that night. Joaquin woke her up twice more to make love to her, each time slower and more tender than the last.

At the end, he curled his fist in her hair and looked straight into her eyes as he glided his way deep inside her, sure and straight and inexorable. He took; she yielded. But he gave back, too, in devotion and pleasure.

Now the sun peeked out behind the hotel's blackout drapes, waking Bailey from her hard sleep. As she rolled over and peeked one eye open, Joaquin sat on his side of the bed, a map spread across the sheets, phone in his hand. He peered from one to the other and frowned.

"Morning, sunshine." He looked clean and put together, like he'd already showered and dressed to take on the day.

"Why aren't you sleeping?" she groaned.

"Too restless. I'm thinking about where Viktor might have taken you to hide what I sure hope is his research. I'm looking all around this map, but there are so many damn lakes."

Grabbing the sheet, she sat up with a grimace. Sitting next to a hot guy with the sweat of their sex still coating her skin and just knowing she had morning breath was something she wanted to correct ASAP.

"Be right back." She hopped up, grabbed the backpack, and headed for the bathroom.

After quickly using the toilet, she hopped in the shower. Ducking her head under the hot spray of water and letting it sluice through her hair and down her body felt like a necessary comfort. She moaned.

Suddenly, the shower curtain whisked across the rod, and a cold blast of air pelted her skin. She opened her eyes. Joaquin watched her with a burning stare that questioned how quickly he could have her in bed with his cock deep inside her again.

She flushed and tried to cover herself with the curtain. "What are you doing?"

"Besides enjoying the view?" he quipped, tugging the curtain out of her hand. "You moaned, and I wondered if you were having fun without me."

She tsked at him. "The water just felt good on my skin, you perv."

"Uh-huh," he drawled, staring up and down her wet, naked figure.

"It did! And now you're shamelessly peeking at me like you're the big wolf and I'm your prey."

"I like that analogy. Let's roll with it." He reached out for her.

Bailey lurched back, wagging her finger at him. "No more until I'm clean and you've fed me. Otherwise, I'll have to call the U.N. or something and complain that you don't follow Geneva Convention rules."

He gave a hearty laugh that bounced off the bathroom's little walls. "Geneva Convention? You're not a prisoner of war, baby girl."

"I'm sure the same rules apply to kidnappers turned sex gods."

"Sex god? I like that even better." His grin widened. "It's your lucky day. I already have some coffee in the little pot near the TV. It's shit, but it's coffee."

"That's enticing," she said, tongue-in-cheek.

"Yep. And I'm sure you'll really love the cardboard muffins I found in the breakfast area downstairs when I grabbed the map."

"Not so much. Who eats that crap every day? You have something against protein?"

He shrugged. "I'm at the mercy of this hotel since I didn't want to leave you for more than a minute."

Bailey sighed. He was right. The choices sucked from a nutrition standpoint, but she wouldn't starve. "Fine. So you're using the map to try to figure out where Viktor took me as a kid?"

He nodded. "Do you remember any landmark you visited on that trip? If so, I should be able to at least pinpoint whether he drove you north, south, east, or west. Right now, I've got nothing."

"Can you give me a minute alone? Your Peeping Tom impression is distracting me."

"Because you don't want me to look at you?" He scoffed. He knew better.

"No. Because I don't want to jump on you before breakfast. I'll get sidetracked and we'll never figure out where to go next."

"Fair enough." He nodded her way, grinning. "I'll get some coffee and muffins together for you so they'll be ready when you're out of the shower. Don't keep me waiting too long or I'll have my wicked way with you again, Geneva Convention be damned."

Bailey shook her head and laughed. "Go. You crazy man."

Joaquin left reluctantly, and she finished her shower, threw on some clothes, then brushed her teeth. With a towel wrapped around her wet hair and her skin scrubbed clean, she felt relatively human again.

As soon as she stepped out of the bathroom, he handed her the prefab breakfast he'd thrown together. "Here you go."

"At least I know you don't mean to starve me for answers." But the muffin sure looked as if it had been mass-produced out of recycled paper products. She might grumble, but she appreciated him trying. Giving him a hard time was simply fun.

"So . . . anything yet?" she asked him, nodding at the map on the bed.

"Nothing. I won't be able to do much until I get a sense of which direction Viktor traveled when you all packed up and left this town. I need to figure it out quickly. Checkout time is at eleven."

"We've got time, right? It can't be that late." Bailey looked toward his nightstand and found the clock. "Ten fifteen? I slept that long?"

"Yep. I guess that means I wore you out." He looked damn proud of himself.

She swatted his arm. "You're impossible . . . but maybe you did."

"Then my day is complete. Well, except the part where I'm supposed to save you from the bad guys. I'm still working on that."

"I appreciate it." She sobered and sipped at her coffee, trying not to choke. "Oh, that is shit."

"Sorry."

Bailey shrugged. "Not your fault. Can I see that map?"

Forcing another sip of coffee down, she picked at the muffin as Joaquin rearranged the map so she could get a better view. But nothing registered with her. She couldn't recall seeing any sign that said they'd left one state or entered another. There seemed to be a big, black hole in her recollections of that trip.

"If I had to guess, Viktor drove north. The Great Lakes would give you lots of possibilities for docks and signs by water. But he might have taken you east to see some sights. There are quite a few lakes along the way if he did that, too. Did you go to D.C. maybe?"

She shook her head. "No. Every place he took us seemed off the beaten path. There weren't many people. None of the places even seemed as if they got a lot of campers. I don't remember seeing a lot of amenities for them. Then again, I was five, so maybe I just wasn't looking."

Joaquin took her shoulders in hand. "I need something to follow. There's no way we can drive around aimlessly until we find something that looks familiar. That's a fucking needle in a haystack. *Anything* you can give me would be helpful."

She looked at the map again, but all the little lines representing the highways and roads just blended together for her. Frustrated at herself, she sighed. "Maybe I should . . . This will sound crazy to you, but if you can find me a place I might be able to spread out and dance, that might help. It focuses my mind and centers me."

"Dance?" He blinked.

Yeah, she'd known that would sound nuts to someone who didn't spend their life *en pointe*. It was tough to explain the way she could let her thoughts just flow as her movements did. Sometimes, when she focused too much on something, nothing happened. But releasing the tension and clearing her head seemed to make her unconscious mind work in her favor. It couldn't hurt to try now.

"Please."

"All right. I think I saw a place when I was downstairs. Let's pack up and head out. I'll even try to find you some protein once we blow this joint."

Bailey sidled up to him and wrapped her arms around the strong column of his neck. Heat flared in his eyes again. Would he ever stop looking at her that way? Gosh, she hoped not.

"That would be perfect. Thanks."

Without a word, they gathered up their stuff and packed it all back in Joaquin's backpack. He opened the door and scanned the parking lot in both directions. It must have been empty because he motioned her out. Sure enough, she didn't see anyone in sight.

Joaquin guided her to a hallway beside the front desk. A variety of meeting rooms shot off from the main walkway on both the left and the right. Some doors had been shut. Voices rose from behind them. Signs in little brass frames standing nearby proclaimed those rooms to be in use.

Joaquin continued leading her farther down until they came to a ballroom. He yanked the door open. It stood perfectly empty except for some tables on their sides, a few stacks of chairs, and a pile of white linens.

"I saw an electronic sign in the lobby earlier. Some sales group is having an awards dinner here tonight, but it doesn't start until six thirty."

"They'll start setting up long before then, but we'll be gone. Can you leave me alone for a few minutes?" Already, she was looking forward to the moment she could turn on her music and become one with it, clear her thoughts and just be.

"No." His denial was immediate and whiplike. "We have no idea who else might be here. I'm not leaving you alone, especially if you're about to put yourself into a state where you're not really paying attention to your surroundings."

"I doubt anyone will think to look for me here," she argued.

"Maybe not, but I'm not willing to take that chance." He

shrugged. "Your choice. Either you dance while I'm in the room or you don't dance at all."

Bailey frowned. She knew he'd seen her before. Dancing wasn't generally a private activity. She did it for audiences. But connecting with her thoughts and using her movement to let go of every pretense and simply breathe? She never willingly did that in front of anyone.

Still, did she have a choice? And didn't he have a point?

"All right. Can I have my phone? My music is on there."

"If you promise to ignore the twelve voicemails."

She blinked as if he'd gone crazy. "Twelve?"

"I'm pretty sure they're all from Blane, except one from a number that's not in your contacts. That one I'm still tracking down, but coming up empty so far."

She blew out a breath. "Fine. But Blane has to be freaking out by now."

"Blane will live. In fact, he's more likely to live if he knows nothing of your whereabouts."

Joaquin had another good point, damn him.

Bailey held out her hand. "All right. I won't listen to any of the voicemails or try to return the calls."

"I'll be watching." He smiled tightly as he slid the mobile into her palm.

"You're being like an overprotective older brother. I'm not Kata."

He shot her a sidelong glance. "If you think I've behaved like your brother lately, then I need to strip you down and fuck you again because apparently you've already forgotten."

She'd never forget. "No, I haven't."

"Good to hear." He winked.

Their camaraderie relaxed her, and when she curled her fingers around her phone, another notch of tension eased inside her. She flipped through the screens, noting the almost full battery. "You've been charging it?"

"Just in case anyone interesting calls."

Bailey didn't love that he'd invaded her privacy, but she understood that he'd done it to try to catch the murderous crazies after her. So she held her tongue and started her music. One of her favorite instrumental tunes had always been a great warm-up song, so as the opening notes filtered through the air, she began stretching and moving, bringing her body back to life. She thanked goodness that Callie had given her stretchy clothes she could be free in.

That song flowed into the next. She lamented the absence of her toe shoes, but she could do plenty without them. So when her muscles felt loose and the music started calling to her soul, she slipped into the vast, empty middle of the room. Industrial carpet wasn't her favorite surface to dance on, and when she found a few dozen wooden parquet floor tiles meshed together with a brass border to resemble a dance floor, she ran, leapt, and executed a jeté onto the hard surface. She immediately stepped into a series of pirouettes . . . and then let the music overtake her body and mind.

One song bled into the next. She tried to open her mind without focusing on the fact that Joaquin watched her. But she could almost feel his fascination emanating from across the room. It bolstered her. For the first time, she felt beautiful and feminine dancing, sort of like a little girl living her fairy-tale castle dreams.

She remembered the times Viktor would let her take over Mikhail's fort with Annika and play. She and her sister would be princesses locked away in a tower. Her biological father would pretend to ride to her rescue. Then he would tickle her. They would all giggle.

The "vacation" he'd taken them on shortly before the murders hadn't been fun at all. No laughing or tickling or levity. She remembered her parents arguing the night before Viktor had taken her to the lake. They'd been to see a big outdoor field earlier that day. But not just a field. There had also been a museum. She frowned, trying to bring the memory into focus.

Another song began. She performed an arabesque, then brought her leg in front of her body in a slow *développé*. The museum . . . it depicted a time when photography had been very new. Lots of grainy black-and-white photos of dead bodies lying in fields. They'd worn uniforms of different colors and—

"Gettysburg!" she shouted over the music, then flipped it off, shoving the phone into her front pocket as she ran toward him. "We visited Gettysburg."

Chapter Seventeen

LIKE the battlefield?" Joaquin asked.

"Yes." She explained her memories to him, and as she did, the pictures in her head became much clearer. "We left the battlefield in the early afternoon. I remember my siblings were hungry for lunch, and Viktor was frustrated with everyone wanting to leave before he'd seen every inch of the place."

"Civil War buff?"

She shrugged. "I don't think so. He seemed more interested in the grounds than the exhibits."

"Like he was looking for a place to bury his research?"

"It's possible. But why on federal land?"

"Maybe because if he could get it buried there, he thought it would be safer. Again, we'll never know. But you think he abandoned the plan?"

Bailey nodded. "He was in a fit, but he relented. We grabbed some fast-food burgers and kept driving. We didn't stop for a couple of hours."

"Before the sun set?" When she shrugged, he rephrased his question. "Do you remember from what side of the car you could see the sun?"

Bailey tried to picture that drive. It was hard when so many memories from that time in her life flooded in, both simultaneous and incomplete. "We spent so many days in the car during that trip, I don't know for sure if I'm remembering the right leg. But I don't think Viktor was wearing his sunglasses. And the backseat seemed hotter than normal, like the sun was beating down on us."

Joaquin grabbed the map from his backpack and knelt, spreading it out. He pointed to a spot. "Here. So from southern Pennsylvania, you traveled east? Do you remember how long you were in the car?"

She shook her head. Her hazy memory was so frustrating. Latching on to the bits she recalled was of life-and-death importance. Yet she didn't really know the details Joaquin needed.

She wrinkled her brow, deep in concentration. "I think I remember my parents snapping at one another because they arrived at the campsite as dark was falling. My birth mother complained they'd have just an hour or two to set up, and that wasn't enough time."

"So . . . some place less than three hours east from Gettysburg. Some place near a lake. Shit," he cursed. "I don't think this map is as detailed as I need." He tossed the paper map aside and pulled up another map on his mobile. "The screen on my phone is awfully small. A computer would be really fucking helpful about now."

"Why not call someone who can help you?" she suggested. "Sean or Hunter. Even Kata."

Joaquin paused. "I usually work alone, but . . . yeah. Good point." He flipped through his recent calls, punched a button, then engaged his speakerphone. Within seconds, a male voice picked up on the other line. "You okay there? Kata is worried about you."

Hunter. Bailey smiled to herself. The former SEAL would definitely get quick answers.

"Fine. Tired and in need of decent food but otherwise alive. I don't think anyone is following us, but I'll keep looking." Joaquin filled his brother-in-law in on everything Bailey had remembered at the house and again this morning. "So I need a lake in eastern

Pennsylvania or the tip of northern Maryland. Can you rattle off a few? I'm also looking for anything that might have a fence painted green near a park around the lake."

"That's going to be hard to find," Hunter commented. "Let me look at some travel sites and maps online."

A few minutes passed in relative silence. Anxiety ate away at Bailey's belly. What if they couldn't find Viktor's research? What if they dead-ended here because she couldn't remember anything more?

"Got a few possibilities for you here, though I don't know if any have a green fence. That will take more digging. The most likely suspects seem to be Memorial Lake, Locust Lake, Crystal Lake, Lake Pocono. If you're just looking for a body of water, don't forget the Susquehanna River, the North East River, the Delaware River. Damn, there's so fucking many of them. Still looking . . . Lake Beltzville, Lake Harmony, Lake—"

"That's it!" Bailey insisted, her heart in her throat as a jolt of recognition rattled down her spine. "It's coming back now. We arrived at the campground just before evening. Remember I said that my parents argued? My brother quipped something to us kids like 'So much for Lake Harmony.'"

"That would fit," Hunter confirmed. "The drive from Gettysburg would be less than three hours. Let me see if I can find anything about a green fence."

"Tell you what," Joaquin said. "You look. Bailey and I have to leave here. It's past checkout time and I don't want to stay in one place for too long and give anyone an easy way to find us. We'll hop in the car and head for Lake Harmony. If you come up with anything else or can figure out exactly which part of the lake that fence might be in, call me. Hopefully, we can put some of this mystery to bed soon."

Hunter agreed, and the men rang off. Joaquin turned to Bailey with a determined look on his face. "Let's go. I have a gut feeling we're getting closer."

Bailey did, too. But she didn't necessarily like it. The nagging fear that had been plaguing her for too long swelled in her throat until she nearly choked. But what choice did she have?

"All right." She blew out a breath. "First, where's that protein you promised?"

He nodded. "I saw a twenty-four-hour pancake place on our way in. Will eggs do?"

Eggs sounded perfect. "Absolutely."

Less than two minutes later, they were gone. Bailey noticed the man she'd seen yesterday still wearing his hoodie. Today, he hung out in the lobby as they passed, engrossed in his morning paper. If he wasn't here to follow her or spy on the cheating wife she'd witnessed, what had brought him here? Could be anything. After all, people with their own business and lives filled this hotel.

Outside, the day was clear, chilly, breezy. They hopped into the SUV, and Joaquin maneuvered onto the road. Within moments, they blended in with the traffic, until they pulled into the mostly empty parking lot.

After nice plates of eggs, bacon, and fruit, they eased back into the vehicle and onto the road. Belly happily full, Bailey lost herself in thought. If they found Viktor's research at this lake, then what? Would Joaquin send her back to her ordinary life and return to his own? Or were they simply too entwined now to part?

She glanced over at his strong profile, blade of a nose, full lips, enviously long lashes. He seemed focused on the road with an occasional glance back in the rearview mirror. Tension rolled through him. Joaquin had done an exceptional job of hiding it previously, but now she felt the gut-knotting tightness hanging in the air.

"Tell me. Best-case scenario if we find this research?"

"We turn it over to the feds. I don't know after that. Maybe LOSS stops looking for you if they know you no longer have what they're seeking. Maybe we have enough to convict McKeevy."

"Worst case?"

"Witness Protection maybe. That's if LOSS doesn't find you first, of course. But I'm going to do everything in my power to make sure that doesn't happen."

"I know." And Bailey did.

When Joaquin had first abducted her, she hadn't trusted him for a moment. He'd drugged her and taken her from the comfortable and familiar, then he'd forced her to look under the façade her adopted parents had given her and truly see herself. She'd hated him for it. How had everything changed in less than three days?

"I know those are terrible options," he murmured.

They were, but they didn't shock Bailey. "So there's a very slim chance I come out of this with a normal life?"

He hesitated, gripped the steering wheel. "I'd love to say it's both possible and likely, but I'd be lying to you."

Now probably wasn't the time to ask about this, but there might not be a later. "What if I'm pregnant?"

"We'll deal with it, whether you have to testify against members of LOSS the feds can convict or we're in Witness Protection."

Bailey's jaw dropped. "But if you came with me, you'd be giving up your family, probably for the rest of your life."

"A week ago, that wouldn't have fazed me at all. Now . . . yeah, it would bother me not to see my mother again or meet her new husband or hold Kata's baby. But I'd still choose you."

His words yanked on her heart until her chest felt ready to implode. In every way except verbally, Joaquin had told her that he loved her. The sentiment warmed every bone in her body.

I love you, too.

The miles and the minutes dipped by. Highway 15 became something else, then they dumped onto Interstate 81 on the outskirts of Harrisburg. From there, they continued northeast, through some deeply scenic territory. Even a few weeks ago, the trees would have looked nearly bare—the ravages of winter taking their toll. Now most spouted the makings of rebirth. Small and tentative and green, the leaves would soon grow and bloom, filling the trees with life again until the next season browned and felled them in preparation for winter once more. The circle of life, she supposed.

Bailey wished she knew where her circle was headed. Hopefully not for an early grave. Or decades of loneliness.

Joaquin veered onto Interstate 80 next, and she swore things were beginning to look familiar.

"We're not far. Do you need a restroom break?"

"I could use one. And maybe more caffeine."

"Ditto." They exited and found a fast-food joint, now dead in the middle of the afternoon.

Bailey turned and saw a silver sedan. Had she see that same car at the hotel? Or was she being paranoid?

"See that car parked at the edge of the parking lot?" she asked him without looking at the vehicle in question, just in case.

Joaquin had the same idea. "The grayish one. Yeah. I've seen him a few times. He seems to stop when we do."

A faint sense of unease became full-on fear. "Do you think—"

"I don't know. The one thing that's keeping me from being too suspicious is that they kidnapped the other victims, then asked questions. I can't think of a reason they'd change their M.O. with you."

She bobbed her head, conceding his point. "We're headed to the Poconos. It's a vacation destination. Maybe he's looking to get away for a few days. We *are* stopping pretty close to the highway." She tried convincing herself. "Maybe he has the same ideas about where to eat and pee."

"We'll find out."

* * *

WHEN they piled back in the SUV to drive the last half hour to the lake, Joaquin watched the silver car. As they pulled back onto the highway, it remained empty and in the parking lot. He relaxed. A red truck and a white hatchback soon pulled onto the highway with them. He kept a cursory glance on the vehicles while trying not to worry what fate had in store for Bailey's future.

For the first time in his adult life, he wanted more than work. He saw the point of coming home to one woman. He'd be thrilled to have a rug rat with her and make certain he or she didn't grow into a defiant teenager. It scared the hell out of him, but he wanted roots and a future with Bailey.

What if LOSS found her and ended that future before it could begin? What if she died while growing the life they'd created together inside her?

The thought made him homicidal and filled him with paralyzing terror at once. Just imagining what it would be like to lose her and the family they might have begun gutted him.

Joaquin reached over and squeezed her hand, reveling in her warm, soft skin. He needed to assure himself that she was well and whole. As he glanced her way, he noticed she looked awfully nervous, too.

"You all right?"

"Evading antigovernment loons isn't exactly as much fun as hanging out with a few friends and sharing a bottle of wine, but I'm managing."

He sent her a faint smile. "Anything look familiar?"

"Not any one thing in particular. I just remember thinking the road up to the lake was a beautiful place. But I'm sure time has changed things."

"Of course."

"And the seasons. It was probably October when we came. I remember lots of fall colors. But now, spring is budding."

"I know. Just keep watching for anything that seems familiar."

A moment later, Joaquin's phone rang. He pulled it from the console and glanced at it before pressing a button to enable the speakerphone. "Hunter?"

"Yeah. It's taken me a while, but I've got some answers for you."

Joaquin's guts knotted up. "Hit me."

"I found a few possibilities. The one that seems most likely is a campground that closed about six years ago. One of the local sporting goods places I called and played dumb with said he remembered a green fence near a dock. Someone else bought the place a few years back and started fixing it up. They've opened the main structure on the grounds as a restaurant. I'll text you directions."

When Joaquin's phone dinged a minute later, he thanked Hunter. "We'll see what we can find. I'll keep you posted."

"Knowing you had your hands full, I called Sean to advise him that you might be onto something. He's alerting the FBI in Philly. They're going to have agents on standby. Call this number I'll text you next if you find anything. They'll get to you in less than an hour."

Another little ding sounded. "Thanks."

"No problem. I wish you had some backup. I'd feel better if you had more than one set of eyes on Bailey."

Joaquin's first instinct was to bristle, but he knew Hunter only spoke from a position of caution. "When we left, I wasn't sure what we'd find, if anything. Now we can't afford to wait."

Hunter grunted like he didn't want to agree but couldn't argue the point, either.

"Besides," Joaquin went on. "Staying in Dallas wasn't an option with McKeevy all set to help at Callie's wedding."

"Maybe not. The photographer who hired him said his new assistant stopped answering calls, so he left a message telling 'Timothy Smith' that he was fired. Sean and a few feds went to his known address, but it turned out to be a dump—literally. He listed some city's garbage facilities as his home."

"Charming."

"That's McKeevy, a delightful sociopath." Hunter huffed. "Keep me posted. If you don't, I'll let your sister kick your ass next time you see her."

Joaquin couldn't not laugh. The idea of a pregnant woman still a good six inches shorter than him beating him up was ridiculous, but if anyone would try, it would be his spitfire sister. "Heaven forbid. I'll let you know as soon as I have news."

They hung up, and Joaquin began following the driving directions to the campground Hunter had texted from his phone. The roads turned twisty and windy, the scenery absolutely stunning. He'd never been to this part of the country, but he wouldn't mind exploring here more. Fall was probably a gorgeous time of year to come.

Within a few minutes, they reached the old campground. It had been converted into a bar and restaurant, but the place looked empty now. He glanced at his phone: 3:38. As he curled an arm around Bailey's tiny waist and led her to the door, he saw that the sign posted said they didn't open until five.

He looked around the parking lot, down the landscaped perimeter, all the way to the lakefront. "Anything look familiar?"

"I see a fence. And a dock." She bit her lip, looking tense, worried. "I don't know. If this is the right place, things have changed a lot. This parking lot wasn't here. It was just a dirt area. The big tree I remember doesn't seem that big, after all."

"Remember, you were smaller, so your vantage point would have been here." He crouched down. "And since it was fall, the tree would have been full of leaves, not just a bunch of spindly branches."

"True," she conceded, easing down to his level and staring up at the treetops. "Is it hickory?"

"I'm not an arborist. It's possible."

She sighed. "It's also possible this is a wild-goose chase."

"Yeah. But in case it's the real deal, we've got to press forward."

Bailey rose and meandered to the fence, stroking her fingers along the top of the pickets, now stained a dark cedar color. Joaquin headed for an old, beat-up sign near the shore that read *No Lifeguard on Duty.*

She looked his way, and her eyes lit up. "I remember that sign."

She glanced between it and the fence again. "It was about that far apart, too. If this fence was still green . . . it would look awfully similar."

"There's a path to follow." He pointed.

"It's concrete now, but if I come to this support post and jump three times to my left . . ." She demonstrated—and wound up precisely in the middle of the path.

And everything seemed to fit into place. A wave of dizziness overcame her.

Joaquin reached out to steady Bailey. "Whoa. You okay?"

"I remember now—and I think we're in the right place. In my head, I see Viktor talking me through this little dance before he headed back to a tiny lump of dirt he'd just made at the base of the tree."

"Are you sure? Because that's exactly the kind of recollection we need."

"Mentally removing the trappings of everything that's changed, I'm thinking we might actually find whatever he buried somewhere around the trunk of the tree. Did we bring a shovel?"

Well, shit. "I wasn't exactly prepared to dig." He took a mental inventory of the items in his car. "I've got an idea. It's not perfect, but it might do the trick."

He jogged back to the car, disappearing behind some foliage for a bit. He hated to leave Bailey for even a moment, but he couldn't see a soul in sight, just lots of nature's wonder.

A green compact that had seen better days speeded into the lot, swinging around a corner and almost tilting over on two wheels. Joaquin tensed as he saw the female driver heading single-mindedly to the lot behind the building, closer to Bailey's position.

A moment later, a harried brunette bolted from her car, carrying an apron and juggling her keys as she locked her vehicle and ran for the back door of the restaurant. The woman let herself into the place, then locked the door behind her with an audible click. With the restaurant opening in just over an hour, it stood to reason that someone had to start cooking or getting the tables set.

Joaquin breathed a sigh of relief, then retrieved the necessary item from the back of his SUV. Then he noticed something that made his blood run cold—the red truck they'd spotted on the highway just after their last stop. Jogging over, he took a quick glance inside. It appeared empty.

After making a mental note of the license plate, he dashed back to Bailey, implement in hand. He was damn glad it would double as a weapon. It would make a nice backup for the SIG shoved into his waistband at the small of his back.

He told her about the truck parked on the other side of the building.

Worry wrinkled her brow. "You think it's the same red truck we saw?"

"Looks like it. But then again, it might be another employee or the owner. Let's stay focused on our task, but we'll definitely keep our eyes open, too."

Her body tensed. She curled her arms around herself. "I wish we could just forget this. I don't have a burning need to know about Viktor's research. So many people have already killed and died for it. Unearthing it may end up being the worst thing we can do for humanity."

"Secrets don't stay buried," he warned. "If we don't find this, someone else will. And we have no idea how unscrupulous that someone might be. You need to dig up whatever he buried and bring light to it. If those are the original—and last—notes about his research, we'll have to make sure everyone knows they've been turned over to the proper authorities. You're the only one with memories of Viktor's plan. Only you can end this."

"I know." She looked crushed by that fact. "Let's just get this done."

He understood how she felt and wished he could take this monkey off her back. "Do you remember on what side of the tree he buried this . . . whatever?"

She studied the tree, wrinkling her nose. "Not exactly. I doubt he did it on the side facing the river. Let's try over here."

When she pointed to the left of the tree, near some protruding roots, Joaquin crouched down to examine the ground. "You sure?"

"No. But he would have avoided either of these sides." She pointed to the back and right of the tree. "Erosion. I'm guessing he wouldn't have put it in front of the tree, knowing that angle would be most likely to be encroached on by people doing things like building a parking lot. Don't you think he'd choose the least accessible side?"

"Yeah." She had been through a lot, and it wasn't over, but she just kept impressing him with her wit, grit, and determination. "Good point. I'll start digging here."

He jammed the crowbar into the soil. The tool didn't wedge free easily. Time and footsteps had packed the dirt down tightly.

Joaquin dug for seemingly endless minutes, Bailey helping out with her bare hands. A sweat broke out at his temples, under his T-shirt, at the waistband of his pants. Beside him on the tar lot, he made a pile of earth. His hands were a filthy black. The sun was heading down and would soon fall behind a nearby mountain.

"I'm starting to wonder now . . ." he admitted. "Maybe we are in the wrong place."

"We're talking about years ago, and I recall that Viktor dug for a while. I really think we're where we should be."

Joaquin had his doubts, but he didn't have more appealing options. If they gave up on this spot, what would he do with Bailey next? Find another hotel room tonight? Take her to bed again and relentlessly plow her delicate curves until neither of them could think straight? Get up tomorrow and procure a shovel so they could cruise around the lake, hoping that something else looked familiar to her? That plan sounded as good as any.

"Ten more minutes. Then we'll have to give up for today. Once the sun dips behind that mountain, it's going to look pretty dark. The only lights in this lot are on the other side, near the restaurant door." He dug into the soil again and scooped out another pile with his hands.

Beside him, Bailey filled her graceful hands with the earth and added to his pile. "I know."

And she sounded so disappointed. Damn it. Once he'd given her a bit of proof about her previous life, she'd believed him, despite how crazy it must have sounded to her. She couldn't produce any evidence out of thin air, but he could still give her the benefit of the doubt until her theory no longer seemed possible.

"I know you're worried and upset. We'll figure it out. This might not be the right spot, but we'll keep looking—"

The crowbar hit something hard and metallic deep in the soil.

Had their luck finally changed?

"What was that?" she asked, hunkered down next to him.

"Help me." He shoved the end of the crowbar into the soil until he could discern the outer edges of a box. It clinked every time he hit the side. Together, they shoved the soil away, frantic to reach whatever they'd found.

"You don't think it's water pipes or a sewer line, do you?" she asked.

"No. The shape is definitely square. I don't know how deep it is yet. Keep digging."

Five minutes became ten. The sun dipped closer to the horizon. Damn it, they had to get a move on. People might show up for dinner or a drink at this restaurant soon and question why the hell they were digging at the edge of the parking lot. He also didn't like the fact that he'd seen that red truck not far away but had no clue where its owner might be right now.

Sweat sheened his skin. His heart beat in rapid thumps of anxiety. His fingers ached from gripping the crowbar and digging into the hard soil, which had been frozen for most of the winter. He'd have dirt under his fingernails for the next six months—and he just didn't care. They might be moments away from the discovery that could save Bailey and allow her to walk away from her past as Tatiana Aslanov.

Joaquin risked a peek at her. A little dewy film covered her forehead and just under her bottom lip. Hell of a time to notice that her nipples strained the purple T-shirt she wore. With her hair in a haphazard knot on her head and her gaze focused down, she still looked beautiful to him. In fact, she always did—at any time, in any setting. He'd do whatever he must to keep her safe. And make her his.

Joaquin reached into the hole they'd dug, feeling his way along the edge of the metallic object. Definitely some sort of box.

Bailey dug around the other side, then looked up at him with an excited smile. "I got my fingers under the edge."

They were close.

"Let me try . . ." He burrowed his digits deeper into the earth, finagling at the edge until the pads of his fingers slipped just under. "I got it, too."

He looked down into the hole, trying to see what he'd only felt so far, but with the canopy of trees filtering out their late afternoon sun, only a shadowy gray yawned back at him.

"Can you pull it up? I think if we wiggle it, we might be able to wedge it free."

Joaquin suspected she was right. "Let's do it. Carefully. I don't think anything is breakable, but let's not take a chance."

They pulled and strained, jiggling one side, then the other. Finally, the sun dropped, seeming to touch the mountain in the distance. Longer shadows fell across the parking lot as he pulled his side free from the hole. Bailey lifted hers up next, and earth trickled back into the hole. The sharp edges of the metallic box bit into his fingers as he held it up to the residual sunlight for a good look.

"There's no lock on it?" Bailey sounded confused by that fact.

"I'm surprised, too. But I guess he had no way of giving you a key and being sure you could hang on to it until you were an adult. Getting you to remember the location of the box was a feat in itself, so he probably didn't want to risk hoping you'd remember a combination on top of it. Besides, with a good pair of wire cutters and some gumption, anyone could snip the lock free."

"Good point."

Joaquin reached for the latch holding the lid shut. As he grasped it, Bailey touched his arm softly.

"Can I do it?" She looked somewhere between nervous and earnest.

This was something she needed to do. Being the first person to set eyes on whatever her father had buried over fifteen years ago would bring her a sense of closure. Hopefully, she'd be seeing exactly what her family had died for, what had wrought so much destruction in her life both now and then. He prayed nothing in here would hurt her or increase her risk of danger even more. But nothing about chasing this crazy needle in this bizarre haystack had been easy or a given. He couldn't take this away from her now.

"Do it." Joaquin handed her the box.

* * *

WITH both relief and a new onslaught of tension, Bailey took the metal container into her grip. It wasn't huge, maybe six inches by four. Caked in dirt, the color was tough to discern, but as she brushed the top clean with her fingers, she suspected it had once been an industrial gray. A sticker of what looked like a mouse was stuck on top, yellowed by time and earth. Viktor had thought of everything in order to tie the rhyme to the location of the box, right down to the little rodent.

Trembling, she took hold of the latch. The rectangular hole in the middle fit over a metal protrusion curved in the shape of a U, which prevented the lid from opening without human intervention.

Her hands trembled as she freed the flap from the flange, then lifted the lid.

Joaquin leaned in with her as they both peered into the box. Inside lay something smallish and square, swathed in layers of bubble wrap. Bailey reached for it, then hesitated.

"Go ahead," he encouraged. "This is what your father wanted you to find."

"What if this . . . whatever it is Viktor left me doesn't make my trouble with LOSS go away?"

"We'll deal with it then, but he kept you alive for this. Check it out."

Anxiety and excitement biting into her belly, Bailey reached into the box and lifted the plastic bundle. She tore into the taped seal of the bubble wrap, her fingers fumbling with nerves and haste.

She nearly dropped it. With a shriek, Bailey bit her lip to hold the sound in as the protective coat finally unraveled from the device.

"Some sort of electronic storage medium," she murmured. "Viktor left me information. It's got to be his research. He left me information that potentially has the power to change the world. Oh, God."

"It's a compact flash disk, kind of a precursor to an SD card. My mom had a camera that stored images on one of these." Joaquin put an arm around her waist to steady her, and Bailey was grateful for his support.

They'd found what her sire had left her, what might secure her safety once and for all. Callie's, too.

"I'll take that," called a voice behind them.

Bailey whirled around to find the man with the hoodie she'd seen at the hotel, pointing a gun directly at them.

Chapter Eighteen

JOAQUIN'S blood froze. Just beyond the man with the gun, he saw the red truck idling. Son of a bitch, he should have realized . . . He should have questioned its mysterious appearance more, scouted around. But he'd let his impatience to help Bailey get in the way of his natural caution. His failure might cost them their lives.

He tightened his grip on Bailey. "Don't."

"Stop trying to be a hero. Just give me the disk," their assailant sneered.

So he could shoot and kill them the moment they complied? Joaquin knew he had to keep this guy talking.

"How did you find us?"

"I followed you from the Aslanov farm. I'd been monitoring the place, hoping you'd turn up. Good to know I was right."

"You were driving the silver sedan at the hotel?" Bailey blurted.

"You're not totally stupid for a ballerina."

Joaquin didn't bother asking why the goon hadn't confronted them then. Of course this guy had waited, hoping Bailey would remember where Aslanov had hidden his research.

She frowned. "Then you traded it for the red truck at the fast-food joint not far from the lake—"

"Again, you figured me out. Congratulations," he drawled. "I'm done talking. Now, dance the disk over to me, ballerina, or you both get it."

"I'll bring it to you," Joaquin offered.

Annoyance flashed across his shadowed features. "This ain't a negotiation. I don't talk to federal agents, even former ones, so fuck off."

This guy knew who he was, too? That set him back and made Joaquin reassess the enemy, who was clearly one step ahead. Their aggressor wasn't big, maybe five-foot-eight, and a little on the scrawny side. The hoodie hid what appeared to be a young face. In a hand-to-hand fight, Joaquin knew he could take the guy, despite the tattoo running up the side of his neck that self-proclaimed him a badass.

Joaquin sized up his limited options. Play along? Jump the creep and hope he could get a good swipe in before a bullet landed between his eyes? Maybe he could draw his own gun and get in a lucky shot before he bit it. Would any of those options give Bailey enough time to run?

Probably not.

They were fucked.

He wished like hell he'd listened to Hunter and come with backup, but this woulda, coulda, shoulda was too late now. Still, he wasn't going down without a fight.

Joaquin tried to ease the arm he'd slid around Bailey toward the small of his back to reach his gun.

"Stop there, asshole," the man warned. "Hands up."

Shit. Joaquin winced. *Now what?*

The criminal trained his gun on Bailey. "Do it! Or I waste her while you watch."

No choice. Any chance he had of keeping Bailey alive, Joaquin would take. He raised his hands above his head.

"Take a step away from her."

Fuck. Did this asshole mean to shoot him and leave Bailey at his dubious mercy? Again, Joaquin didn't see a choice. He took one step to his left, away from her trembling body. He sent her a look that told her he'd do whatever possible to keep her alive. If they could just find a way to distract the guy for a few seconds . . .

"Good. I like cooperation," the man in the gray hoodie snapped. "Keep it that way."

Then, without warning, he pulled the trigger of his weapon, hitting Bailey in the neck.

Panic fired Joaquin's blood as she staggered back. He watched her crumple to the ground and fell to his knees at her side. What had happened? She couldn't be dead. His thoughts jumbled. His heart chugged.

Joaquin inspected Bailey. She wasn't bleeding. Instead, a little dart protruded from her neck. He realized the gun hadn't discharged with a loud bang but a quieter hiss.

Their attacker started laughing. "Psych! It's a tranq gun, you moron. You couldn't tell?"

The parking lot had been too shadowed for him to get a detailed look. Joaquin thanked goodness she wasn't dead, but he was absolutely going to have to shoot this bastard to get her out of here in one piece. Luckily, he had no problem with that.

"Bailey," he called.

"Hmm." She sounded barely coherent.

Worry torqued Joaquin's gut.

"She can't hear you," the bastard in the hoodie sneered. "She'll be asleep for the next twelve hours—at least."

"I'll give you the research." Joaquin reached for the disk. "You want it?"

"Don't touch it!" their assailant shouted. "Get away from her and put your hands in the air, damn it." He transferred the gun to one hand and reached into his hoodie pocket with the other, retrieving a semiautomatic. Instantly, he wrapped his finger around the trigger. "I need her alive. You? Not so much. Get on your knees. I'm itching for the chance to waste a scumbag who made a living as a federal agent."

Joaquin scrambled to his feet and stepped away, knowing that if he knelt again, he wouldn't ever get back up. His best chance to save himself, Bailey, and the research was to take cover and shoot this asshole.

"Yeah?" he challenged. "I'd like the chance to waste the scum trying to tear this country apart."

If he was going to get out of this alive, he needed a distraction. On the edge of an empty parking lot, his choices were few.

Joaquin sank to one knee, as if he meant to stoop down. Instead, he quickly grabbed at the disk and tossed it across the asphalt.

"You fucking shithead!" the criminal yelled and tore after it.

Joaquin tried to lift Bailey and haul her with him to some cover, but he couldn't hold her and his gun at once. *Damn it!* A glance up proved the guy in the hoodie had retrieved the disk and was now shoving it in his pocket.

Joaquin hauled ass toward the cover of the wide trunk of the tree. As dark as the lot had become, he wouldn't be an impossible target to hit, but he would be a much more difficult one. As if to prove him right, the separatist shot at him. A bullet whizzed past his shoulder.

With a curse, the attacker came after him. He'd probably rather take Bailey and the disk, then flee. But he wouldn't leave a loose end alive if he could help it.

Another bullet zipped past his ear as Joaquin reached the trunk and stood sideways behind it, then grabbed his gun from his waistband. He peered around the tree and saw the guy in the hoodie racing toward him. He popped off a shot and obviously missed because the assailant fired again—now closing in. This time, the bullet pinged off the bark.

Joaquin took a chance and crouched down, then leaned around the tree to take another shot. Just as he did, a second man opened the door of the red truck in the distance, gun in hand. The new psycho bore down in Joaquin's direction, his features shadowed by the falling dusk.

Together, the two separatists fired a hail of bullets at him. Joaquin hunkered on the ground, inching toward the lake. If they both came at him at once, guns blazing, he might not have any fallback position except the water. But damn it, he didn't want to leave Bailey to them. God knew what they'd do with her. Still, he was more use to her alive than dead.

Since he had limited ammo remaining for his gun, his options were also limited.

"You're a dead motherfucker," one of them shouted.

Joaquin eased closer to the water. He hoped like hell the woman inside the restaurant had heard this barrage of gunfire and called the police. It might be his only chance to leave this parking lot alive. Without that, he was outmanned, outgunned, and out of his mind with worry for Bailey.

"Grab her," the second assailant, wearing a black T-shirt, said, approaching the tree, gun at the ready. With a tattoo of a burning American flag on his forearm and a mean expression, he looked as if he'd lived a hard fifty years. He also sported a smooth-shaved bald head and a familiar face.

McKeevy. *Shit!* Joaquin's heart stopped.

"I can't get to her with this asshole firing at me," the guy in the hoodie complained.

"Oh, I'll do it, you whiny fucking bastard," McKeevy spit.

Joaquin peeked around and found that he'd flung Bailey over his shoulder fireman style. *Son of a bitch.* She was in the arms of a sick fuck who enjoyed torturing young women to death in the most gruesome ways imaginable.

The hoodie-wearing asshole nodded. "Good. I'll dust this guy."

Joaquin didn't have a moment to waste. He crawled on the far side of an adjacent bush, then stood, caught the younger criminal in his sight line, and pulled the trigger. At the same time, the man fired, but aimed toward Joaquin's previous position, closer to the tree. He missed, then staggered back as Joaquin's bullet went into his chest and rattled around his rib cage. Blood spurted from his wound as he toppled to the ground.

Not wasting a second, Joaquin raced over the man's limp form, toward McKeevy, now darting fifty feet ahead of him for the red truck. Bailey's limp body hung over his shoulder, her torso flopping along his back. He'd run too far for Joaquin to get in a clean shot without risking her, especially with dwindling sunlight, but if the crazy separatist got her in the truck and left, Joaquin doubted he'd ever see her alive again.

Planting his feet, he tried to steady his shaking hands. *Calm. Focus. Breathe.* He lined up his shot and fired—once, twice. From this growing distance, he hit just wide of the moving target.

Thoughts raced. Options dwindled. He'd been tentative with McKeevy to protect Bailey. He had no problem shooting the asshole's tires.

Altering his aim slightly, Joaquin pointed the gun and fired again. The first shot pinged off the rim. The second seemed to hit its target. McKeevy would make it out of the parking lot, but he wouldn't get too far without stopping for air or a patch job. Just for good measure, Joaquin fired at the tire again, hitting it. Then he balanced once more, waiting for the moment the asshole would throw Bailey in the truck, then try to climb in himself, leaving his back vulnerable.

Three, two, one . . . As his finger tightened around the trigger of his P229 and he squeezed, the bastard he'd previously shot jumped on his back and wrestled him for the gun. Joaquin fought back with an elbow to the gut and a right hook to the jaw, followed by another shot between the eyes. The hoodied goon fell to the ground, finally dead.

By then, McKeevy was peeling out of the parking lot in the red truck. Cold dread filling him, Joaquin gave chase on foot, but it was too late to keep the madman from stealing Bailey away—maybe forever.

* * *

THREE hours later, Joaquin paced the local-yokel sheriff's station, going out of his fucking mind. He scrubbed a hand down his face, worry eroding his guts like acid. How was Bailey feeling? Was she still alive? Was McKeevy, even now, beginning to tear her delicate body apart?

He couldn't think that or he'd go homicidal and insane.

"Coffee?" Deputy Williams offered with a sympathetic glance.

"No." He'd probably puke it up.

As soon as the red truck had disappeared from sight, Joaquin had raced to his own SUV and tried to give chase, but McKeevy and the dead dipshit had already slashed his wheels. Even with the tires on McKeevy's truck compromised, Joaquin doubted he'd be effective at catching him and Bailey.

Still, he'd tried, but he hadn't caught sight of them before he'd reached a fork in the road. Though lost and worried out of his mind, he'd refused to give up, exiting the remote, parklike area the same way he'd entered, all the while calling the number for the Philly branch of the FBI as he speeded down the two-lane road.

Still in mid-conversation with the feds, Joaquin hadn't encountered any sign of the red truck—just a police barricade. He'd been tossed out of his SUV, slapped in cuffs, and thrown in a cruiser faster than he could blink. Every one of his protests and explanations had fallen on deaf ears.

Quickly enough, he found out the waitress in the restaurant had called the sheriff about a shooting. Joaquin provided details and advised them about the body laid out in the lot. LOSS member Andrew Vorhees had perished on the asphalt. *Good riddance.*

For the past two hours, Joaquin had tried everything possible to prevent being charged with murder and to start a manhunt for Bailey before it was too late. After a few calls from Sean's end, the police had finally listened to reason and a pair of feds from Philly had entered.

They were working through the last of the red tape now and had ruled Vorhees's death self-defense. Soon, Joaquin would be free.

But McKeevy had three hours' head start.

"We found the red truck abandoned in an industrial area about five miles from the lake."

Joaquin let out a curse, trying to hold everything else in. "McKeevy wouldn't have been prepared to have his tire shot, and he may not have known that he'd be confronting us today, so I'm not sure he would have had a backup vehicle ready. Any reports of stolen cars nearby in the last few hours?"

A deputy tapped a few things on the ancient computer. "A new red Mercedes convertible and a minivan that's about two years old."

"He'd take the minivan," Joaquin assured him. "He's got a hostage to transport, and he wouldn't risk fleeing in the flashy-ass convertible."

One of the feds from Philly—Joaquin couldn't remember his name, so he'd dubbed the guy Generic Suit Two—nodded. "McKeevy will be heading west. We studied Vorhees's burner phone. He had a few text messages. He and McKeevy had orders to bring her and Aslanov's research to the LOSS leadership at their compound in a remote section of Decatur County, Iowa. We're calling agents in Kansas City and Omaha to see if they can seal off the roads around the compound. But even if he goes there, a barricade may not work. Remember, these are separatists, so they're survivalists, too. They grow their own food, slaughter their own meat. They've also made their own roads and tunnels."

"Would he fly?" Joaquin asked.

"Unless he's going to fly VFR, that would require him to file a flight plan." Suit One grimaced. "And that's if he found a plane and a pilot at the last minute, but we'll follow up on private pilots in the area. Still, I doubt he's flying, even though it's a long-ass drive to Iowa."

Joaquin agreed. And if McKeevy managed to get her on their land, Joaquin and the feds would have to find a judge and secure a warrant to search the property. That could take a day, probably more. Even if they obtained one within a few hours, McKeevy would still have Bailey all to himself for far too long. Once the sick bastard reached his hidey-hole, she'd likely endure hours of terrifying torture before he snuffed her out.

Ice ran through Joaquin's veins as he contemplated his next move. Technically, he wasn't a federal agent anymore. He certainly wasn't assigned to this case. The odds of them letting him tag along were zilch. But he couldn't sit on his hands and wait for one of the "big boys" to be Bailey's hero.

He had to get as close to that damn compound as possible.

"Am I free to go?" he asked.

The deputy looked at the sheriff, who nodded, then looked at the two suits from Philly. They both nodded as well.

"I need a ride to my car." Joaquin was already calculating how quickly he could get to Iowa.

"It's in the county lot. Maureen will take care of you," the deputy supplied helpfully. "But the tire's gone totally flat."

Joaquin didn't have time for vehicle repairs now. "What's the easiest way to rent a car?"

After a couple of suggestions—all of which would take hours—he felt as if his head might explode. Suddenly, his phone rang. Sean's number popped on the screen.

"Hey, can't talk now unless you've got an update." He'd spoken to Sean after first being dragged to this sheriff station, so he wasn't expecting a lot.

"Where are you?"

"Still at the Carbon County, Pennsylvania, Sheriff's Office."

"Hurry up. I'm sitting on Xander's private jet at the Philly airport, refueling and waiting for you."

They'd come to help him rescue Bailey.

Relief lifted a mountain of crushing fear from his chest. God bless Xander for lending his plane. And bless Sean for leaving Dallas and his fiancée less than seventy-two hours before his wedding in order to help.

"I owe you, man. Big. I'll get there as quickly as possible."

"Good. From what I hear, we need to get to Iowa."

No shit.

They rang off, and the suits agreed to give him a ride to the airport since it wasn't far out of their way, as long as he promised not to interfere in their investigation. Joaquin agreed. Of course he lied through his teeth, but hell, he would have sworn he had four heads to secure that ride.

The tense drive seemed to take forever. Joaquin kept looking at the time on his phone, thinking of all the moments slipping by that could be Bailey's last. Where was she now? He had no way to track her. They had a license plate of the stolen minivan they suspected McKeevy was in, but what if they'd miscalculated? What if he'd already ditched that car?

Abject fear ate at him from the inside, cracking the hard shell of his composure. He had to get it together for Bailey's sake.

As soon as the agents dropped him off at the terminal that serviced the private jets, Sean met him.

Having slung the backpack the sheriff had returned to him on his back and ensured his weapon was secure, Joaquin shook the man's hand. "Thanks for being here so quickly. I know you're getting married—"

"Callie understands all too well what Bailey is going through. We agreed immediately that I needed to be here."

After a decade running from LOSS, the heiress probably understood better than anyone. Joaquin's respect for her went up another notch. "If we get Bailey back and recover the research, Callie will never have to worry again either."

"Right now, she's just concerned about your girl. I have instructions to text Callie the second I have news. Thorpe is trying to keep her calm."

"You didn't have to do this."

"Any family of Kata's is family of ours." Sean clapped him on the back.

Stunned silent with gratitude, he followed Sean through the building, out to the tarmac. Why would people he'd met a handful of days ago disrupt their wedding plans to help him rescue a girl they hadn't known last week? He wasn't totally sure, but he thanked fuck they were willing.

After a quick trek up the airstairs, Joaquin's thoughts still raced. He ducked to enter the cabin and saw Stone banging away on a computer. He never looked up. "Hi, man. Sorry I keep accompanying the bad news."

"Not your fault," Joaquin assured him.

"I'm looking to see if LOSS has any sort of private network I can hack. If I can see their internal communications, we'll be better informed so we can plan our next course of action."

Good thinking. Stone had located Bailey once. Maybe he'd be helpful again. "I appreciate it."

Stone shook his head as if to wave him away and kept pounding on the keys.

To his right, Hunter rose to meet him, hand outstretched. "We'll do our best to get her back."

Gaping, he shook his brother-in-law's hand. "Why are you here? Your wife is having a baby."

"His wife is not giving birth in the next five minutes," Kata said, exiting the restroom at the back of the plane. "My obstetrician okayed travel for another two weeks. So after a short discussion—"

"Temper tantrum," Hunter corrected.

"My husband and I came to help." Kata went on as if Hunter hadn't spoken. "I'm not just his wife; I'm your sister, too."

And she shouldn't be here. This mission could get dangerous. He looked at Hunter as if the guy had lost his mind. His brother-in-law shrugged. “She agreed to stay out of harm’s way. Stone will keep watch over her.”

Joaquin’s gaze fell to an older man beside Hunter. They looked remarkably similar, right down to the rugged face and shocking blue eyes.

The man stood and stuck his hand out. “Caleb Edgington. I’m Hunter’s father.”

Numbly, Joaquin shook it. “My mother’s new husband?”

Why the hell was this guy here? Yeah, he looked athletic, especially for his age, but they didn’t have time to help Grandpa if his back went out or he needed Jell-O.

“Yes.”

“I appreciate the offer to help, but this could get really physical and dangerous.”

Caleb’s expression iced over and he suddenly looked like a mean motherfucker.

Hunter cleared his throat. “My father served the army for twenty-four years, retiring as a full bird colonel. He fought in Kuwait and Afghanistan. He’s participated in combat training and clandestine missions all over the world. For over a decade, he’s consulted as a military specialist and owned his own private company of operatives. He’s a tactical genius.”

The older man crossed his arms over his chest. “I came because my wife asked me to.”

Joaquin couldn’t quite decipher Caleb’s tone. He seemed very straightforward . . . but underlying grit and a hint of disapproval laced his voice. Naturally, he’d side with his wife, who probably wished her deadbeat son would call or visit more. Joaquin shoved the sting of guilt aside. No time to think about that now.

“Sure. Thanks.”

“You and I have never met, but we’re family now. Family helps its own.”

Mind-blowing. More people willing to go out on a limb to help a relative stranger, just because there happened to be a little blood mixed in along the way. He'd seen this group's closeness over the past few days, but he'd never expected it to include him. Against his will, he felt humbled.

Knowing he didn't have time to examine the sentiment now, he addressed the group at large. "Do we know anything else?"

"The Kansas City and Omaha offices have been alerted," Sean assured him. "The known roads into the compound are on surveillance. They're worried a barricade will signal LOSS that we're onto them and they'll send McKeevy elsewhere. So there's an APB out for him. The highway patrol in every state between here and Iowa will be on the lookout for anyone matching his description. They're circulating pictures of Bailey, too. Other than that, all we can do is wait."

The captain announced moments later that they were taking off and everyone would need to buckle up. Joaquin's gaze fell to the only available seat on the plane—next to his sister.

Dropping into it, he set his backpack between his feet and strapped in. Within moments, they were airborne and reaching their cruising altitude. The silence felt crushing.

"I've done a lot of digging," Stone said suddenly, still tapping computer keys. "LOSS doesn't have any sort of internal hub or electronic communication system."

"We know they're using burner phones," Sean tossed out.

Stone nodded. "I've checked all the private charter companies within a fifty-mile radius of Lake Harmony. I'm not seeing a record of any last-minute flights. That doesn't make it impossible, but less likely."

"So he's probably driving," Caleb mused aloud.

Joaquin nodded. "That explains why they tranqued Bailey."

"Yeah, he wouldn't want to drive all night with an uncooperative hostage," Hunter added.

Joaquin was thankful to have something constructive to think about. "He'll have to switch vehicles often, and if he's smart, he has a stash of plates or steals some every time he swipes a new vehicle to keep any pesky highway patrol off his scent longer."

"Absolutely," Sean agreed.

"If he takes Interstate 80, it's the straightest shot," Stone pointed out. "It's possible someone will spot him if they know which vehicle to look for at any given time, so I'll try to keep up with reports of stolen cars. But some folks may not realize their car is missing until tomorrow morning when they try to head for work."

"Aren't parts of Interstate 80 a toll road?" Kata asked hopefully. "Maybe those cameras will catch something."

"Which is another reason he'd be switching out the license plates," Hunter informed her.

"You're right." Joaquin's sister fell back into her seat again with a sigh.

"And cameras in toll booths don't usually capture an image of the driver," Stone added. "Besides, I'd have to hack into multiple states databases and watch hours of footage."

Hours Bailey might not have.

"McKeevy is wearing a black T-shirt, if that helps." Joaquin raked a hand through his hair. "But even if a camera snapped an image of his face, with night having fallen, the picture won't show much."

"True." Stone twisted his lips in thought. "He'd be smart enough to hide his face. He also might take a few back roads for a little insurance."

"In his shoes, if I could afford the extra time, I would." Sean reached for his nearby water bottle.

"So chances are, we're going to reach Iowa way before McKeevy." Joaquin said what everyone had to be thinking. "We just have to wait for him to show up? Where?"

And Joaquin wondered how he would avoid going batshit crazy.

"We'll get some sleep and food," Sean said. "It will give us an advantage. McKeevy doesn't dare stop for much of either with a hostage. Since you killed Vorhees, the driver he would have passed the wheel to won't be with him. He'll be limping in tired and hungry."

"And probably with a horrific need to pee." Stone snickered.

"He'll have to stop to get gas," Kata pointed out.

"The bureau is doing everything it can to watch public places along the expected route."

"What about a roadblock or a checkpoint along the road, away from the LOSS compound?" She looked at Sean expectantly. "Call it a sobriety check."

"The second the truckers encounter one, they'll be chatting that up on their radios. I'm sure McKeevy will be listening in and will act accordingly." Sean shrugged.

"So don't try at all?" Kata asked, her tone hinting that suggestion sounded ridiculous.

"No, better to let him think he's getting away with something and grab him at the expected destination, rather than spook him early. God knows what he'd do then."

Kata sighed. "Too bad we can't just trace her phone."

Joaquin's head popped up. He snatched up his backpack and rifled through it, but he already knew he didn't have it. Bailey did. If McKeevy was smart, he would have ditched it long ago, but maybe he was too busy driving and laying low to search an unconscious woman. Maybe he was too panicked to think about the fact that the phone could be traced.

"It might still be on her," he told the others, focusing on the hacker.

"Number?" Stone barked.

Joaquin flipped through his own phone, then rattled off the number. And he held his breath. *Dear heaven, please let it be this easy.* Please say he could have Bailey back with just a simple trace of an iPhone and a call to some authorities.

Stone's fingers flew over his keyboard again. He waited. He looked puzzled. He frowned. After typing a bit more and swiping his thumb over the keypad at lightning speed, he sighed. "Looks like McKeevy dumped it off the interstate near Milton, Pennsylvania."

Joaquin's heart sank. Nausea turned his guts. Having his hope dashed was almost as cruel as having her taken in the first place.

"The good news is, McKeevy is definitely headed west, exactly like we thought."

"Any idea how long ago he dumped it?"

Stone clicked around a bit more. "About three hours ago."

A definite dead end. Dread swam thick in his chest, congealed in his belly until he swore he'd throw up. He fucking couldn't lose her now.

Without more logistics to discuss, everyone fell silent. Sean texted furiously, probably to Thorpe or Callie. Stone tapped the side of his laptop—an annoying tic that made Joaquin want to break his fingers. Hunter and Caleb both reclined their heads as if they'd closed their eyes and kicked back. He envied soldiers' ability to catnap in most any situation. Joaquin felt too panicked and wired to try. Beside him, Kata stared out the window.

Now that Joaquin couldn't do anything active to recover Bailey—he simply had to sit and wait until he arrived in Iowa—he felt like he was going to crawl out of his skin. He hated feeling helpless and hopeless, wondering again and again if Bailey was suffering while he couldn't be there to save her. The only bright spot was that McKeevy had tranquilized her. She'd be out for hours still. Joaquin had to believe the sick fuck wouldn't hurt her until he had a chance to question her.

Suddenly, Kata reached for his hand. He turned to look at her, watching her unconsciously stroke her belly. Funny, a few days ago he'd had something close to contempt for Hunter and his sister setting up house and having a baby. Now he envied them like hell. What would it be like to look at Bailey every day and see her caress the growing baby bump they'd created together? To kiss her every night, hold their children, grow old together?

"I'm not going to give you platitudes," Kata said. "You're freaking out and you have every reason to. I can see you feel responsible—"

"I love her," he gasped out.

"I know. I could tell at Thorpe's party. I've never seen you care that much about anyone, so I'm here to help you save her. She's good for you, and after almost two decades, I want my brother back."

"I can't help her and it's killing me. What kind of protector does that make me?" And what the hell would he do if he couldn't save her?

"Don't think the worst," she advised. "I know that feels impossible. But I had a psycho put a gun to my head as Hunter watched. I fell two stories out of a window. If that asshole who threatened me hadn't unwittingly broken my fall, I'd be dead."

Joaquin hadn't known that. Even through his panic for Bailey, the thought disturbed him. He could have lost his sister several years ago and he hadn't known it. *Son of a bitch.*

"But we got through," she assured. "We played as smart as we could, and fate smiled on us. You can't lose faith."

"Bailey is unconscious. She's defenseless." He heard the alarm in his own voice and winced.

"But McKeevy is alone and we have every indication that he's driving. You know his number one goal right now must be focusing on the road and not getting caught. His next order of business will be to read whatever is on that disk."

His head knew that. His heart? He wasn't sure it would survive.

"I can't lose her," he choked out.

"These guys will do everything possible to make sure you won't. You may not know them that well, but I do. I promise, they'll do everything humanly possible—along with some shit you might not have believed at all doable."

Joaquin didn't doubt that. He simply hoped it would be enough.

Chapter Nineteen

BAILEY awoke slowly, in stages. A chill settled over her skin. Her feet felt like blocks of ice. Because her muscles seemed to weigh a million pounds, moving would take superhuman effort. The dark blanket of sleep lulled her back, but her bladder protested that she *had* to get up.

Vaguely, she recalled trying to wake earlier and would have sworn she'd been in the back of a moving vehicle. She had a vague recollection of a man crouched over her and a needle pricking her arm . . . then nothing again. Had that been a dream? Or like everything else, a bad memory?

Mustering her strength, she tried to shift to raise herself up. But her arms wouldn't budge. They felt glued to the table. That made no sense.

She opened her eyes wide, taking in her surroundings. What she saw made her gasp in horror. Dim lighting illuminated the small room everywhere but the dark corners. She didn't see a single window. She lay on a cold, hard surface that gleamed like stainless steel. A surgical table? Yes, and she'd been strapped to it. Plastic covered the floor beneath. All manner of blades hung on the walls—axes, knives, scalpels, and scissors. She saw other implements she didn't have names for, but they terrified her.

Where the hell was she?

The door opened and a vaguely familiar man strode in, wearing a light blue military uniform she remembered seeing once as a child, the last time she'd seen Viktor. It didn't look like one that belonged to any regular branch of the military, but that garb was indelibly printed on her memory.

He shut the door behind him with an eager smile. "Morning. I've been waiting for you."

With another glance around, Bailey was afraid to ask what for.

She studied his face again, wondering why it looked familiar. Then it hit her. Joaquin had shown her a picture of this man. As a child, she'd watched him drag her father from their house for the last time. This was Joseph McKeevy.

Her body turned icy in terror.

"Where is Joaquin?" Her voice shook.

"If you mean the former federal scum you've been fucking, he got away. Don't worry. I'll track him down and cap his ass—as soon as I take care of you."

Bailey didn't want to know what that entailed. "Where am I?"

"Some place you'll never escape," he promised smugly. "Since you're the one strapped to the table, I'm the one who asks the questions. So you better shut up unless I ask you to speak. Women are like kids, better seen and not heard."

She wanted to tell him what a misogynist he was, but didn't dare. Instead, she consoled herself with the notion that he wouldn't understand her insult anyway.

After a long moment of silence, he smiled. "I'm glad you're learning your place real quick. The ones who do feel a lot less pain. Do you need to pee?"

"Yes." And any chance to be unstrapped from this table might be a chance—no matter how slim—to escape.

He released the Velcro on the straps around her wrists and ankles with a loud ripping noise, then he dragged her to her feet. Dizziness swamped her, and Bailey reached out to steady herself, but found only air. Then McKeevy pushed her toward a door standing slightly ajar on the far side of the room. When she fell and scraped her knees, he laughed.

"Some ballerina. You can't even stand up straight, you stupid bitch. Go on." He gestured to the door. "You got two minutes or I come in there and it gets ugly."

She let herself into the tiny bathroom and flipped on the dingy light. The room didn't have a window. The cabinets were empty. Everything looked old. It smelled that way, too, but she managed to do her business, then shimmy back into her jeans. After quickly washing her hands, she inched out of the room, to find McKeevy waiting.

"Hop on the table." He patted the cold, metallic slab.

"Can I stand?"

"Nope."

His answer sounded more like a growl, but she knew if she simply lay down, he would kill her. All the implements on the wall were beyond her reach. She couldn't try to jump or rush him. She lacked the strength to overpower him, and the element of surprise wouldn't be enough to counter that. So now what? Bailey hesitated, her thoughts whirling.

"The longer you stand there, the more you're pissing me off. The more painful I can make your last hours."

So her death wasn't a matter of "if" but "when" in his head. Still, she didn't want to just lie down and die like a good little girl.

"I'm so thirsty. Water?"

"What do you think this is, a hotel?"

"No, I'm just so dry. I'd hoped—"

"Jesus, you're a pain in my ass." He sighed and bent to a bar-size fridge under the wooden tool bench built along one wall. He never took his stare off her as he reached in and plucked out a bottle, then put it into her hand.

Slowly, Bailey unscrewed the cap, looking at any available option she might have to escape. He'd placed his big body between her and the main door. Everything else was walls. As she took a swig of water, she tried to tamp down her frustration. There had to be *something* she could do to save herself. She clung to the knowledge that if Joaquin was alive, he'd be looking for her. Until then? She took another sip, still thinking, but came up empty-handed.

Suddenly, McKeevy grabbed her wrist and seized the bottle from her hand, slamming it on the counter. "That's enough."

Before she could fight, he slung her back on the table and straddled her. She struggled and writhed, bucking to be free, but he slapped her hard. Bailey's head reeled and her cheek throbbed with pain. Since he outweighed her, he easily pinned her to the cold table. In less than a minute, he had her immobilized again with the straps.

McKeevy laughed at her once more. "Stupid cunt. For that, I'll make sure the end is a screaming terrible time for you."

The chill that swept through Bailey's blood wasn't just the low ambient temperature in the room. His words filled her with savage terror. Joaquin had shown her pictures of the carnage he was capable of. Even now, he was probably thinking about all the possibilities and going out of his mind.

She wished she could reassure him or at least say good-bye and tell him that she didn't blame him for the way things would likely end. She hoped he wouldn't crawl deeper into his self-isolation if the worst happened. If he learned instead that life was short and love was worth sharing for as many days as he had on this earth, she could go peacefully. She'd be comforted by the idea that her death could bring him more life.

Tears sprang to her eyes, and she closed them. McKeevy was going to strip her of skin and bone, blood, heartbeat, and life. She refused to give him her dignity, too.

He didn't seem to notice or care that she shut him out. Instead, he moved away and then returned. Bailey cracked one eye open. He held a pair of gardening shears, snapping them together in his meaty hands.

"Normally, I like to start by taking fingers off one at a time. They're sensitive and people start thinking then about the loss of a normal life if they ever get free. I do the first one slow like, so they really feel it. I take my sweet time getting around to the second so they have plenty of time to dread it. They're far more likely to cough up any information they've got then. But I'm going to bet you value your toes more."

Bailey's heart stopped as he slid down the length of her body with an evil grin and grabbed her left foot. "We'll start with the little one and work our way up if you can't tell me what you know."

She could barely find her voice through her terror. "You have the research. I was five when he died. I don't know anything more."

"Are there any more copies of this disk anywhere?"

"I don't think so. He didn't give me another clue to follow or any other indication of a second hiding place. I know from the news that he gave one copy to Daniel Howe, who funded his research. Howe destroyed it. Viktor kept the other copy and you have it. That's all I know."

McKeevy ran a hand along the scraggly dusting of hair on his chin. "Who else knew about this copy of the research?"

"That we found it?" She shook her head. "You took it too quickly for us to inform anyone."

"But that former fed you were bedding down with knows people. Who was he talking to before you found it? Who do you think he's called since?"

Bailey refused to tell him the truth. She didn't want to implicate Sean and put him or Callie at risk, in case he hadn't made that connection. She was likely going to lose her toes—and her life—anyway, so what was the difference?

"I don't know. A fed. He never used names. He didn't trust me. I was just his hostage."

"Yeah." He scoffed. "One who put out a lot. I took the hotel room next to yours last night. I heard all that screaming."

Horror screeched through her veins. He'd *listened* to them making love? Bailey didn't know what to say exactly. "I . . ."

"Save the excuse. Muñoz seems to like you well enough. I'm not buying that you don't know anything about who he's talking to. I'll give you one more shot. Tell me what his plans were once you found the disk. Who was he going to give it to? And before you lie again, remember that I can skip ahead and start removing organs while you're still alive. That always makes for an agonizing, scream-filled death. I know which ones to remove first to make you beg for the end. I've had lots of practice. So, what's your answer?"

She bit her lip. The moment she opened her mouth and spit out her next lie, he was going to carve her up. "You have to understand. I met him when he drugged me and took me from my house in the middle of the night."

"The fucker beat me there by a few hours. I had a plan, and he fucked it up. I knew then you had to be Tatiana Aslanov."

"I don't know anything. I'd hoped that sex would appease him."

"You didn't offer me any," McKeevy snarled.

Bailey couldn't tell him that psychos with stained teeth and body odor issues weren't her thing. That wouldn't end well for her. Still, she couldn't bring herself to offer her body to McKeevy. It would only postpone her execution, not stay it. And for her short time left, she'd end up hating herself.

"He had sex with me unprotected. I don't know if he has any diseases . . ." It was weak, but all she had.

He scoffed, then shook his head. "If we had more time, I'd demand a damn blow job, but I know he's going to come for you. And he's going to bring feds. Besides, I don't want his leftovers. Start talking."

"I swear that I don't know anything. I can't tell you information I don't know. Please . . ." She hoped begging would appease him. He seemed like the sort who enjoyed preying on the weaker.

He dragged the sharp edge of the gardening shears up her foot, drawing a thin line of blood. "Are you sure?"

It stung. Bailey sucked in a breath, trying to keep a lid on her panic. "I swear."

"And you don't know anything about Aslanov's research, how to read his notes, what the formulas meant?"

"I was five." She tried not to cry, but the terror was beginning to swallow her whole.

"We captured a few research subjects in South America. I've got one jailed in the mine below the compound. We need to understand your father's notes to continue our tests. But if you can't help me . . ."

McKeevy reached behind him and ditched the gardening shears for a scalpel off the wall. He set the sharp edge right against her breastbone and began to press. Bailey didn't dare thrash for fear he'd cut her deeper. Instead, she whimpered, wishing she could go out with more grace. God, if she could just get one more opportunity to be uncuffed and fight back, she'd make the most of it.

Suddenly, someone banged on the door. "Joe!"

"I'm working the prisoner here." He sounded annoyed, his scalpel hand shaking.

Blood pooled between her breasts.

"We've got a big fucking problem. Klein is gathering all the officers."

"For fuck's sake." He slammed his implement on the table just above her head, then sneered down at her. "Don't go anywhere."

Then he turned and left. The second the door closed behind him, Bailey dragged in a sharp, ragged breath. Relief spilled through her, leaving her trembling. She knew this reprieve was only momentary, but she'd take it. She wanted nothing more than to close her eyes and mentally escape, but she had to keep her wits about her and find a way out of here.

She jerked her gaze all over the room and thrashed as hard as she could to see if there was any give in her bonds, but she was irrevocably tied down and had no means of escape.

As she reached that terrible conclusion, the door creaked open again. She craned her head around to see if McKeevy had come back to finish up her terrible death. Instead, a very young pregnant girl entered the room. Bailey figured she was probably sixteen and at least six months pregnant.

"Don't ask questions. Just listen. Otter Klein, the leader of LOSS, just found out the feds have the compound surrounded and that they've obtained a search warrant from a judge. Otter, Joe, and the rest, they won't go down without a fight."

Bailey welcomed the news that help was on the way, but wondered why this girl was telling her—and if that help would come too late. Or was this girl setting a trap? Maybe, but Bailey didn't see that she had much choice except to listen.

As she waited for more, she realized the girl was loosening the strap around her wrist as quietly as possible. Bailey began wiggling her hand to speed up the process, fighting to be free. Moments later, she pulled her left hand from the bindings and reached across her body to release the right. The girl moved to her ankles.

"Why are you helping me?" she asked.

Her rescuer turned sad blue eyes on her. "I ran away from home at fourteen after I got in a fight with my momma. Joe picked me up off the street, promising me a ride to a friend's. Instead, he brought me here and raped me. This will be the second baby he's put up in me, so I can't go nowhere. I won't leave my boy with him. But if you get out, will you tell my momma that I'm still alive? Here's her name and address." The girl teared up as she pressed a piece of paper into Bailey's hand.

Her heart broke for the young woman who'd been so trapped and abused. Bailey couldn't imagine just how hopeless she must feel. "What's your name?"

"Destiny." Her voice cracked.

"How old are you?"

"Just turned sixteen. Look, I'm going to get you out in the hall. At the end, there's a table with flashlights. Take one and go to the stairs. All the men are holed up, trying to decide what to do about the feds coming. If you stick to the shadows, you should be able to make it out that door. Once you're through, you'll find a tunnel. Run straight ahead. Don't veer off. And keep running. That leads to an open field just off the compound. Joe brought you in that way. The nearest town is a few miles south, but the feds will probably spot you before then."

"Come with me," Bailey said, grabbing her hands. "Get your son. We'll do this together."

"Can't." Destiny held back her tears. "The women are gathering to make survival packs in case we have to abandon the compound and hike into Canada. If I don't turn up real soon, they'll come looking for me, then no one will get away. I'm supposed to be rounding up the little kids now. The bigger kids are helping me."

Bailey wanted to ask a hundred questions. Were all the women here against their will? How many people lived in this compound? She stifled her curiosity. None of that information was relevant now.

"I will do everything I can to get out of here and see your mother, I promise. And if I can do anything at all to free you, I will."

Tears splashed down the girl's young cheeks. "I'd appreciate it. Billy, my boy, he deserves more than this life. He's barely a year old, but I'm already worried about him. And if Joe knew I was here, he'd kill me."

"Then let's go."

Bailey couldn't find her shoes. They'd sure help with survival in the wild, but she'd ten times rather take her chances out there than in here.

The girl nodded, then opened the door, peeking out and looking both ways. She opened the door wide and motioned Bailey toward another door, at the end of a long, narrow hall.

"That way," Destiny whispered. "Out the door and keep going."

"Thank you." Bailey squeezed her shoulder. "I'm going to make sure you get your life back, too."

"God bless you." The girl picked up her long skirt and dashed away in the opposite direction.

Down that part of the hall, Bailey could hear men shouting about the fucking feds. A loud crash sounded, followed by the sound of fists connecting, then some grunts. A door creaked open and footsteps darted down the hall. Someone shouted again, this time an ugly curse. Had she already been spotted? Had someone discovered her missing?

Bailey didn't hang around to find out. With her heart thumping, she turned toward the door and hugged the shadowy wall, darting down the industrial tiled floor. With every step, she could only pray that she'd make it to the door before anyone caught her. If not . . . well, she knew the consequences.

* * *

IT felt like thirty years had passed since Joaquin had awakened next to Bailey, rather than just over thirty hours. The nightmare seemed never ending.

He paced the county sheriff's office in Leon, about ten miles up the road from the LOSS compound, then turned to Sean. "I don't like the strategy of executing a search warrant when we never saw McKeevy drive in. Securing it probably alerted LOSS that we're onto them. What if they end her quickly for it?"

Sean tossed his hands up at the question. "I wish I knew what the hell was going on. He should have arrived hours ago. We found that SUV stolen just outside of Davenport abandoned about two miles from here. The local sheriff has a K-9 unit. They're picking up Bailey's scent all over the vehicle. She made it that far. Where else would he have taken her? Somehow, he got her into that compound without traveling that road. We've got agents and deputies combing the area now. We'll figure out how and rescue her. You have to believe that or you're going to lose your mind."

"Do I need to remind you what this monster is capable of?" Wondering what she might be enduring even now kept slaying him over and over. Even if he got her back alive, would she ever be whole again, inside and out? The worrying and not knowing were killing him.

Hunter approached from behind and slapped him on the back. "Breathe, buddy. Worrying isn't going to help her."

His head knew that he couldn't help Bailey if he didn't stop freaking out. But he hadn't let himself really care about anything or anyone since his father. He'd forgotten how much loss could hurt. Hurt, hell. He was hemorrhaging. The fear was eviscerating his fucking soul.

Joaquin tried to take a deep breath. "Is there anything new?"

"No. We should hear something in the next hour. The special agent in charge is going to let us ride down with the folks serving the warrant. We have to stay a quarter of a mile away from the compound while they go in, but we'll be close in case Bailey needs you after they extract her. I know you wanted to go in. I did, too. But we're lucky we got this concession. They won't budge another inch."

Joaquin knew it was more than he should have expected and probably a hell of a protocol breach since neither of them were federal agents anymore, but yeah, he'd wanted to be part of the crew who rescued Bailey . . . if she was still alive.

"When are we leaving?"

"In five." Sean tossed him a protein bar, then followed that with a bottle of water. "You haven't eaten anything all day, so until you do, you're not going."

He really didn't think he could, but if it meant the difference between going and staying, he'd choke it down. "Fine."

Sean's phone beeped. He lifted it and shook his head. "Callie . . ."

He tapped out a reply and read it aloud. "'News soon. Patience, lovely. Or you'll learn it from Thorpe while I'm gone.'"

As he hit send, he grinned and walked off. Sean's life was looking up in every way. Joaquin didn't know if he even gave a shit that he had one after today.

Forcing himself to swallow the bar and water, he made sure his gun carried the fresh clip Hunter had given him and tucked it away. The troops started gathering near the door. The FBI had overrun this little sheriff's office. That was about the only thing that gave Joaquin hope. They damn sure wanted whatever was on that flash disk. He hoped to fuck if they recovered it today, they would destroy it.

Sean motioned to him, and he joined the group as they filed out the door. A cluster of black SUVs waited in front. Joaquin didn't know where they'd come from and he didn't care. Hunter kissed his wife, and they shared a quiet moment. He assured her he'd be back and smoothed an affectionate hand over her belly. Joaquin wondered what would happen if his sister's husband didn't make it home. She would be devastated, kind of like Joaquin himself felt right now. She'd turn in to herself in grief and maybe never come out. Joaquin wouldn't blame her. Yet she smiled and kissed her husband as she took the terrible risk. He didn't understand.

The short ride south covered some remote prairie land. Joaquin tried to divorce his mind from the wretched fear eating him alive.

After what seemed like an interminable trip, the agent driving exited the main road and turned onto a bumpy dirt one. "Here's where I leave you. We'll be back to get you as soon as possible. Don't walk to the compound. Don't interfere." He looked at Sean. "We're only allowing this as a favor to you, so don't make us regret it."

"Understood. Thanks," Sean answered, climbing out of the front seat of the vehicle.

Hunter followed, opening the right rear door. His father scooted over and eased out next as Joaquin opened the back door on the left and stepped out into the stiff breeze. As evening approached, the four of them turned and began trekking into a wide open, grassy field. He had a feeling it was going to be a long, miserable night. Putting one foot in front of the other was a challenge. Even breathing felt like a chore. He had to keep going for Bailey.

Sean waved off the fed, who drove away in a cloud of dust.

"What *are* we allowed to do?" Joaquin asked. The restrictions chafed.

"We scout around a bit," Sean offered. "Stone just texted me information about some abandoned limestone quarry not far from here. I'm going to bet LOSS has made use of those tunnels and dug a way out, aboveground. Paranoid paramilitary loons usually have an escape route."

"Absolutely," Hunter agreed. "If they have any idea you're coming, they'll use it, too. Do the feds know about the tunnels?"

"I'm sure they do. Now, whether they've put two and two together and decided that LOSS is making use of them . . ." Sean shrugged.

"If we find that opening and surround it, we'll be prepared in the event the separatists send their soldiers out to wage war on the FBI."

"I hope that's exactly what they do. Stone also did a little research today and told me that over the past year they've purchased enough explosives to rig this entire compound to blow into a million pieces. Let's hope they don't take the nuclear option."

Joaquin's blood froze over as they began walking in the direction of the coordinates Stone had sent Sean earlier. The walk dragged on as the sun inched down. The feds should have arrived by now. He listened for sounds of gunshots, but heard only eerie silence. Somehow, that grated on him even more. Were they too late? Had LOSS already abandoned the compound in the dead of night? Had McKeevy secreted Bailey somewhere else entirely so he could take her apart at his leisure?

A million scenarios all zipped through this head, each uglier than the last. He swallowed down the panic threatening to rise again. How the fuck had he let his guard down and fallen so deeply in love with this woman in just a handful of days? A damn stupid move—especially since he'd thought he knew better.

As the sun began to dip lower, Sean and Caleb both extracted flashlights from packs they must have grabbed at the sheriff's station. They paired up, Hunter veering off with his dad over a rise. Joaquin followed Sean as they scouted the area around Stone's coordinates.

Grass and shrubs coming back to life from the winter dotted the gentle hillside. Behind a cluster of foliage, they found the SUV that McKeevy had most recently stolen and abandoned. Every door was wide open, as was the hatch in back. The FBI had been through it with everything but a microscope and planned to tow it off shortly, so Joaquin knew he wouldn't find Bailey or any sign of her here. But knowing she'd come this far in the vehicle helped him feel closer to finding her. Of course, the K-9 unit couldn't tell him whether she had still been alive when she'd left her scent in this car. But he refused to think that she hadn't.

Static filtered in over the radio the agents had lent Sean, then muffled voices. Sean lifted it from his belt and held it ear-level between them. As they listened, the agents approached the compound, discussing the electronic gates designed to deliver a stunning jolt to trespassers. The perimeter of the compound was surrounded by fences less expensive and off-putting—simple chain link with barbed wire—but attack dogs roamed the premises and had already sniffed out the feds, barking relentlessly.

Joaquin closed his eyes. The FBI's strategy of playing official and making nice didn't feel right. The feds would have to force their way into this compound—and that would be more difficult now that they'd lost the element of surprise. *Son of a bitch.*

"We've got to find a way in there," Joaquin insisted. "Now. They're going to fail."

"They can deal with fences and dogs. This is nothing unexpected. Be patient."

"Would you be patient if Callie was trapped in there?" Joaquin demanded.

"I'd be whatever I needed to be in order to get her out." Sean sent him a dark frown. "Get your shit together."

As the other man stalked off with the flashlight, Joaquin followed, cursing. Sean was right.

Sean ascended the top of a gentle rise, then frowned. He shined the flashlight directly down, kneeling to shove aside long strands of grass swaying with the wind. "I found some sort of metal flap. It's been painted a dark green to match the grass." He shoved his palms under the lip and tried to lift it. "I need your help."

If this door was a way into the quarry, they might be able to get into the compound. This might be Joaquin's way to rescue Bailey.

He knelt beside Sean. Together they tugged and pulled. The sucker was heavy and stuck good.

"Damn it. Why won't it open?"

"There may be a latch on the inside," Joaquin mused. "We need a damn crowbar. I had one in my SUV. If I had thought for a second we'd need it, I would have—"

A deafening roar exploded a moment later. The ground beneath their feet rolled. A fireball lit up the sky. It had come from the direction of the compound.

Bailey.

Joaquin staggered back, staring at the twisting wall of flame in the distance. With his heart thundering, he charged toward it, icy disbelief washing through him. "No!"

Sean chased him down and grabbed him around the neck, holding him back. "Where do you think you're going, man? That fire is probably a thousand degrees. You have to stay back."

A blaze like that would instantly kill anyone near it. Those on the perimeter of the blast might be lucky to only lose a limb or two, but the falling shrapnel could slice skin open wide, or be sucked into lungs. Or the blaze might just cook them alive. Any of those could kill a person more slowly.

And every bit of intel they had put Bailey inside that compound. Or she had been until it blew into little pieces.

Ash and debris rained down nearby—part of a chair, a children's toy, the handle of a rake. Sean put his hands over his head for cover and ducked. Something heavy landed in the shadows about a hundred feet away with a resounding, metallic *clunk*. Joaquin stood in mute horror, gaping at the flames licking high into the darkening sky and struggling to breathe.

His mind screamed that he'd lost Bailey and his life would never be whole or right again.

Sean's radio filled with curses, another explosion, then static. Everything sounded chaotic—lots of fumbling and disbelief.

"Let's get back to the main highway and find someone to call for backup and emergency services." Sean pulled Joaquin away from the carnage.

He couldn't leave Bailey dead here like she hadn't mattered. Like he accepted that she'd simply become a part of the ground. Was he supposed to just leave behind his heart? The potential seed of his family and future?

Please God, let me have a miracle. Let her be alive.

Even as the thought crossed his mind, he knew better.

The numbness of shock gave way to the crushing wall of pain then. Bailey was gone. Dead. No more. He hadn't been good enough, fast enough. He hadn't saved her. Her tragic childhood, her lie of an adolescence, her finally learning the truth of her identity—all for nothing.

Joaquin didn't know how he'd live without her. This crippling agony felt like his father's death, only worse. As a boy, the feelings of helplessness and hopelessness had been hard to swallow and difficult to process. As a man, this twisting anguish was impossible to comprehend or accept.

He'd. Failed. Her. No way to sugarcoat that.

Yeah, he supposed he should take comfort that an explosion had probably taken Bailey, rather than McKeevy's blade, but he couldn't be grateful for a single fucking thing right now.

"I lost her." His voice sounded gravelly and raw as he sank to his knees.

Standing right beside him, Sean helped him to his feet again. "You don't know that for sure. It's possible that explosion is meant to deter the agents or she wasn't near the actual blast."

"Bullshit!" He whirled and focused all his disbelief and fury on Sean. "You said yourself they'd rigged the whole compound to blow. An explosion that big is the whole fucking place going up in flames. They committed mass suicide and took her with them. She's dead. And I fucking didn't stop it." He pointed to himself. "I took her from her bed and I dragged her into this shit—"

"She would have died days ago in Houston if you hadn't abducted her. I know it's awful. I know you're angry. I wish I could say something to change that. Maybe . . . it was just her time. You did the best you could."

"It wasn't good enough." He beat his chest. His eyes stung. "I never let myself care because the pain of loss is too fucking difficult to bear. She slipped under my guard . . . Her and those dancing shoes, those blue eyes, her big fucking heart . . . The one goddamn time I let myself care, I led her right to her death. She's probably up in heaven right now hating me."

God, the pain was enough to implode him.

Joaquin dropped his face into his hands. Shockingly, tears fell. They pricked his eyes like a dozen needles, scalded his cheeks like trails of flame. When he swiped them away, more of the fuckers just tumbled. Why wouldn't they stop? How the hell did he shut this down? How could he get back to being numb and alone, not giving a shit about anything or anyone?

"She's not hating you." Sean tried to console him. "I won't give you false hope. She's likely gone. But the Bailey I knew cared about you too much and wouldn't want to see you hurting."

Joaquin heard the man. Sean might even be right. But he just couldn't take more solace now. Maybe not ever. He didn't deserve it. "Go the fuck away."

"I'm not leaving you here."

"Do it. Just fucking do it!" He clenched his fists. "I don't want you. And don't send Hunter. I don't want anyone. Do you fucking hear me?"

"Stop this, man! You can't bury yourself with—" Sean stopped, looked at something over his shoulder, then charged past him.

Joaquin turned. Silhouetted against the sun now kissing the horizon ran a slender woman with a beam of light shining from a flashlight in her hand, her long hair blowing wildly in the breeze, glinting with a hint of gold. He knew the outline of that face, of that body. Dirt smeared across one cheek. Blood pooled on her chest.

He blinked. His jaw dropped. It wasn't possible. It just wasn't. He was hallucinating. She was a ghost. Something.

But she kept coming closer.

"Bailey?" His voice came out no louder than a whisper.

She nodded, sucking in a sobbing breath, then ran for him. He crept closer, still stunned with disbelief.

She crashed into him, throwing her arms around him and nestling her head on his shoulder. Her chest heaved with another sob and she curled closer as if she took comfort in his nearness.

Joaquin stood unmoving. Tears still rolled down his face.

Sean spoke into his radio, telling the agents that Bailey had escaped the blast.

Seconds later, Caleb and Hunter jogged onto the scene. Hunter pulled her away and held her by the shoulders. He and his father asked questions. Yes, she was mostly unharmed. McKeevy had definitely been in the compound. So had the disk with the research, as far as she knew. Sadly, there had been other people inside, including women and children. Bailey began crying again and Hunter pulled her in close, soothing her.

Joaquin stood, unblinking. Thank God she was alive. For that miracle, he could kiss the ground, repent all his sins, and be grateful every day for the rest of his life.

But he couldn't endure the agony of losing her again.

Within minutes, a slew of black SUVs roared up to the scene. A horde of agents climbed from their vehicles and charged toward her. They would take her away now. They would ask hours of questions. She would be in far better hands than his.

Hunter and his father shadowed her protectively as the feds asked many of the same questions the Edgington men already had. Joaquin watched, shock and pain still reverberating through his system.

Sean sidled up to him. "Go to her. She's going to need your strength."

"I don't have any to give her," he mumbled, unable to take his eyes off her. Even after a harrowing near-death experience, she still had to be the most graceful, beautiful woman he'd ever seen.

"You're just in shock and talking nonsense. You need one another," Sean insisted. "Especially now."

He jerked his head from side to side. "I don't need anyone, and she's better off without me."

Emergency vehicles arrived then. The local sheriff stepped out of his car, gawking at the destruction as smoke rose high above the fire, painting the sky orange.

An EMT cleared a path to Bailey with a gurney. Another followed along, and the pair of them helped her onto the table. As FBI agents continued to bark questions, the medics forced them aside, taking her blood pressure as they inquired about her injuries. She pointed to her chest. Joaquin desperately wanted to know what had happened and how bad it was, but he'd be less crazy if he didn't. *Downshift, dismiss, divorce your mind.*

It didn't take long before they hoisted her into the ambulance and shut her inside. Joaquin flinched as they slammed the doors, then he steeled himself and turned away.

"Aren't you going with her?" Sean asked incredulously.

Why? So he could worry himself into a panicked frenzy and ruin her life even more? She'd have a nice future without him. He'd check on her in a month or two—from a distance—make sure she hadn't gotten pregnant. If she had, well . . . he had to find another job. He'd pay her whatever she wanted in child support promptly and like clockwork.

"How the hell do we get out of here?" he asked.

Sean shook his head, but managed to grab someone with keys. Together, they shoved Joaquin into the vehicle.

"I think you need to see a doctor," Sean suggested. "You really are in shock."

Yes, but not medically. This was the sort of shock from which he knew he'd never recover. "Not at all. I'm perfectly myself again."

Sean shook his head and settled back in his seat, then directed his attention to the other agent. "Can you take us to the hospital?"

So he would see Bailey again, ache to hold her, worry himself sick, and fall a little more in love? No, thank you.

"On your way, drop me off someplace I can catch a fucking shuttle to the airport. I'm done."

* * *

BAILEY woke in the hospital, her lashes fluttering open slowly. The room wasn't big, just very white. The bland beige drapes had been closed against the dark of night. A blue privacy curtain cordoning off her area from the other empty bed in the room had been thrown back. She wasn't alone.

Hunter, Kata, and Sean all hovered nearby, along with a man who looked like Hunter in twenty years. She didn't see Joaquin.

She remembered instantly what had happened. The explosion still rang in her ears, jarred her bones. She remembered running down the dark tunnel, dirt crumbling in on her head. She'd been terrified that she'd be buried alive. She'd literally run into the end of the tunnel, fumbled around for a catch, then pushed a metal door out, relieved to see Joaquin waiting for her. She'd known then she would be all right. Curling up against his chest, she'd been sure she could set McKeevy and her past as Tatiana Aslanov to rest. That her world would finally be perfect.

"How are you feeling?" Kata asked.

Her head hurt a little. She felt somewhat groggy. But otherwise . . . "Fine."

"Good." Hunter jumped in. "We've been worried. Hell, my dad has never even met you and he's been pacing."

The older man smiled and introduced himself. "Sorry. Once a father, always a father—even if you're not my kid."

She smiled faintly. "I appreciate that. Where's Joa—"

"The doctor has been to see you," Kata cut in. "He says you're in good shape. He was able to put a butterfly bandage on your foot. Your chest needed two stitches and you've got a bit of bruising, but otherwise, you're okay."

"I hope you don't mind," Hunter cut in sheepishly. "I lied and told him that you're my sister so he'd update us on your medical."

Some people might feel as if Hunter had invaded her privacy, but he'd been concerned. They all had. Bailey found it touching and didn't mind at all. She just wanted to know where Joaquin was. In the bathroom? Getting coffee? Hurt?

That possibility washed her with panic. She tried to shove herself to a sitting position.

Caleb put a hand on her shoulder and eased her back down. "You can't put too much pressure on those stitches, hon. Relax."

"Okay." She glanced around the room with a frown. "I'm just wondering, where's—"

"The doctor will be around again to discharge you soon," Kata assured her. "They gave you a mild sedative while they stitched you up. Apparently, you already had something heavier in your system?" She spoke the statement like a question.

Bailey nodded. "McKeevy drugged me."

And she didn't want to think about him more than that. Already she knew she'd have nightmares about the psycho and the terrible day she'd spent at his "mercy." Honestly, she didn't wish death on anyone, but she could say unequivocally that she was glad he no longer walked this earth. She hoped he met all his victims in the afterlife and they gave him hell.

"I've spoken to the agents on your case," Sean offered. "As soon as the doctor consents, they'll be coming around to ask you some questions. Just so you know, the LOSS compound was utterly destroyed."

She thought of Destiny, her swollen belly, and her little boy. Such a terrible, saddening waste. "A girl helped me escape the compound. The only thing she asked of me was to contact her mother. I put her address in my jeans."

Sean smiled. "Actually, Destiny has already called her mother. Apparently when some of the women figured out the men meant to blow up the compound with everyone inside so no fed could 'sully' their premises, many of them grabbed their children and ran into the mine. Nearly thirty people escaped. They also rescued a few other prisoners. Those people will be able to provide us a lot of information about LOSS's operations, finances, weaponry, and plans, along with their uses for Viktor Aslanov's research. In fact, one of the men they freed was a former soldier they'd once made into a research subject."

"McKeevy told me about him."

"His name is Dante. He's been there for nearly a year. The doctors are running tests on him now. I'm sure he'll be transferred to D.C. at some point for future testing."

"So my father's research really worked? This man's DNA has been altered?"

"We don't know for sure. Based on Dante's statement so far, I'd say it's possible." Sean shrugged. "Time will tell. But since LOSS didn't have any electronic e-mail or file storage system, the research Viktor was killed for died with McKeevy and that group of fanatics. As far as we know, there are no more copies. So your past should never come back to haunt you."

She could close that chapter of her life. It would be impossible to forget that she'd been born into this world Tatiana Aslanov, but she could spend the rest of her days as Bailey Benson in peace.

"Thank God," she breathed. "I'll bet Callie is thrilled, too."

Sean nodded. "Best wedding present she could have, I think. She's ready to be a 'normal' girl—as much as she's capable of that."

"There's a media storm gathering," Caleb warned. "Once you're discharged, we'll have to sneak you out, but we'll get you out of here and on a plane back to Texas tonight."

That sounded fabulous. If she could return to any sort of decent shape, she had an audition in Dallas next Tuesday. Beyond that . . . all she wanted was to spend her days and nights with Joaquin forging a future. Who knew? Maybe someday, she'd be Mrs. Muñoz. But right now, she was happy to take things one day at a time, find out what their new normal together was. And she couldn't wait to get started. All she needed now was Joaquin himself.

Bailey scanned the room again. "Hey, where's—"

"Joaquin is gone," Hunter said solemnly. "As soon as he found out you weren't injured, he found a ride to the airport. We don't know where he was headed."

Shock slithered through her. After all the times Joaquin had sworn he'd be by her side? "He just . . . left? Without a word?"

The collective grim expression, liberally laced with pity, worn by everyone in the room, hurt even more. Joaquin had seemingly shared more than his body with her. He'd bared so much of his soul. They shared a bond—or so she'd thought. Had she been wrong?

Sean clasped her hand. "I was with him when he thought you'd perished in the explosion. He lost his mind, Bailey. Completely came apart. He railed at himself for not protecting you and said you'd be better off without him. I think he's beating himself up in the worst way right now. I tried to stop him from leaving. I couldn't. I'm sorry."

Humiliation stung, but his abandonment carved a crater in her chest and filled it with acid pain. He'd left her, just like Viktor Aslanov, like Bob and Jane Benson. Now she could add Joaquin to the list of people who had come into her life, altered her in ways she could never undo, then left without a backward glance. Bailey couldn't pretend she didn't know why. If he'd been so deeply impacted by losing his father that he hadn't cried in nearly twenty years, he certainly wasn't going to risk heart, soul, and sanity for a woman he'd met a few days ago. She'd been stupid to hope otherwise.

She'd been even stupider to fall in love.

Everyone stared at her like they all expected her to fall apart. In the past, she probably would have. She still might later, when she was alone. Right now, she was too damn shocked. And furious.

"I'm not surprised," she managed to mutter and not sound bitter—much. "Damn him."

"It's a totally chickenshit move." Kata picked up the verbal torch and ran with it. "When I get my fingers around his neck, I'm going to squeeze hard. He'll learn the value of family if I have to choke it into him."

Hunter cut a sidelong stare at his wife. "Pregnancy has made you bloodthirsty."

"Am I wrong?" Kata asked, her voice picking up volume and emphasis.

"No, honey. But you don't have to choke him. I'll beat the shit out of him for you."

Kata crossed her arms over her chest. "Thank you. Make it hurt. He'd better learn something, damn it. I'm tired of my brother running for the exit all the time."

"He doesn't know how to grieve," Bailey said. "He isn't sure how to deal with the pain. He doesn't do it to hurt you. He just works so hard to preserve himself."

"I don't give a shit. He's not twelve anymore. He's a damn adult, and this is unforgiveable." Kata wagged a finger at her. "Don't you dare defend him."

"Just explaining because I understand." Her issues of abandonment were the reason she'd never had any close friends herself. Bailey saw that clearly now. She understood Joaquin's belief that pulling away would make him feel better. He had just proven what she'd begun to suspect after meeting him: Self-isolation didn't do anything but create misery and loneliness. "I can't defend it. But I can't hate him for it, either."

She could, however, be crushed and cry and wish with everything inside her that he'd come back to her, offering his heart. But he wouldn't. Instead, she would learn from her time with him and from his desertion. The only life worth living was one in which she opened herself, bared her soul, and was surrounded by love. Going forward, that's what she'd do. She would spend tonight mourning what could have been and say a prayer that Joaquin would find life and love in the future. Then she'd let nothing stop her from finding her own.

Chapter Twenty

JOAQUIN woke in his apartment Friday morning after three hours of broken sleep. His hangover wasn't a welcome friend. Neither was his past-due rent notice.

With a groan, he sat up. His head hurt. The sunlight filtering through the blinds he hadn't bothered to close threatened to split his head open like an overripe melon.

Grimacing, he stooped and dragged himself to the bathroom, where he yanked open the medicine cabinet. No pain relievers. *Great.* Just like he'd gone looking for food in the fridge last night and found it empty.

Until last night, he'd never realized how little it looked as if someone lived here. He couldn't escape noticing it again as he shuffled back to bed. Not a single picture on the walls or nightstand. Nothing personal around the place. No family mementoes, no record of achievements, no gag gifts from friends or reminders of loved ones. White walls, a generic black leather sofa, a chocolate-brown comforter, and an inch's worth of dust on all the garage-sale furniture surrounded him. It had never looked so fucking sad until he'd imagined what kind of place he might have shared with Bailey, if he were a different man.

Last night, he'd made a run to the liquor store a few miles down the road, thanking fuck that it wasn't Sunday so he could still get a bottle. Joaquin hadn't cared much what type. He'd been all kinds of eager to numb the constant tide of pain of being without Bailey and worrying if she was all right.

Had she been released from the hospital? Did she hate him half as much as he hated himself right now? Or had Sean been right? Knowing her, she'd understand him all too well. She'd feel sorry for him. Jesus, that idea almost hurt worse.

This morning, Joaquin understood far too clearly that he couldn't drink enough to numb the torment of being without her. He'd really hoped he could pass out last night. Instead, he'd damn near thrown up after three-quarters of a bottle of Cupcake vodka. What the fuck had he been thinking? And what the hell was he going to do now?

Shaking his head, he flung himself back on the bed with a long, shuddering breath. God, he felt old. He probably looked it, too. And what did he have to show for his age? A crappy apartment he'd get evicted from if he never came home often enough to pay his bills. And . . . not much else. Hell, he'd never even wanted the commitment of a pet. No, might as well be honest. He hadn't wanted to risk loving a four-legged friend and suffering its loss well before he found his grave. He really didn't know how to find his mother anymore. His youngest sister was, no doubt, plenty pissed at him right now.

What if he'd died in Iowa? What would his legacy have been? Would his father have met him at the pearly gates, shaking his head in disappointment?

Fuck, he hated this much self-examination.

But the tough questions just wouldn't stop rolling through his head. What had Bailey been feeling when she'd awakened in the hospital to find him absent? Had she been saddened, crushed, or simply resigned? More than a vague shame filled him.

With a curse, he flung himself off the bed and paced to the bathroom. As he flipped on the light, he braced his hands on the bathroom counter and hung his head. He had to find another job. Maybe then he could bury himself, feel nothing . . . and die young and forgotten. Crap, wasn't that a cheerful thought?

Or, a voice in his head whispered, he could stop having this righteous freak-out, figure out how to put on his big-boy britches, and find Bailey. He could apologize and figure out how to deal with the fact that death was a part of living. Maybe.

Wasn't that heavy shit?

He looked up at himself in the mirror. Bags sagged around his eyes. Crow's feet he hadn't noticed before creased his skin. He had a permanent wrinkle between his dark brows where he frowned. Hell, he even spotted a little gray at his temples. His own mortality didn't bug him, just the passing of time. One day he'd look up and, if he still roamed the earth, everyone he loved would be gone, if not literally, then figuratively. His mother was aging. What if he wasted the years he had left with her? His sisters had their own lives.

And Bailey . . . He couldn't expect her to pine for him while he figured out how to get over himself. If it took him another decade to snap out of it, she'd be married, a mom, settled and happy—all without him.

Joaquin stood right in front of the fork in the road. He had to pick a path and take it now. Tomorrow might be too late.

Swallowing his nerves, he flipped on the shower and stripped down. The spray felt good, but he didn't linger. He had a lot of thinking and driving to do. He also had more than a few phone calls to make.

In twenty minutes, he headed out the door and drove east on Interstate 10, enjoying the cloudless blue seventy-degree day. He didn't relish three hours of being trapped with his own thoughts, but he figured he needed it. Two phone calls distracted him a bit. Stone made him laugh and gave him the information he needed. As soon as Joaquin hung up, he was right back to realizing just how hugely he'd overreacted yesterday. And how badly he'd screwed up.

Just before he reached his destination, he stopped at a grocery store and picked up some flowers. He had no idea if the gesture would mean anything . . . but Joaquin figured it would at least show that he was trying.

His GPS led him to the right house, and all too soon, he was knocking on the unfamiliar door. Nice place. Good neighborhood. Well kept. Pretty flowers.

Shit, he was really fucking nervous.

He expected his mother to answer the door. That wasn't who he saw.

"Caleb. Hi." Okay, that sounded stupid. But how else was he supposed to greet his stepfather, whom he barely knew?

"Hi." The older man stood, bracing one beefy arm on the door frame and staring at him as if he was as welcome as a salesman. "What do you want?"

"To talk to my mother." Joaquin didn't expect this to go easy, but how else could he possibly figure out how to get past the hurdle of his father's death if he didn't—gulp—talk to someone who'd been there and suffered more?

"You might have called first," Caleb drawled.

And give Carlotta Muñoz Edgington a reason to dodge him the way he'd done her for so many years? "Sorry. I just . . . I kind of need to see her."

Caleb stared at him with those intense blue eyes. Now he knew where Hunter and Logan got their macho. Joaquin resisted the urge to fidget.

"I'll see if she's free. But before I let you in my house, I want you to understand, I'm doing this for her. She misses you. But after the way you've behaved as long as I've known your mother, I've got no respect for that."

Join the club. He looked down, shuffled his tennis shoes against the brick stoop. "I want to make it up to her. I've got to start somewhere."

"You turned your back on your family and left them in the hands of a neglectful, controlling, verbally abusive prick."

Joaquin gnashed his teeth. "I always hated Gordon. I tried to talk *Mamá* out of marrying him. She wouldn't listen."

"She wanted to provide for you kids in a way she couldn't alone."

Joaquin had known that. Watching her ex-husband eat away at her self-confidence and autonomy until he turned eighteen and left the house had just about killed him.

"I did everything I could to prevent their marriage and help her financially. But if you've been married to my mother for more than five minutes, you know that sometimes she can be downright stubborn."

With a hint of a smile curling his lips, Caleb stepped back and let him into the cool interior of the homey place. "That I can't argue with. Carlotta definitely has her own ideas. She just came off a shift at the hospital. I'll see if she's up to talking."

That took Joaquin aback. "She's working again?"

Caleb nodded. "Her choice. I'd be happier to have her all to myself, but this is good for her self-confidence. She's made new friends and gained back a lot of her self-respect. I'm worried she works too hard, and I don't like that she sometimes works nights, but I'd never take it away from her."

It hadn't taken his new stepfather long to understand his mother and give her what she needed. He supported her, putting his own worries aside so she could be fulfilled. Joaquin hung his head. That's exactly what he should have done for Bailey.

"Then I'm sure you've been good for her and I appreciate what you've done. I know I haven't kept up my responsibilities as a son." He rubbed at the back of his neck. "I'm . . . um, hoping to turn over a new leaf."

"Have a seat." Caleb pointed to the beige sectional.

Joaquin saw his mother everywhere in this room. The dark hardwood floors gleamed. The area rug in cream and taupe had a pattern with some soft lines, yet the room didn't seem too feminine. Flowers sat in a crystal bowl on the coffee table. Accents in earth tones blended with shiny, somehow more modern crystal. He saw the old and new mixed here, warmth and cool sophistication coexisting.

"Thanks." He sank down to the sofa, perched on the edge, elbows on his knees. Shit, he really was nervous.

"I'll find Carlotta for you."

"Wait." He called Caleb back. "Tell me . . . She's happy now, right?"

"Finally. Your sisters and I are close. We share a lot of family occasions. There's never a frown during holidays or gatherings."

Joaquin smiled, swallowing down the ugly realization that he'd missed so much while he'd been busy avoiding and wallowing. "Good. That's what her life should be like."

"Yep," Caleb agreed. "But I know she'd feel complete if she had all her kids here more often."

She wasn't the only one who would probably feel more complete, but Joaquin couldn't make himself say that to Caleb. This conversation was already awkward enough, and some stuff he had to say to *Mamá* alone.

Instead, he nodded.

Caleb departed, and Joaquin resisted the urge to fidget or pace. Was this gesture too little too late?

The wait seemed forever before he heard the rustle of clothing at the edge of the room. Her perfume—that something spicy and floral he'd always equated with her—hit his senses first. He rose, turning. There stood his mother in pink scrubs. He hadn't laid eyes on her in damn near three years. She looked exactly the same, yet totally different. Yes, she'd dropped a few pounds, probably trying to keep up with her very fit husband. And her hair was a little longer, which suited her. More than anything, she looked different because she glowed with a happiness he didn't ever remember seeing on her face.

Her radiance totally belied the frown she wore now. "Joaquin, why are you here?"

That wasn't the greeting he'd expected from his mother. Then again, why should he have expected open arms after the way he'd turned his back on her and the family?

"Because I . . . realize I've been a shit and I wanted to say I'm sorry."

Her expression turned considering. "Apology accepted. I thank you for delivering your words in person."

"Here." He extended the flowers to her, feeling so damn uncomfortable. "These are for you."

She took the flowers in hand, the plastic crinkling. Her dark eyes lit up for a moment, then she blinked and the light was gone. "They are lovely. Thank you."

Joaquin watched his mother walk out of the room. Frowning, he hesitated. Follow? Don't follow? Was she too pissed at him to say more?

Finally, he decided to see where she'd gone. When he trailed behind her and rounded the corner, he found himself in a large kitchen with white cabinets and light marble counters. Chrome fixtures blended well with the soft gray subway tiles and gleaming stainless appliances. The ranch house was far too old to have a kitchen this new and stylish without her hand.

"Wow, you've done a lot of work on this place."

Carlotta reached for a vase and filled it with water. "I have. How did you know?"

"It looks like you, cozy and pretty and . . ." There he went, sounding like an idiot again.

"Caleb helped me. We moved into this house late last year and have been renovating since. I'm glad you like it." She put the flowers in the vase and set them in the middle of the rectangular island. "They look pretty. I am glad you stopped by. It is always good to see you."

Her tone sounded somewhere between distant and dismissive. Joaquin gritted his teeth and reminded himself that he was only reaping what he'd sown.

"*Mamá*, I came to talk to you, if you can spare a few minutes. Please. I know I've been a lousy son—"

"Let us be clear. A good man . . . but not the best son."

The mother he'd last known would never have stated her feelings so bluntly. Joaquin supposed he had Caleb to thank for that. "I'm not even sure I've been a good man. I met this woman . . ."

"So I heard." Her voice turned cold again.

And Caleb had undoubtedly struck on that front, too. "Your husband told you about Bailey?"

"He did."

His mother wasn't going to make this easy for him. He shouldn't have expected that she would. "I'd like to talk to you about her. You understand women . . . and you understand me."

"What is it you wish to know? Do you need me to tell you that you have behaved like an ass? Because I will. The girl has been through a great deal."

"She has." He couldn't disagree.

"And you put her through more still, leaving her when she needed you."

Joaquin hung his head. "I know. I realized this morning that I'm afraid to, you know . . . care about people."

"Your father's death came at a difficult time in your life. You worshipped him. I always believed that you struggled to recover from the shock and sorrow."

Yep, his mother understood. "I didn't recover at all."

"You did not. I tried to help you, but you refused to let me."

He shrugged. "I shut you out. Hell, everyone. I really never let a soul back in. And now, I don't know what to do."

"Kata said as much."

For once, Joaquin was glad that his little sister had meddled. "I almost lost Bailey yesterday."

His mother took a long moment in answering. "You did. Be

thankful that her harrowing experience and near death did not affect you because you have not allowed her truly into your heart."

Her crafty answer took him aback. "Um, that's not true."

"So it did not hurt because you have no wish to commit to her and do not love her?"

Joaquin winced. "I thought protecting myself from emotion would prevent me from feeling anything, but yesterday, when I thought I'd lost her? I couldn't take it. I felt as if my whole life had ended. As if I couldn't take another breath without her. It scared the hell out of me."

Those terrible moments when he'd been sure she was dead stabbed his heart all over again. The sheer, utter terror was something he'd never, ever forget. The worst part was that he needed to stop shutting himself off from everyone and he didn't know how.

"Her life almost ended as well. Do you not think she was frightened? Did you not think she would need comfort and support?"

"I didn't think at all." And that gnawing shame ate at him. "How did you do it? You loved Dad. How did you cope when the other half of your heart was no longer there?"

A sad smile flitted across her face. "At first, I did feel as if my life could not go on. I felt sure I would never smile or love again. After a time, I realized Eduardo would never have chosen such an existence for me. He was always full of life and love. I missed him terribly each and every day. Sometimes, I still do. But after his death, I had to be available for you kids. I had to learn to go on. I had to allow myself to heal and risk loss again. You must enter any relationship knowing there will be pain."

"I don't know how to set myself up for that. It seems stupid to stand there and wait for something terrible."

"Maybe so, but you will miss everything good if you never get involved with anyone. You will miss the years of smiles and warmth, of touching, support, kind words, laughter, and consolation simply to avoid that one moment of pain."

"Dad's death has lasted more than a moment. It's been forever."

"Because you never tried to move on. To live or love again. Do you think that is what your father wished for you?"

He already knew it wasn't. He shook his head. "I don't know how to apologize to Bailey. Hell, I don't even know where she is."

His mother plopped down onto the stool beside him and finally sent him a genuinely warm smile. "You say 'I'm sorry.' You say 'I love you.' You say 'I want to spend forever with you.' And you hope she says yes. If she does not, you will survive. You are strong, Joaquin. The pain of loss will not break you, unless you choose to let it."

Her answer sounded so simple, and her strength humbled him. She'd been a widow in her early thirties. She'd been married to an absolute douchebag for over a dozen years. Finally, she seemed to have found some happiness. She looked as if she had settled into a peace he envied. Was it really as simple as embracing the life in front of him, enduring both the good and bad, and letting go of all the ghosts of the past?

Slowly, he nodded. "I've got nothing else, and I don't think I can stand to be without her. Like you slyly pointed out, just because I hadn't told her how I felt didn't make her absence hurt less, not when I thought she was dead. Not last night when I found myself completely alone and realized I'd really screwed up."

"I want you happy, son."

That was the first thing she'd said that sounded like the mother he'd always known talking to the boy he'd once been. "I'm glad you *are* happy, *Mamá*."

"What will you do next?"

"Find Bailey, do my best to scrape and grovel, I suppose. And pray a lot. I'll need to find a new job. I don't want another paycheck where I'm trotting the globe all the time."

Carlotta smiled, then reached across the space between them to grab his hand. "Does that mean you will come visit your *mamá* more often?"

"A lot more. I've missed you." He dragged her into an embrace, patting her back when she sniffled softly.

Gently, she pulled back and cupped his cheek. Her dark eyes welled with happy moisture as she sent him a radiant smile. "I have missed you. I think for the first time in almost twenty years that I have my son back."

"You do. I'm not going anywhere this time." He nearly got choked up and had to swallow it down. "And what about those crazy sisters of mine? I'd like to see them, too."

Carlotta rose from the stool and almost ran to her cell phone. "I will call them and see if they can meet us for dinner soon."

"That would be great. I'll let you know how it goes with Bailey."

Mamá sent him a secretive smile. "I believe Kata might have mentioned something about a wedding tomorrow in Dallas? Bailey intends to be there."

"Callie and Sean's."

That made sense. Bailey and the heiress had bonded over their mutual tragedies. They'd both risen and overcome. They both had chosen to move forward and seek a new future.

Time for him to do the same. He really hoped that Sean and Callie didn't mind if he crashed their big day.

"Thanks, *Mamá*. I love you."

"I love you, too, son. I wish you all the luck with your lovely girl tomorrow." His mother stood, kissed his cheek, and drifted toward the back of the house.

So . . . that was that. A little abrupt, but overall the reunion had been better than Joaquin had hoped.

He rose and made his way out of the kitchen, toward the front door. With a puzzled frown, he let himself out and headed for his car. As he approached, fob in hand, he heard the strains of classical music coming from the backyard.

Mamá had always liked spicy Latin tunes and anything upbeat, with an occasional romantic ballad. Caleb seemed a little older, but

Joaquin hadn't pegged him for the classical music type. He shrugged. Maybe he'd gotten it wrong.

Suddenly, the music stopped.

"Again," a young male voice insisted from behind the fence. "That's much better, so I want to see it again."

Joaquin had heard that voice once before, on a voicemail of Bailey's.

Dashing toward the sound, Joaquin hoped like hell he'd remembered that voice correctly. That meant Bailey had to be near.

Anticipation jerking his heart, Joaquin searched for the gate to the backyard. When he found it, he lifted the latch slowly, peeking through a crack. He didn't want Caleb or his mother to think he was spying on them, but he could swear the voice he'd just heard was Blane's.

Or was he so desperate to see Bailey that he'd make up shit in his head now?

When he first peeked into the backyard, he didn't see anyone. He just observed a long stretch of grass with a bunch of patio furniture stacked around one edge. A big slab of flagstone had been covered by some sort of rubbery black pad. What the hell?

Then a tall man with a boyish face and a killer physique stepped onto the dark, spongy surface, wearing nothing but a pair of icy blue tights and a smile before he swallowed down a bottle of water.

"Come on." He waved at someone who stood frustratingly out of sight behind a built-in barbeque. "I think you've got it."

But Joaquin could only think of one reason Blane would be at his mother's house. Bailey must be here, too.

He waited, impatience biting at him, and hoped that he was right. But if that was the case, why hadn't Caleb or his mother told him she was here?

Well, dumbass, let's review. Abducting her, forcing her to remember a violent past, and almost getting her killed probably hadn't made her list of top first dates. Most likely, she didn't want to see him again.

He'd have to do whatever it took to change that. He refused to spend his life alone if he could have her in his arms.

A second later, she stepped down from the outdoor kitchen area, onto the rubbery mat—the most graceful creature he'd ever seen. She wore a pale pink leotard thing that covered her from slight breast to delicate toe shoes. Her hair was arranged in a haphazard bun on top of her head. She looked tired and so incredibly beautiful. At the sight of her, his heart threatened to cave in.

Bailey.

Blane held out his hand with a flourish, then set himself in a pose. She took his hand and settled into a stance of her own.

A moment later, *Mamá* appeared, lifting a portable music player up on a half wall between the barbeque and the step-down patio. She pressed a button on top of the unit. The strains of the music began again.

Bailey fluttered away from Blane, her face coquettish but teasing as hell as she held an arm out to him, then curled it back to her chest and lifted her leg behind her in a strong, spectacular line, back arched. Blane pursued, reaching for her, but Bailey put herself just out of his reach by executing a magnificent leap.

Blane gave chase again, in some sort of manly ballet walk-step that looked commanding, but his face reflected an anxious longing. He feared Bailey would reject him.

Joaquin understood that worry.

Bailey allowed Blane to catch her for a moment. He wrapped a hand around her wrist and pulled her against his chest, then caged her to him by encircling her delicate waist with his arm. Her expression was vulnerable, yearning. She wanted to surrender herself and to love him, but she was afraid.

That could very well be another instance of art imitating life.

Blane stroked her arm, nestled his face against hers.

Bailey turned, meeting the other dancer's stare, and Joaquin saw every trembling vulnerability in her blue eyes. Every moment of desire and uncertainty, her ache to trust. He'd seen that on her face before when he'd taken her beneath him and made love to her.

This dance looked every bit as elegant as the one she'd done in her living room in Houston, but this version . . . Joaquin remembered Bailey's words about the importance of expressing emotion during dance. At the time, he'd pretty much dismissed it. If she could technically do the steps, he'd failed to see how the rest of it mattered. But witnessing the difference for himself? In that moment, Bailey swept him up in her character's plight. He held his breath, worrying for her happiness. He rooted for her. He stood mesmerized by everything about her.

Suddenly, a large hand fell on his shoulder. "That's as far as you go."

Caleb. *Shit. Busted.*

"Why didn't you tell me she was here?"

"Neither Carlotta nor I think you deserve to talk to her until you get your shit together. Do you know what you're going to say to her?"

He didn't have every word planned, but he wanted to tell her that he loved her. Did it need to be more complicated? "I think so. I want to see her."

"She's practicing now. She needs this before her audition on Tuesday. She wants this part. Right now, dance is her life. It's helping her heal."

The audition meant a lot to her. Joaquin knew that. He could *see* how much she'd laid her soul open now, how hard she'd worked to open herself up. He couldn't stand in her way. He'd stupidly, selfishly left her in Iowa. If she was important to him and this was important to her, he had to respect her dreams.

"I know. She's staying with you?"

"Yes. After the doctor released her from the hospital, she answered the feds' questions, then declined a press conference. She doesn't want the world to know her as Tatiana Aslanov, the Russian scientist's daughter. She wants them to know her as Bailey Benson the ballerina."

Fierce pride flowed through Joaquin. She hadn't let anything—not him, not remembering her past, not near death—break her. She'd put pain and fear behind her to embrace the future she wanted.

Damn, he could learn a lot from her.

He smiled, unable to take his eyes off her. "Isn't she amazing?"

"Yes. Your mother likes her very much. Your sisters, too. She met Mari this morning. They hit it off."

In every way Joaquin could think of, Bailey was perfect for him. Now he just had to find some way to tell her, show her, prove to her how much he was ready to let go of the tragedies in his own past and take her hand into the future.

"You're right. I need a plan. Words aren't going to be enough."

"Probably not. You have a lot to make up for."

"No denying that. But I'm determined." He actually respected Caleb for putting the truth out there. They didn't know one another well, but Joaquin already liked his new stepfather. He was obviously good to his mother and for this family.

It occurred to him that Hunter wasn't just his brother-in-law anymore, but his stepbrother, too. Logan and his wife were now family as well. While he'd been burying his head and hiding from his past, so much had changed. He couldn't wait to catch up.

Caleb sent him a considering glance. "I heard you lost your job trying to save more women from dying. That true?"

"And avenge a friend's death, yeah."

Joaquin missed Nate and always would. He would also regret that he hadn't done more to deepen the friendship before it was too late. But he swore he'd never make that mistake again.

"You got a line on any jobs yet?"

"Nope. I'd planned to start looking as soon as I left here." Today was Friday, but he wanted to get a jump on his search before the weekend rolled around. Why wait to start his new life?

"Good. Come with me. Hunter and Logan just arrived. I've got a proposition for you boys."

Joaquin frowned. Why would Caleb throw him a bone of any kind? The man's first impression couldn't have been stellar.

With a shrug, Joaquin took a last, lingering glance at Bailey. "She's staying with you tonight?"

"Yes. She's riding with Hunter and Kata to the wedding tomorrow."

He breathed a sigh of relief. "Sure. Then I'm all ears. What did you have in mind?"

Caleb put his hand on his shoulder. "I've decided to retire completely and turn my military and personal security business over to you three boys. I plan to persuade Carlotta to travel with me more, so we can enjoy our years together. Jack Cole will have to do without Hunter and Logan, but he's a resourceful man. He'll figure it out. You in?"

It sounded like the perfect line of work for him and the sort of thing that would allow him to stay closer to home—and Bailey, if she'd have him.

"Absolutely." Joaquin stuck out his hand. "Thank you."

Caleb nodded. "Let's find Hunter and Logan and drop the bomb on them, shall we?"

Laughing for the first time in ages, Joaquin nodded, took one more glance at Bailey's beauty, then headed toward the garage with his stepfather.

* * *

BAILEY stared out the huge picture windows of the wooden chapel, framed by white flowers. Sunlight poured in from the cloudless bright blue sky—the sort she swore she'd only ever seen in Texas. Around her, about forty people were gathered to witness the ceremony. She sat beside Kata, who rubbed her belly with a smile. On the other side, Tara clasped Logan's hand, and they shared a grin. Carlotta and Caleb had been only too happy to watch the twins today.

She saw a few other familiar faces from the bench seats. Happiness flowed through the place, and Bailey was touched that Callie had invited her to attend one of the most momentous occasions of her life. Everything was perfect—or would be if Joaquin were by her side.

Refusing to let her sadness ruin the moment, she shoved the thought aside. The faint background music suddenly swirled to a crescendo, and a romantic classic filled the air, played beautifully by a string quartet in the corner.

A little blond princess, probably four or so, walked down the aisle in a frilly white dress. Her blue eyes looked saucer wide, but she braved a path forward, throwing a mixture of red and white rose petals on a gray velvet runner.

"Aww . . ." Kata groaned beside Bailey. "Isn't Chloe precious?"

"She is," Bailey murmured. "Adorable."

"That's Luc and Alyssa Traverson's daughter." Tara pointed discreetly to a couple across the aisle from them.

Bailey had heard of the gorgeous, famous chef. His wife was stunning. They looked like such proud parents.

Behind the little girl walked two boys, one bigger than Chloe, one a bit smaller. Both carried little pillows with shining rings on top.

Tara giggled. "The bigger one is Cal, Deke and Kimber's son."

The imp had big eyes a shade somewhere between blue and green, golden-blond hair, and a mischievous mien. He all but danced up the aisle.

"The other is Tyler's oldest son, Seth. He's going to be just like his daddy—trouble," Kata vowed. "OMG, did you see him wink at Sweet Pea?"

"Yep. Just like his daddy." Tara leaned forward and shook her head at Kata.

"Shh," Logan warned as the kids sat in the front row.

London came down the aisle next, draped in a gorgeous Tiffany-blue chiffon that floated over her pregnant belly and flowed to the ground. Her blond hair was tucked into a feminine, romantic updo, complete with tendrils at her temples and nape.

She was escorted by Thorpe, who cut a gorgeous, commanding figure in a black tux.

Sean waited at the altar, smiling at Thorpe and nodding London's way. They both took their places, then turned to look down the aisle. The music changed. Rather than the traditional wedding march, the strains of something haunting and lovely filled the room.

Callie appeared in a stunning beaded white dress that took Bailey's breath away. Sean and Thorpe's, too, judging from the looks on their faces. A long white veil floated on top of her train. Even the thin tulle over her face couldn't disguise her big blue eyes or the sublime joy stretching her smiling red lips.

She wore her blue-black hair upswept in a do like London's, except it looked more intricate and was studded with crystals that played off her dress and artful clusters of baby's breath.

Bailey had never seen a more radiant bride.

"Oh, wow . . ." Kata breathed. "I'm jealous. I wore a leather skirt and the first shirt I plucked out of my suitcase to my wedding."

"You looked great," Hunter assured her.

Bailey turned to look at the pair. She would love to know that story someday.

Callie glided down the aisle, graceful and strong, then passed her flowers to London. Sean took her hands, and they looked into each other's eyes. The love between them filled the room, sweetening the air. Impossible to miss the hope and anticipation for the future decorating this celebration of their joining.

The ceremony didn't last long. Their vows made Bailey cry. No use lying. She envied Callie's happy ending, but knew the woman had been through hell and thoroughly deserved it.

The officiant pronounced them husband and wife, then instructed Sean to kiss his bride. He let out a great big whoop. Everyone laughed, and the photographer moved in and captured their first tender, passionate kiss as man and wife.

When they broke apart, Sean shuffled to Callie's side and Thorpe moved closer, taking her shoulders in hand. The smile he bestowed on her made Bailey's heart catch. Not just love, but pride and devotion and an abiding commitment to their future. He might not be the groom, but in that look, he vowed to stay by Callie's side and be every bit the partner to her that Sean had just sworn to be. She mouthed that she loved him. Sean wrapped a hand around her waist as Thorpe kissed her forehead, then bent to take her mouth in a sweet, lingering kiss of promise.

Then the three of them held hands and turned to face the crowd. Tears of joy streamed down Callie's face. The men's expressions both beamed with happiness and pride. Their guests clapped. Bailey found herself tearing up again. She'd bet there wasn't a dry eye in the place.

The officiant announced Mr. and Mrs. Mackenzie. The trio made their way back down the aisle, man and wife and—as Thorpe was fond of calling himself—the only other man.

The reception would be hosted outside in the gardens, so the crowd began to spill out through the tall, ornate chapel doors. Bailey watched wistfully as everyone took his or her spouse's or lover's hand and they smiled fondly at each other, sharing a glance full of past secrets and future promises.

Where was Joaquin today? Bailey knew she should stop tormenting herself about the man and what would never be, but she doubted he'd ever leave her heart. Their few days together had been intense. When he'd dragged her from her bed in Houston, she'd never imagined falling in love. Parts of the last week had been harrowing, even terrible. But she'd come out on the other side, stronger and more certain than ever who she was. Like Callie, she'd adopted this haphazard group of friends and relatives as her own. She might never have the man, but she wouldn't be alone again. There was comfort in that.

"The weather is perfect for the reception," Tara said, rising and casting a glance Logan's way. "We should have waited for an April wedding. August was terrible."

"I'd already waited since high school, Cherry. I wasn't waiting another nine months," he quipped.

Tara laughed. "You barely waited five minutes."

"Hey, I was more patient than Hunter. He didn't wait more than five minutes—literally."

Hunter turned a little red as they filed out of the row and headed to the doors. "I saw the woman I wanted and I went after her. Why put off starting the rest of our lives?"

"Um, you might have waited until I was sober," Kata put in.

Now Bailey *really* wanted to hear this story.

"And give you a chance to get away? Never." He grinned.

Kata stroked her belly again. "You got your wish. Now it looks like I'm not going anywhere."

"Not if I can help it."

They shuffled out of the chapel and into a receiving line. With a small ceremony, it didn't take long, but a crowd of people were pouring into the gardens for the reception.

Sean hugged her first. "Bailey! I'm glad you could make it. Feeling all right?"

"Fine. It was a beautiful ceremony. I wouldn't have missed it. Thank you for including me."

Callie nearly reached across her new husband to grab Bailey and draw her close. Bailey embraced the woman in return, so thrilled for her new friend's joy.

"You look stunning," she murmured.

The lovely brunette's smile only widened, her blue eyes sparkling with profound peace. "It's easy when you're this happy. I'm hoping for the same for you, doll."

Bailey's expression filled with regret. "Maybe someday."

"I really believe Joaquin loves you. Sean is convinced, too. Don't give up, huh?"

"It's your wedding day," Bailey reminded her, changing the subject. "Don't worry about me! You just enjoy the rest of your life."

"Text me after your audition Tuesday and let me know how it went," Callie demanded. "Promise?"

"I don't want to interrupt your honeymoon."

"If we're busy, I'll read the text later. We can't do *that* for two weeks solid." Callie flushed.

"Wanna bet?" Thorpe drawled, taking Bailey's hand and moving her up the line, into his embrace.

Callie giggled. "You're incorrigible, both of you."

Sean leaned over. "You mean insatiable."

"That, too." Thorpe nodded.

The two fist bumped, then looked at the bride as if she was their world.

Bailey envied Callie all over again, but she forced herself to paste on a smile and regard Thorpe. "Congratulations."

He hugged her. "Thank you," he murmured, then frowned. "You look sad. Feeling lonely?"

She swallowed. Why would Thorpe ask now? He was supposed to be enjoying this day of commitment. Besides, he had to know she was. Surely, it was all over her face.

"Yeah, but I'm determined to move on." If Joaquin wasn't ready to face his demons and embrace whatever he felt in his heart, she couldn't make him.

"You deserve a future full of everything wonderful. I know you'll do well in next week's audition."

Fingers crossed. She'd worked hard. Blane had been so thrilled with her progress and the way she'd finally been able to emote through her dance. For the first time, Bailey felt completely herself and free. Yes, sad . . . but at peace with her past.

"Thank you."

"I sure would like to see you smile and mean it. I know someone else who would, too." Thorpe pointed past a gorgeous Italian fountain to a gate on the side of the gardens, surrounded by a profusion of blooming bougainvillea.

There stood Joaquin in a dark gray suit, staring straight at her as if she were the only person on the planet.

Bailey's heart stuttered, skipped. She gasped. Why was he here? Just for the wedding. If he didn't want to see her, she worried it would crush this little mental Zen space she'd worked so hard to achieve.

She tore her gaze from Joaquin and sent a searching expression Thorpe's way. "Why?"

"He called me last night. Hear him out, okay?"

Callie laid a hand on her arm. "Men are stubborn." She sent a meaningful glance Thorpe's way. "Sometimes you have to be patient and forgiving."

Bailey didn't know if she had that in her. She should probably resist, retain her pride, but she wanted to see Joaquin so damn badly. So she nodded.

With a gentle hand at her back, Thorpe eased her on her way. As she put one foot in front of the other, almost in a daze, she had nowhere to look but at Joaquin. Still, her heart wouldn't beat quite right and her stomach knotted with anxiety as she tiptoed across the garden.

He barreled toward her, reaching her in a few long strides. "You look beautiful."

Callie had been kind enough to lend her a dress this morning. She still hadn't been to Houston to clean out her house or reclaim what was left of her things. She'd have to do that after the audition—and figure out where to go from there. Right now, she was thinking she'd move somewhere she could be near her newly adopted family.

"Thanks." Bailey didn't know what else to say. He'd obviously made it back from Iowa. No idea what he wanted to say to her. She probably shouldn't be so eager, but she desperately wanted to know.

"Can I talk to you?" he asked. "I know I don't deserve it, but I owe you an apology at least."

Bailey felt her eyes begin to swim in tears. She didn't want to bare her heartbreak. She wasn't sure she could live with herself if she did . . . but she was also struggling to hold it back.

"I know why you left." Damn it, her voice was shaking. "You don't have to say anything more. I caused you worry you didn't need and—"

"My fear that I'd lost you stripped me all the way down to my soul. I was already struggling with how I could deserve you or show you that I love you. I wasn't prepared to lose you, Bailey, especially when it was all my fault."

She blinked at him, gaping. "I . . ."

He loved her? Had he just said that?

Her thoughts raced. She swallowed, then opened her mouth and tried again. "It wasn't your fault. You did your best."

Joaquin shook his head. "I should have shot McKeevy in the parking lot. I should have laid down my life to keep him from touching you even once."

She didn't need or want Joaquin's guilt. If that's what had brought him here, she would absolve him now and send him on his way. "I'm fine."

"Any more nightmares?"

"Surprisingly no. I've had some panicked moments where I've been afraid to be alone, especially at night. I'm told that's normal. I'm thinking about getting a dog." Where had that come from? Great, now she was rambling. "I'm going to talk to a therapist about what happened to me as a child, so I can work through everything. But you don't have to worry about me."

He frowned fiercely, his hazel eyes looking mysteriously moist. "I will always worry about you, regardless of what happens today. But if you give me another chance, I will stay and care for you every single day. I will never, ever leave you again."

He grabbed her hands, and she felt the shock of his touch all the way to her heart—a bittersweet homecoming. Bailey felt her knees go weak.

"I'm sorry. I miss you. I love you." His chest buckled, and he looked as though he held back tears. "I want you forever."

It took all of Bailey's self-control not to leap into his arms and admit that she loved him, too. But he had to understand how she felt. "It's not that simple, Joaquin. I've been left by everyone I've ever loved, including you."

He closed his eyes. "God, if I could take that day back, I would, baby girl. In a heartbeat. When I thought I'd lost you forever, I freaked out."

"I know. Just like I know you didn't mean to hurt me when you left me. But you did." She sighed. "I'm human. I could die tomorrow. I can't do anything about that. I can't live with wondering if you'll run away every time you're overwhelmed by potential pain and loss."

He shook his head, looking insistent and determined. "I want every moment I can get with you, until fate decides it's time for one of us to take our last breath—whether that's tomorrow or a hundred years from now. But I can't live another second without telling you how much I love you. I know you might reject me, and I'll have earned it. But at least I know I've faced my fear and been one hundred percent honest with you."

God, he sounded like a different man. Bailey scanned the familiar, masculine angles of his face and marveled at the resolution there. "What changed?"

"You," he said as if the truth was obvious. "You make me want tomorrow. You make me ready to face whatever comes next, good or bad." He pulled her closer, and Bailey didn't resist. "I want you to know . . . I spoke to my mother. We're on good terms again. I called Kata and Mari this morning. I've apologized. I won't let my family down. I even reached out to Nate's parents to offer my condolences. I think they needed it."

"That's great." Bailey really meant that. For Joaquin, those were *huge* steps. Maybe he was truly serious.

"Caleb gave me a job. Hunter, Logan, and I are going to take over his business. The three of us spent a lot of time talking last night, planning. I'm really looking forward to . . . belonging again. But life would be so much better with you beside me."

"Joaquin . . ." Bailey's tears spilled over. How was she supposed to resist that?

"Can you forgive me?"

There was one fundamental difference between him and nearly everyone else who'd ever left her: Most had gone without much thought for her feelings. Joaquin was reaching his hand across the chasm between them to bring her into his world. He hadn't plotted to leave her, but he'd come up with a plan to coax her back into his life. It touched her.

"Yes."

"Oh, thank God." He pulled her against him and filtered his fingers into her hair. "Bailey Benson, marry me. Please put me out of my misery, put me in my place when I need it, and take me into your heart, the way you're in mine. I swear, I won't let you down."

He couldn't have been more earnest if he'd tried. The swell of need emanating from him bowled her over. And she loved him so much it hurt.

Joy brought another rush of tears to her eyes. "Yes!"

Joaquin smiled at her, so full of joy and life—and relief as he reached into his pocket and slipped a gorgeous diamond solitaire on her finger. She glanced down at the winking gem, then back up to her new fiancé. He beamed, so clearly embracing their future together. Elation brimmed between them. She couldn't be more thrilled.

As he sealed their new bond with a seeking kiss that quickly turned demanding, Bailey warmed against him and melted as the wedding guests around her clapped. She laughed and cried at once, feeling as if she'd finally found her family.

Don't miss the next Wicked Lovers novel from *New York Times* bestselling author Shayla Black

Wicked for You

Ever since he rescued her from a dangerous kidnapper, Mystery Mullins has wanted Axel Dillon. When he returned her to her Hollywood father and tabloid life, she was grateful . . . and a little in love. Mystery wasn't ready to let Axel go, even after the soldier gently turned her away because, at nineteen, she was too young.

Now, six years later, Mystery is grown, with a flourishing career and a full life—but she's still stuck on Axel. In disguise, she propositions him in a bar, and the night they spend together is beyond her wildest dreams. Mystery steels herself to walk away—except the sheets are barely cold when her past comes back to haunt her.

Once he realizes Mystery isn't the stranger he thought she was, Axel is incensed and intrigued. But when it's clear she's in danger, he doesn't hesitate to become her protector—and her lover—again. And as the two uncover a secret someone is willing to kill for, Axel is determined to claim Mystery's heart before a murderer silences her for good.

Coming soon from Berkley Books

Dear Reader,

Intrigue. Drama. Passion. Danger. Secrets. For Lexi Blake and me, those are the ingredients of a page-turning book. One night, over a bottle of wine (which is how much of our collaborating starts), we thought . . . what if? What if we wrote a series with all those elements? We started with a sexy romance, then added nail-biting stakes along with politics, wealth, and edge-of-your-seat action and surprises. From that, our new series, The Perfect Gentlemen, was born.

We're thrilled to introduce to you a group of brothers-by-choice and the strong women who stand beside them to solve a shocking murder and uncover a long-buried scandal that will rock the foundations of their friendship—and America. Each book will be set in a dazzling city with a new couple to cheer on, but will bring back the characters you know and love as the friends confront a criminal force set on the destruction of everything they hold dear. Turn the page for a sneak peek at the first book in the series, Scandal Never Sleeps, *which releases on July 7, 2015 from Berkley Books. We hope you'll love the Perfect Gentlemen. Happy reading always!*

Shayla and Lexi

EVERLY Parker looked around the swanky bar and felt out of place. This wasn't her crowd, even though she worked with some of these people. She wasn't a big bar hopper. She didn't watch the clock and wait for five p.m. so she could hit her favorite watering hole. No, she was a work-long-hours-and-go-home-to-a-good-book-and-hot-bath kind of girl. But tonight, she wanted to be someone else—anyone who hadn't buried her mentor and friend an hour ago and wasn't now staring down the possibility of losing both her job and the roof over her head soon.

"Hey, are you going to nurse that drink all night long?" Scott leaned over and gave her a wink. He was on his third margarita. "Because I think you should down a few glasses of wine and be my wingwoman. Harry from accounting is here and I swear I'm going to die if I don't go out with that hunk of man soon. He's the only truly beautiful boy at work. He should be mine."

Everly smiled. After she'd started at Crawford last year, she'd met Scott during her orientation. Initially, she'd mistaken his playful nature for a come-on. But he'd finagled her into having coffee with him shortly thereafter and apologized for giving her the wrong impression. He'd admitted that he hadn't been himself because he'd just been through a rough breakup with his boyfriend. Scott sometimes used his happy-go-lucky face to mask his somber moods. To finally see him let go of his lost love and dip his toe in the dating pool with a hot guy thrilled her.

Honestly, Everly wasn't sure she believed in true love. Attraction and affection, yes. But love? Her father had been burned by the concept. He'd taken the profound loss of his wife's abandonment to his grave. Her mother had always seemed so distant, as though she'd spent her life up until the moment she'd walked out on them longing for something else. "Scott, I don't even know what a wingwoman would do."

He sat back and thought about it for a moment. "Well, first you're going to have to go over there and talk me up. Tell him how perfect I am, what a great guy I am, then slip him a roofie so I can have my wicked way with him."

She rolled her eyes. Sometimes Scott had a vivid imagination. "Sure. I'll get right on that."

"I tried," he said with a long sigh, his gaze trailing to the back of the room.

Everly's stare followed. A waitress in a female version of a tuxedo carried what looked to be a cheese plate past a large black man wearing a nondescript suit and aviators. He guarded a door that led to what she could only imagine was a VIP section.

"See that? I heard a rumor," Scott whispered in her ear. "While you were in the bathroom, Marty from processing stopped by and told me the craziest story."

"You shouldn't listen to him. He's a horrible gossip."

"Do you want the scoop or not?"

She was kind of afraid that the next big scoop after this one would be "Wonder Girl Gets Fired After Kindly Employer Dies." She'd shot through the ranks like a comet, and now she was going to hit the ground with a great big thud. She wasn't sure what she was going to do when the new boss came in and found out his or her head of security was a too-young-for-her-position hacker who everyone except Maddox Crawford thought couldn't handle the job. Maddox had been her champion, her mentor in this crazy corporate world. He'd also been a surprising friend.

At first, she'd been devastated by his death. But now, almost a week later, her brain had begun working overtime, and she had questions—the sort no one seemed to want to answer.

Maddox Crawford had been an experienced pilot. Had his death really been an accident?

Not according to that mysterious, inexplicable e-mail she'd received last night.

"Sure. What's the big scoop?" Everly decided to disregard her own advice. She would listen to any gossip that took her mind off her troubles. She needed one good night before she faced whatever crap tomorrow would bring.

She took a healthy gulp of the Sauvignon Blanc she'd ordered. Scott was right. She needed to live a little before the hammer came down on her head. If things went the way she suspected, she would be lucky to afford box wine next month.

"You know how the Great Crawford had some seriously powerful friends, right?"

She didn't follow the gossip rags the way everyone else did. In fact, she purposefully avoided that tripe. Why fixate on the problems of celebrities when she had so many of her own? Besides, when it came to people like Maddox, more fiction than truth filled the tabloids. They wanted a good story, and real life tended to be too boring. The Maddox she knew had worked hard—ten and eleven hour days, often six days a week. He'd cared about his employees. She bet no one reported on that. "He knew a lot of people. Men in his position often do."

"He also knew one very *powerful* person," Scott whispered.

She wasn't sure what he was insinuating. "I don't doubt that. He was in a very lofty position, Scott. It's not so surprising he knew key players."

Scott huffed, his frustration evident. "Damn it, don't you know who I'm talking about? Zachary Hayes, the forty-fifth president of these United States, the hottest man to ever hit the White House. They were friends as teenagers, according to rumors. I've heard the president is a sentimental man. I think he attended Crawford's funeral and is even now somewhere in this bar."

Maddox had told her once that he'd attended the same prep school as the current president and that they'd been close back in the day. The two of them had been part of a small group of friends who had dubbed themselves the Perfect Gentlemen. The rumors of their hijinks had been the stuff of legend . . . and come up in some really low-blow preelection campaigns against Hayes. Everly wasn't sure if they'd meant the name to be ironic, but she suspected so, given Maddox's reputation.

She let out an exasperated sigh. "Yes, the president of the United States is here. I'm so sure."

Scott looked pointedly back toward the VIP room. "Have you seen the surprising number of men in black suits hanging around here?"

"Scott, it's a wake. The majority of people in this bar came straight from the funeral. Are you really shocked they're wearing dark suits?"

"And the sunglasses?" Scott shot back. "How many people besides crazy, scary feds do you know who wear sunglasses inside a crowded bar at dusk?"

She turned and caught a glimpse of two overly large men standing by the entry to the back room. When a woman stumbled toward them, they gently but firmly turned her away. Everly caught a glimpse of metal. Maybe Scott was onto something. "Holy shit. I just saw a SIG SAUER."

Scott's brow rose. "Who is Sig?"

Clearly, Scott hadn't been raised around firearms. "It's the weapon the Secret Service uses. I know because my father was a cop and a complete gun nut. I knew how to shoot practically before I could walk. I don't know if that guy is actual Secret Service, but he's carrying a similar piece."

Scott stared at the doorway being guarded by the aforementioned black-suited, aviator-wearing bodyguards. "Just think, the hottest of all the commanders-in-chief might right now be sitting in that room, downing shitty tequila."

"Somehow, I think they'd give him the good stuff. And it's probably not him. More than likely, it's some pretentious CEO or trust-fund playboy Mad knew. Surely, the president would go someplace more secure. Besides, if he was here, the press would be crawling everywhere."

Scott shrugged as if he saw Everly's wisdom but still liked his own theory better.

Grinning, she canvassed the room to see who else from Crawford Industries had come to pay their liquid respects to Mad and noticed Tavia coming her way. The stunning, polished executive dashed toward them, her standard professional smile in place.

"Good to see you here, dear. I thought you'd go back to Brooklyn after the service." Like many raised on the Upper East Side, she said the word *Brooklyn* as if it were a virus she didn't want to catch. Those poor deluded people thought the city only existed between Midtown and Harlem and wouldn't dirty their designer shoes by walking on the rest of the island. But in every other way, Tavia had proven personable, if a bit high strung. The woman couldn't sit still for anything.

"Scott convinced me to stay for a while." It hadn't taken much. Her loft had been so quiet for the last five days. The silence had become intolerable. She hadn't realized just how much she'd come to depend on her boss's friendship.

Over the last couple of months, he would show up on her doorstep out of the blue and uninvited with some project to talk about. They'd spend hours gabbing and eating. At first, she'd worried that she would have to fend off a lecherous boss, but he'd actually been surprisingly sweet. Kind, even. He'd taken a profound interest in her, but not as a lover. Somehow they'd fallen into a comfortable companionship, as if she'd known him all her life. There had not been a single spark between them.

She was going to miss him so much. The ache she felt at never seeing him again definitely hurt. Everly took a sip of wine, wishing again that she was someone else and somewhere else. Escape sounded great about now.

Tavia tapped a Prada wedge against the floor. The shoes might be a few years old, but they still looked sleek and classy. "Hey, I wanted to pass on a little insider info. Crawford's lawyer is meeting with the executor of his will tomorrow, so it looks like we'll have some news about the company's future soon."

Scott went a little green. "So the pink slips could go out in quick order. God, I don't want to look for another job. It took forever to find this one. And it has so much potential."

Tavia shook her head, her pale hair jerking over her shoulders. "There's always a shake-up after someone new takes the reins, but you should be fine in the executive development program. They usually take out the players at the top. The new guy tends to like to bring in his own leadership team because he's sure he can trust them. It also serves to show everyone who's the boss. If anyone's going to get the boot, it will be me and Everly."

Scott rolled his eyes. "It could be any of us. I'm not exactly a peon, thank you very much, just rotating through all the departments until the program ends."

Surely Tavia knew that. Three margaritas and a funeral had left Scott prickly and morose.

"Which means you'll be valuable, Scott," Everly assured her friend. "You know something about every part of Crawford, having spent six months in most of the major departments. You'll be fine."

"Exactly," Tavia agreed. "But before I'm kicked to the curb, I need to make sure the new boss understands the importance of the foundation's work. It's excellent PR, and we all know Crawford Industries needs that now. With all the turmoil, our stock is down substantially. I'm hoping the new head honcho will think it looks bad to fire me two weeks before the annual fund-raiser. If he keeps me until then, I'll have a little time to convince whoever takes over that I'm worth what Maddox paid me."

The fund-raiser was the most important social event of the year at Crawford. Two weeks didn't seem like a long time to sway a new boss, but Tavia was right. Crawford Industries' support of her International Women and Girls Education Foundation was a true public relations gem. For a playboy like Maddox to give generously to fund educations for females in third-world countries had bought him a lot of good press and goodwill.

So why had Maddox told her privately that he wasn't going to the gala this year? Everly frowned. He'd said it casually over dinner one night when they'd been going over her plans to strengthen their cyber security systems. He hadn't exactly explained other than to say it was complicated. Then again, everything was complicated with Maddox Crawford.

He'd spent time with her, but he hadn't trusted her with his secrets. And she'd understood that—right up until his plane had gone down and she'd received that mysterious e-mail.

Before his death, Everly had suspected he was hiding something. Now, she was almost certain of it. She wished she'd asked more questions and pressed harder, because needed answers now.

But she wasn't going to be able to unravel all his mysteries tonight. Starting tomorrow, she'd probably have lots of time to figure out what Maddox had been up to . . . and find a new job. Tonight, she just wanted to get blitzed enough to sleep through the night.

One white wine wasn't going to accomplish that.

"I'll be right back." She stood and scanned the place. The bar was packed and seemed hopelessly understaffed. It wasn't likely the waitress was going to make it back anytime soon.

Everly couldn't help but notice a couple of well-dressed waitstaff coming in and out of the back room, but they didn't stop to help anyone else. If she wanted another drink, she would have to fend for herself.

Everly moved past the tables of coworkers. She stopped and said hello to some, but could barely handle the speculative stares of the rest. She knew what they thought. She wasn't stupid. Despite the company being a large multinational conglomerate, the corporate office of Crawford Industries still functioned like a small town. Gossip abounded. There was no one they liked to gossip about more than the boss.

She'd been linked to him from the moment she was hired. Her first day on the job, he'd shown her around personally, sparking the rumors that she was Crawford's mistress. When he'd bumped her up to head of security after only six months on the job, the chin-wagging had become unrelenting. Though that made her job difficult, Everly had put her head down and worked. She'd stopped a corporate spy and helped the FBI track down a ring that had used Crawford subsidiaries for phishing expeditions. Still, no matter how effective she'd proven herself, the employees still speculated that she'd slept her way to the top.

Everly sighed. That was a joke. She hadn't slept with anyone in well over a year, and her long dry spell didn't look like it would end anytime soon. At least the tabloids hadn't printed the rumors of her torrid affair with Maddox. She had to be thankful for that small miracle.

She elbowed and nudged her way up to the crowded bar and tried to get the bartender's attention. Unfortunately, she counted only two people working.

She held out a hand as one headed her way. "Can I get a drink?"

He walked right past her, but he did stop for the two blondes at the end of the bar. They were thin and gorgeous. Story of her life.

She'd always been short and slightly more plump than fashion dictated. Damn it, that didn't mean she didn't need a drink as much as the skinny chicks.

The bartender turned and headed her way again.

"I'd like a glass of wine, please."

Nothing. Not even a "hey, I'll be with you in a minute" that she wouldn't believe. He just walked to the opposite end of the bar and started prepping what looked like Cosmopolitans. The female bartender walked by, even more dismissive than the first.

The male walked by again and delivered the drinks to the two supermodels at the end of the bar. This time she was ready. She leaned over, because maybe he just hadn't heard her the first two times.

"Hello, could I get a glass of . . ."

He started to stride past her again, but a large hand zipped past her and over the bar, stopping him in his tracks. "I believe the lady needs a drink. I'd appreciate it if you would help her now."

That was the deepest, sexiest voice she'd ever heard in her life. It was attached to a really masculine-looking hand.

The bartender's eyes widened. "Of course, sir." He finally turned his attention to her. "What can I get you, ma'am?"

At the moment, Everly wasn't interested in wine.

She glanced over her shoulder at her rescuer. The sexiness didn't end with his voice. Vaguely, she noted that while she'd had to shove her way through the crowd, the mass of humanity had seemingly parted for him. He stood alone, though closer to her than strictly necessary. Tall and broad, with close-cropped golden brown hair and the bluest eyes she'd ever seen, her Good Samaritan stared down at her with a bit of a smile. Her tummy knotted.

"He needs to know what kind of wine you'd like. Let me guess." He gave her a considering stare. "A sweet red?"

She shook her head. "No. Um, a Sauvignon Blanc. I prefer the taste of white wine. Red tends to upset my reflux."

Way to go, Everly. That was a super sexy comeback to the hottest man she'd ever met. Of course he wanted to know about her digestive issues.

"Well, we wouldn't want that." A hint of amusement lurked in his voice. "The lady will take a Sauvignon Blanc, and I'll have a Scotch. The Glenlivet fifty."

The bartender immediately went to work.

"Thanks." She felt herself blushing. She probably looked like an idiot schoolgirl to him and could only hope she hadn't drooled. She'd never seen him before, but she would bet he occupied the VIP room. Maybe he was an actor. He certainly looked good enough to be on the screen. "I couldn't seem to get him to hear me."

Mr. Gorgeous's lips curved up as he leaned against the bar. "I don't think his ears are the problem. The man seems a bit blind to me."

Everly wasn't sure what that meant, but she found it impossible to look away from him. "I guess he's really busy tonight. The place is packed. I even heard the strangest rumor that the president is here."

The man laughed. "Ridiculous. I'm sure the leader of the free world can get better booze at the White House." He held out that big hand of his. "Name's Gabriel."

Like the archangel except in a really well-cut suit. His name was fitting. She put her hand in his, and he immediately covered it with his other. He swallowed her hand between his palms, the heat from his skin warming her own.

"I'm, um . . . Eve. It's nice to meet you."

She didn't like the idea of this man calling her the same thing as all her business associates. Only her family and closest friends called her Eve. Tonight, she didn't want to be the woman worrying about her job and how she was going to afford her loft. She'd rather be someone whose only pressing concern was to flirt with a hot guy. This conversation was likely to go nowhere, but she could fantasize about the handsome stranger.

Everly knew she was something of a wunderkind computer geek, but maybe Eve could be a flirty seductress. Eve could drink her wine and pretend that the gorgeous man beside her found her irresistible.

Yes, she would like to be Eve tonight.

About the Author

Shayla Black is the *New York Times* and *USA Today* bestselling author of more than forty sizzling contemporary, erotic, paranormal, and historical romances produced via traditional, small press, independent, and audio publishing. She lives in Texas with her husband, munchkin, and one very spoiled cat. In her "free" time, she enjoys watching reality TV, reading, and listening to an eclectic blend of music.

Shayla's books have been translated into about a dozen languages. She has also received or been nominated for the Passionate Plume, the Holt Medallion, Colorado Romance Writers Award of Excellence, and the National Readers Choice Award. RT BOOKclub has twice nominated her for Best Erotic Romance of the Year, and also awarded her several Top Picks and a KISS Hero Award.

A writing risk-taker, Shayla enjoys tackling writing challenges with every new book. Find Shayla at ShaylaBlack.com or visit her Shayla Black Author Facebook page.